FIGHT NOT FOR GLORY

About the Author

Emma Felling has been an avid reader and lover of history from a young age. After studying social sciences at university, she moved north to Newcastle. There she became a victim of the 'Great Unpleasantness of 2020' and after being forcibly bedridden, she found herself with a story that would not leave her be. *Fight Not For Glory* is that story and her debut novel.

When not being pestered by stories, she can be found dressed up as a medieval person and participating in living history events. Or online gaming with her friends.

FIGHT NOT FOR GLORY

EMMA FELLING

Copyright © 2025 Emma Felling

The moral right of the author has been asserted.

Apart from any fair dealing for the purposes of research or private study, or criticism or review, as permitted under the Copyright, Designs and Patents Act 1988, this publication may only be reproduced, stored or transmitted, in any form or by any means, with the prior permission in writing of the publishers, or in the case of reprographic reproduction in accordance with the terms of licences issued by the Copyright Licensing Agency. Enquiries concerning reproduction outside those terms should be sent to the publishers.

The manufacturer's authorised representative in the EU for product safety is Authorised Rep Compliance Ltd, 71 Lower Baggot Street, Dublin D02 P593 Ireland (www.arccompliance.com).

This is a work of fiction. Names, characters, businesses, places, events and incidents are either the products of the author's imagination or used in a fictitious manner. Any resemblance to actual persons, living or dead, or actual events is purely coincidental.

Troubador Publishing Ltd
Unit E2 Airfield Business Park,
Harrison Road, Market Harborough,
Leicestershire. LE16 7UL
Tel: 0116 2792299
Email: books@troubador.co.uk
Web: www.troubador.co.uk

ISBN 978 1836281 306

British Library Cataloguing in Publication Data.
A catalogue record for this book is available from the British Library.

Printed and bound by CPI Group (UK) Ltd, Croydon, CR0 4YY
Typeset in 11pt Minion Pro by Troubador Publishing Ltd, Leicester, UK

For Jim Turner
You never stopped believing in me

Prologue

Scotland, 1312

There is nothing as inescapable as death, and nothing more precious than love. At a table in a small manor sat a man who understood that well. Childhood malnutrition had stunted his growth and aided a sharp mind. As he wrote, his two children sat at his feet, as different from each other as night and day. A red-headed girl of five played contently with a rag doll. Her bored ten-year-old brother, with his father's dark hair and dark brown eyes, messed with his father's chess pieces. The man paused.

'It's time for bed. Go say goodnight tae yer ma. I'll follow shortly.'

The girl was quick to stand and obey his instruction while his son lingered. The man shot the older boy a warning glare that hurried him along. He finished his work and took a moment to compose himself before following the children.

In a chamber above the hall, a frail woman sat propped up in bed, her skin translucent and her eyes sunken with chronic illness. She kept her breathing shallow and hid the wince when her daughter cuddled into her side. The boy stayed away but stared with morbid curiosity.

'So what story will it be tonight?' the man asked as he arrived, putting on an air of cheer.

'Phoenix!' demanded the little girl.

The boy rolled his eyes. Their father carefully settled on the bed next to his daughter and wife.

'Och, of course, it has tae be that! Now let's see, how did it go? Ah yes! Not too long ago, a splendid kingdom was ruled over by a ruthless and greedy lion who wanted to expand his own lands. Many tried to stop him, but only one held the true right tae do so. This lion was brave and just. He called upon noble eagles, mighty bears and cunning ravens to stand by him. Eager to win, the Ruthless Lion also called upon his animals, bidding them to work under a cruel dragon. The no-good sons of—"

'Thomas,' came the weak voice of his wife, touched with warning notes.

He shifted, uncomfortable at having been caught out. 'Aye, right. Well, the Ruthless Lion had them attack the Just Lion and his animals while they rested. Amongst them were wolves belonging to the Just Lion's own kingdom. The Just Lion never forgot their act of betrayal.

'Shortly after that battle, the Just Lion turned to one of his best ravens. He instructed the creature to fly high over the carnage caused by the Ruthless Lion and report on what he saw. The raven did as he was instructed, and found the Just Lion's lands destroyed. The delicate flowers had been trampled into the ground by his mighty paw, and fire had destroyed the rest. The bird wept bitterly at the sight.'

Thomas fell silent, lost in old memories. His daughter used her foot to poke him impatiently.

'It was then that the raven spotted her. Amongst the ashes stood the most beautiful creature he had ever seen. A phoenix, brightly coloured and full of life. She was very scared, but the raven fell in love with her and encouraged her to go with him.'

'And the phoenix found herself falling in love with the raven,' said the woman, her voice even weaker than before. She used what strength she had to reach out and take Thomas's hand. He squeezed it gently.

'And her with him,' he agreed, eyes glistening. 'But the phoenix held a great secret. She carried a gift that that held the power to unite or destroy the kingdom. When the Just Lion found out, he didnae ken what to do. It was seeing their love for each other that helped him make up his mind. The raven was instructed to fly somewhere safe and protect this gift. He knew this would be no easy task but he accepted, for he loved the phoenix so. Naebody kens where they went, but it is whispered that they are still out there, waiting for when the gift is needed most.'

The room was silent for barely a moment before the boy spoke up, contempt in his voice. 'Tis a foolish story with foolish animals.'

He stalked out of the room without so much as a backwards glance at his parents. The little girl's mouth dropped open in indignation. She quickly hugged the woman in the bed before sliding off it and chasing after the boy. Her voice could be heard berating him from their separate bedchamber, followed by the nursemaid instructing the girl to hush. Father and mother stayed silent, listening to their children being prepared for bed.

Thomas spoke up. 'Ye need yer rest too, Annabelle.'

'Nae, Thomas.'

She started coughing; her body shook from the effort but barely any sound came out. Thomas got up from the bed and rushed around the side to a nearby table. Picking up the jug that sat there, he poured some watery ale into its accompanying earthenware cup. When he returned to her side, Annabelle barely had the energy to wave it away. Settling at her side, he took Annabelle's hand again and gently kissed it. It was colder than it had been before.

'My love, promise me.' Her voice was barely a whisper.

'I promise I will continue to protect Sorcha and love her like I love you.'

A soft smile formed on her lips as her eyes closed. Silent tears trickled down his face. Her last words hung heavy in the air. In his mind's eye, he returned to a camp near Loudoun Hill. He had never been able to bring himself to tell her what lay in store for their daughter, and now it was too late.

*

Loudoun Hill, 1307

A bear of a man pushed his way through the teeming camp. His dirty blond hair lay plastered to his forehead with sweat. He still wore mail over his padded yellow *léine*. Both were heavily stained with mud and blood, but he cared not. His eyes were focused on the yellow standard emblazoned with a galley. A crowd was gathered in front of it, attacking something. They jeered and egged each other on. Somehow, they had found the energy, post-battle, to vent their frustrations with fists.

He shoved one of the men out of his way. The man was about to retaliate but fell silent as the pained scream of a boy pierced the ruckus. The man-bear started shoving others out of the way in crazed desperation. The crowd moved without hesitation, clearing a path through the mob. If the man-bear had taken a moment to look down, he would have seen a dead English knight stripped of his armour, a fatal wound to his mid-torso. He would have also recognised the dagger that killed him.

The tent, if it could be called that, stank heavily of blood, alcohol and burned skin. Near its centre, on a bed of gathered heather, lay a boy, now unconscious; a fifteen-year-old who was more limb than muscle. His head had been tilted to the right and his shoulder-length, dark blond hair plaited to keep it from his face. From the outer edge of his left eye, across the cheek and down to just under his mouth lay a blackened, burned line of flesh.

The man-bear stilled long enough to take in the sight, before his anger took full hold. He turned on the red-headed man standing next to the boy.

'Aonghus Óg, ye promised me that my son would no battle this day!'

'I kept that promise, Grann.' The man remained cool-headed as he stared into the blue eyes of the boy's enraged father. 'It's because he didnae battle that he is like this.'

'Ye talk nonsense, man. What did he do? Sneak away?'

'He saved my life.'

Grann spun around and immediately fell to his knee. The voice belonged to the victorious Robert Bruce. An average-looking man with broad shoulders and a politician's mind. He sat on a chest, making no effort to move.

'Forgive me, Yer Grace, I didnae see ye there.'

'I ken all too well how a father's pain can blind a man.' The king stood and joined Grann, clasping his shoulder.

'Cailean here is a credit tae yer clan. He had his wits about him and saw that the prisoner knelt afore me had no been properly stripped. Yer boy pushed me out of the way but in doing so, he exposed himself. His unwavering action also brought the man down.'

'He is of Kermac Macmaghan's blood,' Grann proudly stated. A warrior amongst warriors, Kermac had helped drive the Norse from the isles and been heavily rewarded for his loyalty to the throne.

'It shows,' agreed Robert. 'When he is of age, he will be knighted for the bravery he showed this day. And tae further show my gratitude, he will be betrothed tae my ward.'

The knighthood was expected; Robert would not jeopardise Clan MacMhathain support by denying it. But Grann hesitated. 'Yer Grace is most generous, yet she is a suckling babe. Surely another would be more suitable?'

'Nae. I will see the legalities addressed as soon as possible.'

Robert's words were final. To drive home his point, the king left the tent without waiting for a response. Grann let out a low growl of frustration as Aonghus Óg gave him a thin smile. 'When Cailean wakes, I'll see him escorted tae yer camp. He cannae train in this condition and it'll help him heal if he's at home.'

'I thank ye. And I apologise for earlier.'

'Och, I'd have thought the same in yer situation.'

The man-bear stayed long enough to watch women dress his son's wound with honey and linen. Then he left, gaining a shadow as he went. Neither spoke until they were a good distance away.

'Ah should have guessed ye'd be here,' Grann said.

'War's good for business,' mused his companion, before the subtle darkening of his brown eyes gave away his real emotion. 'But ye ken that's no why I'm here. Robert sprung that on me as much as yerself.'

'Why am I no surprised?'

'He needs tae keep his options open, but I fear for both our children.'

Grann's lip twitched in a slight smile before he became serious again. 'Ah ken ye're already thinking, so share it.'

He folded his arms and waited patiently. The smaller man was still thinking.

'There is something we could do, but I'm no sure ye'll like it.'

'What?'

'I need an apprentice and ye have two sons.'

Grann rubbed the top of his nose. 'There is no hurry, aye?' he finally asked.

'None at all.'

'Then I will think on it.'

Chapter I

The Scottish Borderlands, 1324

Men on horseback broke the peace of the surrounding countryside. Above them flew the lion rampant of an absent Robert Bruce. In his place was a hard-built man with heavy scarring over half his face. Beyond that, his strong jaw, straight nose and dark blue eyes were classically appealing. While his dark blond hair fell to his shoulders, curling lightly there, it did little to soften the toughness of his naturally downturned face. He, like most of his retinue, wore the *léine* and trews of a Highlander and carried his green-grey plaid pinned to his shoulder.

His companion had the same facial features and was just as tall. However, his lithe frame, pale blue eyes and light blond ringlets made him more boyish, an effect further accentuated by the sparkle in his eyes and his upturned lips. Also, unlike the man, he wore the courtly attire of cotehardie, hose and hood in bright colours, the latter rolled up and sat at a jaunty angle upon his head.

'Ah still dinnae understand this, Cailean,' the happier man said, his Highland accent tinged with irritation. 'Why would Robert send us oot like this?'

Cailean did not respond, watching the track ahead. Not that it stopped his brother.

'Orderin us both tae fetch the daughter of some self-made border laird. What's so special about him? Or her?'

A twitch of his lip, an extended silence, then: 'Alasdair, I'm nae fallin for yer tricks. Ye ken the Brus gives orders and naught else,' his familial brogue slurred by his impediment.

'So dae ye no think it's related tae yer mysterious betrothal?'

'No that again! They want tae keep me in check. Nothing more.'

'Then why hae ye no married?'

Alasdair smirked at Cailean's death glare. Chief at twenty-one, his people had been concerned by his youth, conveniently forgetting that he had already been handling the majority of the old chief's work as *tanist*. He had ascended with several conditions, all bar one of which had now been lifted.

The chief spotted something. He called the retinue to a halt and reined his horse so it stood across the path. A more subtle movement brought forth a cat-like man with dark hair.

'Aye, *mo ciann*?'

Cailean reached for his flask. 'I saw movement ahead. Seems to be just one.'

The scout nodded and returned in the direction he'd come. The rest of the retinue followed Cailean's lead.

Pretending to be stiff, or wanting to piss, they stretched limbs or dismounted. Alasdair joined in the pretence, describing a 'rare flower' he had found at the English court. The reappearance of the scout further up, unharmed and bemused, caused a collective muttering of discontent. Cailean broke away, joining him.

'Shoddy job and gone when I got there,' the man reported, holding up a bit of torn white linen. Cailean's frown grew deeper, and his mount started to fret under him. They should soon be seeing the hamlet.

The retinue found it hugging a hillside. Locked-up wattle and daub houses greeted them. Tools sat discarded and livestock strayed unchecked. The few locals caught outside refused to acknowledge them. The brothers glanced at each other. Near the end of the hamlet was a single open house where the men did not look away. They glared, openly hostile. Next came a small kirk, and beyond, a cruck-framed manor house. Once just a stone hall, it had been extended on one side. A complex of other buildings and fenced pastures spread behind it, filled with horses in all stages of life. Most grazed but some were being worked by men.

Waiting for them was a small man, slightly stooped with age. He wore a rich claret robe, and an embroidered coif covering his thin, grey hair. Next to him, a woman only half a head taller stood inflexibly straight. Her grey, shapeless surcoat, wimple and veil were frumpish in comparison. She clasped her hands in front of her and met the gaze of no one.

'She cannae be the maiden; she looks like a younger Aunt Bernice!'

There was a hint of disappointment in Alasdair's voice. Cailean discreetly studied the woman as they approached. High cheekbones and a slightly upturned nose scattered with freckles paired with bottom-heavy lips were what he found. Had he been asked, he would have said she was not unpleasant.

The brothers dismounted and approached as one. They were met with bent knees, the woman's a little overeager. Alasdair returned the gesture but Cailean barely dipped. Before any could speak, the manor doors burst open. Out strode a stocky, piggy-eyed man. His black hair shone with grease, and he struggled to buckle his belt over his cotehardie. He panted as he brushed past the older man and thrust out his soft hand.

'Welcome, welcome! A retinue o the king's men on my doorstep. What a pleasant surprise! Tae what dae I owe the pleasure?'

Again, the brothers shared a glance. The older man looked on in stoic resignation while the woman stayed unnaturally still. Alasdair quickly produced a dazzling smile and an overtly ornamental, low kneel. The young man preened with delight, unaware of the blatant mockery.

'Greetings, Laird Gilchrist. I am Alasdair Macmaghan. I will gladly explain why we are here, but no on the doorstep like this.'

'Of course not. Where are my manners? Please do come in, and call me Michael.'

Michael guided Alasdair inside, currying favour by asking about his fine clothing. The older man, and true laird of the estate, looked heavenwards. He waited until they were out of earshot.

'It appears we are doing things backwards,' he muttered. 'Please forgive the insult, Sir Cailean. I am Thomas, and may I introduce my daughter, the Lady Sorcha.'

She stepped forwards, meeting Cailean's eye. She did not shy away, or show repulsion, or any other emotion aside from a bright intelligence in her eyes. Cailean's lips lifted for a fraction of a second. He did not break the gaze until forced to. Neither spoke. If Thomas noticed, he said nothing and escorted his guest inside.

The great hall was small with a central hearth, trestle tables and benches erect and set for the evening meal. In pride of place hung a lone Burgundian tapestry; above, the original lord's chamber had been enclosed. Michael and Alasdair were not there, and Thomas cursed mildly, gesturing to a side door that led into the family solar. In this intimate setting, the scattering of poorly completed needlework and carvings revealed a father's hidden pride.

Everyone but Michael displayed discomfort. Cailean stood, joined by Sorcha, leaving a reluctant Thomas to take the only remaining free chair. Michael bragged about the land and the good hunting it provided. And then about 'his' well-stocked buttery. No one but he and Alasdair spoke. Cailean was too busy appraising the situation; something that seemingly did not unsettle the younger brother, who deftly changed the conversation.

Alasdair first encouraged talk of how the kingdom was once again flourishing under their king. Then about himself, and how much of an honour it was to be chosen to work for the Bruce. The prestige and wealth it brought.

Cailean snorted at that, not that it dissuaded the ensnared Michael.

'I am, therefore, here on behalf o the queen tae offer the Lady Sorcha a position as a maid of honour.'

All Michael's warmth evaporated. Cailean's hand shifted to his dagger.

Michael jumped up. 'Never!'

Cailean shoved Sorcha behind him, blocking any path. Neither Thomas nor Alasdair flinched. The hostility seeped from Michael's pores, the sound of Sorcha's heavy, startled breathing unnaturally loud.

'I… I mean she—'

'Sit down.'

Thomas had not raised his voice, nor shifted. Just its tone was enough to settle the unruliest of youths, including Michael. Sorcha showed herself but appeared reluctant to move anywhere near her brother. Ignoring his son, Thomas addressed Alasdair.

'As ye say it is an honour to hear that the queen has chosen my daughter. As her father, *I speak for her*, and she humbly accepts. I also apologise for my son's poor conduct. I thought I had educated him better.'

Again, Michael shot to his feet. He made a show of destroying his chair before slamming the door on his way out. And again, Thomas did not flinch. The brothers met eyes again; the Bruce had not warned them. The tension was broken by a female voice drifting up from the floor.

'Hey, Highlander, dae ye dae that tae every lady ye meet or just tae me?'

An uneasy round of chuckles. Cailean helped her

up and she avoided his gaze. Her skin flushed. The door opened and a nervous boy entered carrying pitchers.

'Please sit, Sir Cailean, and let us discuss arrangements.'

The chief kept his eye on the maid as he righted the chair and took it. She moved deeper into the room and sat at the window bench, her face turned from the men. No matter what they discussed, or how much it involved her, it never turned back.

*

The light but simple provender suited Cailean's tastes. It reminded him of simpler days. He was further blessed by Michael's absence. But the strange atmosphere was worsening; even his *leuchd-crios* wore their swords. Not that his host appeared to care. He dried his hands and searched for his trencher partner. Sorcha was an intriguing puzzle. She was not there. Grabbing his goblet to mask disappointment, he lifted it to his mouth.

She sat down next to him. He choked, stunned by her ability to outsmart him.

'Dinnae tell me that I, a mere woman, startled the Highland warrior?'

He stared at her; her mischievous glint held no malice. An improvement on her earlier appearance. Thomas growled her name in warning, the glint died, and she murmured an apology. Why did that annoy him? Damn propriety. He cut their food. Not being an idle talker, he remained silent. Sorcha talked, mainly of trivial matters. Then of his mount – she was well versed in *chevalerie*. He blinked, though he should not have been surprised.

It was her father's trade. Her language, though. Not one question overtaxed his speech.

Her attention strayed so he followed it. On his other side, Thomas and Alasdair were engaged in a lively discourse. An intellectual match for his brother?

'For one with your job, Alasdair, I am surprised that you have never philosophised the nature of chess before. See not the board as two opposing armies but of those in power.'

His brother was thinking as he chewed.

'The king is considered the most powerful piece but must rely on the others around him tae do his bidding?'

'Exactly. The queen too is powerful, but it makes her vulnerable. Use her too much and she will fall. But what of pawns?'

'They are the lowliest of his court?'

'Not lowliest, most expendable. He can afford tae lose them tae gain what he wants yet he forgets that through perseverance, they can raise tae great power.'

Why was Thomas staring at his daughter? But his brother had not finished interrogating their host. 'Please go on. What o the knight? I see his loyalty sending him everywhere.'

Thomas nodded. 'Aye. Blinded so, he disnae see what the king intends for him. While the rook is granted the most freedom, making him the hardest worker.'

Why was Alasdair chuckling?

His brother continued. 'The bishop serves more than the king. So his actions are sideways?'

Ah. Their host did not laugh, souring the mood. Sorcha suddenly, and quietly, excused herself. He stared down at his trencher; he just liked the game.

Cailean savoured the cool evening. He rolled his shoulders while glancing around. The place reminded him of those occupied by Longshanks. A well-groomed, middle-aged priest emerged from shadow. *Intent on catching his eye.* He cautiously followed the man into his chapel. Dark, save for a few lit candles at the altar. And no ambush awaiting him. At the front, he knelt on a prayer stool.

'I apologise for the subterfuge, but we fear it is necessary.'

'We?'

'Come now, good sir, ye ken better than that.'

Robert's spies. And worse, a man of God. If he was here, then it confirmed Alasdair's idle chatter. This was no favour for the queen.

'The king kens that I dinnae care for deception.'

The priest prepared to bless him.

'Aye, a real Arthurian knight so I hear. Ah'm no here tae change yer mind but tae warn ye.'

'I was warned. I dinnae ride my destrier for fun.'

'No fully, ye weren't. The men out there, they want the lass. Dinnae ask me why, for I am no privileged tae that information. But ye must understand that is Robert's real motive for sendin ye.'

'Tae save a damsel in distress? Anything else?'

And why did Robert care? Damn it, he would not get involved. Do the job and go home. The priest launched into the blessing as the door opened. Light footsteps. From the corner of his eye, he recognised Sorcha. She stopped and placed flowers upon a stone. He stood up, muttering amen. Time to act as though he liked the damned priest.

'Thank ye, father. Will ye share a drink?'

'Aye, I think ah shall.'

Cailean took a few steps before jumping back into the shadows. The door crashed open. The cursing priest joined him. So much for sanctity. Stale ale assaulted his nose. Michael passed, his evil eyes on Sorcha. Cailean stepped forward but the priest stopped him. *He was to watch?* She was pale with fear, having risen to face her attacker. If she wavered any longer… She bolted. Michael caught and backhanded her, sending her crashing to the floor, lip bloodied.

God's balls, this was wrong! He hardened his jaw and dug his nails into the palms of his hands.

'Now look what ye made me do,' Michael slurred, spreading his arms wide. 'Why dae ye insist on doing this tae me? I had everythin planned and ye had tae ruin it, like everythin else ye do.'

The scum gave Sorcha no time to respond. A swift kick to her side. Winded, she curled up into a ball.

'And no only that, ye manage tae get yerself a cushy place at court! Damn you, ye sluttish whore!'

Michael grabbed her by her arm, forcing her to her feet. She had not yet uttered a sound. He withdrew his eating knife and pressed it to her throat.

'Tell me whose cock ye sucked tae arrange this?'

'Go tae hell!'

Enough! Cailean sprang forward, his dagger already to hand. Wrapping his left arm around Michael's neck, he rested the point of his blade under his ribcage. The scum's knife fell to the floor. He must stay in control, even as he recognised what Michael was. He was the kind that only targeted those weaker. This should be enough to scare him.

'Dinnae move and shut up,' he growled into Michael's ear before calling out to Sorcha, 'Are ye alright?'

She held herself up with the altar. Shamefaced, then nothing but a distant stare. A post-battle stare that some men never returned from. And this... whelp... had done it to a woman? She walked past, acknowledging no one. Gutting the fool would be so easy. And now he had pissed himself! Cailean swung him around.

'Move.'

Outside, Cailean silently cursed. His *leuchd-crios* stood braced for a fight. Opposite were the men the priest warned about – they were outnumbered. He flung Michael towards them, and the snivelling whoreson stumble-ran the rest of the way.

'You're mad, Highlander! Attacking yer host unprovoked in a church! I should kill ye where you stand!'

The worm's swagger had returned. He was not worth the time. War and his father's belt had taught Cailean that. He sheathed his blade and walked down the middle. Thomas arrived at his door, giving a subtle nod of thanks.

'Michael, need I remind you that these men are here under the king's banner? No to mention from a powerful clan? I have no desire tae see blood drawn or start a feud we cannae win. Control your *friends*.'

One of the 'friends' spat; hah, they had no feelings for Michael either. Were they hired or something else?

'Who is yer chief?' Cailean demanded. The man

responded by lifting his right fist high and placing his left hand in the crook of the elbow.

"*S e' Galla Bhruis a th'annad!*'

He shook his head; calling him Robert's bitch was hardly original. And it created more questions than answers. Their clothing was too rough to draw a conclusion. Yet Gaelic had been declining around the border. And these men disliked the king. And finally, that was a French gesture favoured by returned mercenaries. He signalled to his men to follow him inside.

He rubbed the bridge of his nose and waited. They filed around him.

'I want a watch kept. If they come, it'll no be more than one tae feign innocence. We'll leave first thing tomorrow.'

His *leuchd-crios* agreed and threw in a few choice words. It brought a slight smile to his lips.

'I'll take the first watch.'

'Ah thank ye, Donald.'

He told them what he had learned and they altered plans accordingly. Yet they had questions which he could not answer. Sharing his frustration. He omitted what had happened in the kirk; they did not need further enticement.

'Nae wonder we were bein watched earlier,' his scout added, slowly.

'Ye think? Honestly, Ewan, ye do like tae state the obvious!' chided Donald with a grin.

He let them ease their tension with jibes. He needed more, but practising swordplay was too risky.

'Where's my *gowkit-cled* brother?' he interrupted. Ewan pointed towards the chambers above the hall.

*

Alasdair ran his hands through his hair – how quickly plans change! He alone should have been escorting Sorcha to Lochalsh. Yet here they both were, escorting her to Robert's court, and His Grace had not had the decency to say why. Laughable, almost, were it not that a fool could detect something was amiss. Now his intuition was begging him to investigate, but it was no good, he needed sleep. Sitting on the edge of the bed, he searched his pouch for a leather thong. Loath as he was to admit it – he was teased enough by Cailean – he had to plait his hair or it was a rats' nest come morning. His fingers grazed something solid. What now? And how in God's name had it got there unnoticed?

He lay on the bed and held the object up to the light. A key with parchment wrapped around its shaft. He let out a sigh. The last thing he needed was another assignment from Robert's spymaster. Dear Lord, please not more of Edward's love letters! That foppish sop's words bored him near to death. The code was not worth breaking. He unravelled the parchment from its shaft, pausing briefly at the sound of footsteps. They were too light to be Cailean's.

Your time to soar is nigh.

This had to be some foul trick! Nonetheless, it was his enigmatic mentor's distinctive spidery writing. His hands dropped onto his forehead. Why couldn't he leave him alone?

Now those were Cailean's footsteps. He returned the items to his pouch, let his head fall to one side and placed his hands on his chest. As the door opened, he relaxed his face and closed his eyes. The door was shut a little too hard and his brother was growling. Oh joy! They may be adults but that never stopped Cailean: the blanket under him was yanked out at such speed, he flew from the bed. Having 'woken' the moment he moved, he landed on his hands and knees. To finish the act, he swung around in anger to spit out some choice words but stopped. It was worse than he feared; Cailean was pacing.

'Tell me what happened.'

Chapter 2

There was no hiding the excitement in the manor the next morning, although the fear of waking Michael was still palpable. The retinue gathered in front, watching the hired driver packing his cart. At the door, Cailean and Thomas were joined by a late-rising Alasdair. Sorcha and her mount were the only ones absent. The driver raised his hand, signalling that he was ready, and a young lad took off running towards the stables. Thomas paused to study the two men next to him. A spark of what looked to be a father's pride shone from his eyes. The brothers shifted uncomfortably under his gaze.

'Aye, ye'll both do. Ye take good care of her now.'

'The lady will arrive safe,' Cailean coolly remarked, before striding over to his mount. Alasdair lingered, jaw set, and gave the slightest of nods to Thomas.

'It will be done. We thank ye for yer hospitality.'

Thomas and Alasdair bowed as equals before the younger man followed his brother's lead.

A man led a chestnut mare towards the group. She

stood fourteen hands high; her lightly dished head, big eyes, deep chest and strong hindquarters radiated good breeding. She stopped for a moment to lift her head high and let out a loud, excited whinny. The man walked her in circles to calm her, as the lad reappeared with a mounting block.

Donald watched the mare's antics from the back of his mount. Outwardly, he looked like a strong but shaggy Highland cow. He could never tame his hair or his beard and, no matter how hard his wife tried, his clothing never sat right. Yet beneath it all, he closely resembled his cousins, Cailean and Alasdair. Leaning forwards, he nudged Ewan.

'What dae ye make o that then?'

The younger man wore both his *léine* and darker hair shorter than most Highlanders. He had cat-like reflexes, except in his speech. In that, he always took his time. He peered over his horse's back and eventually let out a low whistle of appreciation.

'Ah'll bet yer new belt that be no palfrey.'

'Well, it's no destrier either, so deal.'

*

Sorcha took a last, long look around her empty chamber. While under that accursed spell of absence, she had somehow travelled alone from the kirk to her chamber. The ailment customarily bade her to remain immobile. She closed her eyes as fear gripped her heart. Why had it come just as she was embarking on a new life? And with a man who had witnessed her impertinence! Perhaps he could not recall that it was a woman's biblical obligation to endure such from her male relatives? If only she knew what she had done to incur Michael's wrath. She had never dared suck her broth, or a bone clean, let alone a cockerel. Yet she must have.

Leaving it, she stopped by the chamber Ma had once slept in. Their guests had left its bed dishevelled, though nothing else had changed. Unlike her memory of Ma, which was as faded as a sun-bleached tapestry. The stone was all she had of her and now she was leaving for a future only the Lord knew. Sorcha quickly crossed herself. Glaistig was whinnying; she could not prolong her departure anymore. She pulled her old green mantle around her before breathing deeply. She *must* resemble a respectable lady.

Pa was there waiting for her and she threw her arms around him. His reassuring strength kept her from further embarrassment. This was not right; she should be staying to care for him in his winter days. He took her by the shoulders and stared deep into her eyes. Pa wanted her to go and do what her brother could not. Her eyes grew moist.

'I'll write often, and I'm sure the queen will let me visit.'

'Och, dinnae ye worry about me, my wee gem. I am old and ye have yer whole life ahead of ye.'

Pa clasped her hands and squeezed them.

'Now will ye humour yer old pa one last time?'

'Anything, my Laird Pa.'

'Wear these when ye arrive at court.'

He gestured to a bundle the cart driver was holding. She dared not speak, so nodded, failing miserably at attempting a smile. Pa gave her one last kiss and murmured into her ear '*stay strong*', before leading her to Glaistig. Her heart now torn asunder, she quickly mounted and was still sorting her skirts when Cailean called for the retinue to leave. Why did he hurry so? It forced her to fall in. As they rode away, she turned to look one last time at Pa. Instead of seeing the strong man who had guided her on the path of goodness, she saw a frail old man waving her goodbye.

She rode in silence for most of the morning, tormented ruthlessly by her heart. Her gallant little steed took no heed and eagerly strode forwards. She glanced to her companion – Donald – and he smiled warmly at her. Did he recognise what she was going through? Yet she could not let melancholy overwhelm her. If she was to survive, she would need people who were like Donald. Her eyes lingered on Cailean, yet Alasdair was more approachable. Nonetheless, how would they react? She urged her mare forwards and between them.

'I assume we can now drop the pretence. Forgive me for being so forthright, Lord Alasdair, but I ken ye are no the great lord my brother assumed ye were.'

Alasdair glanced at her in surprise before he reined his horse over to give hers more room. Thankfully, he showed no hard feelings at her words. Cailean's laughter, however, had him staring past her in slack-jawed disbelief. Were her words really that foolish? He composed himself before answering.

'I am Lord Alasdair Macmaghan, the king's ambassador. That tittering oaf is my brother, Sir Cailean Macmaghan. Earl of Kintail, Chief of Clan MacMhathain,

Constable of Eilean Donnain and, if we are being pedantic, Laird of Lochalsh.'

Alas, Cailean was so far above her station, he would have little interest in helping her. Yet he had seemed to enjoy her company at the table, and he had not reprimanded her for her insolence. She glanced at the earl. Why was he staring daggers at his brother?

His gaze shifted to hers and he nodded in confirmation.

'Forgive me, my lord, for appearing so importunate, but I do not understand. Why am I being escorted by one so far above me?'

'Ye tell me, lass.'

Cailean's stare was intense, yet she had nothing to hide! The intensity softened, replaced by what she had seen when they first met. Sorcha still could not put a name to it, but she enjoyed seeing it. He broke away, coughed and shifted in his saddle. She suddenly felt like her twelve-year-old self, when she was besotted with the new blacksmith!

'We'll make for the old road tae Glasgow. Through the city and on tae the king's manor at Pillanflatt.'

'Oh... is that far?'

She caught herself – that was not how a lady spoke. Thank goodness he had not noticed! Instead, he looked behind them. At what? All she could see was Alasdair reading a piece of parchment. The earl sighed.

'Did ye no travel?'

'My pa permitted me to travel tae the local market on occasion but nothing else.'

Sorcha gestured in the opposite direction from their route. It had never struck her as an odd practice. She had not wanted for much. Except pins, she was always needing pins. No matter what she did, they rarely stayed put.

'What about education?'

'My father hired monks and every summer a lady would visit for a few weeks tae teach me what was acceptable for my age.'

Cailean gave her a most peculiar look. She had not spoken out of turn so she checked her veil. It was intact and her dress was modest. What else could it be?

*

The call to make camp was greatly welcomed by Sorcha. She rode almost daily but never in such long stretches. It made for an ungainly dismount and her legs would not hold her weight, much to the amusement of Cailean's men. In that sense, they were no different to the stable lads. Though they were less crude in their language. She politely declined their offers to care for Glaistig. She had looked after her since she was a yearling, she would not hand her over now. Besides, the mare could be… challenging… at the best of times. After checking one last time that she was securely tied and hobbled for the night, Sorcha approached the campfire.

Cailean stood there, watching his men. They were gathered around an unfolded tent, arguing. From under it came Ewan's curses. Sorcha scuffled the floor to catch Cailean's attention; he was too close to the fire to be startled. He undid his plaid and laid it on the floor for her to sit on. She thanked him. Alasdair approached with a sack. He took an apple from it before setting it down. After likewise sitting, he cut the fruit and shared it with her. They were both so courteous to her, a complete stranger!

'Still at it ah see.'

'Blathering gowks, the lot o them,' muttered Cailean in response.

'Ye chose them!'

'Dinnae remind me.'

The earl joined them and picked up a leather flask from his bundle. He pulled the lid off and took a sip, his eyes never leaving his men. She glanced between the brothers.

'Why do ye no help them?'

'Ye dinnae ken much of Highlanders dae ye?' Alasdair answered. 'The males have a terrible affliction called pride. It gets in the way o accepting help and is usually resolved with a few hard knocks tae the face.'

Such sarcasm! It even made Cailean grunt in annoyance. Or was it agreement? Sometimes they sounded the same. Alasdair continued to explain that they themselves rarely bothered with large tents, preferring lean-to shelters or just their plaids. When they did have them, it was often camp followers putting them up.

'Cailean here is no one for all the pomp and ceremony that comes with his titles. Our elder chieftain had to nigh box his ears tae get him tae agree tae always travel with a full *leuchd-crios*. A remarkable feat considering that by then the man was half in his grave!'

'He was allowed tae do that? I was led to believe that the chief of a clan held the authority.'

Cailean suddenly seemed interested in their discussion.

'Aye and nae. I have authority because the clan gave it tae me. Likewise, they can remove it. A good chief listens tae his chieftains.'

'But a good chief can also be a stubborn fool, who needs a reminder or two from his great-uncle.'

'Aye well, I was younger then.'

The *leuchd-crios* let out a cheer and backed away from the tent. It stayed up, though it did sag in a couple of places. She hid the concern from her voice as she thanked them for their work. Alasdair, on the other hand, got up and made a great show of studying it.

'Dinnae ye dare say a thing,' growled Donald, 'or ye'll be gettin intimate with its damned pole!'

Alasdair chose to stay silent; it made her reluctant to ask how intimacy with the object could happen.

The answer dawned on her later. After sharing a meal, the men started to relax. They had been guarding their language. It was hardly warranted; she knew the crude words and had helped Pa on the stud – been there for many coverings and geldings. So, where she knew the words, she laughed along. At several points, Donald tried to ask about Glaistig, forcing her to quieten. Thankfully, he never pressed. At other moments, she found her gaze lingering on Cailean. While his face remained staunch, his eyes shone.

*

Cailean returned from relieving himself. How quickly the dour damsel had changed! Like a spring flower. Oh great, he sounded like his brother. Sorcha was no longer there. He glanced to the tent. The candle she was using illuminated her, though not enough to ruin modesty. Good. And disappointing? He shook his head and focused on the ground. Alasdair was watching him; he could feel it.

'Lost something?'

'Aye, some bugger's stolen my plaid.'

He looked towards Alasdair, who looked around and shrugged. Then he disappeared under his own plaid. The *tyke* was getting his revenge. Cailean grumbled to himself and arranged his sheepskin in front of the tent. Not because he distrusted his men, he just… He sighed and stared up at the night sky. Sorcha snuffed the candle. In the still that followed, he heard her subdued crying. Homesickness was never easy.

Something was happening; he opened his eyes. A few inches above his face was Glaistig's nose. She sniffed him before snorting. He pulled his hand out to push her away. Abruptly sitting up, he stared at his plaid. He should have woken when Alasdair returned it. He used it to wipe his face and paused. Since when did his brother use lavender?

It was no use trying to sleep again, so he joined Ewan.

'Why is she loose?'

'She'll no stay tied tae the line, *mo ciann*. Ah reckon it's why she be hobbled.'

Cailean stared at the mare again; she had followed him like a doting hound. Begrudgingly, he accepted the hobble.

'I see. What about Alasdair?'

Ewan glanced at him in confusion before returning his attention to the trees.

'When did he return my plaid?'

'Twas there when ah was woken for my turn.'

A growl was all he could manage; no other would dare trick him. Ewan's voice dropped low.

'We're being watched. They've just changed their scout.'

'Just the one?'

'Aye.'

He grunted at the news. The men after Sorcha were eager to fight but not foolish. They had apparently been acting like reivers, biding their time. Only instead of a full moon, they got a storm and lost their prize. Surely they'd follow the prize and reconsider the options. But what made Sorcha their prize?

'They'll no attack here. Quietly alert the others as tae our next camp.'

'Aye, *mo ciann.*'

He stayed with Ewan until the sun rose. Again, Alasdair was the last man up – he always had been a sound sleeper. He packed away what he could but stopped to break the fast. Better porridge than sickness from dubious street foods. The smell must have woken Sorcha. She emerged from the tent half-asleep; dear Lord, he could wake to that face. He shot up and glared at the others. Their gentle teasing of Sorcha stopped. Multiple pairs of questioning eyes. Damn, it wasn't their behaviour but his thoughts!

'If you're no eating, ye can prepare the horses. Put the *crotals* on; the route will be busy.'

He was sharper than he intended to be. Still, he included himself in the orders. Taranis, his destrier, fidgeted. Before this damned mission, he treated women like they treated him. Completely uninterested. But she – she was getting under his skin. It was a folly, yet maybe he could… no; he needed to put a stop to it and distance between them. He turned to stare at Alasdair, who had followed him. His brother froze like a rabbit, looking at him from the corner of his eye.

'Och, no. Ye're giving me that look. Why is it always that look? I never like what's coming when ye give me it.'

He folded his arms but said nothing; his brother flung his arms up in exaggerated annoyance.

'Fine! What is it ye want me tae dae?'

Chapter 3

They set off earlier than they had the day before, reaching an extraordinarily hard and wide path. Sorcha's companion, Alasdair, explained that it was an old Roman road leading directly to Glasgow. It certainly made travelling faster. More often did they trot, the jingling *crotals* drowning out her conversation with the ambassador. He spoke of life at court and how it differed.

'There is little kinship tae be found at court. It disnae matter if ye're of the same clan or no, the king cannae be seen sitting and drinking with those who dine in the lower hall. 'Tis the complete opposite in the Highlands as a chief will break bread with any of his clan. And for that, they respect him greatly.'

'Perhaps if the powerful condescended to do so, there would be less war.'

Less, greed, less famine too. Alasdair scratched the back of his head and looked somewhat ashamed.

'Och, well, ah'm no sure about that; honour is everything. And honour can only be defended in a square clash of blades, or fists. Then there's the need for good arable lands as we have less useful land than yer hale Henderleithen. More so after the war.'

She brought Glaistig to a dead halt; cries of alarm followed in her wake. He knew nothing! They too had survived on what little could be foraged! She lifted her chin to stare him down.

'Do not dare to assume that my home prospered during the war! It has been greatly affected by Scot and English alike! Both of their armies needed feeding, and both have men who care not for honour. Do ye even ken what happens when they leave and there is nowt but a single grain left? A man will do anything to feed his starving family.'

Cailean rode between them, his face flushed. No, no, she had gone too far! Who was she to berate the noble?

The earl growled, 'Alasdair, get yer damned arse tae the rear. Now! Donald, up front. Lady Sorcha, ye'll ride with me.'

He swung his horse around and alongside Glaistig. The stallion nickered softly as they got closer, only for the mare to flatten her ears and squeal. He reached out to sniff at her, and she nipped at him. Please, not now, behave yourself Glaistig! Sorcha looked down at her hands as they set off again.

'I apologise for Alasdair's behaviour,' he said, after they had ridden in silence for a good while. 'He likes tae goad people.'

Her head shot up. No, this was not their fault but all hers!

'Nae, my lord. It's me who should apologise for my outburst.'

'Ye were right. War destroys land.'

She could not take it, she had to tell the truth.

'Alas, Lord Alasdair was correct and myself too impetuous. We were more fortunate, for the powerful on both sides left my father's lands alone. However, he would never turn away those in need. It was never charity, for that hurts a poor man's pride. In exchange for food, he offered them a bit of work. We would often see the same people going back and forth. Driven out from wherever they tried to settle. And then when the harvests started failing, he continued tae do what he had always done.'

He listened, but did he believe her, now he knew her to be a scolding liar?

'A good man, but charity disnae stop attacks. Who protected ye?'

She shifted in her saddle. There were always the outliers – usually small groups of foraging men – but she dared not speak of them.

'The clans around us. I suppose my father indirectly helped them all. They never took our animals, rather the opposite. If those from farther afield took them, then they would often reappear. Or, I assume, were replaced by them returning the favour.'

'Shrewd, too.'

She glanced at him, but he was lost in thought. What did he mean by shrewd? Was there more to it than she thought? Come to think of it, there must have been. Why had the armies not simply taken the horses they needed? There had been so many people coming and going back then. As she got older they had greatly diminished, but the poor weather had continued.

The closer they got to Glasgow, the more distracted

she became. The road grew crowded with fellow travellers, animals and tradesfolk. It reminded her vaguely of visits to the local market, but on a grander scale. They crested a hill and she let out a gasp. Alasdair had called it scarcely a town, but there was nothing scarce about it! Cailean coughed, catching her attention. Was that a hint of a smile on his lips?

'Hand me yer right rein.'

He could take both; she had not the slightest understanding of riding through such numbers! She urged Glaistig closer, accidently brushing her leg against his.

'Oh, I'm sorry!'

Why was her face so warm? Cailean merely grunted and took the rein.

Closer to the city gates, they slowed to a shuffle and the road transformed into a sludge that resembled mud in appearance but smelt far worse. Still, the smell was somewhat tolerable. The noise, however, was such a din! Bells, animals, talk and shouts; she could even hear music somewhere!

Their standard drew many towards her. Rosy-cheeked boys ran alongside. Their pleas of 'spare a coin, sire' were met with threats to kick backsides. Such blatant wantonness! Next came those who could carry their wares – umble pies, small tokens, even relics from the cathedral. She did not possess the coin they wanted.

Further away, people pushed pots of ale on carts. Shouters advertised their inns – and, Lord have mercy, brothels! Thank goodness, there were also preachers. One man stood on top of a cart, trying to sell his cure-all concoction; he claimed that his brew of iron was sure to restore vitality both in and out of the bedchamber. A wise woman had once warned her of such individuals. But there, amongst them all, was a small child. Her dress too small, her face grubby, and her cheeks sunken. She was alone and lonely with naught to clutch but a worn basket of wildflowers. Cailean stopped and called her to him. He must have given her a whole penny, for life sprung to her eyes as she handed over a posy.

Out of all the sellers, he had chosen the one who needed it the most. His eyes had not lied; there was so much beyond that scowl. And now he was awkwardly handing it to her!

'Here, lass, ye will need this.'

'Oh... I thank ye!'

She took it and raised it to her nose, trying to hide her no doubt foolish smile. His eyes suddenly widened, before he looked away.

*

For Cailean, Glasgow was just another port. But Sorcha's excitement was oddly intoxicating. She was constantly twisting in her saddle. And her innocence was obvious. He willingly answered her questions. Yet she was oblivious to the riches sold, save for a longing stare at a manuscript seller. Most odd for a woman. She soon lost her vitality and quietened. No, when his head turned but his eyes lingered, she winced. How had he forgot her beating? All that twisting must be hurting her stomach. He stood up in his stirrups; the retinue was scattered. He could just make out Ewan and Iain.

Clear of the west gates, he called for them to halt. He

handed back Sorcha's rein before approaching Donald. The man was married; he'd understand women better. The nearby inns were overtly sordid. So carry on or go back to his representative's townhouse? There she could sleep in a proper bed.

'We've lost our rear and the lass is exhausted.'

His standard-bearer sniggered.

'Jesus, Mata, how old are ye?' scolded Donald. He took a moment to think it over. 'There's nae point turnin back, *mo ciann*. If we canter, we'll be at the site well before the others. She could rest there?'

It made sense. Sorcha sat oblivious, fiddling with her back.

'Lady Sorcha?'

'Aye, my lord?'

The lass blushed so easily.

'We're riding fast now.'

She pursed her lips before agreeing. Cailean nudged Taranis's side and the horse shot forwards. Glaistig easily matched pace; she was a plucky, if mischievous, beast. He kept an eye on Sorcha as they rode. Peculiarly, she always held her upper back stiff. Her lower back was now the same, and she hovered just above the saddle.

The site came into view. A designated place to sleep that was free. He chose a firepit and immediately laid down his plaid. Sorcha was struggling to dismount. He reached up to her.

'Come, you're hurting; let me help.'

She hesitated, likely due to pride.

'Ye're bruised and havenae ridden this far before. Dinnae be so rash.'

She relented. He held her steady until she gained her feet. How had he not noticed her hazel eyes? The gap between them decreased. Catching himself, he blinked and withdrew sharply. Internally cursing, he grabbed Glaistig's reins.

'Go and rest on my plaid. I'll look after yer mare.'

Again, his tone was gruffer than he intended. Not waiting for a reply, he led the horses to the river. They drank their fill, oblivious. Damn Alasdair for being incapable of the one task he'd set him! And where had it led him? To nigh-on kissing her! Should he ride back and sate his lust on some blind whore? No. It would not work. Clicking his tongue, he led the horses to a post. He was joined by a wincing Mata.

'*Mo ciann*, how do ye no strangle Donald?'

He blinked before snorting, 'There are worse forms of torture.'

Donald never could hold a tune. Not that he cared. Cailean glanced to the firepit. Sorcha lay with her head on her arm, seemingly impervious. He sat at her feet; ah, she had fallen asleep!

'Hush, Donald.'

He nodded in Sorcha's direction before rearranging her mantle. Her stillness, along with her pallor, did not bode well. Yet her forehead was cool. She was a primrose – appearing so delicate but so hardy.

'Poor thing. Do ye think we'll be moving from here?'

He took his time answering. 'Maybe, but I'll no force her.'

Pillanflatt was too far. Dumbarton could be reached before the gloaming, but all respectable inns would be full.

And what of those following her? He cast his eye over the campsite. He had never stayed there before. There were numerous pens for livestock. Already one was being filled by a drover. Hardy men who may be eager for a fight, or mistake attackers for suicidal reivers. Aye, they would not risk it here.

Slowly, he was reunited with his men. They chose quiet activities or also napped. Though they should stop glancing at Sorcha; he was handling it fine! Alasdair finally arrived with the cart. His jaw hardened; it reminded him that they needed to speak. But first the tent.

'Och aye, what's this then? Getting cosy while we slogged through the city?' Alasdair approached.

'Wheesht yerself. She's no used tae riding so much,' Donald replied.

'Of course she's no used tae it, she's a maiden!'

Damn him! He sprang to his feet. His brother took a step back before kneeling. His eyes lowered respectfully. Cailean's *leuchd-crios* shifted uneasily before also kneeling.

'That's twice ye have insulted the Lady Sorcha. There will no be a third time.'

'Aye, *mo ciann*.'

'Need I remind ye that she is under our protection?'

'I apologise, *mo ciann*.'

His men glanced at each other. He ignored them. 'We camp here tonight. Get the tent up first.'

Sorcha still slept; as he checked her she muttered sleepily and flicked his hand away. Thank the Lord! Not illness, just bone tired. He sighed. Reprimanding clan members was bad enough, but his brother? It was uncharacteristic of them both. Had he been too harsh?

The tent was up. Ewan caught his gaze with a smile and wink. Apparently not. Donald, too, motioned for him to stay put. There was to be more 'punishment' – normally something harmless but embarrassing. Staring into the fire, he waited for them to confront Alasdair.

'It's finished? We can go do the horses?'

'Aye.' That was Donald.

'But ye're no goin near them.' Mata's voice.

His brother's shout was muffled; his men had attacked. He glanced at Sorcha; she slept on. Indistinct chatter… further protests. Alasdair's garments flew into sight. So that was their plan. He piled more wood onto the fire. A splash suddenly rent the peace. He cursed as Sorcha sat bolt upright.

'What… where… did I…?'

'Aye, lass, ye slept. My brother bathes, tis all.'

*

Cailean sat with his back to the tent. Mercifully, Sorcha had been quick to retire. He pulled a small flask from his belongings, tossing it to his petulant brother – he was in naught but his plaid. Served him right. Still, he had made a promise and he would uphold it; the flask contained medicinal *uisge beatha*. Alasdair sniffed at its contents before nodding his thanks. They stared at each other before simultaneously cracking. He loved the daft sop too much to stay angry.

Ewan and Donald caught his attention. Glaistig refused to be unsaddled. She would swing away or quickly towards them. His lips twitched in amusement. When they pincered her, she shot back. They quickly retreated, likely fearing broken reins.

'Let's untie her an try tae unsaddle her as she walks,' suggested Ewan.

The mare put her head down and charged, tongue over bit. It took their combined effort to stop her. He blinked. She meekly returned to the post. Donald tried to get the saddle again. Glaistig halted, squealed and started to bounce. He bolted up, calling a warning. Ewan sprung back as she reared up; her hooves striking where his head had been. Using brute force, Cailean grabbed her bit and swung her head around to unbalance the mare. She followed the movement. He held her head to his chest. Glaistig calmed instantly; what the devil? As he relaxed and she sniffed his plaid, he growled. Of course, it smelt like Sorcha! He looked up. Onlookers had gathered, as had his men.

He kicked himself. She had not been acting mulish. His men could fight from horseback but lacked chivalric training. And Thomas had warned him that Glaistig's training was thorough. Likely aided by having one rider her entire life.

'I'm sorry. The blame lays with me.'

'Surely she was just overheated, *mo ciann*?' asked Donald.

'Nae, Taranis would do similar if he didnae ken ye.'

Why was his cousin handing Ewan his belt? Surely not a bet? He dismissed their behaviour; this moment was better used to teach.

'Iain?'

His foster came forwards.

'This is one reason why we aim tae kill a horse and no just its rider.'

'Cailean?'

A soft voice called out; facing its owner, his mouth dropped open. It was not the mare that was the fairy. She stood barefoot in the grass. The sun setting behind her illuminated her legs through the linen shift. Slender ankles, thick calves and a blanket covering her full chest. He was drawn to her pale face; framed with brilliant auburn curls that flamed in the evening light. *God's balls, it was no fae but Sorcha!* What was she doing outside the tent? And where had her breasts come from? He growled; it was not right! He shoved the now placid mare's reins into Ewan's hand.

'Cailean… is everything well?'

He strode across the grass to block her from everyone else's view. She smelt strongly of lavender. He imagined running his hands through her hair before lifting her…

'Aye, lass. The mare just forgot that we're friends. Get ye back tae bed.'

The last sentence shot from his mouth. And where had that tone come from? Sorcha lingered there, looking up at him. Her eyes wide and her lips barely parted as she searched his face. Could she not see what she was doing to him? After an agonising eternity, she accepted what he was saying. His eyes betrayed him; they fell to her backside as she turned and entered the tent.

Once she was safely inside, he tore towards the river. Stopping short of the water, he ran his hands through his hair. Never had he been so distracted by a woman before. And it had nearly cost Ewan his life. Then when they were safe, he had abandoned them again for her. He wanted her, all of her. And not just to sate his damned raging erection! He started pacing with ferocity and almost ran over a pedlar. The stooped, aged man gave him a knowing look.

'It's never easy, aye? But ah think I have what ye need...'

*

The world slept, oblivious to the torment plaguing Sorcha. A fever like none she had felt before radiated from her privy area. She softly moaned. It wanted to be fed but she knew not how, and it forbade her from staying still! Had her back not suffered enough? Her breast bindings were bloodied! She abandoned her pallet and paced. Mayhap her humours were unbalanced by the journey. Just beyond the tent's flap, Cailean let out a snort. Her breath caught in her throat – he slept outside her tent entrance again! She fell to her knees and spied on his sleeping form. He lay on his back, his face peacefully angelic.

She backed away and stared at the tent's flap. If he woke and found her there, what would he think? Still, she desired to press herself against him. Sorcha gasped. She wanted to know him carnally; to roll around like the maids and stable lads! Alas, that was sin! Unless... There had been no mention of a wife. No, it could never be. He was an earl and she low-born; men like him married for power and wealth. The devil mocked her. He tore away the lustful heat and replaced it with a cold emptiness. She returned to her pallet and pulled the blanket over her head to hide her wet cheeks.

Sorcha awoke to the sound of others breaking camp but made little effort to move. Despite sacrificing her wimple, the cloth smeared in her ointment had done little to ease her back. And her insides still carried an emptiness that no food could fill. She hugged her legs and rested her chin on her knees. They would arrive at court today and she could barely rouse any enthusiasm. She should turn back home while she still had a chance. But alas, she had to honour Pa by taking this opportunity to repair their family name.

The new ensemble was so extravagant; it must have cost Pa a month of earnings! The first piece, a pale blue kirtle with silver buttons up the arms. Holding it up to examine it, she recoiled with horror at what she saw. She knew the garment's cut. It would not work with bound breasts! Dear Lord, please no. Let it not all be so revealing! It was worse. The rich woad surcoat was sideless and would show the shape of her hip. But she had promised Pa and he had gone to the trouble of thoroughly completing it with hose, garters, an almost translucent veil, and a rich caul of royal blue thread and pearls.

Having dressed, she stood fidgeting with it for a good while. Nothing she did hid how exposed she was! Pray the mantle would work. It too was opulently lined with the winter coat of mountain hares. What was Pa thinking? As for her hair, she settled on a simple plaited crown, the rest tucked neatly into the caul and covered with the veil. She stared into her small looking glass – she was like a suckling pig dressed for some high table. A new life and a new semblance had been forced upon her. What else was she expected to change to appease others?

Cailean stood talking to Donald when she stepped out. The latter fell silent, his eyes widening before he dipped his head in a greeting. It made Cailean turn around. Sorcha felt her cheeks grow hot. She glanced to one side before lifting her eyes to his. Her greeting caught in her throat. He looked furious! She stepped back; for sure Pa would understand if she did not honour his wish. Alasdair blocked her. He offered her his hand with a reassuring smile. Was he making sure she kept her promise? She reluctantly took it.

'Ye look as beautiful as the broom that blooms on the side of Loch Alsh.'

He lifted her hand and placed a kiss on the back of it. What did he think he was doing? She snatched it away and looked back to Cailean. Tears blurred her vision, for he was gone.

'I… I need tae see tae Glaistig.'

She lifted her skirts and fled towards the horses. At least they were not so complicated.

Chapter 4

Much to Sorcha's distress, Cailean remained in his foul mood. Any attempt to converse resulted in nothing but grunts. And while the men behind them spoke jovially of home, she felt as jovial as the condemned. What had she done to deserve this? Pa had told her to stay strong, and who was stronger than a warrior in battle? She must take heart from that image. The fancy clothes would be her standard, the façade of a demure, obedient maiden her armour.

Her battleground, the king's residence, sat in its own grounds close to the river. A resplendent rectangle of joined buildings, the largest of which formed a double-ended great hall. To the left of it stood a stone kirk, and hidden away at the back were many other buildings. All were no doubt vital to daily operations – she dared not imagine the size of the buttery! Her heart sank further, for the stables were some distance away. Although it was mid-afternoon, the area pulsed with activity akin to Glasgow's streets. Individuals came and went past numerous guards. Somewhere, men trained and falcons shrieked. She already hated it.

Cailean guided them around the building and into the courtyard at the back. They halted in front of the steps leading to the main entrance. Most peculiar was the lack of interest in her arrival. A lone, rotund man with an equally round face awaited them. His countenance was welcoming at least, though it appeared that he was not one for idleness. She slid off Glaistig and before she could do anything, a young stable lad took her mare's reins.

'Oh…!'

She tried to stop him but Cailean caught her hand. Her heart jumped, only to be crushed: he was avoiding her gaze. She too was being led away and, like her mare, she could do little about it. They stopped in front of the waiting man.

'John, this be Lady Sorcha Gilchrist of Henderleithen.'

He lowered himself almost to his knees and she did likewise, respectfully correcting him. She would not put on airs just because Pa's estate granted her the title of Lady.

'Greetings, Lady Gilchrist. I am the seneschal of Pillanflatt; it is at His Grace's request that I help ye tae settle here.'

'That is most kind of His Grace.'

Once more she donned the measured tone of one well-educated. She clasped her hands and looked at the floor ahead of her.

'His Grace thanks my lord for the safe delivery of the Lady,' John told her escort. 'He also wishes to speak with ye and the ambassador on the morrow.'

'Ye jest? Can he no let a man go home?' Cailean took his leave without so much as a goodbye. Did he have to hurt her so?

'If my lady would care tae follow me?'

Care to? What other choice did she have? John led her into the first of the bigger buildings. Corridors led away from the antechamber, no doubt to residences for those like Cailean. She had to find the strength to put him behind her or she would surely drown. They continued straight into the great hall. Despite the abundance of fine hangings, there was nothing pleasant about this place. She felt the cold, hard eyes of those she passed. It was no better than picking a ripe, juicy apple and cutting it open to find nothing but maggots within. If only she could discard this place like she could an apple.

They passed the dais and through an ornate door into a chamber that mirrored the entrance. Only this included padded benches where the door had been. The royal quarters. He was taking her straight to the queen! After leading her up some steps, John stopped at a nearby door. He shifted his overstuffed bag and glanced around.

'My lady must be in good standing. For down there are the queen's quarters and back that way are the king's.'

Not the queen then – but why here and what was he talking about? She had never met the king, let alone made an impression. He must have confused her with someone else, for surely her place was a pallet *outside* the queen's door? Before she could contradict him, he opened the door and ushered her inside. The chamber left her dizzy and speechless. It was so bright! The walls had been whitewashed and then painted with fake brickwork and flowers. There were glass windows and a bed so thick with mattresses it must be like sleeping on a cloud! The rest of the furnishings were brightly coloured and ornately carved. This one chamber must cost more than Pa's manor. She bit her lip. There really was a grave misunderstanding!

'I apologise for speaking so loudly just now. His Grace insisted upon my doing it for your safety.'

Shuddering, she tried her best to correct him.

'I beg yer pardon for I fear these are not my chambers. I am nothing but a trader's daughter, here tae serve my queen.'

The last thing she wanted, or needed, was to get in trouble on her first day at court. Yet the seneschal showed no interest.

'My lady, I just do the king's bidding. He also wished for ye tae have a maid – this is Ailis. She has just finished her training and comes from a most trustworthy merchant family.'

The chamber suddenly felt far too warm. Would she be punished for this mistake? Or sent home to further disgrace Pa? He had suffered enough with Michael. A brown-haired girl of fourteen approached and knelt. She still retained a childlike shape, and was pale, like she too would swoon.

'Ailis... what a beautiful name!'

It was all she could bring herself to say. She tried to follow it with a warm smile. From the look she received, it had not worked. Well, that made two of them. John rustled loudly through his bag, searching for something. He chuckled when he found and pulled out two missives, and a set of keys. He passed them to her.

'These are yours, my lady. Ailis will see tae any needs and show ye around. Now before I go, there was one last thing... Ah yes! His Grace wishes tae see ye in the morning before ye begin yer duty to the queen.'

As quickly as he spoke, he bowed and left. She surveyed the room once more before examining the items. At least one of the seals belonged to Pa. She ran her finger over the wax before turning to Ailis.

'Ailis, I think there has been a misunderstanding.'

'Forgive me, my lady. I was hired tae serve Lady Sorcha Gilchrist. Are ye no her?'

She was as timid as a mouse!

'I am that woman.'

The maid relaxed; Sorcha bit down her frustration and strode to a window. She threw it open and embraced the breeze. She rubbed her temples, mind racing like a hare chased by dogs. Behind her came a knock at the door, and Ailis hurried to answer before she had the sense to say anything.

'My lady, yer chests are here.'

So preoccupied was she that she did not at first register the words. Turning, she gasped. Several men had carried into the chamber two large chests along with her single, small one.

'Wait! They are no—'

It was too late.

She let out a defeated sigh and unpinned her mantle. It looked like she was staying there for the day at least. Ailis was suddenly upon her, whisking her outer garment away. Sinking into a chair, she tried to think again. It was hopeless with the maid flittering around!

She sent Ailis off to enquire about Glaistig, with instructions for the marshal. Without her there, she hoped he would take heed. Now she studied the missives. The unfamiliar one may hold a clue as to who the chambers were originally intended for. Yet could she bring herself to break the seal? What if it spoke of something treasonous or was highly personal? She was backed into a corner – what other hope did she have? Carefully she opened it, to find a bill of sale.

'*Laird Thomas Gilchrist, acting on behalf of Lady Sorcha Gilchrist, ordered...*'

Praise the Lord that was all it was! She read on. A complete collection of new gowns, shoes and accompaniments. All to be placed in two provided chests and forwarded on to Pillanflatt. Another excessive gift from Pa. He really should not have spent so much on her! She would write and gratefully admonish him.

Wait.

To send the trunks, fill them up, and have them arrive in four days was impossible. Let alone send a missive that arrived ahead of her. She read through the receipt again. It had been arranged six months before and paid on her behalf by the steward of her property. She ran to the window, but it was no use: it was not poor writing or a misspell. Henderleithen was her brother's inheritance, not hers. Her stomach lurched and the room span. Pa had planned this, but why? His missive must contain the answers. She breathed slowly and deeply. Now was not the time to swoon, or worse – she needed to know!

Giving herself no choice, she grabbed the missive and tore the seal. The letter started warmly, with Pa stating that he loved her and always would. A pang of homesickness unexpectedly caught her, but she forced herself past it.

'*...My dearest child, there is a concern that I must address with you. It has weighed heavily on my heart to keep it from you for so long. Alas, I made an oath to our beloved king and only now has he granted me license to tell you the truth. For the sake of the realm, I raised you in secrecy as my own daughter. Your mother, God rest her soul, was a widow when we met and with child. You are of noble blood and your father...*'

Her chest tightened and she gasped for breath; as the world closed in around her, her legs slowly buckled. It could not be true, yet here it was in his own hand!

*

A freshly washed and changed Alasdair entered the great hall. It could not match the likes of the great Palais de la Cité, but it was one of the most richly appointed halls in the kingdom. And, whether he liked it or not, his second home. He caught snippets of conversation and hid a smile. Sorcha had the rumour grindstone pounding away. He would no doubt be accosted at some point by those who worked it the hardest. He kept his head down, not wishing to speak with anyone. And to avoid the angry gazes of fathers whose daughters cast coquettish glances.

He successfully made it to his place at the table just as the hall fell silent. The door to the royal quarters had opened. Whoever entered was unimportant, for the hall quickly filled with voices again. No, that was not true; the tone had changed. He tried to see over people's heads, but whoever it was stood small. Then the crowd parted and Sorcha appeared, led by her maid. Only this woman was not the Sorcha he knew. Where was her delightful radiance? Surely Cailean had not stolen all of it with his mood?

'My lady, this is yer place,' the maid said quietly.

'I thank ye, Ailis. Ye may go.'

Sorcha finally noticed him. A flicker of relief washed over her features before disappearing. He stood up and dipped his knee in greeting before smiling. She dipped in return, but nowhere near as low as she had before. Indeed, she was sitting above him.

'Lord Alasdair, it is pleasing tae see a familiar face in a crowd of strangers.'

'The pleasure is all mine, Lady Sorcha, for ye are far fairer on the eye than my old trencher companion.'

His flirtatious comment garnered no response other than her sitting down. Further away, Donald caught his eye. The man looked deliberately at Sorcha before looking at him again. Alasdair gave the slightest shake of his head and raised his shoulders just a fraction before they fell again.

During their meal, he pointed out a select number of individuals sitting around the hall. From who held the king's favour to who Sorcha should avoid. She politely listened but made no show of emotion of any kind until the end of the meal.

'I dinnae see Sir Cailean anywhere.'

'Ye willnae. He only dines in the hall on days when it's required of him.'

'Oh... I see.'

He glanced around before lowering his voice and leaning ever so slightly closer to her.

'Sorcha, I ken we barely know each other, but I like tae consider myself yer friend. What ails ye?'

She looked down at the trencher between them. For a good time, she stayed silent.

Finally, she spoke. 'Truthfully, I cannot say more than this: I ken not who I am.'

The words were murmured and the minute she concluded them, she departed. Alasdair sat back and watched her go. So much for leaving the mysteries of Henderleithen behind him.

*

Robert Bruce sat staring into his bedchamber's fire. For everything the crown had given him, it had robbed him dearly. The man he saw in his looking glass each morning still had broad shoulders, but his hair was mostly grey, his nose misshapen and his cheeks red. Add his crippled joints, and he was outwardly but a shadow. His sharp mind remained though, and even now, few could defeat him at chess or riddles. *That* was what kept his kingdom from falling. He nodded to his steward to proceed.

At his man's prompting, his ward entered and knelt in his presence. While she had the distinction of becoming his first ward as king, he had never met her. Her conduct was becoming and her clothing discreetly wealthy. Good. He gestured for her to rise and approach him. She neither lingered nor hurried as she came closer. Stopping a few feet away, she lowered herself once more, before standing with her eyes politely up, but not directed towards him. It was undeniable, Thomas had raised her well.

'Come closer, child, I'll no bite ye.'

She silently followed his instruction. He studied her face now that he could clearly see it. The resemblance was startling, though she appeared paler than her mother. No wonder Thomas had insisted that she remain hidden until needed. Now what was her name again? Ah yes, Sorcha. An interesting choice for such a timid flower.

'Och, Thomas was right about ye. Now I trust ye ken why ye here?'

'I received a letter, Yer Grace, instructing me that I am yer ward. The child of the late Lady Annabelle and… another.'

'Yes, this situation is rather unfortunate. I had my reservations about it, but yer stepfather convinced me otherwise. I believe Thomas treated ye well.'

'He… he was a father tae me.'

Her voice cracked and he softened his tone. Women often accepted their duty better when men displayed some sympathy for their plight.

'Ye are here until I can see ye safely wed tae a good man, Lady Sorcha. It will take me time tae find the most advantageous match. As I believe one should stay busy and the queen agrees, she permits ye tae join her entourage as a maid of honour. Should ye please her, ye will, upon your marriage, take the position of lady-in-waiting.'

Aside from a flicker of emotion in her eyes, she kept her face neutral. Excellent. A woman who accepted authority without question was a gift indeed. Nor was she aware of her betrothal.

'As Yer Grace wishes.'

'From yer estate I will permit an allowance of two pounds a month. Out of which ye must pay any whose service ye employ, yer horse's keep, and any other frippery ye women need these days. Yer meals will be provided for ye, though you are welcome tae supplement them. My clerics will keep a book for ye.'

He paused to let the scribe make a note of what he said before continuing. 'I believe ye ken Lady Evelyn Campbell? She is tae be your chaperone.'

'Aye, Yer Grace. The lady kindly tutored me on etiquette.'

She did not even know it was he who'd chosen Evelyn. The old hen was notoriously maternal towards anyone she considered a waif – including himself during his early campaigns. She was also loyal, making her ideal; for that, he would overlook her occasional slides in decorum.

'Good. Now away with ye, my wife is waiting.'

She knelt once more before leaving.

Robert stroked his chin in thought. He had not believed his seneschal's report when he first read it. Having seen her for himself, it rang true. Again, Thomas was correct – there *was* more to a horse than its breeding.

Next came the tedious formality of welcoming or releasing individuals from the court. Of which, only Baron Macnachten was of interest. Though he had officially forgiven the man, he was wary. Why was he really here? It could not be just to find a suitable match for his daughter. He toyed with him, before permitting him to stay.

Then came the Macmaghan brothers – his genuine allies. Cailean had been his first choice of foster as king.

And Alasdair, well, he was on the rise. Whereas others he could trick with disinterest, it never worked on that pair.

He graced them with a smile. 'Tell me, how did it go?'

'Och, well…'

Oh joy, his earl was in a sarcastic mood.

'…the son led a fine welcoming party that shadowed us upon our return. No blood was drawn.'

He already knew of those men; what he wanted was their impressions. He turned his attention to Alasdair. The man looked apologetic.

'There was an altercation, Yer Grace. I was no present tae witness it. I can only confirm that no blood was shed.'

That left him no choice but to debrief Cailean, and getting blood from a stone was easier. He sat up in surprise as the earl spoke without prompt.

'Gaelic speakers with no love for Yer Grace. And accustomed tae French practices, so mercenaries. I am certain they are Highlanders.'

Cailean's report was a bitter brew, confirming what he feared. Yet he was not about to waste the opportunity it provided.

'Until we ken more, ye are tae remain at court, Sir Cailean. I want all my advisers at hand.'

He kept his laughter contained as Cailean's countenance shifted from surly to sucking gooseberries. The man was predictable, though restrained, and would need a suitable outlet. He called to his scribe to have his armourer double the usual stock of pells. Even Alasdair struggled to contain his mirth at that order.

'What of this son? Ye spoke that he led them.'

'If I may, Yer Grace,' Alasdair interrupted, 'the son

of Laird Gilchrist is a prattling, foolish, *drukkin* wastrel. He fancies himself as a lord but is as base as a common swineherd.'

'The men used him, no more,' added Cailean.

His ambassador liked his insults, but he had never heard him use so many. No wonder Thomas spoke so little of his son; the shame he must carry.

'So, he is irrelevant?'

Both brothers answered at the same time, giving differing responses. He tapped the arm of his chair in annoyance.

'A bully o the weak, no more.'

'A possessive individual, yer Grace. He may try to be of nuisance, as he regards the Lady Sorcha as his property.'

Grains of truth in both answers, no doubt. For those who bullied the weak did not like their toys taken away. He would, of course, fail but contingencies must be planned. And what of the mercenaries? He needed to speak to Alasdair alone.

'Sir Cailean, ye are dismissed; Lord Alasdair, I have missed our games of chess and it would please me to engage in one.'

The men knelt in unison, and murmured their acceptance of his wishes. Further away, his vassals prepared a table with his chess set and drink. And his scribe packed up, knowing this game would go unrecorded. He sat at the table and bade Alasdair to join him.

'I met with my ward earlier. She kens nothing and I assume my earl is the same?'

'Aye, Yer Grace, though there are some interesting developments regarding that.'

'Pray tell.'

'I believe love is taking its course.'

His eyebrows shot up. Cailean cared not for wooing women or whores. Perchance this change had loosened his tongue? Indeed, Alasdair explained how he had meddled to assess this situation. His brother had not been amused and had defended the lady's honour.

Robert chuckled before making his opening move.

'The chieftains wish tae ken of the lady's character. I assume they will now push for the betrothal tae be enforced,' he added.

That gave Robert pause. As eager as he was to see the couple wed, he needed more time. And he wanted to witness their courting for himself. Nothing to do with a wager he had with his nephew.

Alasdair made his first countermove.

'Ye're no tae act on it until ye receive my word,' Robert ordered.

'Aye, Yer Grace. May I humbly enquire as tae why?'

'Ye will one day ken all, Alasdair. Until then, I have a matter of utmost urgency. There is a man here in my court that I fear is plotting against me.'

Chapter 5

What gave Alasdair the freedom of the court he never knew, but it aided him immensely. He could come or go at any hour – or, like now, he could sit in wait like a cat hunting its prey. Indeed, the cushioned window seats in the royal quarters were a pleasant spot to do so. In the enclosed garden below, the queen took air with her ladies. All, excepting Sorcha, were enjoying themselves. Her ability to mask was impressive, but he would be a poor spy if he could not see past it.

He hardened his jaw. Robert had revealed little more than that he already knew. Though she had not been told that until she arrived. Jesus, she had not asked for the world she'd been dragged into any more than he had. And yet, here they both were. He would do his damned best to protect her until Cailean could.

His chosen 'prey' was approaching. The Good Sir James Douglas held the esteemed position of being Robert's closest friend. Alasdair began to rise, only to be waved down, so he dipped his head to acknowledge Sir

James's seniority. Both in rank and in fashion, for it was his French choices that Alasdair copied. Flattery goes a long way. Feigning disinterest, he turned back to the window; it caught Sir James's curiosity.

'Ah, dinnae tell me ye too are enamoured with our newest arrival?'

'Nae, more like concern, my lord.'

Alasdair spoke genuinely, sensing how it made Sir James draw closer.

'Ye fear for her?'

'She is cut from the same cloth as Cailean, but lacks his strength.'

'Then it is good that they are tae wed.'

'He is but a man, with his own weaknesses. I fear Robert's plans for them.'

The warlord fell silent. A thinker like himself, it was Sir James's ruthlessness in battle that set them apart. After some time, he swung away from the window to smile gravely at Sir James. For Cailean, and now Sorcha, he would use every trick he knew.

'I will do nothing tae sway Robert's path, Alasdair, but ye are right to be concerned. For Cailean and for Thomas's sake, I will help where I can.'

So few words, but they spoke volumes! Whatever Robert was planning, Sir James did not approve. Alasdair gave a short nod, for brothers were not just of the womb: Cailean had, by pure chance, become the babe of their brotherhood. But what of Thomas? Who was he to Robert and the good sir? He dared not push the man any further. Once again, he would disturb the keeper of the king's records for breadcrumbs. As a trade, he let slip news of who Edward had offended lately. There was a longstanding wager amongst many of the lords on who would be the next to rise against England's lousy king.

*

Thomas was nigh-on non-existent! The majority of what Alasdair found consisted of bills of sales and land taxes, the latter having been honestly procured. Furthermore, his acquisition of harnesses and horseshoes post-battle was hardly suspicious. Yet he had been there for every major skirmish. That required a lot of either luck or knowledge. Alasdair would be a wretched dog to give up on this bone. But he could only do so much in a day, and Cailean's incessant brooding made asking him impossible.

He quickened his pace, heading towards his quarters. A wash, a nip from his stash, and something not so straining would end his day well enough. Rònan fell into step with him. When did he return from Norway?

'He flies no more for Robert,' his fellow ambassador and spy informed him.

Alasdair convulsively closed his fist tight; the key and scrap of parchment were still on his body.

'It has been confirmed?'

'Aye, we but wait to see who takes his place.'

He worked to keep his face and pace the same, but he could not stop the bile that rose within. Thanks to that distinctive hand, Alasdair had quickly learned that his enigmatic mentor was Robert's spymaster. He had thought it normal. But now? Had it been because…? Jesus, no. He was no leader of men. Just being Cailean's second was so difficult that, unconventionally, he shared the position with Donald. Yet everyone seemed intent on insisting he was!

Alasdair stopped outside the ambassadorial quarters. 'He will make himself known. I would keep ye company were it no for the fact that ah've spent most of the day amongst manuscripts. And now, I fear, the night draws in.'

'Then I have kept ye long enough. I bid ye goodnight.'

Everything in this damned role was a *double entendre*. Let them think he was busy with their not-so-savoury duties. For certain they would not disturb him. His companion parted with him in the small hall while he continued further into the building and into his chamber.

Something was off. And no, it was not caused by his kin or the chambermaid. He slowly bolted the door; the boxbed and trunk were clear. His tapestry lay flat against the wall, his panel window was locked, and his table uncovered. There was nowhere else to hide. Sinking onto his stool, he studied the room again. Everything looked undisturbed, apart from the carved flower. Kneeling at the base of his bed, he twisted it and the panel gave way. Inside there were two new objects: an ornately bound book and a simple box.

Alasdair set them on the table and placed his chin on his hands. For how long he sat there staring at them he could not tell, but stare he did. To be a child again, driving his mother to distraction! He took the key from his pouch. It fitted the box. To open it would be to confirm his worst fear, so he ignored it and focused on the book. A bestiary of some sort, decorated with glass beads, under each of which was an animal. A bear, a raven, a dragon and an eagle. He studied it closely but found no method to open its clasp. Only the glass beads gave way, but none opened the book.

Damn it, the box likely contained instructions. Its lock opened with a soft click. He was going to be sick. Instead, he reached for the small bottle of Cailean's *uisge beatha* he had filched last winter. A good dose of liquid courage helped him open the lid. Under it sat the tool of his newest office: a seal stamp bearing a raven's head. *Now he was the king's spymaster.*

He reached for another mouthful of the drink before reluctantly stashing it away. Falling into a stupor would do nothing. He was honour-bound to accept his promotion. Until then, he had been in a loch sheltered by the greatest of mountains. Now he faced the deepest depths of the open sea. If he did not act appropriately, he would drown before he had begun to swim. Alasdair ran a hand through his hair, his finger tracing the small scar on his skull. An old habit. And heaved a sigh before reaching for his writing supplies. He had no choice but to tell them that the new spymaster had taken flight.

*

Several days later, Alasdair stood in an alcove, whispering sweet nothings into the ear of a chambermaid. He flicked back her veil and ran his fingers through her hair, making her moan for more. *Double entendres* and *mummeries* for the rest of his life! He loathed playing the flirtatious, debauching *sumph*, but it ensured few men took him seriously. And paired with his looks, it opened many a neglected wife's, or daughter's, mouth. They knew more than many men realised.

He hoisted the maid onto his hips and trailed his lips down to where her neck met her body. Ravishing it with kisses, he watched, through his curls, the antechamber behind her. Two men came to a stop in front of him, merely glancing in his direction in disgust. Perfect, for one of them was Baron Macnachten; the man was as slippery as an eel.

'The children of St Cuthbert's need more funds, Macnachten. They have lost the support of a patron after a greater cause led them to leave his lands.'

'I would give more but ye ken how bad the harvests have been lately. I'm holding on by the skin of me own teeth.'

'Ye ken that the rewards for supporting the Lord's cause are far greater than that.'

'I will try my best. That is all I can say on the matter. Now about yer son and my—'

'Och, nae!'

He squeezed the maid's backside; it was her cue to cry out and her lustful pleasure was most convincing. She was another spy, for many overlooked the serving staff. To complete the pretence, he rocked his hips.

'Damn that whoring Macmaghan. Ah dinnae ken why the king keeps him in his employ,' cursed the baron.

His companion agreed, before they split up and went their separate ways. Alasdair let out a snort of laughter before setting the maid down.

'Thank ye, Magda. Ah sincerely apologise for holding ye up with yer chores.'

'Nae, thank ye and remember, any time ye actually want tae, well, ye ken.'

She stood on tiptoes to kiss the corner of his lips and he gave her one of his dazzling but fake smiles. He watched her go, leaning against the alcove. He'd be damned to believe that whoever 'The children of St Cuthbert's' were, they were linked to a Christian cause.

'Tae hear me name sullied again!'

Cailean's voice preceded him from around the corner. Jesus, he was still in that foul mood! It was bordering on ridiculous. Even so, Alasdair's office was a lonely affair, and his brother was the most authentic person at court. He plastered a bright grin on his face and bowed in the preposterous manner he used when appeasing fools and foreign kings. It normally got a good-natured eye-roll from Cailean.

'Forgive me, *mo ciann*, for bringing our name intae disrepute; I will strive tae dae better.'

'God's balls, Alasdair. One day ye'll tryst with the wrong woman and leave me tae pick up the pieces. Again!'

He kept the smile there to hide the sting of his brother's words. Why was Cailean hurting? And hurting enough to lash out at Alasdair's own grief and guilt? He gestured in the direction of Cailean's chamber. Whatever was going on, it needed to come out *now*.

Chapter 6

Cailean grabbed a bottle of *uisge beatha* from the gaudily-painted cupboard. What was wrong with unpainted wood? Earthier colours in general? Or for that matter, simplicity! One chest was all he needed. His weapons, armour and tack were more important. He nodded at Iain – an unusually calm lad – who sat cleaning them, before joining his brother at the table.

'Och, is it really that bad?'

He sent a withering glare in Alasdair's direction, and filled two goblets. That damned pedlar and Sorcha, the conniving bitch! He tossed the waste of good coin across the table. Alasdair picked the ring up and examined it. Cailean gulped down his drink and refilled it. The burn of the *uisge beatha* soothed his pride. It would also loosen his lips. He needed this out before it rotted his core.

'She looked me in the eye.'

'Aye, I ken she did.'

'But she's nae different tae the rest of them!'

Alasdair stared, slack-jawed. Iain too had stopped

cleaning. A quick reprimand was all it took to make him work. He raised his goblet in salute, muttering a *'slàinte mhath'*. Still the words refused to come. He abandoned the goblet for the bottle.

'Ye've seen her clothes! Parading... partridge!'

'Fetch the others,' ordered Alasdair.

Cailean blinked. He was not their father; drink did not make him that unpredictable! Nor would he throw himself on his sword for any woman. Damn her. Damn him for wanting the whore. He closed his eyes and took another mouthful. It was working! He should have seen this coming like Alasdair had. All those jibes! He knew women, and had seen through her pretence.

He found the words, 'I finally thought ah found someone, ye ken? Someone who saw past this and cared no for status. Yet now look at her. She wears nowt but rich gowns and frippery. Sits above even ye, and dances with the nobles! Ye ken she's wheedled a bedchamber in the royal quarters? They say Brus is fond of her because she's his bastard.'

'I highly doubt that.'

'Makes sense though, doesnae it? Couldnae have the English stealing another daughter!'

He fell silent, hugging the bottle, but Alasdair had barely touched his. More fool him! He should be pleased that he'd found out before marrying the she-devil. The bottle was almost empty; he needed another. This batch was a fine one. He staggered to his feet as the door opened. Lifting the bottle in greeting, he encouraged his men to join him.

'Come, come! There's drink enough for the lot of ye!'

He squinted when they got closer; they looked far from happy. His cousin had folded his arms.

'Och, we're celebrating, are we?' asked Donald.

He grinned. 'Aye, to no getting trapped by that harlot, the she-devil Sorcha!'

'Ah see. Is this why ye called us, Alasdair?'

'Nae,' responded Alasdair. 'Ah needed ye tae bear witness so he cannae banish me for doing this.'

What was his brother blethering about? He would never banish him. Alasdair appeared in front of him; he could move fast when he put his mind to it. A brutal blow to the jaw caught him. Where in the Lord's name had that come from? He fell onto his bed. His bottle was not so fortunate. How dare Alasdair attack him unprovoked? How dare he waste good drink? It would not go unanswered! He got to his feet and swung. The little *tyke* avoided him! He roared and charged after him. The wind tore from his lungs. He was on the floor under his men! How dare they pin him down? They should be apprehending Alasdair! He could not shake them off.

'God's balls, Alasdair, I'll skelp yer arse and feed yer balls tae a corbie! As for the rest of ye...'

He spluttered as cold water fell over his head. He spat out a rose petal and blinked the water from his eyes. Damned ewer! He sighed and slumped.

'I'd normally no agree tae such things, Alasdair, but ah think in this case it was warranted.'

His men agreed with Donald. The lot of them had fallen under her spell! Cailean snatched the linen cloth from his cousin.

'I kenned Grann tae be a *ranten drukkin*, but I never

thought ye would. What in the Lord's name is wrong with ye?'

Damn it, that hurt. Something had changed in his father after Loudoun Hill. Always strong-willed and hard on them, he had grown worse. Their mother's death had been his final downfall. He caught Alasdair rubbing his sore hand. Served him right.

'He's blinded by jealousy, and it seems he's taken up listening tae gossip,' Alasdair answered.

'Gossip? Nae wonder ye wanted tae skelp him.'

They helped him to his feet and over to the table. He sank into his chair, cursing whoever had had the forethought to move Alasdair's goblet. His mind was murky. What did they mean by jealousy? He had been tricked! But then the way she looked when she just woke and the way her hair fell…

'Ah, I see you're right.' Donald's voice softened.

'Huh?'

Lude-smitten sumph.'

He rubbed at his jaw and felt Alasdair's hand on his shoulder. God's balls, he was not some lovestruck youth! She was just a woman who needed protecting and was pleasing to the eye.

'Cailean, she's no Robert's bastard or Thomas's daughter, but a ward. Sorcha is highborn and is living according tae her station. Robert is just parading her around tae find a suitable match.'

He blinked; he could not fault that reasoning. But then if she was a noble orphan and available… he could make her his! But his chieftains… the contract.

'But she—' he protested.

'Is miserable and hiding it too well, ye *drukkin sumph*. Ye only have tae watch her to see that she performs as she did around Michael. No tae mention that she spends most of her free time in her chamber, like some other fool I ken of!'

He fell quiet and knocked his forehead with the heel of his palm. Guilt clawed at him. He had ripped Sorcha from a bad situation and abandoned her in another. Failed her as a knight and as a friend. Then he had the audacity to besmirch her. No wonder Alasdair had punched him! She needed protection, not scorn. He hit his head harder. Think!

Across from him sat Donald who was trying not to laugh.

He scowled. 'What is so damned funny?'

'Och, nothing, *mo ciann*.'

'Yer lips are no the only thing that loosens when ye drink.' Alasdair looked like their disappointed father. It was not helping.

Cailean glanced towards Iain; he had suddenly developed the ability to mind his own business. Typical. He would have to ride this out and plan accordingly. Let the court know she was his and off the market. It would involve playing their games. But it would be worth it.

A knock at his door startled him. He waved his hand, then remembered to speak. Sorcha's timid maid entered and lowered herself.

'Forgive me, my lord, for interrupting yer evening. My mistress, the Lady Sorcha, wished tae repay ye for the kindness ye showed in escorting her here.'

The maid handed him an earthenware jar. She was

struggling to keep her composure. Was he really that scary? He took it and waved her away.

'It is ointment to ease the tightness of scars. My lady apologises for the delay. She had to wait for the ingredients tae arrive.'

'Uh… thank the Lady Sorcha for me.'

She all but fled the chamber.

Cailean's fingers refused to work properly. Several attempts later, the waxed linen came off. Lavender filled his nose; Sorcha must love that plant. He dabbed a bit on his fingers. Its fatty substance spread easily, and a gentle heat radiated from it. The guilt returned tenfold. He could not just sit there. Despite his ridiculing her, she had sent him a gift. He needed to apologise right this minute!

*

Cailean followed the maid back to Sorcha's chamber. He pushed his damp hair off his face and knocked. The hall was rolling like a boat. Since when had it done that? She opened the door; a heavy robe covered her undressed state. Her hair was uncovered though regrettably still up. He stepped forwards, filling the door's frame. Why was she so nervous? She did not have to fear him.

'Greetings, my lord. I hope I didnae offend ye with my gift.'

'Cailean, me name's Cailean.'

He corrected her softly. She stepped back further into the chamber, inviting him in. He eagerly followed. Her skin, so perfectly soft in the evening sun. It had to be touched. His fingers lingered on her cheek. Her eyes widened; Lord help him, he could bathe in them.

'Then Cailean it is.'

'And it is I who should apologise for my unchristian behaviour. I have been a *sumph*. Please, Sorcha, say ye forgive me.'

The gap between them was gone. She stayed there. How had he not noticed how small she was? Then she licked her sweet, delicate lips. How they had plagued him!

'There... there is nothing tae forgive.'

She radiated heat; it burned him through his *léine*. He had to know her. Their lips met and there was no resistance. He cupped the back of her neck. His tongue slipped between her lips. At first she shivered, then naively tried to join him. He growled. Grabbing her waist with his free hand, he pulled her close. Dear Lord, she was made for his arms.

'My lady!'

'*Mo ciann*!'

The mixed cries of Ailis, Alasdair and Donald broke the moment. Their lips parted. He stared deep into her eyes and damned his chieftains. Betrothal or not, Sorcha was his and he would make it so. She broke away and lowered her face; no doubt not wanting the others to see what he saw. She burned for him too.

'Sorcha... ah need tae tell ye...'

Cailean tried to close the gap and his legs refused to do his bidding. He staggered, trying to stay upright in a now-spinning chamber. That damned *uisge beatha*! What was it doing to him? He held out his hands to her but all he saw was woven rushes. They were getting closer...

Sorcha gasped in horror as Cailean landed face-first on the rush matting. Drink had claimed yet another victim and he fair reeked of it. Afeared of what she would find, she could not bring herself to approach. Donald rushed into her chamber and hauled his chief over onto his back. Cailean's loud, drunken snores were music to her ears! She rushed forwards and knelt next to him. Her hand lingered on his cheek. Despite his state, there had been no tomfoolery in his actions. Her head reeled and her heart rejoiced!

Remembering herself, she backed away as Alasdair approached. He nudged Cailean with a toe before turning to her in disbelief. 'Lady Sorcha, I must offer ye my humblest apology. My brother is nae one tae often indulge like this.'

'I believe I can see why.'

Her voice shook but no longer from fear. That devilish torment clawed once more at her innermost privy areas.

'We were sat with Cailean, tae watch over him. After receiving yer gift he unexpectedly bolted. If we had kenned that he was going to come here and… well… ravish ye, we would have tied him down!'

She could hardly admit her feelings! Not trusting her tongue, she smiled politely. Alasdair bowed before helping Donald haul Cailean up. She clung to her robe in alarm; they held him like a sack of grain.

'If word spreads, we will defend yer honour, Lady Sorcha. And if none does, then we will no speak of this incident. Agreed?'

Sorcha nodded a bit too eagerly before motioning to the pale Ailis, who hovered in the background. 'Ailis, help them to escort Cai… the earl back to his chambers. Take them through the service passage and bid whoever ye meet no tae speak of what they saw.'

As soon as they left, she closed the door. Oh, Holy Mother of Christ, he had ravished her and, sin or not, she wanted more! She sprinted across the chamber and jumped onto her bed with a giddy squeal. Her fingers traced her swollen lips. Was it also a sin for her to wish that talk did spread? Surely then the king would have no choice but to see them wed!

*

'Ah said I'm coming!' Cailean's voice was a hoarse whisper.

He had woken in a dreadful state. Still dressed and reeking of drink. He could not recall how he had got there. Only *that*. Cradling his head, he lifted the latch. Alasdair entered with a steaming cup. Ignoring him, he returned to packing his bundle.

'I didnae think Robert had freed ye.' Alasdair's voice was too loud.

'He hasnae, but I cannae stay here.'

His brother frowned and thrust the cup at him. Willow bark, thank the Lord.

'I've shamed meself and the clan.'

'Wheesht! Think ye're the only *sumph* tae drunkenly kiss a maid?'

'Damn it, Alasdair, I'm no just any *sumph*!'

He was a coward too. Misleading them like that, forcing a kiss on Sorcha. All because she treated him well.

Yes, she was pretty, and naive, and… no. Nothing else. Alasdair could protect her. He fastened the rope around his sheepskin. The damned bark was not working fast enough.

'Well, I cannae stop ye. But will ye first help me with something?'

What now? His brother was still not smiling.

'Fine!'

'Just…'

Cailean glared at his brother.

'…put more than yer undershirt on!'

Finally dressed, he followed Alasdair outside. The sun taunted him mercilessly. He kept his head down. Where were they going? The scent of horse was getting stronger. He glanced up. The destrier barn? It contained the best loose stalls around. He blinked and welcomed the darkness. In the aisle lay a body. Without prompt, he approached the person. Dead from a blow to the head. And multiple other wounds. He turned the head. A single milky eye stared back at him. He cursed.

'So it's one of them then?' Alasdair asked.

He nodded. Standing, he focused on the stalls. Two stood empty. One with the beam down, the other split asunder. *Outwards.* He looked around at the horses. Taranis and Glaistig were missing.

'Where are they?'

The approaching stable marshal answered. 'Having a great time in the enclosure outside, Sir Cailean. The stallion will no leave the mare alone.'

The lucky *tyke*. If only his life was so easy! He gestured to the lowered beam.

'Lady Sorcha's mount?'

'Aye.'

It was a warning; they knew what Glaistig meant to Sorcha. And they were aided by an insider. The men here were meticulous about admittance; this stable held the most expensive horseflesh. God's balls, he could not leave her here with them. She needed proper protection. A husband with men to command. *His clan.* The chieftains would understand.

Alasdair interrupted his thoughts. 'The lady is no tae be told of this attempt on her mount. Any idea as tae which killed him?'

'Damned if I ken. Likely both.'

He cast another look at the broken beam. His own stables were going to need work.

The marshal sighed. 'We'll treat the mare like a seasoned warhorse. I dinnae suppose ye have any idea how tae separate them?'

'Aye, Lady Sorcha Gilchrist.'

'She's o *that* Gilchrist?'

Alasdair answered for him. 'Stepdaughter. Trained the mare herself.'

He was done here; he spun around and left. His brother caught up and they stepped off the path. He stopped under a tree and leaned against its trunk. The willow bark was wearing off.

'Jesus Christ,' cursed Alasdair.

He silently agreed.

They exchanged theories. And speculated on who could be assisting them. He rubbed the bridge of his nose; he needed rest. Unpacking could wait. Unfortunately, his damned drunken plan could not.

'Alasdair, do me a favour?'

'Aye?'

'Send one of my men tae me. And,' he sighed, 'inform the king that my men are guarding her.'

'Brus will no like that.'

His hands clenched.

'I care not.'

Chapter 7

Alasdair had no issue finding Donald – and, consequently, Ewan. At court they had little to do but train and entertain themselves. He leaned against the wall and waited for the game of bones to finish. Donald was a fiend and no one at home would play him. Alasdair struggled to hide his yawn. Once he was sure Cailean would not choke on his own vomit, he had returned to his chamber and worked through the night. Alongside missives re-routed to him, he was receiving replies from his sources closest to court. As he feared, some familiar names were emerging. But nothing on Thomas.

He fiddled with his signet ring as Cailean's men broke off and approached.

Donald spoke first. 'Is this for you or Cailean?'

'Mmm, a bit of both. Ewan, he's in his chamber.'

'*Sair heid*?'

'Aye.'

Ewan sighed and left for the manor. Alasdair motioned for Donald to walk with him. He discreetly passed the ring to his cousin. Donald hesitated before slipping it onto his own finger.

'Ye ken the boat will arrive at Dumbarton tomorrow?'

'The one with Cailean's missives?'

'Aye. I have sessions. Would ye?'

'I do miss my wife so. I wonder if she has sent any word with the crew.'

Alasdair surreptitiously took one last look around. There was no going back, but Robert's orders be damned; his brother needed all the help he could give him. 'And if there is any word from the chieftains?'

'Well then, ah'd assume it was for Cailean.'

He gave the slightest of nods.

'The weather's been favourable,' added Donald. 'Ah'll ride out now. With luck, she'll have arrived early.'

'If not, stay at the Rose. They're discreet and the crew ken tae find me there.'

He bid Donald a safe journey and headed back towards the manor. The death at the stables still plagued him. Insiders would have been needed to find the horse. But if the dead man had been seen with one, they would be remembered. He had to have been told, but then, how did he get past the watch? Alasdair stopped at the bottom of the steps and observed the guards. They *seemed* attentive. Jesus, not another task.

Turning sharply, he walked headfirst into a woman's bosom. Upon extracting himself, his jaw dropped. She stood almost as tall as him, albeit higher due to the steps. Her blonde hair flowed free and long under her veil, though she looked older than the average maiden. Plain-faced and blue-eyed, she justifiably looked furious.

He gave her a dazzling smile, sure to melt her heart. Her stance did not change. A most courtly kneel? Nothing.

'Forgive me, my Lady, but tae accidently walk into yer bosom was a blessing indeed.'

'Ah'm no "yer lady", Alasdair Macmaghan, and ah'm no some frivolous hen ye can woo with yer foolish prancin aboot.'

He could hardly believe what he was hearing. This Lagertha of the sagas stood before him and just as savagely cut him down. How invigorating!

'I see ye ken me but ah've no had the pleasure of gettin tae ken ye.'

She narrowed her eyes before letting out a humph and stepping to one side to get past him. He watched her walk away. For one so tall and strongly built, her hips swayed delectably.

'Och, lad, ye have no chance with that one.' The seneschal appeared at his side. 'She be Mordag Nicnachten and her reputation precedes her. Scared away nigh-on a dozen suitors. Her father is at his wits' end trying tae find some poor cur who will take her.'

Nicnachten? She was the baron's daughter? Just his luck!

'I can see why, John. She's stunningly fierce.'

Abandoning his thoughts, Alasdair faced the jovial man and tucked his thumb just inside his cotehardie. Retrieving the missive he had hidden there, he deftly passed it to John.

The seneschal deftly hid it in his always-overflowing bag before making a great show of searching for something.

'I have some missives here for ye. I believe one is from yer tailor. I also hear that the wolves are getting bolder this year again, no doubt driven by their hunger.'

Alasdair flicked through the small pile. 'Perhaps. Have any been found too close?'

'Just the ones ye ken of.'

He blinked and glanced at John. *Double entendres* again, and since when had his tailor ever written to him? Jesus, he needed sleep. Tucking the missives under his arm, he made his excuses.

*

A whole day wasted in bed and Cailean was still as weak as a babe! Poor Iain was being kept busy with his orders. He pushed away his midday meal. A couple of bites and he could not stomach it. Alasdair would soon bring news from home. Sorcha's gift caught his attention. It was worth a try. He rubbed some into his scar; the heat eased its constant ache.

'Enter,' he responded to a knock.

Wait. He had left the door unlatched – Alasdair typically rushed in. Donald entered with his satchel.

'Did Alasdair no go for it?' he asked.

'He had a session, *mo ciann*, and I hoped for news from Bridget. And he only went and recommended the Rose on Grapien-cunte Lane.'

Cailean blinked. The districting around the inn must have altered. No wonder their profits had improved.

'What other news?'

'Bridget wishes me home before autumn. No doubt

tae keep her warm. And young Donald is now at foster. I dinnae ken where the time went with him.'

'Blink of an eye, Mither would say.'

'Aye, Moira was right about that. Aside from that, no much else. Harvest is already faring better this year.'

'And?'

Something was being held back. Donald sighed and handed him the satchel. 'Ah'm told there was a meeting held in yer absence.'

That was odd. He reached into the bag and felt something hard. 'Damn the lot o them tae hell and back!'

That was why they met! He threw the satchel onto the floor. Again, others were dictating *his* life!

Donald coughed awkwardly. 'Ah, I thought it may be that.'

'I'll no do it, Donald. I've sacrificed enough for clan and king.'

'*Mo ciann...* Cailean...'

'Nay. They will accept it this once.'

Not once had he done anything without consulting the clan. Not once! They owed him this. He tightened his jaw and got up. He would write back immediately. He would not marry some shallow woman. Donald took the betrothal agreement out of the bag and stood reading it. The pendant seals of his father and king mocked him. Just burn the damned thing!

'This indenture made... between King Robert Bruce... and Laird Grann Macmaghan...' Donald skipped the legal verbiage, '...agreed for a marriage between Cailean Macmaghan... and Sorcha Gilchrist, ward of the state...'

'Dinnae mock me, Donald!'

'It's written here plainly. And again "make tae the said Cailean Macmaghan and Sorcha Gilchrist"…'

He ripped the document from Donald's hands. *Sorcha Gilchrist*. He staggered backwards; it could not be true. But there it was. The oddly shaped cross that was his father's signature. *God's balls, she really was his!* He laughed and Donald smiled. Could it be any better? And did she know? No, she could not.

Alasdair walked in and latched the door behind him. He looked at the betrothal agreement and cursed violently.

'Jesus, ye ken. Donald, I told ye tae wait for me!'

'Wait, what? I thought ye… never mind. *Ye* can explain tae Bridget why I spent the night in a brothel!'

What? Alasdair had known? They had never kept secrets. But why? Come to think of it, why had he not been told sooner? *By anyone?* He slumped into a chair. And raised a hand to silence Donald's blathering.

'Och, dinnae look at me like that, Cailean,' countered Alasdair. 'I was oathbound tae Father, as were the chieftains that kenned. All he told us was that the betrothal was a reward for saving Robert's life. And that her name was Sorcha and that she was of suitable status. Nothing else.'

'Did ye no press?'

'Of course I did, but just mentioning it was enough tae enrage him. Do ye ken how close I came tae a skelping? Especially after his first apoplexy.'

Cailean stopped pinching his nose and winced. They should be celebrating. Instead, it brought more riddles. 'Robert forbade him.'

'I cannae confirm that.'

'And ye,' he muttered as Alasdair sat down. 'I'll no tell

her. None of us will. And no using Donald – or anyone else – tae get around these orders.'

His cousin was still muttering to himself. He glared at his brother.

Alasdair sighed. 'Donald, the Rose helps pay yer stipends. Tae save money, we have as many stay at our properties as possible.'

'Ye damned *tyke*, why did ye no say that in the first place?'

'I use it for other things and wish tae keep its owners hidden.'

Cailean looked heavenwards; why was he not surprised?

'So why now?' He altered the conversation.

'I dinnae like this, Cailean.'

They talked about Alasdair's concerns for several hours. But it did not change his plan. She was his; he'd force Robert's hand to honour it. And get her away from this damned place!

*

Alasdair sat in the hall of his residence, nursing a drink. The noise around him was a welcome companion. Cailean's reaction – well, it was not what he'd expected. His brother was often shouting, usually to keep people away. But not this time. Being quiet meant two things: he was either dangerously angry or he had a plan. Or worse, both! But why had he not shared it? Was it because of him keeping his knowledge a secret? No, surely not. But still. He could not lose his brother because of what he had become. His family would, God willing, be around long after Robert was feeding the worms. And what of Robert's line? If Elizabeth did not give him a son, it would be a Stewart on the throne. They may not want the Raven.

So be it; let it be known that he was for his family first. Now and always!

Someone grabbed his earlobe and dragged him from his seat. 'Och, ow, ow, ow! Uncle, please! I'm no a child!'

To a chorus of laughter, he was dragged outside and let go. Rubbing his sore ear, he came face to face with the chief of Clan Domhnaill. Jesus, he looked unhappy.

'Dinnae "please, Uncle" me. Now, tell it tae me straight.'

'Pray tell, what "it" is that ye speak of?'

'I told ye no tae act the fool with me, lad. Ah ken about her. I was there! And I ken the king ordered him tae fetch her. But there's been no announcement.'

Had someone been eavesdropping? But that door was too thick, their voices too low, and the windows were closed.

'I swear on the Bible, I ken no what ye speak of.'

'Is Cailean trying tae woo her without kenning who she is?'

Thank the Lord for neutral faces! But wait, that meant his brother was playing courtier! He burst out laughing. He must see it for himself!

'What's he done?'

'Sent her some trinket this morning.'

'Och aye, he showed me something a couple of days ago. I didnae expect him tae send it.'

'Jesus Christ on a ewe's arse. Why did the pair of ye have tae turn out as contrary as Moira?'

He sniggered some more but Aonghus Óg ranted on.

'Damn it, I owe Randolph a fat purse. We bet summers ago that Cailean would never try tae win a woman's heart. Unless…'

'Och, no. I'm no stopping him!'

'Then ye better find a way tae pay my debt.'

'Wheesht! Did you no learn the lesson the first time a Macmaghan outwitted ye?'

The string of curses made the jibe so much sweeter. His parents' story was sung throughout the west coast and isles for it echoed the ways of the past. And as much as his uncle bemoaned it, he had been happy for them. Alasdair started walking away, and then stopped. What had Aonghus Óg said?

'Will ye walk with me, Uncle?'

There was nowhere in particular that he wished to walk but keeping moving made it hard for ears. He asked his uncle for the events that fateful day. But there was little that he did not already know.

'I'm sorry, Alasdair. For the most part, Robert kept his own counsel. I kenned that her just being alive made trouble for him, but not the how or the why.'

'I fear he has shifted that trouble onto Cailean.'

'I believe that Grann feared the same.'

Chapter 8

Sorcha stared at the cross and struggled to concentrate on her prayers. After their kiss, she had tried desperately to sleep. Yet her head was rife with indecent thoughts, and the heat that clawed at her would not cease. Worse, she longed to seek him out when sober to be ravished once more! Lord have mercy, she could not bear another night like it. But prevail she must. Alas her queen, the fair Elizabeth, had not helped. One would think that she was teasing her by having her read romances aloud on a daily basis. But that was absurd; the queen was already heavy with child and just needing to rest.

Although…

She studied the silver ring that she wore and ran her finger over the cool opal. Such a beautiful stone. And better, it was from Cailean! He had sent it several days ago, causing much agitation amongst the ladies-in-waiting. The very women who insulted and chided her for being the lowest amongst them had been falling over themselves to see it. Only the Lord knew why! Worse still was the behaviour of the men. They had been but curious before, but they now swarmed around her, giving countless little tokens. The likes of rings, brooches, polished looking glasses, and even a small book of hours!

Evelyn, who now steadfastly remained at her side, had explained this was expected behaviour. Especially with Cailean being so powerful. Such heartless, petty gestures were the preposterous backbone of this wretched place. Even she had been encouraged to buy gold rings as favours. May the Lord free her from this place, where power and wealth ruled supreme! She started out of her thoughts – they were moving. Falling in behind Elizabeth, she kept her gaze on the back of the lady in front. It helped deflect some of the attention she was receiving.

'My lady queen, I trust ye are well.'

Sorcha quickly lowered herself as Robert addressed his wife.

'As well as expected, given the situation, my lord the king.'

'It pleases me tae hear that. I have arranged for games outside, after noon. I would be most obliged if ye joined me.'

'I will endeavour to be there, as the air should soothe your restless son.'

*

The queen was true to her word. After a light repast and a change of gowns, Sorcha accompanied her mistress to the lawn in front of the manor. Colourful pavilions, light music and laughter welcomed her. Almost the whole court was in attendance, yet it felt as carefree as the May fair her father would host. She lifted her face to the sun and savoured the rare warm day – Elizabeth had freed her to partake in the festivities. And she had done likewise to Ailis.

'My lady, would ye care tae play a game of quoits with me?'

'If Evelyn doesnae mind, then I think I shall.'

'Och, ah'd never say no tae a bit o fun. Just get one o the strapping laddies tae put a bench near it for me, Ailis.'

Sorcha should have seen through the innocent guile for Ailis did excel at the game! As poor an opponent as she herself was, her spirits soared. If only she could be so free all the time. After losing a third game, she laughed and begged for mercy. Iain too must have been permitted the afternoon off for he approached and bowed politely.

'My lady, if ye permit it, ah would be delighted tae play with Miss Ailis.'

'Please do, for I am sure ye will be a worthier opponent.'

She joined Evelyn on the nearby bench to keep a watch over the pair, who appeared most taken with each other.

Her chaperone lacked her usual merriment. 'The knaves are circling like hounds again.'

They would not spoil her enjoyment.

'I ken, but what can I do? They do no wrong for I am no yet betrothed.'

'There is a lot ye can do, lass. Dinnae think for a moment that our king and queen dinnae watch ye tae see who ye warm tae. And while I ken it, lass, it's no so obvious tae the others.'

Her fingers found the ring and she bit her lip. How had Evelyn guessed?

'The ring, ye foolish filly. Ye wear it and no other. Why no make it clearer so they'll stop trying?'

She inhaled sharply, for her chaperone was right. She could not bear to wear the trinkets that decorum decreed she could not return. One of them adorned Ailis's finger. Still, dare she be as bold? Whyever not? The court was full of people taking what they wanted through fair or foul means. Alas, she was no sinner, so that left but one option. She gazed upon the royal couple; together, they watched the festivities. But what if the king did not wish it – or worse, laughed at her impudence? Surely, they of all people could understand love. Perhaps not Robert, but definitely Elizabeth.

'Please excuse me, Lady Evelyn.'

Having crossed the lawn and arrived at the royal canopy, her wits abandoned her. She quickly lowered herself and moved to the benches just behind Elizabeth's throne. Just walking up to them would be no good. She needed to have the queen's ear without the king being present. Hopefully, he would get up soon. She fiddled with her skirts as she sat down.

'Well now, Sir Cailean, this is a welcome surprise. To what do we owe this pleasure?' Elizabeth asked.

Mercifully, Sorcha caught herself before she fell backwards off the bench. What was he doing here? She must not stare, or even look at him!

'Yer Grace. Yer Highness. I beg permission tae escort the Lady Sorcha to the archery range.'

Her mouth filled with wool. Please, Elizabeth!

'If my maid permits it, then you are welcome to. Now, I feel this is quite pointless, but I will say it nonetheless: *I am watching you.*'

'I thank thee.'

Her breath failed her as Cailean stepped aside and approached her. He bowed awkwardly, though his eyes never left hers. She knew that look; she had seen it on Michael's face, though it lacked his anger. She shivered.

'Lady Sorcha, would ye care to accompany me?'

'I accept yer offer, Sir Cailean.'

She tried to keep herself calm and composed, but then rose far too quickly. Perhaps, instead of telling Elizabeth, she could show her? Finally, a use for all those romances! Though they walked without touching each other, she got as close as she dared.

'I wasnae expecting to see ye here.'

'Aye. I see ye like the ring.'

'It is beautiful, and I will treasure it always.'

Cailean half-halted to stare into her eyes again, and Sorcha's heart fluttered. She swore she saw a slight upturn of his lips as he grunted in approval. When they arrived at the range, he grabbed a bracer and she held out her arm for him to fasten it on.

'I want tae taste yer lips again,' he murmured. 'But until I can...'

'I want ye tae... oh!'

Her words came out before she could censor herself, and then Cailean placed a kiss on the inside of her wrist. Oh, dear merciful Lord! Her skin felt like she had touched something metallic but far more welcomed and powerful. What she had thought was a small smile shifted into a real one. Somehow, as captivated as she was by its beauty, she managed to force her words out.

'You should smile more often.'

'Only for you.'

He took a bow and stepped behind her. What was he doing? Oh my! He was pressing himself against her back! What had Evelyn called her? A foolish filly? Of course, he was helping her notch and shoot. Still, the feel of him, so sinfully perfect. And if she leaned back into him? He growled softly into her ear, his breath soft and warm, sending shivers down her spine.

'Lower your elbow, there, that's it. Now let the string slide from yer fingers.'

The arrow flew true and firmly planted itself in the target. She laughed and fidgeted with delight. Cailean's responding chuckle sounded a little hoarse. She wanted to bathe in his sight, but he was already encouraging her to notch another arrow.

It was over far too soon for Sorcha's liking, but there were no more excuses for them to linger close to each other. She thanked him for his escort and returned to the royal canopy. Judging by the whispers and looks, it was not just her guardians who witnessed her wantonness. Evelyn had joined the royal couple so she sat next to her chaperone, but she sought Cailean with her eyes. He was talking to the Lord of Islay and looked less than thrilled about it.

'Dear Mother of Christ, forgive me for no being so clear! I said tae make yer wishes known, not tae mark each other as yer mate!'

'I dinnae ken what ye mean.'

'Wheesht lass, dinnae play me for a fool.'

She glanced at Evelyn; despite the harshness of her words, her eyes sparkled with mirth. Sorcha smiled coyly, for she could hardly feel guilt at such approval. Indeed, she felt so invigorated she could not remain seated. Evelyn accepted her offer to fetch them both a drink. Was it possible for a person to grow taller in half a day? As she stood, she could have sworn she'd gained a couple of inches.

Inside the food pavilion, she approached a side table with pitchers. Nearby stood two ladies – she could not recall their names. They had not seen her approach, nor did they turn when she filled the goblets.

'Can ye believe he turned up here?'

'Aye and she went with him!'

'Ye dinnae think?'

'Perhaps. I suppose someone has tae wed the beast.'

'Can ye imagine staring at—'

She slammed the jug back down. How dare they try to ruin a beautiful thing with their venom? Grabbing the goblets, she stormed out of the tent.

*

Sorcha's last duty of the day was to bank the fire in the queen's chamber. Elizabeth must have been just as invigorated by the day's events as herself, for she stayed up late. She lowered herself to the closed bed curtain before backing out of the chamber. At this hour the hallways were empty save for the odd guard or page sleeping at a door. She welcomed the peace and safety it brought; few could enter the royal chambers at night. Though tonight she would not linger; wicked as it was, she was eager to recall her closeness to Cailean.

Only she was not alone.

Whoever it was, she could not be trapped in her chamber with them. Sorcha continued into the musicians' gallery above the hall. Below her, the floor was covered with sleeping bodies. She would hurt someone before she found a place to hide there. Nor could she wake them, for they'd surely dismiss her concerns as a woman's folly. What of Cailean? She walked past the doors to the quarters for the nobles, but Iain was nowhere to be seen. He must share Cailean's bed like Ailis did hers.

Perhaps then, she could outwit them? She headed back along a servants' passage and into the lower wing of the royal quarters. Sorcha caught the guard's attention with a nod. Dear Lord, they made it past them without so much as a murmur. Certainly not one of Michael's friends, or himself. Could it be one of the courtiers, insulted by her overlooking them for Cailean? Whoever they were, they surely meant harm. And her options were diminishing. Think. This is what all those special lessons with Pa were for. Hastily, she re-entered the area where her chamber was – maybe she could run to it and get inside. Bolt the door before her pursuer saw where she had gone.

'My lady, ah've been looking for ye.'

Thank the Lord that Ailis's voice was quiet. Sorcha placed her finger to her lips and pulled the young maid behind a doorway. There was no time now, so she focused on Pa's second plan. Around her, there was little of use except an ornamental targe. She had seen enough swordplay to know that shields were more than defensive. They could do what they liked to her, but no one was going to lay a hand on her maid. She lifted it down, finding it to be about the same size and weight as a barrel lid. She held it high.

The bulky figure of a man stepped through the doorway and paused. Sorcha flung herself towards him, aiming at his face. Success! And better still, he was caught off-guard. The sickening sound of nasal bone crunching was followed by a thud as his body crumpled. She lowered the shield and panted heavily – a tree would have been a softer target! God willing, it would never have to happen again.

Ailis timidly peeked out. 'Is he dead?'

'Nae, just unconscious.'

She examined the man more closely. There was something familiar, though his new appearance made it difficult to place him. Ailis uncovered her candle and shone the light over him. Sorcha openly cursed, just as Alasdair appeared. He looked to her face and then down at Donald. She all but hissed when he guffawed.

'Och now, this looks like an interesting story. Ailis, ye best get some water and a cloth. This old beast will be waking with a mighty *sair heid*.'

'I'm glad ye find it amusing,' Sorcha said dryly.

Why had he been following her and why had he not spoken up? Still, she had no desire to see him choke on his own blood. Alasdair was at least helpful on that regard; Donald was as heavy as a cow! She sat back in her heels and prayed that he – and Cailean – would forgive her.

'Dinnae fret, Sorcha, I should have warned Cailean ye may recognise that someone was following ye. I'm guessing he got too close and with Ailis with ye, ye did the next best thing?'

'Cailean ordered this? Why?'

How dare he; did he not trust her? Not even Michael had stooped that low! She folded her arms and glared at the ambassador. If he made any more jests, she'd use the shield on him too.

'He wants tae protect ye. For now, this is the only way the *sumph* can.'

She let out an exasperated sigh. 'I'm safe here, Alasdair, I dinnae need a guard. And now look, I've *skaithit* Donald because he wishes tae play fair Galahad! I have it in mind tae—'

Alasdair's jaw hardened, as did his eyes. It brought her tirade to an unexpected halt. She lifted her chin to dare him into contradicting her.

'He never "plays" at being a knight, Sorcha. God damn him, he abides by every last letter of those damned codes and has earned respect for it too – Sir James jests that Cailean is his conscience when they raid England. And he cares for ye in a way I've never seen him care for a woman.'

She flinched. How could she have been so quick to judge? He was caring for her and had she not, just moments before, believed herself in danger? He really had treated her with the respect the Arthurian tales talked of. Ailis approached with a bowl of water and some cloths. She took them and moved around to Donald's head to gently wipe the blood clean.

'I am sorry, Alasdair, I spoke out of turn. Cailean is an honourable man and disnae deserve my wrath.'

'Dinnae ye worry, I ken it was yer fear talking.'

When she was finished, Ailis held out the bottle

containing her comfrey decoction and a fresh cloth. Sorcha explained to Alasdair that the herbal remedy would reduce swelling. He looked grateful for her tenderness while she felt nothing but guilt. She would have to make it up to Donald. A groan drew her attention back to him; he was slowly coming around. The man lifted his hand to hold the cloth she had laid over his nose in place.

'God's toes, woman, what did ye do tae me?'

'Nowt that's no been done to ye before,' Alasdair told the warrior before helping him to sit up. He glanced at Sorcha. 'Get ye tae yer bed. I'll look after the oaf.'

Chapter 9

Robert stared at the bloodstained targe, torn between admiration and laughter. That quiet little mouse had more guts than half the men in his court. Alas, what had transpired was of greater concern than a noble assaulting another noble. The man should not have been able to enter the royal quarters upon the nod of a lady – let alone one who was not accompanying him!

He sighed. 'Is he well?'

Alasdair glanced up from making his move. 'Aye, just a wee headache and a busted nose.'

'Does he wish to seek restitution?'

'He is reluctant to bring this before the court, Yer Grace. Pride, I suspect. He would have tae admit to being bested by a woman.'

'Aye. Nae Highlander would wish tae admit such. Let alone Cailean's best man. Is there anything she can do to make amends?'

'Well, he did lose his belt recently. From what I hear,

he lost it in a bet. So as a gesture of goodwill, she may wish tae replace it.'

After studying the board, Robert made his move. 'It will be done. And speaking of Cailean, I ken about his drunken escapades, and of the trinket he sent her. Paired with their joint performance in the afternoon, one would think that ye had told them both, Alasdair.'

He stared him down, but the younger man did not waver under his gaze. Rather, he made a cunning move on his well-guarded king. 'Check, Yer Grace. And no, I havenae told him. The path Cailean takes is his own making. In this instance, he is as headstrong as our father and lacks the finesse most men learn in their youth.'

Alas, he spoke the truth. Robert had assumed Cailean's foster after the battle at Loudoun Hill, though there was little left to teach the boy. He was confident with a sword but painfully conscious of his scar, and Robert had been unsure of a remedy. Randolph and James, however, had no such qualm. He had found them with their ears to a door. Upon enquiring, they had informed him that within was Cailean and a clean 'woman', having tricked the boy into sharing the chamber with her. He could not recall the result of their scheme, but it had never happened again, and Cailean did find his voice.

'That is fortunate for us and them. I do find courting to be the foundation of a strong marriage.' Robert smiled and blocked the attack on his king with his knight. He observed Alasdair as he studied the board. He looked fatigued, likely from learning his new office, yet there was a subtle change in him. 'Now, tell me more about my lax guards.'

*

Thomas watched a young raven take its first flight from his bedchamber window. He had done everything he could and now things were no longer in his hands. It was only right. Espionage and war were games for those younger than himself. Sorcha too was an adult and needed to live her own life. The brothers had grown into fine, strong specimens, even if they did not recognise it in themselves. Ah, Grann would have been justifiably proud of them had he still been alive.

His surroundings matched his decline. As expected, Michael's 'friends' had followed Sorcha, leaving him to descend into a drunken stupor. That had driven away all but those most loyal to Thomas. Dirt and debris followed, and he made no effort to stop it. Gone too was his beloved stud. He gifted the horses to his long-term customers and the clan that had kept him safe. A last thank you. The best of his breeding stock, he sent to Sorcha's lands.

As for Michael, well, he was done trying. Had he not risked much to place him in a good household only for him to be sent home in disgrace? The boy would never be a man fit to carry the Gilchrist name. Much like Thomas's first wife, Michael carried a darkness within him and lusted for the pretentious life of a fake noble. Let his son now learn what hard work was and let him be responsible for the multitude of bastards he had created. He could have Henderleithen, but Thomas would be damned if he would give him anything else.

Quietly, and quickly, he had stripped the manor of most of its furnishings. The profit paid for prayers for his soul. His espionage had left him riddled with sin and he could not confess for fear of revealing too much. Sitting on his bed, he regarded the few possessions left; on the morrow, he would leave for some distant monastery to spend his remaining days worshiping the Heavenly Lord.

Picking up two letters from the pile, he read once more their contents. The first informed that the chieftains of Clan MacMhathain were moving to enforce the betrothal. The second was from his dear Sorcha, forgiving him for keeping knowledge from her. She had a goodly heart and spirit to match. Poor old Patch had never forgiven him for being her first lesson pony; everyone thought he had but two paces – plod and shuffle – until she went flying by on him.

It had not been easy keeping his promise to Annabelle; all those childhood sicknesses and then the scalding incident. Even now he saw Sorcha laid out on his bed, her upper back a mix of blisters and exposed flesh. Delirious with fever, she had been begging forgiveness for being in his bedchamber. And she had never revealed that it was Michael's doing.

Much like the devil himself, just thinking of Michael brought him into one's presence. His son's shouts for more wine had gone unanswered and his heavy footsteps were getting closer. Bracing himself for what was to come, Thomas faced the door.

'The useless servants have grown slovenly. They dinnae come when called,' Michael growled as he burst into the chamber.

'There are no servants tae call. Ye drove them away or I dismissed them.'

'Ye louse-ridden *sumph*, why the devil would ye do that?'

He rarely let his anger get the better of him; now he brandished it like a sword. He had nothing to lose and maybe, just maybe, everything to gain from the action. 'Look about ye, Michael, I have done much. I am retiring, and I leave this manor in the state that suits ye, for ye have never worked a day in your life. Instead, ye bullied others tae get what ye wanted. Look about and see what it gets ye!'

Michael cast his gaze over the chamber, his sneer quickly replaced with bulging eyes and flared nostrils. The boy had always been an open book.

'God damn ye! What have ye done with my home?'

Filled with a vigour he had not felt since his youth, Thomas once again turned on him.

'*Yer* home? What of yer money paid for this place? Instead ye choose tae squander mine, while spouting that it was never good enough for ye! Ye always wanted more. And when ye didnae get it, yer jealousy made Sorcha's life hell! Aye, I kenned what ye did tae her. Well, you've made yer bed so now ye will lay in it. Ye are no son o mine!'

Michael lunged at Thomas, purple with rage.

He had waited all his life to run this God damned hellhole and his father dared take it away from him? He grabbed the foolish sop and flung him against the chamber's wall before kicking and stomping on the useless whoreson. He would finally teach him a lesson he would never forget.

'Yer camp-following whore deserved tae die. Instead ye raised that bastard child as yer own and gave her our family name! Spending all yer money on fancy tutors and ladies tae educate her. And now where is she? A position at court, when I dinnae even get tae be a squire!'

Fight back, God damn it, fight! He grabbed Thomas by the jaw and pulled him to his feet, but still the man did not defend himself. By God's knees, how was this *sumph* his blood? Mother could have done so much better. And to think she died for him. The whore. The old man dared to stand up and laugh in his face? The laughter fizzled out with a cough. Hah! But Thomas still smiled – he would wipe that gong-eating look from his face.

'Sorcha was never yer blood sister,' Thomas wheezed. 'She is o noble blood and a far better person than ye will ever be. No only does she serve a queen, but she's tae marry an earl! As for those men ye pompously used, they don't give a rat's arse about ye and were using ye tae get close to her. Whatever they promised ye, ye'll no see it.'

No! No he did not, would not believe it! That bitch was nothing but a whore's bastard. What nonsense had Annabelle conjured up? The devil's witch! That and the bitch's inheritance, no wonder the old man had been holding out for so long. He'd wanted it all for himself! Michael grabbed his knife and a red mist fell over his eyes. He stabbed repeatedly at the form in front of him. Following the useless sack to the floor. Let it feel his hatred for that whore Sorcha. A rattling sound came from somewhere and he fell back. It was a beautiful sight! So much blood and torn flesh. His best work yet! No one would dare mock him again! He was king!

He wiped the blood from his face. That had taught the old man; and to further humiliate him, he grabbed

Thomas's chin and stared into his eyes. 'Dinnae ye worry about yer precious bastard. I'll get her, bring her back here and kill her in front of ye before taking what is rightfully mine.'

Chapter 10

Cailean stood facing Ewan, blunted knightly sword in hand. His knees bent, he held it in a defensive position and waited. The rest of his men, and Alasdair, also trained with the blade. Next time it would be the axe, and so on. Ewan favoured axe and sparth but had grown weak with the sword. Cailean favoured the latter. His scout attacked. He caught the blade, then wrapped it with his arm. Ewan relinquished his sword. There was no need to follow through.

'Sloppy. Again.'

He handed the sword back. After two successful evades, he let Ewan return to free sparring. He ignored the small crowd that had formed to watch; they were at a safe distance. As they sparred, he called out corrections. Soon his man was on a more equal footing. It forced him to work harder. Cailean locked blades with Ewan. Grabbing the flat of his blade, he flicked the pommel upwards, stopping short of hitting Ewan's head. The man cursed as they broke apart.

'I should like to go but I have nae escort.'

Sorcha's voice. She stood at the end of the group, watching him attentively. God's balls, the impudent *tyke* took advantage! Behind on his defence, Ewan quickly overcame him, levelling his blade at his throat. He grinned as Cailean pushed the blade away. They faced the audience and quickly bowed. The queen was amongst them.

'Do not tell me that the mighty Earl of Kintail is easily distracted by a lady?'

'There is none as rare as this lady, Yer Highness.'

Where had *that* come from? Alasdair was the damned bard. And worse, he had made a fool of himself! Sorcha bit her lip and dipped her head. Even she had cringed! Elizabeth stared at him hard.

'A rare creature indeed. Come, ladies, I wish to rest.'

He tensed and turned away as the women left. Ewan coughed and nodded his head; Sorcha was approaching. He kept his guard up. She tucked something into the neck of his mail.

'Personally, I hope tae see more of yer swordplay.'

Was she flirting with him? She shyly caught his eye; she was flirting with him! Sorcha hurried after the ladies before he could respond. He pulled the item free. It was a square of linen – a token. He clutched it in his fist and suddenly recalled his men. Several were struggling to contain laughter. Alasdair most of all.

'Who said ye could stop?' he roared. Damn the lot of them; they could train for another hour for that! 'Alasdair, with me.'

*

Training ended earlier than Cailean had planned, though he did make Alasdair and himself sweat. His brother was a fine warrior and had the heart of a leader. He would welcome the day when he saw it for himself. Until then, Cailean did what he could – like a private meal post-training. He sent Iain for their food.

'Dinnae forget behind your ears.' He threw a washcloth at Alasdair, who stopped stripping to catch it.

'I'm no the one who smells like a midden.'

''Tis called hard work. Of which I ken ye are doing too much.'

He waited his turn at the basin; Alasdair rolled his eyes.

'Och, dinnae fash, *màthair*. It will settle soon.'

'We cannae have ye wasting yer beauty sleep, *little* brother.'

'Jesus, I'm no yer "little" brother!'

There were few phrases he could use against Alasdair; that one had worked since his voice dropped. The drying linen was thrust into his chest as they passed.

'So ye do need yer beauty sleep?'

That got him a withering stare.

The cool water left him refreshed. He joined Alasdair at the table as the food arrived. He kept the mood light, jesting about the Rose's newly dubious reputation, and Aonghus Óg's displeasure at his behaviour. Apparently, he owed the man ten cows. He had refused; his uncle could afford to pay his own debts.

His brother, too, was eager to share stories.

'I just cannae believe I met a lass that didnae fall for it.'

'I ken this will pain ye, but no all fall for ye.'

'Very humorous. I ken that, but I couldnae even raise a smile.'

'A proper facsimile of our aunt?'

'Jesus no, she was… I cannae describe it.'

He put down his bread; Alasdair rarely lost his words.

'So why are ye no pursuing her?'

'Wrong family.'

What was being held back? Once, when blind drunk, his brother had admitted his deliberate celibacy. Though he had not remembered upon waking. So Cailean kept his secret. He took his cup and held it up. 'May things change.'

'Aye… And talking of pursuing, are ye going tae escort Sorcha on the morrow, or no?'

He blinked and set his cup down.

'What? Where?'

'I swear that skull o yers is thicker than a tree trunk. Ye were only distracted by her because she purposefully spoke loud enough tae do so.'

He stared at the linen she had given him. That had been a message?

'The king fancies a bit o sport and will be hosting a stag hunt. Elizabeth has freed her ladies tae attend, but only if they have someone tae ride alongside.'

'And she chose me?'

'Rejoice! For the Lord hath opened his eyes!'

Yet Sorcha had not given an impression of being interested in blood sports.

As if reading his thoughts, his brother continued, 'I doubt it is the game that holds the Lady Sorcha's interest. I imagine that it is the allure of horse riding.'

Now that was logical and better suited him. Hunting on horseback was dishonourable; better to face the beast eye to eye. He wiped his fingers and mouth on his napkin. 'Aye, I'll escort her.'

*

With sword at his side, Cailean met Sorcha the next day. It garnered odd looks, which he dismissed. If those mercenaries had been forewarned, they may lay in wait. Likewise, he had rejected the offer of wine. And he had borrowed Alasdair's rouncey; it was accustomed to hunting and battle. Though Alasdair's thoughts behind calling it 'Legs' bewildered him.

He focused on Sorcha as the party headed for the woods. She wore a green brocade gown and a bycocket over her veil. Muted compared to the rest of them. It suited her. She would match him well. As she would his mither's old chair – she'd be engulfed in one his size. With Alasdair's guidance, he now knew her courtly façade. It had dropped that afternoon, and again now. She was genuinely happy to be out. He would endeavour to ride out often when they returned home.

The hunt spread out before coming to a stop; the dogs were let loose to harry a stag. He rested his hunting spear on his foot.

'I thank ye for the ointment; my scar disnae feel so tight.' A nice safe start.

'I'm gladdened tae hear that… Cailean. It is something I spent many a night perfecting.'

His name on her lips; as sweet as the first honey!

'Ye enjoy herbs?'

'At first, no. It was necessary tae ken how tae treat injury and fever. Now, I think I may enjoy learning more someday.'

He bit his cheek; damned foolish question. She'd needed to know how to heal from Michael's beatings. Was engaging a woman in conversation always this hard? And he had upset her! Sorcha sat fiddling with her reins. His jaw hardened. He needed a new safe ground, but what?

'How is Donald doing? I hadnae realised it was him following me. Oh, please say he is well!' she blurted.

'I dinnae ken what ye speak of.'

'The night after the archery. I didnae realise it was tae protect me. I feared ill-intent, so I hit him in the face with a targe.'

He blinked; that was not Donald's explanation. He clasped a fist to his lips. Now was not the time to laugh. Once composed, he replied, 'Donald's fine. The thick-skulled *sumph* has survived worse.'

She blushed and looked away. He frowned. Accidents happened; she need not blame herself. The hounds' cries broke their conversation. Cailean gestured for Sorcha to set their pace. She gave Glaistig her head. The mare kept up with dogs and huntsmen alike. As her mount settled, they returned to a more leisurely pace. Alasdair had been right. She wanted to ride, not hunt.

The stag got away.

While waiting on the dogs again, he asked about horses. Her eyes sparkled, though she curbed her enthusiasm. Thomas's training secrets were safe with her. Good. She did, however, stress the importance of a yearling's inquisitiveness.

'Most behave because their curiosity is sated, but those with intelligence can become a handful.'

'Like Glaistig?'

'Aye. She taught herself how tae escape. We didnae ken until Pa found her in the hall. She had followed me there like a lamb. Unfortunately, he wasnae so impressed with her newfound talent.'

'I can imagine.'

The hunt set off again. Sorcha did not increase their pace. She wanted to talk with him. And had she not wanted to kiss too? He had made an oath. But he could take measure of her feelings; ask about approaching the king.

'Sorcha, I...'

'What of... oh!'

They had both spoken at once. He coughed and shifted awkwardly. Damn Legs's awkward gait.

'You first,' he offered.

'Oh, well, ye ken some of my past, yet I know nothing of yours. How did ye spend yer youth?'

He blinked. No one had ever asked him. Was this politeness or more?

'It was spent doing my father's bidding,' he said slowly. 'At six summers, I was sent tae a lowland monastic school.'

'That is unusual?'

'Aye – it was under Edward's influence.'

'It must not have been easy for ye.'

'Ah hated it, but now I understand. To defeat an

enemy, ye need tae ken their thinking.' Adjust yourself to match them, 'or else'. He had refused. 'When Wallace became guardian, I returned home. Studied with Alasdair instead. At twelve summers, I went tae foster with Aonghus Óg Mac Domhnaill.'

The horns announced a successful kill. Thank goodness! She did not need to know about the battles.

*

The hunt continued while they turned back. Cailean spoke of his seat near Loch Achaid na h-Inich. Though the fort was smaller than Eilean Donnain, it was his heart's home. Tradition dictated his birth there; God willing, he would die there too. The forest behind it held much game. And it overlooked the gathering place. Sorcha listened attentively, though he lacked the words to do it justice.

'Will ye return there when ye leave court?' she asked.

'Sadly no, I winter at Eilean Donnain. Tis more central.'

'Spring then?'

'Summer. After the baptism.'

'Oh aye, Her Highness is due then.'

Her enthusiasm diminished. Surely she feared not childbirth?

'I'll have been here several months by then.'

Ah, no. She feared still being stuck at court.

Outside the manor, followers sat awaiting news, Elizabeth amongst them. She bade Cailean stay with them. He did not complain. He would not – could not – stop being with Sorcha. He chose a bench as far from the group as he dared, though Evelyn quickly joined them. Sorcha spoke of being a maid-in-waiting. Of differences between households. And how much she had learned.

'Truth be told, while I am confident in handling expensive goods, the glass vessels terrify me. I fear doing something foolish while carrying them.'

'As do many – myself included. But every highborn *must* have them.'

She smiled at his cynical observation. He twitched his lips in return.

'A good morn tae ye, *mo ciann*, Lady Sorcha.'

His eye-roll came to an abrupt stop. Alasdair's jaunty voice was betrayed by his eyes. What was keeping him up so late? He nodded his greeting.

'And tae ye, Lord Alasdair. I trust ye are well?' Sorcha asked.

His brother ignored his glare and continued the conversation. 'Well indeed. Was the hunt successful?'

'We didnae witness the kill,' he answered, and the fool grinned. Just great.

Sorcha changed the subject. 'Do ye share Sir Cailean's love of the fort?'

'Ah yes, though I prefer the Kyle of Lochalsh. From it ye can see the snow-capped peaks of Skye and the rugged waters of the Inner Sound.'

He raised his eyebrow at Alasdair.

'I should much like tae see yer homeland. It sounds beautiful.'

'I'm sure ye will someday.'

Damn it, he did not need his brother's help with wooing.

Several people cried out. Cailean stood, hand on sword, and looked around. A man was approaching at a gallop. For once, the guards did their job; they surrounded the queen. The rider came to an abrupt stop and dismounted. Sorcha shot past him. He caught up and grabbed her, pulling her back.

'Let him through! He's my father's messenger!' She struggled against him.

He glanced to Elizabeth, who nodded. He relaxed his grip on Sorcha; a glare was her thank you. Well, damn.

The pale-faced man was uncertain who to approach first.

'My lady.' He chose Sorcha; kneeling there, he held out a missive.

Cailean caught the stench of sweat. It could not be good news. Enough of this pretence! He looked pointedly at Elizabeth. *Send word to the king.* Good, she understood.

'What is it, Arthur?' Sorcha asked, her hand hovering over the missive.

Did she too fear his word?

'I bring bad news, my lady. It is yer father. They found him de—'

Her wretched wail engulfed him.

*

Pa was dead! What would she do now? She had no one! Someone caught her as her legs buckled – it was Cailean. Her knight, her protector. She buried her head in his neck as sobs wracked her body. Shouts broke out all around and she gripped Cailean's *léine*, silently begging him not to leave her so very alone in this cruel place. Did Pa get the letter? Did he know that she loved him? They were still shouting. Cailean's voice so authoritative as he carried her. To where, she cared not as long as he was there. Oh Lord have mercy; her heart was torn asunder. The pain was too great!

She cried out as he put her down, but heard nothing of her own voice. *No! That must not happen now!* But there it was, the familiar mist creeping in, and with it came a dreamlike calmness. She looked down at her incapacitated body, laid out on her bed. The blurry forms of people rushed all around her, their words an incoherent murmur. Except one that sounded like a Gaelic poem. No, it was a lullaby, and it was Cailean reciting it to her. He was still there!

She focused on his voice and it steadily became clearer. She gasped as her grief hit her like a gust of strong wind. It would be so easy to retreat once again, but his voice… She clung to it. Her view altered as she was lifted up. Wait, she was already back in her body? That never happened so quickly. Bitter-tasting *dwale* was poured into her mouth. Please no, not again! She couldn't spit it out for her tongue would not work. She had to swallow or choke.

Laid back down, her eyes searched for Cailean. He was there, having pushed his way back to her side. He saw her and ordered everyone back. Focusing on his face, she felt her extremities slowly return to her. He took her hand in his and called her name. She squeezed as hard as she could before the black clouds of sleep descended.

Chapter 11

Hot tears warmed Sorcha's cool cheeks. Pa was gone, Ma was gone, and Michael would sooner see her destitute than call her his sister. Cailean too had left. She was alone, save for her appointed chaperone who, in the still of the night, had fallen asleep on a nearby chair. Just as she had that fateful summer. Only this time Pa would not return to find her in his bed. He would never return. Why was God testing her like this? Was it because she was enjoying not having Michael around? Or for desiring Cailean so? A sob caught in her throat, stirring Evelyn.

'Hush now, lass.'

'How… how did they find him?'

'It disnae matter, child. Yer father is at peace and reunited with yer mither. He loved her greatly, ye ken?'

Evelyn leaned over and stroked her hair; they must have removed her veil at some point. Why weren't they telling her anything about Pa's death? The physician's orders? Her eyes were growing heavy again. Her mind drifted back to her childhood. They were all in a bedchamber and Pa was telling them stories…

Sorcha awoke to hushed voices beyond her drawn bedcurtains. Her head ached terribly, like she had drunk too much wine. She wanted nothing more than to linger there; to let her grief shroud her as the cloth likely shrouded her pa. But the voices. Who were they and what were they doing in her chamber? Her call for Ailis silenced them. Her maid greeted her as she pulled back the curtains. Lord have mercy, her chamber was busier than the great hall! Two of Cailean's men were standing at her door and Evelyn sat nearby, messing with Sorcha's blue gown. The physician stood talking with Cailean. She clutched her coverings to her chest for they were all staring at her.

'Pray tell why ye all think it is acceptable tae be in my chamber?'

Her voice was unintentionally sharp, but judging from the shameful looks on the faces of Cailean's men, it had worked. Perhaps she should let it out more. She no longer had anyone to upset. The physician looked even more proud of himself, if that were possible.

'Ah good, the black bile hasnae risen,' he preened. 'Ye keep her in bed for a few more days now and ensure she eats the meals I've ordered. She'll be sound and ready for the big day.'

The big day? And why was he addressing Cailean and not herself? How dare he ignore her; this was her chamber – her home now, and the earl was not her guardian. No, this would not do. She would not be swept away. Her pa had raised her better than that! She got up, ignoring Ailis's pleas to at least put some shoes on.

'Get out!'

The physician dared look to Cailean once again, only leaving upon his nod. She glared at the men, who took one look at her and abandoned their chief. That left Cailean. She lifted her chin and marched over. Standing toe to toe with him, she looked him in the eye.

'I ken not what ye're playing at, *Sir* Cailean Macmaghan. Ye may be an earl, but this is still *my* chamber. And who do ye think ye are, speaking for me? Ye're no my husband. Does the king even ken ye're here? In his maiden ward's chamber?'

His eyebrow rose in surprise. Did he not see? She could not surrender her control and lose what little she had left.

'Och, my wee *fiadh-chat*, much happened while ye slept.'

Dear Lord, he was now kissing her! He grasped her hair and bent her back as he claimed her mouth. So much strength, and oh, so much better when he was sober! She clung to him and moaned as her privy became flushed with heat. Please, her body begged, please take her back to bed. Douse her wantonness with whatever it was that made the maids cry!

But no – this was not the time or place. The cur! Her pa was dead and here he was seducing her! She balled her fists up and slammed them against his chest, resisting the hand that held her head. His eyes were dangerously dark as they broke the kiss. He did not like her denying him. And why was Evelyn not stopping this?

'Enough of this madness! Ye will explain yerself,' she demanded.

'When ye are washed, dressed and back in bed, I'll explain everything.' His voice lowered, like it did the night he ordered her to return to her tent.

Her breath caught; no, not this time! Evelyn let out a warning cough and he growled before stalking outside. What was that about? Ailis was immediately upon Sorcha; she stopped the maid.

'Ye will dress me correctly and then prepare the chamber for a visitor.'

It was the best she could do.

*

Sorcha sat in a chair and watched Evelyn. The lady had said nothing, but nonetheless she felt supported in her endeavour. Alas, it filled but a small corner of the hollowness caused by her grief. She fiddled with her paternoster and sent a short prayer for Pa's soul. When she was done with this distasteful matter, she would send coin to the chapel for prayers and candles. She nodded to Ailis to let the pacing Cailean in.

His face darkened upon seeing her. 'Lass, I told ye—'

'Lest ye forget, *Sir* Cailean, this is my chamber, no yours.'

He hesitated and then bowed; finally, someone was listening to her. She motioned to the empty chair opposite. Was he pouting? He was, and why did it look so sweet? She dismissed the thought; she must not crumble now. Ailis brought over goblets of mead for them both.

'Now tell me. I ken of nothing after… the *dwale*.'

'Ah tried tae stop them.'

'I ken. And I thank ye, Cailean. Truly. I cannot abide the concoction, but people oft insist upon it.'

Like Pa, she had set the ground, there was no need to stay distant. She smiled as he relaxed; the Cailean she had grown to know was returning. Though he appeared to be struggling with something.

He sighed. 'Sorcha, Thomas's death was no natural. And Michael's missing. We ken not if it's him or his "companions".'

She gripped her goblet tighter. He could not, could he? Yet all those animals, and the girls he took. Tears clouded her view. 'I should never have left.'

'I dinnae want tae hear that from ye ever again, Sorcha. It wasnae yer fault.'

No. If Michael had her to keep in check, Pa might still be alive. Michael was right. Noble or not, she wanted more than she deserved. So dreadfully selfish.

'Whatever this is, it started well before our ken.'

Sorcha stared blankly at the wall. He was speaking nonsense. She was a wicked orphan thrice over and worth only the sum of her land. Let her forfeit it to the king and become a nun. She heard Cailean set down his drink and rustle some parchment. He knelt in front of her and held out the vellum. It was some contract dated from the year of her birth. She lifted her eyes to his. There was something there. Regret, perhaps, for being dragged into this sordid mess.

'Read it, lass.'

She failed Pa again, for she had no fight in her. It would tell her nothing that she did not already know. But to appease Cailean, she read it. The words cruelly mocked her. Concealing her origins was one thing, but also conspiring with Robert to hide this? Who was he really? Once again, Pa had looked her in the face and unashamedly lied.

'Robert said there was no betrothal.'

'I didnae ken until recently either.'

She watched him from the corner of her eye. How could she trust his words?

'Tis true, Sorcha. I'll no hide that I want ye, but I'd no be so dishonourable.'

She squarely met his face. It must be true, but dare she hope? Better wed to someone she knew than a stranger, yet this was dreadfully wrong. He suddenly pulled her onto his lap. She clung to him, and her tears came again. She cried for the man she once knew. The one who had raised and loved her. Not for the man the king made him be.

Cailean did not stop her or push her away. 'Hear me, Sorcha. Ye are mine now. And I will have the answers tae yer questions.'

She knew not how long they sat there but, eventually, he carried her back to her bed and stayed with her. Evelyn fussed around her but did nothing to stop them; had she also known?

'Unfortunately, there is more.' Cailean broke the silence.

Lord have mercy, surely there could be no more?

'We are tae be wed within the week. And my men are tae guard ye at all times.'

'Why would Michael come for me here?'

Cailean did not answer her; had she not been so fatigued, she would have pressed him. He wished for the guards to be inside the chamber, but that would be her choice. She wavered between relief and guilt.

'Robert orders that until we wed, Evelyn will be yer bedfellow.'

He did not sound amused, so she glanced at her chaperone; Evelyn was being discreet as always but her shoulders were shaking. Lord have mercy! Did they think she had no control? And what about Pa? When, amid all these arrangements, was she permitted to mourn him?

It seemed she was not. Alasdair arrived, followed by a page carrying her approved meal. He settled on a stool and waited for her. She sent the page away to bring food for her companions.

'It's good tae see ye about, Sorcha. Ye gave us quite the fright.' Alasdair's tone was, as always, good natured.

She smiled politely.

'Two last things,' interjected Cailean. 'If ye will have us, we wish tae keep ye company. And Alasdair is determined tae play *sennachie*.'

'I would love tae have both your company and will gladly listen to stories,' she admitted.

Alasdair grinned. 'I cannac tell them, as our *sennachie* will murder me for taking away his right. Rather, I think it would be a great benefit for ye tae learn our lineage.'

She supposed it made sense and they lapsed into silence.

Sorcha stirred the broth, heavy with a meat and, by the smell of it, verjuice. Though he did not order it, she knew Cailean was wanting her to eat it. Well, she had eaten far worse after such episodes. Ah, the meat was pork.

'What news?' Cailean again broke the peace.

'Nothing much. Robert is still in his cups and will see no one but myself, Sir James and his wife. Apparently, Thomas was one of his best men…'

She glanced up from her spoon. Pa had never talked about Robert beyond the likes of taxes and rents. Or news shared with pedlars. Alasdair sighed a surprisingly heavy sigh.

'Judging by yer look, I'm guessing that's news tae ye too.'

'I truly wish I could tell ye more. Pa, God rest his soul, spoke not of any such matter.'

'After everything else, I'm no surprised he kept it hidden.'

He smiled a weary smile. Everything else? What did Alasdair do when not abroad? She looked to Cailean, who seemed unconcerned, and struggled to keep her frustration from returning.

*

Being too far away to attend the funeral and with no masses said for him at court, Sorcha mourned Pa by spending time amongst the horses. There, the men respectfully joined her in mourning the loss of a great horseman. After a couple of days, she felt stable enough to return to her duties. Surprisingly, Cailean supported her decision. Now she knelt in front of her queen.

'Yer Highness. I am most grateful for yer discretion. May I return tae yer side?'

Elizabeth bid her to rise. 'I am gladdened by your return to health, Lady Sorcha. We have much to do before you say your vows.'

She kept her countenance in check, though what did Elizabeth mean? Suddenly, Sorcha was surrounded by the other ladies. Not to comfort her for the loss of Pa, but giddily discussing the celebrations. Oh, how that stung! She glanced back at Evelyn, who carried the gown Sorcha was to wear. The blue one. The flock suddenly fell upon Evelyn.

'Och, Sorcha, what a perfect colour – and the cut! Give him a glimpse of what the night will offer.'

'Will ye wheesht? Discussing innocence and seduction in the same sentence!'

'That new daisy chain embroidery is perfect!'

'Shame it'll no mean a thing the day after.'

'It also means loyal love and patience.'

'And dae we no all need that with our husbands!'

They clucked away like hens, hypocritically admiring the gown they had once derided. Still, all that mattered was Cailean's opinion, and he'd confirmed that it was his favourite the minute she'd stepped from the tent. She quietly left to see to whatever of her chores still remained. Small mercies! There were enough to keep her away until the ladies had calmed down.

Upon her return, there was one reading to Elizabeth. And the rest, aside from Evelyn, worked on refreshing a gown for the queen to wear. They shooed her away – and she could hardly blame them, for her embroidery was appalling. Instead, she was tasked with sewing an undershirt for her future husband. They insisted that it proved she was a suitable wife. Would repairing one not prove that better?

But alas, that was the least of her concerns. After a light repast, all the maids save herself were dismissed.

While some of the younger ladies stifled giggles, others looked on sympathetically as Elizabeth beckoned her.

'Lady Sorcha, your mother passed when you were young, correct?' Elizabeth enquired.

'Aye, Yer Highness.'

'Then as you are my husband's ward, I will assume it is my duty to prepare you.'

'Forgive me, Yer Highness, but the bishop has already instructed me on my wifely duties.'

His monotone sermon had focused primarily on subservience in all matters – she swore her guards had fallen asleep on their feet.

Laughter surrounded her until silenced by a single look from the queen. Most uncharacteristically, Elizabeth took Sorcha's hands in hers. It was almost motherly. Had she done this for her step-daughter?

'The price we pay as Eve's daughters is the pain and the blood we spill upon the breaching of our maidenhood. But if your husband is considerate, he will warm ye first. We crave that warmth, for it numbs pain and releases our seed. Only then can it join with his.'

Sorcha shook her head. That made no sense, she already overheated just thinking about Cailean. How could she get any warmer?

Evelyn chuckled and added to Elizabeth's words, 'It means they'll make it enjoyable for ye, lass. Dinnae ask me how or where the men learn tae do it, but the good ones do.'

She gasped. 'The Church says tis a sin.'

'Crusty auld celibates, what dae they ken?'

Elizabeth coughed. 'The physicians disagree, and I am

inclined to believe them. God is love, is he not? And what perfect way to conceive a child than through the pleasure of lovemaking? Now, as we are not your mother, we can divulge few little secrets that will improve your chances of conceiving.'

'And dinnae say it is a sin, for surely it keeps them from being unfaithful,' one of the ladies said laughing 'Tae start, there are more ways than just what the Church teaches…'

*

Cailean hesitated outside Sorcha's chamber. It was happening; he would wed on the morrow. But before that, he needed to know. Would she respect the tradition? He pushed open the door. Inside, he found Sorcha staring out of a window. Well away from the others. Through her veil, her hair shone in the evening sun. In their private space she would go uncovered, he would order it. Alasdair nodded in greeting; he was teaching Ailis chess. Next to them, Evelyn napped.

He touched Sorcha on her shoulder. She started; such a deep thinker.

'Come, sit with me.'

She followed him to the bed, her eyes wide with curiosity. So innocent. He kissed her hand.

'What plagues ye?'

'I'm so afeared… not because of ye, but because…'

'Ah ken.'

Oathtaking should never be superficial. Especially where God was involved. He took the circlet from under his arm. It represented so much love and hatred. Indeed, battles were fought over what it symbolised. To give it to a MacMhathain man was akin to proclaiming a *tanist*. And now he knew why his mother had stopped wearing it when she did. Cailean unwrapped it and held it out to Sorcha. She gasped.

'This was gifted tae our ancestor by a great Celtic queen,' he explained.

'It is beautiful, Cailean.'

'It is said tae bring luck tae the chief. But only if his bride wears it on her wedding day. And until she is welcomed by the clan.'

He watched her reaction. Good, she understood.

'Will ye do me that honour, Sorcha?'

'Aye, Cailean. I am honoured tae carry the tradition on with you. And Lord willing, tae our future son.'

He savoured her words. Then placed the circlet on her head, over the veil. The triskeles and sapphires shone brighter than before. Forget the ceremony. Here and now. This was his vow. To her and God alone. Damn the plans they had needed to make. He would take her now if he could, and seal their agreement. Cailean kissed Sorcha's forehead, just below the circlet. Just as his father had once done. Ideally, this was how he would have told her. Though not in her chamber. Outside, under a tree. Sitting on his plaid. Or better yet, after stealing her away.

He would have left then, had she not insisted. Instead, they joined the others. He raised an eyebrow at Alasdair's pretence of playing chess poorly, though Ailis was charmed by it. And he shared Sorcha's drink of choice. The mead was growing on him; it needed no spices like the imported grape wines. She recited poetry and he surprised himself by joining in. The sun had set by the time he withdrew. Alasdair by his side, he walked along the musician's gallery.

'Are evenings always like that?'

'With a wife?'

'Aye.'

'They can be. Assuming ye're both getting along. Ye recall how Ruth used tae be fond of sweetmeats?'

'Aye.'

He stopped on the other side of the great hall and waited. Whatever Alasdair had once had with Ruth, he wanted it.

'I would pay for the ingredients and for cook tae make them. Then we would sit for hours on the bed, eating them and just talking.'

'I think... I understand.'

'Cailean?'

'Aye?'

'Dinnae be thick-skulled with her. She's no one of yer men.'

He blinked. What did that mean? Since when was he thick-skulled?

'*Mo ciann*!' Ewan distracted him, having returned from Dumbarton.

'He's there?'

'Aye, and ye'll no guess where he's staying.'

The Rose. The drunken, and likely murderous, letch must have despised sleeping outside.

'He better pay his tab,' he all but growled, while Alasdair swallowed his laughter.

'Nae. Let him run up a big one. Remember our plan.'

Of course! The bigger the debt the better. He clasped his brother's arm, then bid them both a good night.

Chapter 12

Cailean inhaled the cloying scent of newly laid, dried flowers. He could not escape it, nor the air of anticipation. Laid out on his bed was his best *léine*, the woad cloth edged with gold-threaded embroidery and lined with sable. Alongside it lay his mantle, embroidered with his heraldry, and his rarely worn coronet. He wanted to be alone, but the day dictated his every move. And was as pompous as Alasdair's outfit. He had not seen the particoloured cotehardie before. Red wool and his weavers' plaid; a sacrilege to their good work! They clashed with Alasdair's saffron hose, blue tippets and hood. Mind, the other lords were no better.

His brother was taking his time: Sir James would drink him dry before the wedding. Once dressed, he was forced to sit – they wanted to brush his hair out like a maiden! He gritted his teeth. If his chamberlain could see him, the man would die of shock. Finally, it was over. He stood. A goblet was thrust towards him, and a hand landed on his shoulder.

'Today, the last of us is shackled tae a wife!' declared the Earl of Atholl to cheers. ''Tis about bloody time!'

Sir James lifted his drink in a mock toast. 'Tell us, Cailean, do ye recall what that "lady" taught ye?'

Heckles and promises to assist in the bedding abounded. He growled, the lewd *tykes*.

'Out!'

He would have his moment of peace. They laughed and left the chamber. Well, all except his brother. Ignoring him, he approached his window. Outside they were already gathering for the procession.

'They're only giving ye what they too were given.'

'I ken.'

He sighed and rubbed the bridge of his nose. He had never doubted becoming clan chief. And he wanted this. So why was he doubting now? Battles were fairly predictable; women were not. He may as well be untried. Yes, that damned whore had taught him some tricks – insisted they would make any woman see past his face. But was it true? And what of maids? Alasdair appeared at his side.

Cailean wouldn't meet his eye. 'I dinnae want tae hurt her.'

*

Sorcha was still waking up when she was ambushed by the queen's ladies. They dragged her to Elizabeth's chambers, where she was ordered to break her fast. Befuddled, she unquestioningly finished the meal before rising to do her duties, only to be stopped and guided to a rose-oil bath instead. Their words finally broke through. It was her wedding day! She must not work, and the chosen ladies were *her* attendants. Yet she was naught but a poppet for them to pull, poke, and dress to their liking.

The food grew heavier within her. Would Cailean approve of how she looked? Would he care? Or would he depart from the festivities after the blessing? She was not Elizabeth – she could not carry such a burden. How did the queen do it? To be wedded so young, then torn from her husband. A pawn in a war not of her making. And then to go on and bear her husband heirs while still a portrait of dignity and grace. If Sorcha could become but a shadow of Elizabeth…

The ladies parted to present her to their queen. Sorcha's hair was left to flow one last time, covered by the lightest of veils, held down by the silver circlet. Her reworked gown included tippets. They fell so long, she was afeared she would stumble. She lowered herself.

'Come, Lady Sorcha, you are ready.'

Was she really? She did not feel it.

As she left Elizabeth's chambers, Donald joined her. She glanced at him, then gave him her full attention. Someone had tamed him! And he looked less than impressed by it.

'What happened tae ye?' she asked quietly.

'Lady Evelyn got her paws on me.' He pulled at the neck of his cotehardie. 'How am ah meant tae wield my sword in this?'

'Pray tell me it isnae needed!'

Donald grinned. As Cailean's best man, he had but one duty. Yet no one would steal her, to attempt it would be ludicrous.

Outside, she greeted the king. He and Elizabeth would lead the procession to the kirk in lieu of Sorcha's parents. Around her gathered her ladies, fussing until the last possible moment, and behind came Donald. Cailean's retinue formed behind her own. But she could not make him out amongst all the men, heraldry and musicians. She squeezed her eyes shut. It was far too much noise. Opening them again, she focused on the common folk who had gathered to watch from afar.

Her chest contracted. What was he doing here? Why?

She intended to warn Donald, but the procession was starting, and then he was gone! Gasping for breath, she struggled to locate him elsewhere. The crowd gave way to reveal the kirk step. She came to a halt and the crowd chuckled. Surely he would not be so foolish?

Cailean's hand suddenly took hers and lifted it high. He guided her to the step and she could not stop him. In front of the bishop, she faced her betrothed. He took an inadvertent step back.

'What is it?' he growled.

Oh no, he was angry at her!

'I... I saw Michael.'

'Are ye sure it was him?'

'Aye.'

He looked to Robert and then to Donald. She felt the latter step closer to her. As did her betrothed, forcing her attention back onto him. He placed a bag of coin into her hands. Yet her dowry had not been read out. This was not right, and what were they doing about her brother? He tugged her hands and she returned her gaze to his. He wanted her to trust him. If only he knew how much trust she had placed in him. Still… oh, the bishop was asking if she came of her own free will! Again, the crowd chuckled as she stammered out her consent. With no godly reason to deny their marriage, their oaths were quick to follow.

'Here before God, I do take ye, Sorcha Gilchrist, tae be my wife and to this I solemnly pledge ye my troth.'

Sorcha echoed Cailean's vow with her own. She smiled up at Cailean as he slipped a simple band onto her finger, over the opal stone. With him at her side, she stepped away from the kirk to distribute the coins amongst the needy. They had walked from Dumbarton upon the mere promise of coin and trencher alms. The entire time, his hand never left the small of her back. Lord have mercy! The marriage had not been blessed and she was already aflame by her husband's touch! When there was coin no more, she was led inside.

There both she and Cailean lay beneath a canopy, foreheads on hands, to receive His blessing. She bit her lip. It had happened; she was married. Cailean was her husband, and she was now Lady Sorcha Nicmaghan. She had taken his name, having no right to Gilchrist. A warmth wrapped around her like a comforting blanket, as though Ma and Pa were also giving their blessing.

*

Sorcha's jaw ached as she smiled her thanks to yet another baron for yet another bolt of cloth. The Glasgow cloth merchants must have had a merry old time. As had the glassmakers and goldsmiths, judging by the tokens Cailean gave in return. She glanced at John.

He spoke as he wrote the inventory: 'One bolt of burnet; one gilded brooch with freshwater pearl.'

Her husband – would she ever tire of saying that? – rolled his shoulders and muttered, 'If this continues, we'll be clothing the whole clan.'

She bit her lip to keep from laughing aloud – a few people were lingering nearby, ready for the feast. They were back in the safety of the hall where, upon entering, she had been reassured to see double the usual guard.

Cailean faced her and tugged at her veil. So much swirled in those eyes. 'Ye look stunning and I cannae wait tae get this off ye.'

Oh, sweet Mother Mary, the bedding! In her apprehension, she had forgotten it – and the knowledge that they were to be watched by Evelyn and Sir James. How could she enjoy such an act with them there? What if Cailean did not know how to warm her properly? And how much would she bleed? He stopped playing with a loose lock of hair and placed his palm on her cheek. The skin felt rough, but his touch comforted her nonetheless.

'Dinnae be so alarmed, my wee *fiadh-chat*.'

After several more gifts – thankfully, no more cloth – the exchange was completed, and the feasting began. The extravagance of the high table made Henderleithen's look like it belonged in a tavern. Ornate silver salt cellars, glass vessels, and not a shared trencher in sight. The foods, too, appeared somehow richer than those served at her usual place, though they seemed exactly the same. Cailean discreetly explained some of the more unusual dishes, stopping her before she mistook pudding of porpoise for haggis.

Between the courses, fools and bards entertained them. One sang not of the glory of the battle of Loudoun Hill, but of a boy who, after it had ended, saved his king's life, only to be grossly injured.

'Poor child. I wonder what ever happened to him,' she mused aloud.

'I believe he's done quite well for himself,' replied Cailean dryly.

Well, of course he would do – to save the king would see him highly rewarded. Assuming he survived. Robert developed a nasty coughing fit, yet he waved away his attendants. She looked between them; men did confuse her so!

After the feast the tables were cleared away, and Sorcha had no way to excuse herself. Instead, tradition dictated that she and Cailean had to socialise with their guests – the entire court. She smiled through yet another jest at the expense of her maidenhood. Must they keep reminding her? Alas, the wine she drank was doing little; someone, likely Evelyn, had ordered it to be well watered down. The closer to the wedding, the more it had become obvious how much the lady mothered her. It left her conflicted. On one hand, she welcomed the matronly support, on the other, it felt like a snub to Ma.

Upon his arm, she could feel her husband – her Cailean – growing tenser. Were the comments getting to him too? Or something else? She had managed to put Michael from her mind, but his behaviour reminded her that they had heard nothing.

Excusing herself, she slipped away to the garderobe. Drinking extra wine to counteract the watering-down was destroying her control. Returning, she found not Cailean but Alasdair awaiting her. He lowered himself further than before – of course, she was a countess now!

'Cailean apologises, he was called away. But I am not upset, dear sister, for it permits me a chance tae dance with ye.'

She tried to mask her disappointment and held out her hand. He escorted her to the middle of the hall. She waited next to him for the saltarello to begin.

'I am also grateful to have this moment alone, Sorcha. There is something I must tell ye.'

She pursed her lips. What was so frightful that he needed to divulge it like this? They knelt to each other, and upon standing again, she took his hand. Side by side, they started the kick-stepped dance.

'As ye have likely seen, Cailean is oft quite reserved. A trait whipped intae him by our father, I fear.'

She glanced at him out the side of her eye as she spun on the spot. Had he forgotten that she had already seen his bluster when angered? He waited until he danced around her to speak again.

'He will work himself up or worse, hide away,' continued Alasdair.

She took his hand and waited until it was her turn to dance around him. 'What are ye advising me tae do about it?'

After a few more kicks, they spun together. Alasdair took his chance. 'Dinnae let him do it, Sorcha. Coax it out of him.'

Sorcha nodded before they separated to join other dance partners. Though truthfully, she had no idea how she could coax anything out of Cailean. And where was he? She tried to catch a glimpse of him as she traversed through dance partners. Re-joining Alasdair, she asked, 'What news of Michael?'

'Dinnae worry, he'll no bother ye.'

He was as bad as Cailean; that was not what she had asked. They knelt and thanked each other as the dance concluded. She glanced around – coming towards her was Evelyn, with her bride's maids. No, surely not! She was not ready!

*

Sorcha was swept up and deposited in her chamber. It had more lit candles than a chapel and there were petals everywhere, their scent sickly sweet. Reluctantly, Sorcha handed her circlet to Ailis and sat on a stool. The women started undressing her.

'Be sure all pins are removed. We dinnae want their time off tae a bad start now do we?' warned Evelyn.

Another superstition like the countless others she had taken part in. Still, she welcomed all the luck she could get. They then fed her bread and heavily spiced wine that lacked the water. Too little of the wine, though – oh why had her desire chosen today of all days to flee her? They made her stand and removed her gowns, mercifully leaving the shift on.

They tucked her in and gave her a sprig of fennel for her breath. Now all they had to do was wait. Oh, merciful Lord, make it quick! He answered her prayer, for she heard the men approaching. Cailean was pushed into the room, already half-undressed. At least the ladies had waited for her! And … his bared legs. So muscular! She stared straight ahead and clutched at her covers as he was tossed into the bed next to her amidst ribald jeers. She could only imagine what he made of that!

The crowd suddenly silenced as the bishop entered. He appeared most uneasy as he stood at the foot of the bed. His blessing was hurried and he departed equally swiftly. Darkness descended as the bed curtains were pulled shut around them. She swallowed nervously. Surely, they would not remain out there? No, the crowd was withdrawing, leaving Ailis lamenting that someone had stolen her mistress's garters. Her maid was hushed by someone.

Cailean shifted next to her and cursed the indignity of it all. He pulled back a curtain on his side. The light from beyond made her blink and turn towards it. He had removed his undershirt! So much hair and chest and, Lord help her, he was getting closer! He gently ran his fingers through her hair.

'Beautiful, my wee *fiadh-chat*.'

She could not speak; he was far too close to her. He cupped the back of her neck and pulled her even closer. He was going to… oh! She could not resist if she wished it! And now she could have all she wanted! Her hands found his chest, her fingers trailing up over his warm skin, behind his neck and grasping at his hair as, tentatively, her tongue sought to mirror his. He growled softly, she shivered. More! She nipped at his lip. Why had she done that?

He pushed her back into the bed, deepening their kiss. So strong! She slipped down onto her back. Like this? Wait! Oh! She tightened her grip as his lips brushed just under her ear. When had her skin ever prickled so? Calloused fingers found the soft skin of her thigh. So wicked! She shut her legs, only for him to purr into her ear.

'Part yerself for me.'

She could not find her words, though her legs betrayed her. Was she already warmed enough? Dear Lord! His fingers lay inside her feminine lips and… Oh! That spot that was so painfully sensitive, how could he? How could she like it? She gasped and lifted her hips from the bed. No, he was rubbing it! Her hips bucked, her body no longer under her control. Whatever had clawed at her before was nothing compared to this. What was he doing? Was this the real heating? Lord forgive her, she wanted more! And yet, she must keep away. Sorcha clawed at his hand.

'Cailean! …I… I…!'

'Ah ken, lass, dinnae fight it.'

Her eyes closed. Oh! It made it worse. She gritted her teeth and still he was relentless! No, he was going faster! She had no strength to tear away his hand. She could not take this. She pulled and twisted her chemise off; it was far too rough against her skin. Cailean growled loudly. His breath on her nipple and then, oh sweet Mother Mary, his lips! She cried out; let them hear how he took care of her!

'Open yer eyes!'

He growled loudly, his voice strained. She opened them and met his gaze. Sweat beaded on his forehead, his eyes darker than she had ever seen them. He was as heated as she! Yet, somehow, she knew there was more. A hunger that must be sated. He had moved; he hovered over her.

'Cailean, please!' she begged, pleaded.

He too was shaking, as something thicker pressed

closer to her maidenhood. There was no way that would fit in... oh! He had entered her, only to stop.

'Sorcha, I dinnae...' Cailean panted, 'I dinnae want tae hurt ye.'

Damn the pain! He hissed as she thrust up her hips, spearing herself onto him. A sharp ripping pain stole her breath, but it was done. Please, chase it away and come closer! She wrapped her limbs around him. He fell onto his elbows with a grunt. Moaning, she tried again to kiss him as he kissed her. He hungrily matched her efforts but would not move his body. They had said there was more!

She ripped her lips from his. 'Cailean, please, join our seed!'

She barely found the words before he pulled back and thrust into her. Then again! Over and over, faster and faster. Stoking the strange hunger that clawed away at her. She gasped and panted; his movements were as rhythmic as a horse's gait. She met his thrusts with her own.

'God damn it, Sorcha!'

He leaned onto one hand and barely brushed that sensitive point again. Oh Mother of Christ, Lord have mercy! Something within her gave way. The pleasure it brought swept through her and she cried out. First in alarm, then pure bliss! She did not know whether to grab Cailean or tear him away as she writhed under him. He thrust one last time into her, his entire body growing stiff. He cried out triumphantly.

Cailean sunk onto his elbows as her wild movements slowed to nothing. Her flushed face haloed by a ring of untamed curls. Her bust and hips equally well curved. Both muscular and soft. Cailean was sure she would be the death of him. Her spearing herself had almost ripped apart the last of his control. The feel of her maidenhood giving way; a part of her that was his alone. He fell to the side, pulling her with him as he went. She was as floppy as a poppet. Her head rested upon his chest. Yes, she fitted him perfectly. She murmured something incomprehensible.

'Hmmm?'

'Elizabeth was right. It cannae be a sin.'

He laughed; so innocent and so passionate. 'With ye it'll never be so.'

He pulled her even closer, pressing the flat of his hand against her upper back. It was not as soft as the rest of her. Scarring. His brows furrowed as he stared at the canopy overhead. Please let it be an accident. Sorcha stirred, then draped a leg over him. Their sweet, sticky seed wetting his leg. She was already half-asleep.

'I found Michael taking my friend Anna's maidenhood; he punished me for interrupting by pouring boiling water over my back.'

His jaw hardened.

'It was my fault. I was a mettlesome child.'

Damn that son of a bitch; damn him to hell and back. That was no punishment. And he had to look him in the eye tomorrow. He deserved nothing but the noose! Thank the Lord she was now his! Her brother would *never* get his hands on her again. Cailean kissed the top of her head, listening to her fall asleep. He let out a polite cough. Hushed voices were replaced with footsteps. From the opposite side, the curtain opened. He caught Evelyn's eye, nodding to where Sorcha had lain. She retrieved the square of linen, the final proof of his wife's virtue.

Chapter 13

Sorcha slowly woke up to a tickling sensation on her ear. Oh! She was still wrapped in his arms. They had joined their seed twice more during the night. She twisted in his arms and winced; her privy felt like she had hit it hard against a pommel. He stirred. With features relaxed from sleep, he was as soft as a puppy. She tenderly kissed his lips.

'Good morn, my husband.'

A lopsided smile greeted her as he came further round.

'Aye my wife, Sorcha Nicmaghan.'

His eyes sprung open and he quickly sat up. She held the bedcover to her; was something wrong? Where was he going? And why was he in such a hurry to abandon her?

'Ailis, come tend to yer mistress,' he called as he rose.

She had only just been dressed in a clean shift by the time he was dressed in the clothes he wore yesterday. Oh, of course! Today was an open court session. He would be needed elsewhere. Sorcha swallowed her disappointment; there would be many more mornings. She sat down on a stool to await Ailis, who fetched her comb.

'Dinnae hide all her hair away, Ailis.'

'Aye, my lord.'

He was instructing her maid again. And to show her hair too! Did he wish her to appear wanton? Unless, yes, she would accept the fashion worn by the other wives.

'Double plaits, Ailis.'

'Aye, my lady.'

Cailean knelt in front of her. He laid a heavy plaid mantle over her legs, its inside lined with catskin. What was he doing now?

'This is for you, my *fiadh-chat*. For yer maidenhood.'

'Cailean, ye dinnae…'

'I do. Ye'll need it for travelling. The sea is a fickle mistress.'

'I thank ye – the sea?'

'Aye, tis faster and easier by boat.'

They were going by boat? Was that not dangerous? Lord have mercy! She had never stepped on a crossing barge, let alone a boat! Cailean brushed her forehead with his lips and departed before she thought to ask him. Sorcha gripped the mantle closer to her. So brusque; where had that man she met between the sheets gone? And what of her? What did he expect from his wife? To confine her feelings for him only to their bedchamber? She may as well already be on that boat!

Donald stood waiting for her outside her door. He fell into a full kneel, his eyes respectfully on the door behind her. What was he doing? And surely not everyone would greet her so?

'My Lady Sorcha, I welcome ye tae the clan.'

'Please, Donald… ye are now my cousin.' She quickly gestured for him to rise.

He smiled as he did so, but still dipped his head slightly. 'Ye are also my chief's wife.'

Chief's wife, countess, lady in waiting – she could not forget. No longer would she lower herself greatly for anyone besides royalty. Well, that was easier said than done. She almost overbalanced several times on her way to join the queen.

No one mentioned the consumption, besides Elizabeth enquiring as to her comfort. A welcomed mercy! As part of her rise in rank, she was now to assist in dressing the queen, and the ladies also watched their tongues. She outranked most of them. It *almost* made court pleasant.

*

At the appointed time, Sorcha escorted Elizabeth to the great hall for the session. Her new prestige further permitted her to take a seat at a nearby bench. Regrettably, it was un-cushioned and unusually uncomfortable. She composed herself, determined not to draw attention. Evelyn, it appeared, could not care less. She sat beside her, lifting from her girdle a pouch of nuts.

'I do hope it's no going tae be a day o land disputes. They are always the most tedious cases.'

Sorcha declined the offer of nuts. A hand landed on her shoulder, and a glance behind revealed Cailean, standing with several rolls of parchment under his arm. He gently tugged on one of her plaits, nodding his approval. Why did that thrill her so? She smiled warmly at him and tentatively placed her hand on top of his. He made no move to remove it.

The court was called to session. As Evelyn had feared, the first cases were land disputes, but on a larger scale than Sorcha had ever witnessed. By the third case, she had to poke the older woman in the ribs for she had begun to snore!

'I call before the king the Earl and Countess of Kintail,' the steward announced.

She felt Cailean move away. Oh! She was the countess! So much for not making a fool of herself. She made haste to his side amidst a ripple of chuckles. Together they both knelt until permitted to rise. What was happening? And why was Robert getting up? He motioned for her to face Cailean, like she had at the kirk. He took from his chancellor a legal document and held it between them.

'In my haste tae finally see this man wed, I overlooked Lady Sorcha's dowry. It's time I right that wrong.'

She glanced from Robert to Cailean; again, he was silently instructing her to trust him. This had been planned before the wedding. But why?

'As part of the dowry of Lady Sorcha Nicmaghan, née Gilchrist, I grant you, Lord Macmaghan, the rights tae the lands of Druim Earbainn.'

So that was the name of her inheritance. While it meant little to her, it meant something to those at court. Some praised, others cursed, and one openly accused her of being Robert's bastard! Cailean tightened his grip on her.

'Enough!'

She recoiled as the king shouted his order; only Cailean's grip kept her upright.

'Those lands were part o a forfeit and would rightly belong tae me. I chose tae be gracious and return them tae their heir. I have confirmed that Lady Sorcha is said heir. If there are those that doubt her claim, they can face me instead of whispering behind my back.'

Thank goodness no one moved! Slowly, Cailean released his grip on her. The king held out the rights again and her husband took them with a dip of his head.

'Furthermore, I add tae the dowry any unspent income from the land.'

The announcement concluded, she stepped back and lowered herself, before Cailean led her back to her seat. Again, he positioned himself behind her.

'That was Robert's wish, no mine.'

Did he have to whisper in her ear so? Her skin tingled and she pressed her legs together. But his words. Had Robert feared a challenge? If so, from whom? Those that owned her blood father's lands before him? Ma's kin perhaps, but she knew not who they were. Pa had left that detail out, and she had never been introduced to any. She glanced up at him and smiled her apology – it was not his fault that she came with such intricacies.

*

The day soon began to drag, and cases merged into one another. More than once, Sorcha unintentionally leaned against Cailean. If it bothered him, he did not say – he did not even move under her weight. How did he do that? And on the occasion that he was called upon to bear witness, he always returned to her. The shadows had lengthened considerably when he whispered in her ear once more.

'Come stand by me side and trust us, we ken what we're doing.'

What was he planning now? And who was he working with? However, she was now his dutiful wife, so did as requested without a murmur. She glanced at Alasdair before giving him a more thorough look. When had he arrived there? He too wore the same garments as yesterday and a heraldic belt. He smiled a greeting and then hurried off to the other side of the hall. Cailean kissed her forehead and stood to block her line of sight.

'I call before the king Michael Gilchrist, Laird of Henderleithen,' cried the steward.

Correction – to hide her from his line of sight! Her warmth fled as her brother strutted into court, although he was struggling with his feet. On either side of him stood a guard. He was unshaven and his hair its usual greasy mess. But the ill-fitting garments he wore were Pa's! How had she not seen that yesterday? She could feel him searching for her and shrank back.

'I'm over here.' Robert's droll words were spoken in a flat tone.

He was not at all impressed by her brother's impertinence. Michael turned his attention to the king and knelt, only to rise without permission. Perhaps it was better that Pa was not alive to witness this humiliation; it would have broken his heart. Cailean took her hand and gently squeezed it.

'Yer Grace, ah've walked all the way here tae spare my sister from a most evil crime! Ah fear my weak-minded father was lied to. He gave her tae a man who falsely rode under yer banner, stole her maidenhood, and forced her tae wed him. All so that he may lay his hands on her inheritance.'

'And who may this man be?' replied a bored Robert.

'The Earl o Kintail!'

Around her, the court erupted into laughter. Cailean's reputation was solid. Nonetheless, she could not let him slander her husband! He stopped her. 'Nae, lass, no yet.'

Robert lifted his hand to silence the court.

'So ye are saying that the Earl of Kintail forged a letter, rode out tae yer home, took yer sister and—'

'And raped her so she had nae choice but to wed him.'

'This is a serious allegation, Laird Gilchrist. Sir Cailean, is it true?'

'It's no how I remember it.' Cailean stepped forwards, taking her with him.

She stayed tucked into his side, just ever so slightly behind him. Her husband raised his hands to demonstrate that he was not restraining her. She stayed still; she may as well have taunted a wild boar. Michael's eyes bulged and he stepped forwards. In spite of the guards stopping him, her stomach lurched. She must not shy away, for she held the upper hand.

'That's no him. He… he must have been working together with him!' Michael pointed to the other side of the hall.

Alasdair gave a roguish wave; again, laughter filled the hall. She quietly groaned, for Michael was not one to be mocked. Indeed, the rage already radiated from him, and he never backed down from anyone he believed to be below him.

'Come forward, Lord Alasdair. Now, Laird Gilchrist, are ye sure ye wish tae continue with this? I ken they are brothers, but I highly doubt they share *that* much.'

Please Lord, let him see the light!

'Aye, they must have planned this whole thing!'

Foolish, foolish man! Once again Cailean took her hand; he looked down at her, and was that a wink? Robert let out a bored sigh.

'Ambassador, I would like tae hear yer version of events.'

Merciful Lord! Alasdair had a finesse with words akin to Pa's. Though he was subtly scathing. He started with their orders to escort her, and her brother's lack of propriety upon arrival. Then he showed her old gown – so that was where it had got to – and explained her modest appearance up until just before her arrival at court. For good measure, he introduced the carter, who bore witness to her sleeping arrangements. The second witness was one of Elizabeth's midwives – she could still feel the woman's cold, probing finger inside her. And then there was the further indignity of last night's witnesses!

'Do we really wish tae shame the countess further by parading her bloodied sheet?' Alasdair asked on her behalf.

Thank goodness the answer was no! If Michael had not already ruined his standing, her brother-in-law would have ruthlessly destroyed it.

'I was fooled from the start!' protested Michael.

She looked away.

'They came tae the door in switched clothing! The ambassador in the clothing of the master and the earl in that of a manservant.'

Sorcha could not take much more of this, for now Michael had insulted every Highlander present. Were it not for the rule of no weapons, he would surely have had a dozen swords in him. And he had blundered the one cause that could have been his saving grace. If only he would stop speaking.

'We treated them well, they drank me father's best wine. Then for no reason other than that he disliked the way a wee family dispute went, the earl attacked me in my church before causing uproar amongst my men! As for my sister, she is a whore! They ken how to trick ye into believing they are but a virtuous maid!'

Cailean growled, the sound the frightening opposite of those he made in bed. She grabbed at his arm – her brother was not worth it! Robert called for quiet.

'So what is it? Yer sister is innocent and was stolen away. Or she's a whore and planned the whole thing despite the many witnesses who speak here?' Robert paused as Elizabeth leaned over and spoke in his ear. 'And yer queen's willingness to release a statement of how well the countess conducts herself?'

Lord have mercy, Michael was enraged now. Dangerous. Like he had been that day… She started to shake.

'Yer Grace, if I may?'

She prayed Alasdair would not push him further.

'Lady Sorcha, please explain to the court how ye learned that ye were our king's ward?'

So this was it: she was to deliver the final blow? Unable to control her shaking, she let go of Cailean's hand and clasped hers together. She tried her best to be clear. 'On the day of my arrival... there was a letter waiting for me. I am quite literate... I discerned that it had come from... from my late guardian, Thomas Gilchrist – the then Laird of Henderleithen.'

She paused to take some air.

'Its contents revealed that... that while he had wed my mother, I was no his birth daughter... This was then confirmed the following day in a private audience with Yer Grace."

'Is Michael Gilchrist yer half-brother?'

Her brother was glaring at her; she dared not meet his gaze.

'Nae... he is the son of Laird Thomas's first wife... Margaret.'

'So he kenned that ye were a ward and had an inheritance?'

How had she not noticed that? Her brother growled a demand that she shut up. She swallowed and met his eye. She would do this honourably. 'Michael Gilchrist was no greater than five years of age when I was born... We were raised as siblings with nae distinction other than that of our sex.'

That look in his eye; that was what she saw when he dragged her to the kitchen. The edges of her vision started to fade into that dreamlike haze. 'I dinnae ken where he learned o such things.'

She fell back, letting out a terrified scream as Michael lunged towards her. The blow did not come; the guards had him on his knees. Her back was pressed into Cailean's chest, his arms around her. But it was not enough. She felt her body going limp.

'I beseech Yer Grace, let me remove my wife from this man's presence!'

Was that Cailean? They were moving. *Focus*. She must not float away. His voice, yes, he was singing to her that same sweet lullaby. Her eyes moved. They were in the hallway of the royal quarters, and she was sitting on one of the benches there. Focus on the song ...

'What is it called?' she somehow asked.

'Thank the Lord! Sorcha, please forgive me... If I—'

She didn't let him finish. Her hands grabbed his shoulders. He nearly overbalanced as she pulled herself towards him and pressed a hard kiss to his lips. She needed him; she needed to feel his skin against hers. To feel herself alive. He lifted her up and she wrapped her legs around him. So effortlessly did he carry her to their bed!

*

Curled up on the bed, Sorcha wore only her kirtle and chemise, her hair pulled back into a loose braid, uncovered upon Cailean's request. She played a relaxed game of chess with Ailis while nearby the brothers were sharing a drink and discussing the case. Like Cailean, Alasdair had apologised for using her so. It was sadly necessary, and hopefully, the result would keep her brother safe from himself.

'Most were ready tae see him hung after that. But the bishop called for leniency,' Alasdair explained, making her warm glow dissipate. '"Doth the Bible not say a man can punish his own?" and "is not woman known tae deceive like Eve?"'

Both men cursed. She abandoned the game and joined Cailean, resting a hand on his shoulder. 'He is right. I oft defied Michael as a child and again today, when I bore witness.'

Her husband pulled her to his side; he was angry. Why? Had she not spoken the truth?

'First, ye were obeying yer husband.'

He lifted his goblet and held it out to her; she reached for the jug to refill it. He stopped her and pressed the goblet into her hand. Oh! He was offering her a drink.

'And second, what he did tae ye was no punishment.'

She stopped drinking. Opposite her, Alasdair sat up sharply.

Cailean continued, 'If I punish ye, I'll put ye over my knee. No cover ye with boiling water!'

Her brother-in-law exhaled sharply. Why had Cailean revealed that to Alasdair? Sickened, she set the goblet down and turned to walk away. He caught her hand and pulled her back. She glanced from him to Alasdair – his jaw had set hard like his brother's. 'Damn him. I'll see him rot in the tolbuith for what he did tae ye.'

Could they not see? Michael was still her brother and, for all his faults, she loved him. Besides, what could Alasdair do about the situation? There were no witnesses to her scalding, and no proof that it had been Michael who murdered Pa. One of those men could have done it or even a thief! She would instead pray for him, that the time he spent imprisoned would help him see the error of his ways.

Chapter 14

Cailean stood with Alasdair, awaiting Sorcha. Never had he travelled home with so much. He had ordered extra *birlinn*! Let this not be permanent, except the tent. Purchased from a retiring knight, it came with all its furnishings. Though he refused to buy the warhorse, which was likely as old as its master. The carts – and Ailis – had left early that morning. Everything should be loaded by now.

'When will ye leave?' he asked Alasdair.

'In about a sennight. I have work tae conclude here first.'

'Then I will send Seumas and nine other men here.'

'I thank ye, *mo ciann*, brother.'

He nodded and stepped back. Sorcha had arrived. She bade Alasdair farewell; he gave her the kiss of peace. Not a single jest? Cailean grasped his brother by the hand and embraced him.

'Take care, and try tae stay out o trouble.'

'Now why would ah do that when ah can just call upon ye tae fix it?'

He snorted. 'Ye dinnae need yer big brother tae chase away *bogles.*' *Nor his chief to lead him.*

Cailean mounted and called the retinue to action. A last nod for Alasdair; he knew what they had to do. Finally, court was behind him! And he flew his own standard – gules and fess wavy abased azure with a rampant ram. Sorcha's shadow be warned: he would fight on land or sea for justice. He looked to her and her bright smile. The night before he had lain awake. Her odd behaviour around Michael had vexed him.

They made good time riding fast towards Dumbarton. Ahead, Cailean spotted a man on the track. He ordered Sorcha to fall behind, and confirmed his men had surrounded her. Hand on his sword, he slowed to a stop.

'Name yerself!' he shouted.

'Ye should not o wedded her, MacMhathain. This feud has nowt tae dae with ye,' the stranger replied.

'Tis a bit late now, is it no?'

'We warn ye, stay oot o it.'

'Who are "we" tae be ordering me?'

Their secrecy was beginning to wear thin.

'That is no yer concern.'

'She is my wife, that makes it so.'

'So be it. The blood o yer clan be on yer hands.'

Cailean would not be cowed. He nudged Taranis forwards, forcing the messenger aside. And kept his eye contact as they passed, only then speeding up. He shouted at those walking ahead. Did they not hear the damned *crotals*? *The blood of your clan.* A slip of the tongue? Or were they acting for their clan? God's balls, not a blood feud!

At the dock, he jumped from his horse. They needed to leave *now*. Too many people about to keep an effective watch. And the men wanting Sorcha would have had plenty of time to arrange reinforcements.

'Get the horses aboard. Untack them when ye sail!' he ordered.

'Bad news?' Donald joined him.

He shared his concerns.

'Do ye ken who the clan is yet?'

'Nae, but I have a good idea of who they're no.'

'Aye, that be mighty handy, like.'

Cailean grunted in agreement, turned, and almost tripped over his wife.

'God's balls, how do ye do that?'

'Same way ye do it.'

He blinked; Thomas had *trained* Sorcha to walk silently. And too damned well! He shook it from his thoughts. She needed to be on a readied boat. And the captain briefed.

*

They left without issue. And considering the lateness of the day, travelled well. Cailean watched the horse transport sail onwards. His *birlinn* was to land each night instead. Better for Sorcha. How many more changes would he need to make? Alasdair had laughed when asked; Donald refused to answer. The clinker-built vessel easily slid ashore; he jumped down and helped haul it further onto the beach. The grassland merged with the sand, ideal for the tent.

He held out his hands to Sorcha. For her first time, she fared well. Only an hour or so spent clinging to the mast, and only when they hit the sea. Though she was eager for dry land. He set her on the hard sand and watched. She was entranced, shooting back when the wash approached.

'It'll no reach ye; tide's going out.'

'But it's coming in… oh!'

He chuckled; he could vaguely recall Alasdair doing the same. Cailean must have been, what, five summers old? He left her watching the white horses. There was unpacking to do.

Several loads later, an oarsman caught his attention. What was it? The lands here were safe. Sorcha? She sat on soft sand, running her fingers through it. He abandoned his work.

'Having fun are we?' he asked, joining her.

'I have never seen sand like this. It's so warm!'

'Aye, but if ye dig deep enough, it's wet and no so pleasant.'

'It is?'

He glanced back over his shoulder; he should be helping set up camp. But her wonder. And, unlike Glasgow, he could show her more. He reached under her skirts to remove her boots.

'Cailean, no out here! At least wait for the tent!'

'Nae, wife, I'm no after that. Remove yer cloak.'

Again, she made him chuckle – such a dubious look! But she complied as he chucked her hose at Ailis. He helped her up.

'I fear the sea air has… My goodness!'

She fidgeted, burying her feet. Just what he had done

as a child. It was compulsive, yet when had he last done it? When had he last enjoyed a sandy beach?

'Come, let me show ye more.'

They ventured away from the others. He searched for the treasures of his youth. Razor clams, limpet shells, perhaps a mermaid's lost purse. And he named the birds. She was as captivated as he had once been. Had he really forgotten such pleasures? But these were not the best! He guided her to soft sand once more. And pulled her close.

'Run!' he growled with laughter.

She took flight, skirts in hand. He walked after her; she was going nowhere fast. Several times she stumbled until her legs gave way. Cailean was there to catch her. They fell together into the sand, her face flushed with happiness. He rolled over and pinned her beneath him. She squealed and tried to escape, her laughter not once diminishing. Dear Lord, he was blessed! He leaned in, kissing and sucking at her neckline. Her laughter became gasps. She responded well to his touch. Were they not so visible, he would have taken her.

The camp was ready when they returned. Seated, she leaned into him; he handed her his flask. Ewan joined them. 'So how do ye like the beach?'

'It is beautiful. So much life!' she exclaimed. 'The Lord has blessed us with such things, as he has me with my handsome husband.'

Cailean took a swig from his returned flask to hide his pain. 'Once he was.'

'He still is. The scar does no define ye like that, Cailean. Ye are far more attractive than ye ken.'

She stood abruptly, and left for the tent. What had he

done to deserve that? He spoke the truth. Did they not call him a beast at court? But his mither had once said the same. But then she would, wouldn't she?

'She be one of a kind, aye.' Ewan had a slight grin on his face.

'She is perplexing.'

'Aye, tis often the way of a wife. They leave ye no kenning if you're coming or going. But ah think she's just what ye need.'

'Maybe. Who put the tent up?'

Yes, he was changing the subject. He just could not talk about… well, them. Was there such a thing? It worked, for Ewan was muttering. Cailean took a guess. 'The seamen did it. And much faster too.'

'Tis no right, that one be far more complicated.'

He glanced at the tent. It was larger, square, and had a small canopy. Ailis left it and headed towards another fire, where food was cooking.

'Aye, but they work with canvas, rope and poles all day.'

'And women ken matters of beauty better.'

Damn the observant *tyke*.

*

In the gloaming, Cailean sat with his men. Sorcha had not returned. Ailis claimed tiredness. He would not pander to such childishness – let her sulk. The men spoke of home, of the harvest. And of the coming opportunities for reiving. He would send Iain with them; the boy had yet to be tested. But then, should he allow parties to roam this year? It would be a good time to attack his clan. If only he knew numbers. Names. Anything! He stood up and took a walk. Donald followed, damn him.

'What?'

'Do ye no think ye've sulked enough?'

He glared.

'Och, *mo ciann*, dinnae give me that look. Ewan told me. And that ye refused tae follow her inside.'

'What?'

'Jesus, Alasdair said ye were wet behind the ears. Aye, she was angry with ye, but she wanted ye too. She was being *discreet*.'

He cursed. Must conversation between the sexes always be convoluted? And was he too late? He hurried back towards the tent, only to pause at the fire. Donald cast him an odd look as the rest fell silent.

'I'm tae bed. Ye all should rest. Especially Donald.'

'What, why me?'

Cailean gestured to his cousin's face. 'Ye must be no well, being bested by a lass and all.'

He walked away from the uproar. Petty? Yes. Worth it? Absolutely. He would be forgiven, eventually.

He was too late. The only warmth came from a lit candle. She had fallen asleep. Just his luck! He stripped down and climbed in next to her. The bed was too small. She murmured but did not wake when he nudged her over. God's balls, she slept as soundly as Alasdair. He wrapped himself around her…

'Please! No, don't!'

Sorcha! His eyes sprang open; he must have fallen asleep. Oof! Something sharp rammed into his gut.

Instinct had him turning for his blade. A small foot landed in the back of his knee. He swung back around, pulling it from its sheath. He blinked. There was no one there. She screamed. Damn – she was having a nightmare! What to do? He dropped his sword and pulled her to him.

'*Mo ciann?*' a guard called.

'Stay out, she dreams!'

She went limp in his arms; her breathing becoming choking sobs. At a loss, he soothed her like a babe.

'I… I'm sorry.'

'Shhh, my *fiadh-chat.*'

She rolled over and buried her head into his chest. Was this an effect of her distancing? Or a separate affliction cause by Michael's hand? The violence of battles past sometimes plagued his dreams. What could such do to a woman? And how in the Lord's name was he to protect her from memories? At some point, she fell back asleep. He was still awake when the sun rose.

Chapter 15

Sorcha nestled with Ailis in the hull of the galley. The weather had turned, making the waters choppy. More than choppy. This had to be one of the circles of hell that Italian witnessed! Oh, what was his name? She pulled her hood further over her head before tucking her hands back inside the catskin mantle. The sailors near her spoke of keeping to the coast and travelling up the Sound of Mull. Whatever that was. She tried her best to stay upright; she really should have forgone breaking her fast! Though the men seemed unperturbed – still standing on the edge and urinating over the side like they had the day before. Oh, to be back on land, on Glaistig's back! A bucket suddenly appeared next to her.

'If ye don't mind me saying so, my lady, ye're looking a wee bit green around the gills.'

She stared inanely at Donald.

'Sickly.'

'I feel it.'

He insisted she got up, ignoring her protestations. So

much for her being his superior! She rose, clinging to him as the boat tried to toss her around.

'Easy, my lady. Keep looking out there and I'll hold ye steady.'

'At what? I see nothing.'

'At the horizon, Sorcha.'

Cailean reached around behind her and grasped her forearms. She looked towards the line and fell backwards against his chest. Donald let go as her husband thanked him.

'Dinnae try to fight it; go with it like ye would a horse,' Cailean instructed.

She bit her tongue. What did he think she was trying to do? Focusing fully on the horizon, she started to move with the ship. She laughed and glanced back at him. He rewarded her with that handsome smile of his and let go. She did not need the horizon for she was one with the boat! She was... Lord have mercy! She barely reached the bucket in time.

Sitting on her heels, Sorcha groaned and lifted her head to the sky with closed eyes. Heavy raindrops splashed onto her face, one or two landing, then falling harder and quicker. She cared not as her wretched stomach had her reaching for the bucket yet again.

When she could purge no more, she huddled once again. How could the oarsmen sing so cheerfully? It was now bone-chilling cold and wet; neither the oiled linen nor the extra furs and plaid could keep her warm. Ailis's attempt at tricking them with verse that spoke of hot summers did little either. She had no choice but to hush the poor girl before she did anything ungodly.

Why did her husband have to come from a seafaring family? He had already warned her that this would be their main transport. Apparently, Highland hills could be so steep, one had to go around them when on horseback, adding days. Well, she had lived as a recluse before, she would do it again before setting foot on another vessel!

Cailean joined them and brought with him worse news. They would not be landing; it was pointless as fires could not be lit. Instead, she was to endure the night under a sail shelter.

Though crude, it was remarkably effective, for it trapped in the heat released by their combined bodies. Alas, it also kept in all the smells. She was quite aware of how distasteful men could be, but had never expected to bear such close witness! Cailean was not much sweeter, but thank the Lord, he was warm.

*

By the fourth and final day of sailing, the weather was doing its best to make amends with Sorcha. They had spent the night on land again, and she had made the most of it. A strip down and wash in the tent followed by a heavy sleep. She should have felt guilty making Ailis boil the water, but she could not. It had felt far too good! That morning she had dressed as Cailean asked, for he knew his people best. He had chosen her wedding garments; must she wear them every time her life changed? Now she stood at the bow, wrapped safely in his arms.

'See the narrowing? On the other side o that is Loch Alsh, the start of our home waters. The northern shore is the edge of our ancestral seat. Where she meets with Loch Duich and Loch Long is Eilean Donnain.'

How different was the landscape! It towered around them like sleeping giants. Sparse, windswept lands intermixed with large areas of dark greens and purples, and craggy rocks. Or woodlands where the trees grew thin and tall. Yet people, animals and crops clung steadfastly to their sides. No wonder Cailean was so strong. She gasped as the boat glided into the loch. In its harshness, there was a raw beauty to it all. Cailean's grasp on her tightened.

'I kenned ye would like it,' he whispered directly into her ear, his voice sending a heavenly shiver down her spine.

She smiled up at him, before her new home caught her attention again. He pointed out various landmarks and the names of the islands. One day, she would explore them all. Get to know the land like she had her childhood home. The islands hid Eilean Donnain from her view until they rounded the second one's point. A large curtain wall interspersed with towers greeted her. Tucked just behind it stood a tall keep. It appeared as harsh as the hills – only: 'Are those glass windows?'

'Aye, and garderobes too. Alaxandair mac Uilliam commissioned us tae build it.'

'Kermac?'

'Nae. But he improved it.'

She strained to see more, but their position made it harder. Along the shore, people ran towards the cluster of buildings and dockside that stood nearby. They dressed in simpler *léines* and ran barelegged. Most were barefooted. They were too far away for her to make out their shouted words, though it was clear their excitement was at Cailean's return and not her arrival. How would they treat her?

At the dock, he was the first to step off. Sorcha hung back; no one had instructed her on any protocol. He held out his hand and, after a deep breath to steady her nerves, she took it. He led her away from the boat to what appeared to be the hamlet's square. A crowd gathered around them. Their looks proved they judged differently from the court, but just as harshly. She could not blame them, for she would have Cailean's ear and could greatly affect their lives. Yet she kept her poise. It was far easier than it had been at court. Perhaps because she knew some of what she was doing?

'Ye see the circlet, ye ken what it means. Meet yer new mistress – Lady Sorcha Nicmaghan.'

Cailean had returned to speaking his birth tongue, Gaelic. A poetic language if ever there was one, though there were noticeable differences from her own Gaelic tongue. She tried her best to be understandable. To make a good impression.

'I am honoured tae be here and to be granted the privilege of being yer chief's wife.'

The crowd murmured and one or two called out 'Sassenach', having recognised her accent, or word choice. Cailean shifted and she quickly squeezed his hand to stop him. Once, Elizabeth had chided another maid for using her father's name to influence people. *'Better to demonstrate with actions than demand acceptance.'* A small boy broke through the crowds. Shyly, he approached and held out a bunch of wildflowers that had been hastily and poorly picked. She let go of Cailean's hand and crouched to the boy's level.

She smiled warmly at him. 'Hello. What's yer name?'

'Ciaran.'

'A pleasure to meet ye, Ciaran. Are these for me?'

The boy nodded and Sorcha took them.

'I thank ye, they are most beautiful.'

When she stood back up, Sorcha sensed a change to one of begrudgingly mild approval. Ciaran left her and ran towards one of the men who had been on the galley. She could not help but smile again at their reunion.

A loud whinny belonging to her dear, sweet Glaistig broke the silence. She must have fared better on the journey! The mare greeted her with a nose to her chest. Sorcha lingered for a few minutes, caressing her between the eyes before mounting with Cailean's help. There was a sparkle in his eye and, though he was trying to hide it, his lips were slightly upturned. She had pleased him!

*

Arriving at the mainland in front of the castle, Sorcha stared in disbelief. There was no bridge over the water, yet she seemed to be the only one concerned. She looked around her as the others stood talking. Were they to stay there until one was built? Surely they should have taken the boat directly to its gates? Cailean leaned across in his saddle.

'See that post out there?'

It stood halfway between the castle and the land.

'Aye.'

'When the white is visible, we can safely cross. Aim directly for it and then for the gates.'

This loch was like the sea? She watched closely; sure enough, rocks started to emerge and soon the white appeared. How ingenious! Their horses splashed through the remaining water, accompanied by Glaistig's squeals of delight. Sorcha groaned; she should have called her Kelpie.

The large and heavy main gate was open by the time they had crossed. Past it, the keep stood upon the highest part of the island. To its left were kitchens and the like, and to the right, a guard hall and other, dirtier, structures. It was all too enclosed and shadowy. Where was the freedom to come and go as one wished? The king's manor had been more open than this!

Many stood waiting to greet their chief, though yet again, their eyes were on her. The outsider wearing the circlet. She struggled to not stare in return. At the front was a ruddy-faced, middle-aged man. Judging by the numerous keys he wore, he had to be the seneschal. She dismounted and he limped towards them, before kneeling awkwardly. Others followed suit.

'Greetings, *mo ciann* and Lady...'

'Sorcha Nicmaghan. Sorcha, this is Hamish.'

Cailean bid them to rise before clasping the man's hands in friendship. Alasdair had been right – formalities were there, but so was a closeness that differed from court. A vast improvement, in her opinion. She smiled warmly but, outside of a greeting, she held her tongue. Now was really not the time to say anything foolish. And Glaistig had already made too much of a display.

'My lady, I look forward to working with ye. And *mo ciann,* ah had everything prepared just how ye wished, including these.'

He handed a set of keys to Cailean, who then faced her. These would not open heavy doors, but rather the chests and strongboxes that contained Cailean's most valuable items. Far more than those she had carried at Henderleithen. Back then, the spice box had been the most expensive item under her charge. She dared not consider what wealth lay within. Cailean placed the keys into her hand and cupped it with his own hands.

'Just as ye trust me to protect ye, I trust ye to run my household.'

And he did, she could see it; she would not let him down. He kissed her gently, and with far more reserve than he would in their chambers. A shame propriety demanded it; perhaps he could spare the time to show her to her chamber. Hamish gave an awkward cough.

'*Mo ciann*, ah'm afraid that—'

The door to the keep crashed open, and out strode a large woman wearing clothes identical to those Sorcha herself had once worn. Right down to the wimple. Sorcha inhaled sharply, for the woman's judgement was clear. She, Sorcha Nicmaghan, was guilty of the most heinous crime of wedding Cailean! Lord have mercy, neither brother had mentioned a mother. Her husband muttered a rather indecent curse before calling out, 'Aunt Bernice, how nice of ye tae visit.'

'It's about time ye arrived home. If it was no for me, the keep would have gone tae ruin. I arrived tae find these *sumphs* wasting yer money by decorating the bedchambers with an abundance of whitewash and frippery. Furthermore, they tried to keep me from my chamber. When I got in there, they had ruined that with indulgences too!'

Hallelujah! This hard-faced beast was not her mother-in-law! But who was she, to be speaking to her chief so? Cailean shot from her side and bounded up the stairs towards Bernice. Reaching the top, he shoved the woman inside. She looked to Hamish for an explanation, but he was mouthing a countdown to her. As he got to one, the air turned sour.

'God's balls, woman, this is no yer home and that is no yer chamber!'

'Dinnae ye dare blaspheme in front of me, Cailean Macmaghan. Ye're no too old that I cannae put ye over my knee. Ye ken full well that ah sleep there when ah'm here!'

'Because ye always break intae it, ye rotten old hag!'

Her mouth dropped open. She thought she had heard him rage on the road to Glasgow but that was nothing. Alasdair could surely hear their voices in Pillanflatt!

Hamish was most uncomfortable. 'I must apologise. The abbess is most insistent when she visits. Ah'm afraid ye have entered quite a war o attrition.'

'She's a lady o the Church?'

'Aye, Bernice joined after the... well, never mind.'

She had to wonder about that. Gathering up her skirts, Sorcha started up the steps, ignoring Hamish's warnings to hold back, and walked inside. In contrast to the bailey, the entrance to the keep was bright and airy. There were benches, and steps leading above and below to the left. It caught her off-guard; perhaps living here would not be so bad. The airiness continued in the great hall, decorated with frescoes of flowers. The windows were high up and large enough to flood the space with light. At the end of the hall stood two doorways on either side of a raised dais. On the wall in between them was a hanging of Cailean's heraldry. She would have continued staring, were it not for their voices cutting the air. Cautiously, she approached. Perhaps a shared love of the Bible would calm the woman.

'I dinnae care what ye think, that chamber is my and me wife's solar!'

'Aye, I heard of yer so-called betrothal tae some low-born border reiver's whore of a daughter. Tis why I came, tae save ye from embarrassment.'

How dare she? Pa had more integrity than this abbess would ever hold! And she was not demonstrating much Christianity either! Just as she could not stand for what happened in her chamber, she would not stand for this.

Chapter 16

'Tae think ye are a bride of God! Yer tongue exudes more poison than the asp in the Garden!'

Cailean swung around; why was Sorcha here? And what did she think she was doing? This was his hall and his concern to address! She held her head high, outraged. Where had she been hiding that?

'Ye speak like ye ken of the Bible but ye ken nothing, ye little witch. Ye dinnae belong—'

Damn Bernice! How dare she attack Sorcha? And how dare Sorcha interrupt!

'Enough!' he roared.

'Christ stood upon the mountain and gave sermon: "To each of ye, I say judge not lest ye be judged; for the Lord will measure ye as ye yourself measure." I try my hardest to live by the commandment, but I know I carry wood in my eye. I fear my judgement at His hands. What of you, abbess?'

God's balls, he now had two women defying him! Only now in Latin! He glared at the two of them, but it did nothing.

'In the last month, I have been uprooted from a goodly, Christian life. Pulled away from the only home I've ever known and dropped at court tae await my fate. Which was decided by a man I had never met before. While there, I was accused of manipulation and promiscuousness, when not once had I sinned or broken the law!' Sorcha erupted, now in lowland Gaelic. 'Furthermore, the man I called my father has died; the man I called my brother likely his murderer. And I have just spent several days soaking wet and freezing tae come up here and be a faithful wife tae the man I wedded!'

Damn it, she had a point, but this was not the time or place. And she was still not finished.

'Would ye still like tae call me a whore and debase a dead man when I have injured ye not?'

He stared from her to Bernice; the latter hmphed and stormed out. He had not dismissed her, and as for his wife, was he not the lord here? He strode towards her, only for her to brush past him.

'Hamish, I will see my chamber now.'

Who was she to…? Still stupefied, he nodded to the seneschal. Then flung himself into his chair. Alasdair had not spoken of this. His men knew not to challenge him thus. Yet thrice Sorcha had challenged. Each time worse than before. Though this time, Bernice was also to blame. He sighed and rubbed his nose.

*

Some time later, Cailean found Sorcha in the solar. She lay on the bed, facing away from him. The chamber had returned to the way his parents had kept it. It only lacked his childhood toys, wherever they had gone. Her back stiffened as he approached.

'Leave me alone.' He braced himself. No, it was not an order but a childlike plea.

'I cannae dae that. Ye're in the wrong chamber.'

'I… I see.'

She sat up and kept her head low. Why would she not look at him? Had she realised her error?

'I plan on moving that bed out o here.'

She flinched. 'Where do ye wish me tae sleep?'

She became as passive as she was at Henderleithen. Damn it. He wanted obedience, but also spirit. Grabbing her, he swung her over his shoulders. The shock worked. Sorcha cried out and kicked at him. He patted her backside and headed for the door.

The chamberlain had tried to soften his chamber. Extra chairs, rugs and furs adorned it. But the plain whitewashed walls lacked warmth. Sorcha could change that. For now, her beauty would be decoration enough. He dropped her into the middle of his bed. Gripping one of the knotwork posts, he watched her. Flush-faced, doe-eyed.

'This is yer chamber. Nae. *Our* bedchamber. Ye sleep with me.' Cailean shifted his weight and folded his arms. 'Rightly, ah should punish ye for interrupting. No tae mention shouting at me.'

The colour drained from her face. Had she already forgotten the difference?

'If ye do it again, I will put ye over my knee, Sorcha. But ah'm no a beast. In here and in there,' he gestured to the solar, 'I'm happy tae hear yer complaints, shouted or no.'

She sat up. Yes, she was understanding him. His father had done likewise, and why not? Still, everything had a place and time.

'As tae why I'm letting ye off – well, you're a canny lass.'

She fidgeted but understood. He sat next to her. Should he tell her his plan for Bernice? Yes. Then she spoke of her concern about establishing herself. It reminded him of mediating his clansmen's disputes. Were women really not that different? Most women, he corrected. Bernice was a law unto herself.

'Whatever happens, ye are my priority now.'

She rewarded him by coming closer. He smiled; the hard work was over. And he had done it without others' counsel. Hah! She reached up and removed her veil – she remembered!

'And tis time I properly welcomed my wife home.'

'How does my husband intend tae do that?'

'Like this…'

He pressed her back into the bed. Her lips still tasted of the sea. Sweet Sorcha. It had been too long since he last sated his need. She was already moaning softly. He tugged her skirt out and ran his hand up her leg. He need not touch her; she was already burning for him. But he wanted to hear her plead! Another damned skirt. He tugged at it, but it would not come free. He growled impatiently and tugged harder.

Sorcha pushed lightly against his chest and broke the kiss. 'Dinnae rip me trews.'

'Yer what?' He propped himself up and stared into her eyes. She was not lying. 'Why is my wife wearing trews?'

'Because the only beast she rides barelegged is you.'

He blinked; it made sense. Her thighs would be as rough as his hands. He growled again before nuzzling her neck, making her cry out and laugh. On her lips, 'beast' did not sting.

'Best take them—'

A loud knock interrupted him. Now what?

'This better be good!' he called out.

Sorcha bit her lip.

'Forgive us, *mo ciann*, we have the chests. And the abbess is tryin tae interfere wi tonight's feast.'

Cailean's head fell onto her shoulder. He had forgotten about the feast. Her hands ran through his hair.

'Give them enough tae drink later and they'll no notice us leaving.'

Sound advice. He rolled off the bed and straightened himself. 'Aye, and there better no be any trews under there.'

*

Lifting his signet, Cailean checked his mark. It had taken well upon the final missive. All of them outlined the threat the clan now faced. He knew not if the septs and sencliathe would be attacked; or if he would need their manpower. The missive invited the heads to a meeting. He motioned to a runner.

'This is tae go to them all. Read it for the ones that need it. Move fast.'

'Aye, *mo ciann*.' The man took it and left.

He motioned to the other runner. 'Tae the Lord of Islay. Wait till ye see him personally.'

As the second runner left, Cailean sat back and looked around the side-chamber. His hound set its head on his lap. He was home. Through the latticework, he focused on the stairs beyond. They were almost solely for him and his closest kin. How often had he and Alasdair hidden in its shadows? Spying on their father's meetings. God willing, his children would do the same. And he too would send them back to bed with a growl. He shook his head to clear the daydream. Voices and footsteps were coming towards him. Ailis and Sorcha.

He rose and headed into the hall. The tables were up and the linen laid. This was the noise he preferred; that of those he loved and trusted. A few called out, welcoming him back. He nodded a greeting and paused; Donald's youngest toddled by, oblivious to him. She had been crawling when they left. He greeted Sorcha on the dais with a chaste kiss. Someone shoved him aside to grab her.

'Douglas?'

Three score and more, the man was still as strong as an ox. And a legend. A head injury had deprived him of his memory-making. He lived permanently at Eilean Donnain, in the guard hall. He was prone to wander from other places. But why was he so disturbed by Sorcha?

'Annabelle, what are ye doing here? It's no safe! What was Thomas thinkin, bringin ye here in yer condition?'

Who was Annabelle? And what of Thomas? Did he mean Sorcha's stepfather? His wife's eyes were shining wet. Yet she was not afeared; she treated Douglas like a dear old friend. 'The unrest at the border is too great. Edward's army's been stealing everything tae feed themselves and in return, the clans are raiding tae survive. Thomas brought me here so Cailean could protect me.'

'Och aye, he's a good lad. He'll watch ye.'

Cailean blinked. Had he missed something? Douglas patted his shoulder and wandered off. Sorcha stepped closer to him; she stared in disbelief. He wrapped his arms around her.

'Ma's name was Annabelle.'

They had been here? Or at least met Douglas? He glanced back towards the man; he now sat expectantly. Always the same spot, regardless of hierarchy. Damn it. The questions and duties would wait; the feast awaited them. He settled Sorcha in her seat. The tables grew quiet, expectant. He looked at them, then to Sorcha.

'No matter how far I roam, there is nae place like my sweet home. Nae storm shall keep me from my bed, for within it lays the lass I wed.'

His lips twitched as cheers filled the hall. Several calls of 'about time' followed. He raised his goblet before sitting down. His butler started serving the dishes.

'For one who speaks little, my lord husband is a bard.'

'It isnae my words. It was composed for my father. I thought it fitting.'

'Indeed,' she teased.

He would return the favour later. When she lay in his bed. He stared into her eyes before taking a sip of… mead? His butler had been busy. And cook had outdone himself again. Yes, it was good to be home. Yet there was a lack of women; no doubt Bernice's doing.

He would not let that stop him. He motioned to the musicians.

Between the courses, the *sennachie* regaled them with tales of their ancestors. After the conclusion of one, Sorcha leaned in. 'Dinnae tell Alasdair, but he makes a poor storyteller.'

He snorted, somewhat tempted to break her request.

After the feast, there was only drink. The hall got livelier. Tales grew taller and dancing began. He permitted all to join upon completion of duties. Noble or swineherd, it mattered not. This time he was eager to join them, though he never needed to say much. Sorcha was as graceful as she had been at court;. she overlooked no one. Neither of them took much drink. He watched the crowd carefully. Several of the stronger men were soon swaying.

'It's time, my *fiadh-chat*.'

*

The door slammed shut behind them, Cailean's lips already on hers. This was the real feast. He guided her back to the bed where she pushed him away. He growled and stepped back. How dare she deny him? Instead, Sorcha dropped her gown over her shoulders and undid her girdle. He did not stop to watch and tore off his own garments.

She stood before him in her shift, her hair down. He could not wait any longer. He pushed her back into the bed. Claiming first her lips, then her neck. His hand found her breast, squeezing it. Her nipple hard underneath.

'Tell me, Sorcha, tell me ye're ready!'

'I have been since we last parted!'

God's balls, he almost spilled his seed. She had burned for him all that time! He shoved the skirt out of the way. She lifted her hips and he slid into her with ease. Damn, she was made for him. He grabbed her hips and thrust hard. He could not stop himself. His wild cat came alive under him. Her flushed face, her gasps. She clawed at his hands and tried to meet his thrusts, but her arousal was too strong. He growled triumphantly. He did this to her; he and no other! He leaned forwards, thrusting faster.

'Cailean!'

'Aye, sweet wife, give in!'

She stiffened and then he felt it. Her release making her cling to his shaft. He thrust through it. Once, twice. And filled her, his gasps mixing with her own.

He pulled out and collapsed onto the bed next to her. He would never tire of her! She was still making small sounds of pleasure. He paused. There was talk that unlike a man, a woman needed no rest. Was she still hot? He propped himself up on his elbow.

'Wha... what is it?'

Her words wonderfully slurred. He ran his hand up her thigh. 'Shh, my *fiadh-chat*. Let me watch ye.'

Dipping his fingers between her lips, he found her wet with both their seed. Her breathing was already increasing. Aware of his own sensitivity, he lightly touched that sweet spot. She bucked hard – 'Lord have mercy!'

Yes. Overly sensitive and alive. It was true!

'Nae the Lord, Sorcha, just me.'

He rubbed it ever so lightly. She hissed and grasped him, her eyes clouding with arousal. This was going to be good. And better, he could watch it all.

Chapter 17

The bed was once again empty when Sorcha woke. Cailean must rise with the lark. He certainly had risen well last night! She could not keep the smile off her face as Ailis dressed her. How much she had changed. No more a blushing maid. She was so very blessed with him. Yet now she was cursed with his burdens too.

'Ailis, have ye been treated well?'

The maid blushed. 'Aye, my lady; Iain has been most helpful. And the butler and cook have already enquired as tae yer tastes.'

'The others?'

'The maids accept me, though some of the ladies…'

It was as she suspected. Ailis was too young and docile to be a threat, but she was still Sorcha's maid. She instructed Ailis to find her as soon as she had finished tidying.

In the solar, a chaplain stood awaiting her. Upon her acknowledgement, he spoke.

'Good morrow, my lady. I am Brother Paul. I am tae assist ye in learning yer household.'

Ah yes, larger noble houses consisted of two halves, the lord's and the lady's, as there would be times that they would be separated. Was it wrong of her to wish it were not so? She bade the surprisingly young man to sit with her.

'I assume we have much tae discuss.'

Indeed, they did. From her allowance to the dispensing of spices, to the arrangements for travelling. She was to have at her disposal horses, men to protect her, and two *birlinn*. Well, they would not be used! Cailean had instructed that she was free to travel anywhere on his lands, and to court when necessary. But to go elsewhere, she must attain his permission. What of her inherited land? Paul could not say. Apparently, Cailean also had a chamberlain – not once had she seen him be dressed by anyone other than himself. It was with him that she should discuss decorating their chambers. That should be fun! She had never had such a free rein before.

After the worldly aspects had been discussed, the chaplain focused on her spiritual needs. Did she know that on the floor above was the lord's private chapel? And that she could take mass there? She did now; and would do so on fast days. Sundays and saints' days, she would attend the kirk with Cailean when she could.

'This leaves but one final, delicate, issue. Ye have yer own ladies, but—'

'My lord husband's aunt. Well, no time like the present, I suppose.'

The longer she waited then the harder it would be. But Lord forgive her, she wanted nothing to do with such a vile woman. Paul gave her an apologetic smile. Perhaps he should pray with her before she did battle? Her stomach knotted as she rose. *Be strong, be like Elizabeth.* She could do that, couldn't she?

'Come, Ailis.'

In the hall she found her ladies with the abbess sitting amongst them as though she were the queen. Nonetheless, she was an imposter that needed to be driven out like Edward had been. Only one rose and greeted her with the respect her status dictated. The rest barely glanced her way. She lifted her chin and kept her face serene. Bernice smiled smugly. Was it unchristian of Sorcha to want to wipe that smile from her face? The only seat left was a stool. She could not accept this further insult. But how to broach it?

A woman addressed the abbess; she was working on a table linen. 'Should I embroider some flowers on this?'

'Nae, that is too opulent.'

'Pray tell why ye would ask a guest that question and not yer lady?' That voice had come back! So level and majestic while her insides churned like the sea.

The woman stammered and glanced back and forth between the two of them.

'Ignore her insolence. My nephew married a useless Sassenach. He'll see sense soon and send her back tae where she came from.'

Their work stopped and all eyes were upon her. They expected her to prove Bernice right. If only they knew that she really was an imposter, pretending to be what she was not. They would cast her aside in an instance. But she would not buckle, nor whine. Had she not taken worse?

'Ye can say what ye like about me, I cannae stop that,' Sorcha started, aware of the abbess already preening. 'However, I am yer chief and laird's wife. If ye cannae respect me, then respect the position.'

'Chief's wife? Ye are no of this clan, lass, and ye never will be!' spat Bernice.

She reminded them that her children would be of Macmaghan blood and, to further her point, listed Cailean's line. *Thank you, Alasdair!* A couple of the women glanced at each other. From nearby, an older man raised his drink. 'That's more than ye kenned when ye wedded, Bernice!'

At least she had his support! Only she could not remember his name. She nodded to him. That worked, for they were used to Cailean's nods. Her attention returned to an enraged Bernice.

'A shame ye have forgotten our chief's words already. He was most adamant that he will not be accepting certain behaviours from *any* of his family.'

An indirect approach was an awful manipulation, but it worked. And like the ladies at court, there was a visible shift amongst the women. They abandoned Bernice's cause like rats from a burning barn. The one who had greeted her now rose and rounded on them.

'Shame, shame on ye all. My Ewan has been singing our lady's praises since he got home. Claims she has nary a drop of bad blood in her. That she can tame wild beasts and that she single-handedly bested Donald! Forgive me, my lady, I am Iona.'

Ah, Ewan's wife, no wonder she had waited. She held one of the lowest positions.

'It is a pleasure tae meet ye, Iona, but I fear yer husband has over-exaggerated.' Sorcha's words were lost as another screeched with laughter.

'Och, it was ye who bested him? My lady, please, ye have tae tell me how! Ah've wanted to do that tae the oaf for years now!' Donald's wife stood up. 'I be Bridget. I apologise for no being at the feast last night. We were instructed to stay away.'

She stepped aside to give her chair to Sorcha, who struggled to keep her composure. She had cracked their outer wall, but could she truly trust their defection?

'I hold no grudge. It cannae be easy for ye all when ye hear of a new lady. Now, please share with me what ye're all working on, yer needlework looks far finer than my own.'

They started speaking at once, all eager. She struggled at first, but slowly, she grasped what they were saying. A new smock for a daughter, fixing garments, and tablecloths for future saints' days. She recommended using the local flowers on the latter. They had looked so pretty from the boat. Yet when she offered Bernice a chance of redemption, it was ignored.

*

The days that followed were fairly peaceful for Sorcha. Bernice either avoided or ignored her, while Bridget and Iona were as friendly as their husbands, although far more outspoken. With their help, she started to take root. First, she spoke to cook about having her porridge with milk. Salt and water reminded her too much of the sea. Then she ordered drapes to be made for the bedchamber, using some of the gifted fabric, for the walls were too cold to be left bare. If they turned out well, she would have matching cushions and a spread made. During the day, she hardly saw Cailean, but he was always there at night. That was *their* time.

Now it was the clan's time. The sessions, Alasdair had instructed, were not the formal gatekeeping sessions seen at court. Indeed, it was more akin to a social gathering, where all wishes and grievances could be heard. And on a far smaller scale to The Gathering, whatever that was. Cailean had expressed his wishes for Sorcha to be at his side and, though no longer needed, she chose to wear the circlet. It was too important not to. Her thought was confirmed by his nod of approval. When he reached for his plaid, she followed him.

'Have ye more than the one?'

His eyebrow rose and he wordlessly pulled out another. She took it and wrapped it over her shoulders, as she had seen the other women do.

'Ye can get one from storage,' he said, after a moment of watching her.

'Aye, but they're no yers.'

'What's that tae do with… ouch!'

He had pricked himself. Sorcha took the brooch from him. It was the one with the two bears, for he rarely wore any other. She bit her cheek to keep from smiling like a fool as he let her pin it upon him. Finishing, she explained, 'They hold yer smell. Tis the next best thing tae being in yer arms.'

He must have liked that too, as he caught her head and kissed her deeply.

The hall bustled with activity but immediately fell silent on their entrance. Cailean escorted her to their chairs and, before they sat, presented her to the chieftains who stood gathered to one side. These must have been the men upholding the betrothal – judging by their looks, they were not just here for Cailean, but to see her! Sorcha kept her head up and smiled as warmly as she could towards them.

At the opening of the session, the same men presented them with a belated wedding gift: a beautifully ornate cradle, decorated with knotwork, Cailean's coat of arms, and long stems of flowers. She marvelled at its detailing and praised the craftsmanship. They had made the most of their advanced knowledge!

'Tis the broom, my lady. It flowers in spring, just like a babe is in the spring of its life,' explained one.

'How delightful, I thank ye all.'

They retreated back but continued to stare, much to her husband's displeasure. 'Have ye no seen a lass before? Away with your *glowren*!'

She bit her cheek to keep from biting her lip in front of everyone. Cailean took her hand and stared into her eyes. That possessive look again. He may as well have been a stallion, roaring at the others to stay away from his mare. She dipped her head briefly to swallow her delight lest he mistake it for mockery.

Thankfully, the men who had come of age stood waiting nearby. She watched Cailean accept their pledges, made on their daggers. So different to the clasped hands those living at Henderleithen had given. But then they were not warriors. Movement to her right caught her attention: Hamish was setting a stool next to her chair. He kept his voice low. 'The causeway is nearly clear so the rest of them will be here shortly. I'm tae sit here and answer any questions my lady may have.'

'I thank ye, Hamish.'

Douglas too had joined her, albeit behind her chair and facing the wrong way. He often insisted on guarding her, or rather Annabelle, until he forgot what he was doing. Thankfully, this morning, he had remembered why she was 'visiting'.

The first grievance was a dispute over inheritance, followed by a couple seeking permission to wed. As much as she tried to prevent it, her eyes drifted. In the musicians' gallery above, she spotted Bernice. The abbess had acquired a guard for the day. Surely she had not questioned his rulings too? Sorcha let out a soft sigh. At least she stood alone there. Her gaze returned to the matter in hand, and she smiled in congratulation. There was nothing impeding their marriage.

Following the newly betrothed came two families, equally roughly dressed. The heads of each stepped forwards.

'*Mo ciann*, ah ask for yer assistance. Our neighbour killed our layin chicken.'

'*Mo ciann*, ah didnae do it in anger. Our crop is late in maturing and ah confused her as me own.'

For ones so poor to kill a laying chicken, they must have been desperate. A glance at the hollow faces of the children confirmed it.

'Why did ye no approach the *tacksman* before this? He could have granted relief on my behalf,' asked Cailean.

'He had his own struggles with the harvest and sick children, *mo ciann*. We didnae wish tae burden him,' stated the struggling man.

The complainant quickly agreed.

'I see. I assume ye cannae compensate?'

Both men looked to each other and shook their heads. The last few years' weather must have been just as difficult for the Highlanders, if not worse. Sorcha had already taken to stopping to appreciate the sun when it chose to shine.

'Ah have nothing tae its value.'

'And ah dinnae have enough work tae accept labour.'

So now they were at an impasse. She bit her lip. For sure, Cailean could give them both chickens and food before sending them on the way. Only that could encourage poor behaviour in less honest individuals. Or he could punish, and ruin one of the families. Unless... Dare she? She leaned over, getting her husband's attention; he looked surprised, but leaned over too.

'I pray I am not overstepping, my lord husband. Could we pay the recompense with a laying chicken and then have the older daughter work off the debt with, say, the alewife?'

She spoke softly so that only he could hear. An eyebrow shot up, but he made no other comment and settled back in his seat. Had she spoken out of turn?

'I will offer a laying chicken in recompense; and some oats to see both families through harvest. I will also ride out tae see the *tacksman*, should he too need support.'

Both men lowered themselves and started thanking him; he held out a hand to stop them.

'With the upcoming festivities, my staff need help. Yer eldest daughter is tae assist my alewife until the debt is repaid. Go now.'

'Ailis, take both families tae the cook.'

She caught herself; had she really just called that out? She glanced to Cailean, but his face lacked any emotion. Was he angry? She looked around the hall. Bernice was glowering, but Donald was smiling. They met eyes and he nodded.

'God's balls, no again,' muttered Cailean.

Her heart leapt to her mouth, but her husband was not looking at her. She followed his gaze. Two older men were bickering as they came up the hall. They paused long enough to lower themselves.

'Burnie stole me coo again.'

'She likely wandered off somewhere while ye were in yer cups, ye clarty git!'

'Och aye, and ah suppose yer wife be takin up lowing, has she?'

'Ye sayin' me wife cannae sing?'

She wanted so desperately to laugh, but Cailean was rubbing the bridge of his nose. She looked to Hamish and the seneschal leaned in. 'It started back when Cailean was knee-high. On Old Angus's wedding day, he ended up so deep in his cups, his new missus went home without him. He was found the next morn wi Burnie's best nanny goat. Apparently, she was no the same after that and in retaliation, Burnie kept stealing the coo tae get its milk.'

Sorcha stared in disbelief, both at the story and at the idea of her husband once being knee-high. 'Why is it still going on?'

'They're both stubborn-headed *sumphs* with reputations for bein tight-fisted. Ye see, by sharing one coo, they each feed it less. The feud is only brought up when one o them tries tae keep it for longer than he should.'

She turned back in time to see Cailean send them off with a flea in their ear for wasting his time. It would no doubt be long dead by the time the other wanted fresh milk. They were the only ones he dismissed thus. Rather, he was highly attentive to each case, just as he had been with her.

Indeed, by the end of the day, few had left. She learned that, unlike the king's sessions, all who had attended were invited to dine with them. Even those punished. Alasdair had been right. Sorcha ordered drinks to be served in the centre of the hall in the hopes of making work easier for the staff. Cailean did not stop her. He had fallen silent, for her ointment could do only so much. She had a lad bring some steeped willow bark in a goblet. He took it and drank without question. Then, with his hand on her back, they joined the chieftains. She could finally put faces to names, and did most of the conversing.

Her father's old messenger came running towards them. He wore an embroidered livery patch, marking him as being in Cailean's employ. How kind of her husband! He knelt and held out a missive to her husband.

'I was no expecting ye so soon.' Cailean's speech, normally only lightly slurred, had grown worse. That and the drink confirmed what Sorcha guessed when they first met; incessant talking made the pain from his scar worsen.

'There have been some unexpected developments, my lord,' responded the astute Arthur.

Had something happened to Alasdair? She watched Cailean's face, but aside from an eyebrow, nothing changed. Then he spoke, his words much clearer. 'He's taken a wife!'

Chapter 18

Several days earlier.

Alasdair groaned as a knocking sound woke him. He rolled over – let Iain or Donald handle it. Alas, the door opened and in strode his brother. He should have stayed in the ambassadorial quarters. No one to share the chamber with meant no one to leave the door unbolted! Why was Cailean not busy bedding his new wife? Jesus, they had not already argued, had they? He buried his head in the pillow as Cailean tore aside the curtain. Silence. He lifted his head just enough to see the mirror of his angry father passing judgement.

'Another late night?'

No more sleep for him!

'Just my work. There's talk o trouble from those who still dinnae support Bruce.' And he'd been writing instruction to his best interrogator about Michael. Cailean shoved his legs over and sat down; Alasdair opened his eyes long enough to give his brother a dirty look. 'So why are ye waking me so damned early?'

'Been speaking tae Robert about ye.'

'Oh, joy!'

'Wheesht the sarcasm. I need ye, and he agrees.'

He cracked an eye open again; was Cailean really talking about him? Nonetheless, he was intrigued.

'I need ye tae manage Sorcha's land.'

Alasdair shot upright. Though he had found no record of who had once owned the land, both Robert and the court's behaviour had confirmed that its inhabitants had not been the king's supporters. To be closer to those he suspected were the source of Robert's troubles. And to have a place and become a chieftain properly…

He sighed and sank back into the bed. 'Ye ken why I cannae accept; I'm no chieftain.'

The sight of his own blood made him swoon and, much to his father's disgust, he could not overcome it. His foster had resorted to rousing him with buckets of cold water. All that had done was teach him to ignore injuries. It meant he could fight, but he would always be a risky right-hand man. And who would follow a swooning leader? Not that he'd endanger men by leaving them leaderless in battle.

'Our father made ye think that, no I. I'll tell ye what ah see, Alasdair. A man who kens how tae prevent unnecessary bloodshed, who can reason with the most stubborn of people. And the best adviser I, and our clan, have.'

He blinked. Cailean was not a man prone to lecture. Slowly he sat up again, and stared at his brother. He really believed all that? It was madness. Yet, to prove their father wrong, would that not be sweet justice? And if Robert agreed, it finally meant an escape from court life and playing the fool. But if he failed…

'I *need* ye for this. Take it and, if ye must, Seumas as yer commander.'

He couldn't argue with that. 'We may both be deluded, but fine, I'll do it.'

'It's yers to run as ye see fit. Ah just ask for the usual rents.'

After dressing, Alasdair joined his brother at the table to discuss the more pressing concerns. Be it battle or espionage, a person should not blindly charge into the unknown. Cailean explained that it was currently managed by an officer. Though 'managed' was a loose term – collecting exorbitant rents appeared to be his main role, as most of the manor was shut up. Thankfully, it was on the edge of a sea loch; refurbishing it would be easier by boat. All in all, he could not fault it, for it looked promising. A nice little family home, if only he still had Ruth to help him fill it.

They stood; Cailean and Sorcha would be leaving soon, and Alasdair wished to see them off.

'Send on my chests when ye get home, aye?' Alasdair asked.

'And our parents' bed; ye fit it better than I do.'

'Tis no my fault ye spent all your time standing in a midden as a wean.'

He grinned and received an eye-roll in return. They could both fit in the bed, but Cailean had indulged in a larger bed – the only real luxury his brother had treated himself to – and had no need for it. Better it stayed in the family.

Mordag flung herself down onto her pallet and screamed into a pillow. Her father had run out of ribald old lechers and was now starting on the downright decrepit! Why could he not let her be? From the moment she developed breasts, all men did was stare. And to think, that whorer Macmaghan had got an eyeful! It made her skin crawl. A small home, a few sheep, a goat and a bit of land was all she needed. But no, she must wed! Damn men, damn them all to hell and back!

Someone was coming. She wiped her eyes and grabbed her discarded embroidery.

'Da says fine, ye can stay here fer now. But ye must be up at the hall fer the evening meal. He's arranged fer Sir Carruthers tae sit with us and he wants ye both tae meet. Ah wouldnae worry about him. The knight looks like he can barely sit upon a horse let alone ride ye. Ah swear he was old when Wallace was fighting.'

'Thank ye, Angus. I dinnae ken if that is better or worse.'

Her younger brother was just on the cusp of adulthood. He was a lanky colt and no matter what she did, she could not stop his *léine* hanging off him. Much like his full head of bright red hair.

'Aye, a couple of thrusts and he'd be deid on yer wedding night. And ye'd be back tae being paraded around like a broodmare.'

She groaned as he mimed the gross actions, chest pain, and death.

'I thought ye were here tae cheer me up, no tae disgust me?'

'Can I no do both? Here, this should help.' Angus reached into his pouch, pulled out half a round of soft, white flour bread and tossed it towards Mordag. She caught it and gasped, smelling its freshly baked goodness. It was a long time since she had last eaten good quality bread.

'Do ah dare ask where ye got it from?'

'Didnae filch it if that's what ye're thinking. Was playing knucklebones with a high-born lad who is here with his foster. He'd brought it with him tae eat and shared it with me.'

Fine, not all men, but he was more boy than man. She offered to share but he was having none of it. He sat down next to her and took some hard cheese from his pouch. He took a bite and chewed.

'I filched this instead.'

'Angus!'

He gave her a grin and she bumped him with her shoulder.

'Any other news?'

'No really, they're still talking about that incident.'

Mordag rolled her eyes. She had not attended the court session, but Angus had. He had told her all about how the Macmaghan brothers had torn down a lowly laird. He insisted that it was justified, but she struggled to agree. He had been too young to remember the hardships Robert had caused their family, leaving their father no choice but to swap allegiances.

'Mordag, ah ken ah'm the last one ye want tae hear this from, but Pa's wrong. There's more tae politics than what he says.'

'Hush, dinnae speak so!'

She got up and hurried to the tent to look out. Thank the Virgin that no one was about! Especially those dubious men their father was speaking to last night! She looked back and shook her head. Their father had spent his spare coin on learning for her brother. She swore he had learned too well!

*

Decrepit? This man lay in his grave and waited for the topsoil. And his breath smelled of it! Mordag shifted as far away as she could. Damn it, she would take the beating when her father caught her later. She stood, claimed some unspecified feminine illness, and hurried from the hall.

She should not return to the tent, he'd find her too easily. But where to hide? Angus had told her that tapestries hid spaces. Something to do with draught or guards – it mattered not. She just needed to hide. Glancing at the floor, she looked for the telltale light flick of fabric being caught by a draught. One showing the king's crowning caught her eye. Wonderful!

A quick glance told her she was not being followed. She slid behind it, facing the fabric. Surprisingly, it made a good lookout. She stepped backwards into something soft.

'Och, lass, we've got tae stop bumping into each other like this,' a flowing Highland lilt in her ear.

Jesus, Joseph and Mary! She swung around and came face to face with Alasdair.

'You!' she hissed. 'What are ye doing in my hiding place?'

'*Yer* hiding place, is it? I dinnae see anything that says it's yers, Mordag. Besides, I was here first.'

She inhaled sharply – how did he know her name? And what was he… Never mind… the childish, grinning fool needed to leave.

'*Get out.*'

'It's no a good idea that ah shift. If ye want tae stay hidden from yer father's matchmaking efforts ye're welcome tae stay here, but if no, then ah suggest ye leave first.'

What the…? How dare he? She gritted her teeth. 'Ah said *get out*!'

He held his hands up in mock surrender. The toad!

'Dinnae say I didnae warn ye.'

As deep as her hiding place was, it was not that wide. She pressed as hard as she could against the wall to let the slimy beast past – he must not touch her! His hand propped uncomfortably close to her head. She looked the other way. He smelt surprisingly clean. How odd. He tried to squeeze past her bosom. It didn't work. *Damn, damn, and damn again, they were stuck!* This was the last thing she wanted, and he looked equally alarmed! She could not breathe. She fidgeted, needing to be free.

'Please, Mordag, I beg ye no tae move!' Alasdair had become taut as a bowstring, his voice just as strained.

Did he not see how uncomfortable she was? And what was that hard thing pressed against her privy? No, it could not be!

'Jesus, lass!' exhaled Alasdair.

Mordag grabbed at the wall and clawed at the tapestry – it was far too hot in there!

She was coming free!

'Yes, yes!'

The hanging gave way with a loud rip, pulling her off her feet. The toad grabbed her waist to stop her. What? No! He too lost his balance. She landed hard on the tiled floor and let out a breathy 'oomph'. Alasdair landed on top, his head wedged between her breasts. She blinked, trying to clear the light from her sight. Oh damn, her father was there!

Alasdair lifted his head. '*Tiom-teasan, gun teagahm.*'

She felt his head land back in her bosom. For once, she agreed with the toad; the whole thing was one big nightmare!

*

Mordag's father faked outrage at Alasdair for 'trysting' with his daughter. The others followed suit. Not one listened to her. Why would they? She was a woman besotted by the known whorer! But why was he just standing there, stone-faced and firm-jawed? His pale blue eyes were dangerously dark. *Angry.* At her? Did he think she had planned this? Trapped the slimy toad in ways no other woman had? Her father grabbed her arms and frogmarched her back towards the great hall. Behind her, she could hear several men trying to do the same with Alasdair. Followed by loud thumps. Hah! He had sent them flying!

'I can walk there meself. I'll no run,' he snapped.

They were taken beyond the hall and up some stairs,

to stop at what, presumably, was the king's antechamber. The steward heaved a sigh of annoyance. He got up from his seat and entered Robert's bedchamber without so much as a word. If only he had asked her first, he would not have needed to disturb the man.

She looked around for a sympathetic ear.

'Angus, nae!'

Her brother slammed into Alasdair, toppling him. She screeched at Angus to get off. He was a sapling compared to the Highlander! Why was no one stopping him? No, he was being stopped, by Alasdair himself! But he was not beating the boy senseless. Instead, he grabbed his hands and waited. It drained Angus's anger and he sat back on his heels before looking to her. She shook her head and he climbed off. Angus must have thought the worst had happened. No, *that* was to come.

*

Alasdair sat staring at the ceiling with a wet cloth to his nose. Caught in a compromised position with the only woman who could not care less. His brother would have a merry old time when he learned of this. So much for not getting into trouble! From the corner of his eye he watched Robert and Elizabeth; the latter was barely containing her mirth. Robert had finished eating while listening to the baron's story. Apparently, both Mordag and he had been meeting in secret for days now. Where had he found the time for that?

'So, Baron Macnachten, as I understand it ye have dragged one of my best ambassadors in here, while

I'm enjoying a private meal with me wife, tae demand restitution. Yet ye did not bring it before the court yesterday?'

'Forgive me, Yer Grace. Me daughter led me tae believe she cared no fer any man or marriage. Ah've only just learned o her devious nature.'

'Did she now? And what says Lord Alasdair on this matter?'

'Yer ambassador rightly has a silver tongue. Ah fear he would put it to great use tae weasel out of this situation. And what with his reputation, Yer Grace.'

'What reputation would that be?'

'Fer seducing ladies.'

This whole farce was laughable! Just get on with the damned thing. Mordag snorted; he could just about see her. Ah, the shield-maiden was not just a pretty face! He glanced back to Robert; oh great, he wanted to play.

'I see. Well, if it is a matter of her maidenhood, I can have a midwife examine yer daughter.'

Poor lass. Judging from Sorcha's face after hers, it was not pleasant. The steward stepped in and whispered into the king's ear. Now what? Robert hid it well, but he was displeased. Yet he let the baron continue.

'As kind as that is, Yer Grace, I fear nothing below a marriage will be acceptable, fer gossip will spread and who will wed a lass touched by another man?'

'True. Gossip does spread. Lord Alasdair, I ken of the custom o your chief having the final word. Would Cailean accept my decision on this matter?'

The cloth on his nose did not make his reply easy. 'Yer Grace, you are our overlord. He is but yer most humble and obedient servant and will accept any decision ye make on this matter.'

She was not of the clan so there was no risk of them being too closely related. Besides, he would be too busy muttering 'I told ye so'.

'Then I will permit the marriage tae go ahead on the condition that yer daughter's dowry is the same as what ye offered Sir Carruthers, and no a penny less. Aye, Baron Macnachten, I ken exactly how hard ye have been trying tae wed off yer daughter.'

He wanted to laugh at how entangled the baron was in his own net. But how could he, when he shared it? The baron reluctantly accepted. Looks like he would be taking a wife to Druim Earbainn after all. And no warrior could assist him with the uphill battle it would be.

'Then it shall be done. Lord Alasdair, when do ye leave?'

'As soon as fresh men and supplies arrive from Eilean Donnain – about a sennight, Yer Grace.'

'Then I will see another Macmaghan is granted special dispensation, and ye will be wed on the morrow.'

Everyone was dismissed, bar himself. As soon as the door shut, a servant checked on him and pronounced that he was no longer bleeding. He gingerly touched his nose. The young lad – Angus – had a good fist on him. Elizabeth rose and bid her husband goodnight before leaving. As she passed him, she smirked. At least she got enjoyment from the situation.

'I am surprised by how quiet ye are, Alasdair,' remarked Robert. 'Cailean would have been ranting an raving.'

'I have my moments, Yer Grace, but why waste me strength? If ye wish tae ken the truth, I'll happily tell ye. Though ah dae wonder though why ye allowed it tae go ahead.'

At Robert's behest, he joined him at the table. A goblet was placed beside him and filled. He felt his king's eyes on him.

'I cannae afford for ye tae be caught up in scandal and talked about,' he said at last. 'Yer predecessor kenned that well and barely visited court for that reason. I dinnae expect ye tae stay away, but with a wife, ye can be seen as tamed and sewing good oats. As for who she is, it may be a way tae learn what's happening. Alasdair, I'm no ordering ye tae bed her, just wed her.'

He kept his face still; why was he not surprised? Robert was already using Sorcha for some game of his, why would he not use another's daughter? They were all pawns to him. He would wed her, and Lord willing, bed her. She was the first to stir him, so why should he not seek some pleasure? Watching Cailean and Sorcha had been agony. But why did she have to be related to *that* man?

'I doubt they will trust me, with both me brother and I being so firmly yer men.'

'I dinnae expect them tae. But a spymaster is more than just the leader o a spy ring, is he no?'

He lifted his goblet in recognition of Robert's words before taking a sip. Wine was rarely pleasant to begin with, but in that moment it tasted particularly bitter.

Chapter 19

Alasdair trod lightly through the king's forest, short bow in hand. Intending to make the best of the situation, he hunted rabbit for the wedding feast. He stopped and slowly lifted the weapon, drawing it taut. The animal sat eating, oblivious. It was dead before it knew what hit it. Like Mordag and himself. He couldn't blame her for the incident. He had seen the truth in her eyes; her anger was as much her armour as it was Cailean's. He approached his kill and pulled out the arrow. Its head was still intact. But what was that, just over there? He strung up the rabbit with the others before investigating.

A campfire surrounded by well-trodden ground. And a hastily torn-down shelter. Someone, or some people, had been staying here for quite some time. Poaching to survive, by the looks of it. He checked the ashes. Cold, but still somewhat fresh. It could not be coincidence that this well-hidden camp was newly abandoned. At least they would be taking the long way round. It was time to get some answers.

'I applaud yer silence, lad, but you're moving too fast.'

For the entirety of his hunt, Angus had been following him. Whether out of curiosity or instruction, he had not been sure. The boy cursed and emerged from the bushes.

'Angus, right?'

'Aye. Mordag told me what really happened. Why did you no stop it?'

'The marriage? She deserves better than being paraded around like she was.'

Half-truths were always better than full lies. Granted, the lad had intelligence enough to be sceptical, but his face was practically a glass window.

'Then why did ye no approach her before?'

'I may no hold a title or knighthood, but I am noble and me brother's heir. There are those who would consider it an unsuitable match. And, well, ye ken yer sister. If you were a suitor interested in her, would ye approach her?'

'Och no, ah'd want children some day!'

Alasdair held out the rabbits, 'With the blessing of the king, these are for the feast.'

As they walked back through the woods, he gently interrogated the boy. Angus was reserved about his father's political views, giving little but distaste away. It was a start. On the other hand, he was most eager to know Alasdair. He relented to some, but not all, of the questions. Yes, he was leaving court and stepping back from his ambassadorial duties; yes, that meant Mordag would have a home of her own to manage. And the like. His future brother-in-law clearly cared for her.

'Mordag willnae like it, but ah think ye are more suited to each other than she kens. Mind ye ken this, Alasdair:

Macmaghan or no, if ye hurt her I'll hunt ye down and truss ye up like a roast hog.'

Indeed, when calm, Angus was most astute. With some training, he could... Jesus, was this how his predecessor found him? No, he would not recruit a boy, no matter how beneficial. Instead, he smiled and patted Angus on the back. 'I promise ye, if ah ever hurt her, I'd let ye.'

*

With Mordag's hand in his, Alasdair stopped at the kirk step. In front of him, the bishop lacked the good humour he'd shown at Cailean's wedding. No doubt annoyed to be conducting another wedding without banns. His bride stood, just as sullen, in the old gown she'd worn the day before, with a hastily woven crown of flowers upon her head. It irritated him more than he cared to admit. He glanced behind her at his best man – one of his uncle's *leuchd-crios*. Now *that* had not been a fun conversation. Mordag's father stumbled over and rushed through the reciting of her dowry.

Jesus, this may as well be a funeral. Was it? It was at the king's bidding, not his. Yet the part of him she stunned at their first meeting – and, annoyingly, his member – was rejoicing. He hardened his jaw and listened to the bishop, ignoring the scandalised crowd that had gathered.

'Here before God, I dae take ye, Mordag Nicnachten, tae be my wife and tae this I solemnly pledge ye my troth.'

He slipped what had once been his mither's ring onto her finger; the freshwater pearl it clasped had come from their land. Staring at it, guilt suddenly claimed him. How could he marry another when he still loved Ruth? But he was determined to honour his vows even if Mordag did not. She tripped over her words; was he really that appalling in her eyes?

The rest of the ceremony was nothing special. As much as he had faith, religious events bored the life out of him. And a wedding blessing was no different, though Mordag did unwillingly accept the kiss of peace from him.

They had a long walk to their wedding feast. Unlike Cailean's, theirs was in a pavilion next to her father's tents. It was to be a simple affair with only a few present, but with plenty of strong bride ale. Having barely had the chance to speak to his new wife, he took the opportunity to drop his pretence.

'Look, Mordag, I ken this is no what either o us wanted, but I intend tae be an honest man. I'll no raise my fist in anger or stray from ye.'

'I will believe that when I see it, *Macmaghan*.'

'Interesting that ye say that. Working for the king and travelling as I dae, I have found certain behaviours are oft but a *mummer's* mask.'

His words brought Mordag to a halt and she stared at him. He held her gaze with his own; like her brother, there was intelligence there.

'Who are ye?'

If only he could tell her the full truth. He sighed. 'No the man everyone thinks me tae be.'

*

The silence that surrounded Mordag while they were undressed was deafening. And neither her father nor brother had followed them to Alasdair's bedchamber. She glanced around the space. The colours were striking and everything was like new. It was too beautiful for what was about to happen to her. The blood, the pain! She should spear herself on that metal sword rather than Alasdair's. The lady left her in her shift and led her to the bed. What did she want now? Spiced wine? Keep it coming until she was in a stupor. Damn it, she took it away after the first goblet.

The bed moved and she refused to look, staring instead at the newly arrived bishop. Their bed did not need blessing. She *would not* be giving him any children. The man of God left too quickly. Was there still time for her to suddenly feel a calling? No. Convents were worse. Alasdair sat there for a moment. He then got out of the bed. What was he doing? She heard the bolt on the door slide shut. Great, there was no escape. He walked into her view, raiding a small box that stood on the table. She pulled the coverings up over her chest. What was that small phial? Poison?

'I have no desire tae bed a woman who doesnae want it. I find the very notion nauseating, so I will no force meself on ye. But for the sake of honour and the fact that a man and wife should share their bed, I will expect that of ye. Understood?'

She could only nod her head. Sharing a bed was not bad. She had slept in the hall at home with many surrounding her. Maybe this would work – only: 'Honour? How is that honourable? Ye would leave me a maiden while ye tryst with every other woman at court?'

Her anger had loosened her tongue. And he just stood there staring at her like she was addled!

'I told ye, I will be an honest man tae ye. Ye are smart enough to ken that I want ye. And I want ye more than I've wanted any woman in quite a long time, but ah'm happy tae wait. Now shift over.'

'Why?'

'I need the linen that lays under ye.'

What was he blathering about? She lifted the covers. Sure enough, there lay a separate cloth under her. What the devil? She shifted off it. He poured the contents of the phial onto it. It spread out and stained like blood.

'Courtesy o the rabbits.'

He was feigning her maidenhood breach! She bit her lip and gingerly pushed the cloth off the edge of the bed. Alasdair then smeared some of the blood into his own hands before wiping them on another piece of cloth and washing them in the washbowl that sat nearby. That was over the top and where had he learned it? To save some maiden he had once ploughed?

She kept her eye on him as he returned to the bed. Jesus, Joseph and Mary, he was taking his undershirt off! A scattering of hair crossed his lightly scarred torso. It trailed down to his navel and… well, he was not lying about wanting her! Her eyes shot to his; he had the nerve to grin!

'I probably should have warned ye that ah sleep naked,' the *sumph* admitted.

He blew out the candles before returning to bed. Thank the Lord he faced the other way. A naked arse was not so intimidating.

'Goodnight, wife.'

She stayed sitting up in the dark; this was the last thing she'd expected. He had not acted like a man who saw women as places to warm his prick. But her father had caught him with that maid. What about Angus, though? He had insisted she gave Alasdair a chance. Normally he was good at judging a person. She sighed; she could not sit there all night. And the bed was incredibly soft. She sank into it and looked toward her – urgh – husband. Those curls! She would have done anything as a child to have some, but her hair only ever fell straight. Annoyed, she reached out and tugged a lock of it. He did not react. No one could sleep that quickly, that deeply, could they?

*

That was one of the best night's sleeps Mordag had ever had. She stretched out her leg and clung tighter to the pillow her head rested on. Only it was rising and falling. Jesus, Joseph and Mary, it was Alasdair's chest, and she was sprawled over him! And he was also awake. She kept her eyes firmly shut. What was she to do? She was not going to lift her head and meet the toad's smug face! Hallelujah, a knock at the door! She rolled over, pretending to have been disturbed. Behind her, he got up to answer.

'I'm sorry tae bother ye, my lord, but I thought ye'd wish tae ken. Baron Macnachten left during the night,' a man informed Alasdair.

'Thank ye, John. Please send for water.'

She should have known he would run as soon as she was no longer his concern. He had never cared for her, and the rejection had long lost its sting. But Angus – she'd not had a chance to say goodbye to him. Please God, watch over him. He was still young, full of childish dreams and encouraged by the stories his tutors had told him. She sat up, clinging to her knees. Alasdair was behind the screen, pissing.

A maid entered with a fresh pitcher and bowl for ablutions. She caught the maid's curious glance; the cackling hens would be out in full force.

'Fetch some food and drink, I wish tae break my fast,' she snapped.

'Aye, my lady.'

Damn it, it was not the maid's fault. She should blame the toad for his slimy reputation. It was a small blessing to be leaving court, at least; she would have gone mad living here.

'A hearty good morn tae ye too, wife,' he called from where he now washed himself.

She rolled her eyes. 'Ah heard nowt hearty about it.'

'Ah, ye overheard that. I'm sorry he did that tae ye, Mordag. No man should treat his daughter that way.'

'Wheesht, he's needed at home fer the harvest.'

She wiped the tears that sprung from nowhere. Alasdair did not believe her. He walked over, now in a clean linen shirt, and kissed her forehead. She had not been prepared to fend him off, yet it felt... comforting? She shook her head.

'I have some missives tae write. And a little later, we shall be receiving a visitor,' he told her.

Not more people like him? She got up and dressed. The maid returned with the food and offered to help

Mordag with her hair. She caught herself before she snapped again. This was her new life now – the fine ladywife of one of Robert's favoured lapdogs. Hah! What was fine about having nothing besides her comb, gravour, pins and thread?

'If my lady wishes tae extend her collection, there's a pedlar set up under the oak.'

'I dinnae—'

'Let him know we will be visiting later, Magda. And when ye go, please take these tae John.'

She glanced towards Alasdair; he watched her. Heat flooded to her cheeks. Damn, what was wrong with her? One pretty-boy glance and some niceties and she was already falling?

Once the maid was finished, she joined him at the table and ate her fill. He still scratched away at his letters. Some he sealed, others he left open. She could not read and barely wrote her name. When she asked him what he wrote about, he smiled. But it was not that foolish smile. It looked honest.

He obliged, telling her that he was preparing for his – their – new life. And about what he did to earn money. Apparently, inns were Alasdair's main source of income. Hadn't her father always said that Robert hoarded wealth and gave it to his closest men? Was he wrong?

Their guest soon arrived, revealing himself to be a tailor. Unusually, his cotehardie was a walking display of all the embellishments he offered. He bowed politely while a couple of younger men carried in a chest.

'I thank ye for coming at such short notice. My lady wife needs garments quickly.' Alasdair spoke confidently.

'Should she find yer work pleasing, then I will order some more tae be delivered tae our home.'

Mordag struggled to grasp his meaning. The man was there for her? She stared at the toad. Why the generosity?

'I was most eager when I heard it was yerself that sent for me, my lord. Yer reputation for elegance precedes ye,' the tailor replied, while taking a good look at her. Though he showed nothing, she knew exactly what he was thinking. Silk could not be made with sow skin.

'My lady is most radiant, though taller than most o me clients. Thankfully, ah keep a few of my pieces unfinished fer moments like this.'

Liar. But wait – of course, that was why her husband was doing this! She was a bauble to decorate as he saw fit. She sat back, waiting for Alasdair to decide, but he did not budge. Instead, he motioned for her to go ahead. Was this some trick? Would he punish her for choosing wrong? She kept a close eye on him as the tailor measured her with knotted string. He had returned to his writing.

'Ah'm afraid that I only have the one garment that will fit ye, my lady. The rest will have tae be cut especially. Thankfully I have many a sample here for ye tae choose from.'

She glanced back to Alasdair. He stopped writing to nod and smile at her. He really was giving her the freedom to choose. She had always just been handed material to sew herself. And here she was now, expected to choose from so many different cloth swatches and fashion dolls. She dared not consider the cost.

The ready-made garments were a dusty pink half-sleeved surcoat and a steel-grey kirtle, and she ordered a cotehardie in a deep blue wool and another gown of blue and green plaid, both with matching kirtles and hose. Sensible, hard-wearing fabrics, but bright enough to please the toad.

'Anything else, my lady?'

'Nae, my lord husband has been very generous.'

My lord husband. Why did the words not taste bitter? His generosity in letting her choose? But it was all a ploy to bed her. It had to be.

'I have a request,' interrupted Alasdair. 'My sister-in-law had one of those gowns without sleeves that is cut to the hip. I should like one o them in that green and gold brocade, lined and trimmed with *gris*, and paired with a matching undergown.'

There it was! He had ordered a gown that made men look! Her skin crawled at the thought. She waited for the tailor to leave before confronting him. 'I ken how scandalous those garments are, Macmaghan. I'll no wear such a thing!'

'Aye, ye will one day, my proud shield-maiden.'

His damned arrogance. What did he know? She grabbed a nearby cushion and threw it at him. He laughed, dodging it easily. Damn the slimy toad! And he was coming closer.

'Come now, Mordag, we have a pedlar tae see. It would be a waste tae wear such fine gowns and not likewise dress yer hair, no?'

She rolled her eyes and folded her arms. Fine, she would go with him. If only to satisfy that giddy child in her that loved looking over a pedlar's wares.

Chapter 20

For Alasdair, the days that followed were most curious. Mordag would raise one portcullis, only for another to abruptly fall in his face. And, like a child, she tried his patience, acutely watching his responses. Yet it became painfully clear that he was all she now had, for she never strayed far. At least it helped keep his reputation, only instead of bedding her each night, he read aloud.

Now he had abandoned his courtly garments and waited for Seumas so he could abandon the place too. He let himself chuckle as he recalled Mordag's shock at seeing him in *léine* and trews. He had grinned at her and gained another similar look for that.

The brown-haired form of his friend approached, leading the retinue. Ever fond of his food, he looked to have gained some weight since they last spoke.

'Seumas, it's good tae see ye! How have ye been keeping?'

'I'm good, me wife's just given me another daughter,' Seumas heartily replied.

'What's that now, yer fourth?'

'Och, dinnae rub it in! Every penny ah make goes straight tae their dowries.'

He grinned – the man adored his daughters – and then gestured to Mordag. 'Come, wife, come meet Seumas.'

'Wife? I didnae think ye would...'

'Well, it happened; this is Mordag Nicnachten.'

'Greetings, my lady.'

'Hello, Seumas.'

Well, she was polite, if not *that* welcoming.

He had unconventionally chosen a sumpter for Mordag's mount. She had little experience, and the beast would plod on regardless. After seeing her mounted, he left her in Seumas's capable hands and returned to John. The seneschal was to forward all material for the Raven. He made his goodbye with one final instruction: to alert him immediately if the baron returned to court. Returning to Legs, he overheard Seumas telling Mordag how lucky she was. If only he knew the truth!

Alasdair kept a brisk pace up along the east side of Loch Lomond. It would be a long journey, without dallying. He took every opportunity to brief Seumas and, as much as he regretted having to do it, he also warned of who Mordag was. She had said nothing, so he knew not where her loyalties lay. They slowed to a walk to give the horses a breather. And Mordag forced her way between them. What was it with women doing that? Seumas flashed him a grin before falling back. His brother would call this sweet vengeance.

'I'll no be kept in the dark, Macmaghan, ah had enough o that with me father. Why are we riding wi enough men tae keep a glenful o farmers in check?'

'Because we may have tae keep a glenful o farmers in check. The place we travel tae is Sorcha's inheritance. She has never visited it, and many believed Robert held it for himself. That in itself would no be an issue, but they lie just south of Inverlochy Castle.'

'Ye expect hostilities from those that remained after the Herschip?'

'Potentially, aye. The land is rich compared to the scarred lands around it.'

It was apparently enough truth to satisfy her. Mordag rode silently alongside him for a moment before speaking up again. 'Me father was rantin over Druim Earbainn after court. That's her dowry, is it no? Only ah cannae recall why.'

He watched her from the corner of his eye, not wanting to give anything away. What in the Lord's name did Druim Earbainn have to do with those plotting against Robert? It was surely too far south-west to be of importance. While she spoke candidly enough, it could be a lure.

'Ye find it in ye to tell me about it, despite what may result?' he tested.

'As much as ah hate having tae admit it, ye are me husband, Macmaghan. I have no wish tae have find another, so ye're more useful to me alive than dead.'

He snorted; never had a person spoken truer words!

'I dinnae mind what ye call me, lass, but ye may wish tae choose a different name. Half the men following us are Macmaghans. And I'm no the chief.'

'Then Toad it is.'

He scratched his head. 'Funny, me mither once screamed that at me while jumping out o bed.'

'What?'

'I'd been hunting them in a pond. Had them in a wee bucket but me nurse was in a hurry and wouldnae let me release them. I left the bucket in my parents' bedchamber and forgot about it.'

She rolled her eyes and he grinned again. His mither could not abide them, and nor could he after his father's thrashing.

*

Alasdair made use of what shelter they could find. The first night was a sheepfold which an enterprising person had stuck waxed canvas over, then charged for the privilege. Though he was apologetic, Mordag showed no discomfort. And she had chosen to cuddle him, though he put that down to warmth.

The following two days were tough, though Mordag stomached it, refusing his help. By the fourth day, he finally convinced his flagging wife to ride with him, though the deteriorating weather more likely persuaded her. It was that awful drizzling kind that slowly soaked a person to their skin and hid the landscape. What a sorry sight he must portray, but it was a necessary sacrifice. If news of his arrival had preceded him, then the folk there would expect him to arrive by sea.

Mordag's head started bobbing. He gently pressed her back against his collar bone; she did not utter a sound of protest, but pressed her face to his neck. The heat of her breath there warmed his skin. It was both welcomed and torturous.

The rain had started to slow when Seumas rode up alongside.

'Good, tis no a nice trek for a lady like herself.' Seumas kept his voice soft.

'Aye, especially after we pass Loch Tulla.'

'I have yet tae cross Rannoch Moor in good weather.'

'That isnae what ah'm concerned about. Sir Cowden has a stick up his arse; he displeased Brus and was sent here. Furthermore, he's a real whorer and sees me as competition. I'll no be stopping here if ah can help it.'

Seumas winced and they continued in silence. Sure enough, as they reached the northern tip of the loch he spotted a gathering of men on horseback. He tensed and his movement disturbed Mordag, waking her.

Alasdair cursed to himself. 'Dinnae look up and keep yer head on me shoulder. This is no a nice man.'

She inhaled sharply, then surprised him by following his request. World-wary indeed. What had his wife witnessed? She buried her head further into his neck, her lips brushing his skin. Jesus, that distraction was the last thing he needed! He quickly pulled his plaid higher up over the two of them.

'Halt! I demand tae ken why ye ride over the king's lands with so many men, Macmaghan.'

For a whorer, Sir Cowden held as much appeal as a leech. The pox-ridden, bulbous-nosed cur.

'Did ye no receive word from Brus and the Raven?' He played the ignorant fool while reining in his horse. 'Ah pass through on business for them both. These men are me brother's, sent tae aid me.'

The knight spat at the ground before his eyes lingered

on Mordag. He had to bite down the sudden urge to growl, for the man's eyes were already undressing his wife.

'I ken yer work and I ken it disnae involve the work o real men. Ah demand again, why are ye here an why dae ye carry a lady with ye? As for the Raven, his hand has changed. I have nae reason tae believe whoever is now writing under his seal has the king's best interest.'

'The lady is *my wife*, no that it's any concern tae ye. As for my work, it varies, but ye're too dim-witted tae understand that.' Alasdair guided his horse forward so their mounts were nose to nose. 'And make what ye wish of the Raven but be careful who hears ye. Brus would see ye a traitor for such words, and ah've heard that the bloody flux is running rife in France. Now move.'

He glared with his father's force. The knight tried to sneer but fear flickered in his eyes. He abruptly gave way. 'I will accompany ye, ensure ye're sticking tae yer path.'

'How gracious.'

The day could hardly get any worse.

*

Once free from their escort, Alasdair ordered an early stop beside a recently abandoned shieling. It would be tighter than the sheep fold had been, but it would be dry. And right now, that was all that mattered. Mordag left to light a fire while he tended to their mounts and arranged a guard. He would stand with his back facing an English army before he trusted Sir Cowden. By the time he made it inside, the fire was blazing, and Mordag had raided their supplies for oats and dried meats to cook. She had them all singing her praises and, for the first time, he saw a smile on her face.

'Yer father's men no thank ye when ye did this for them?' he asked as he sat down.

'Nae, twas expected o me.'

'Expected or no, they should have had the decency tae thank ye.'

Jesus, she looked so radiant, and was that a blush?

After a meal that rivalled those served at court, he lay propped up on an elbow and talked quietly with Mordag. She confirmed what he suspected. After her mother's death, she had taken over the majority of duties for their small household. And she was expected to work hard with little praise. Had she feared the same with marriage? Or was there more? Her reaction in his arms earlier that day certainly suggested it. He reached out and tucked a stray wisp of her hair away from her face. She did not stop him.

'What have I done to deserve such a wife?' he asked her softly.

'Wheesht, ah told ye ah dinnae care fer silver tongues.'

'Tis no a silver tongue. I leave that for persuading men. Now ah speak the truth.'

'Like yer garments and whoring?'

'Aye, like them. They are simply the tools o my trade.' She doubted him so he added, 'As Robert's ambassador, I've mostly worked with England. Edward is a sop when it comes tae courtly romance. It makes my task easier if a reputation precedes me.'

She was *finally* listening to him; another portcullis was raising! He lowered his hand to Seumas's pouch.

'A reputation is like a *mummer's* mask? But what o that maid me father saw ye with?'

He reached up to his oblivious friend, who sat next to him playing dice, and pulled a coin from his ear. 'Here, ye dropped this.'

Seumas snatched the coin back. 'Stop robbing me!'

Mordag's eyes widened, and he smiled; they never saw him do it or felt it.

'A person will see only what they wish tae see, Mordag. Never forget that. Only, I used tae practise on Seumas, so he disnae count.'

Sweet Jesus, she was laughing! Not a deep belly laugh, but still, he would take any victory he could. And now, those blue pools were no longer on his eyes but his lips. Her innocence shone through in how she licked her own. Testing the waters, he leaned forwards ever so slightly and she mirrored it. Did he dare? He hungered to truly taste her. The kiss of peace had been but a tantalising scent of a sweetmeat. He cupped her chin with his fingers and ran one along the jaw. Again, she did not pull away. He leaned in, and knew immediately that he was the first man she had kissed. Gently, he guided her with his tongue and earned a gasp in return. She tasted of sugared almonds and he wanted more. But he could not scare her; he broke the kiss. She was startled, leaving her lips slightly parted. Dear Lord have mercy on his tormented soul!

'There, my shield-maiden, that wasnae so bad…'

She lunged towards him, forcing him back onto the floor. Her kiss was rushed and ungainly. He pushed himself back up, heady with the taste of her. He reached for his *léine*, wanting it off before her hands tore it.

Seumas coughed awkwardly.

Jesus Christ, what had got into them? As much as it pained him to hold back, he had to. This was no place for her to lose her maidenhood. Nor would he torment the men. They tore apart like cats separated by a bucket of water. Her face was bright red. Angry with himself, he pulled her towards him and protected her from shame. She kept her face buried in his chest. Glaring at his grinning commander, he lay down and pulled his plaid over them.

'Shh, lass, dinnae fret. We have all the time in the world, and we'll have a proper bed too,' he murmured, before kissing her head.

Alasdair stayed like that until the games and talk ceased, and Mordag had fallen asleep. As much as he tried to blame his irritation on the men taking their sweet time to settle, and then that particularly whiny snore, he could not fool himself. He wanted her more than the starved wanted food.

Giving up, he left her to sleep and headed outside. The rain had subsided, but the clouds still lingered. He sent the man on watch to his sleep. As the sun crested a distant hill, Seumas joined him.

'Ye Macmaghans get it bad, eh?'

'What dae ye mean? And last ah looked, yer mither was one!'

His commander snorted. 'Ah was talking with one o the oarsmen. Our chief's new wife has him so in love with her, they were playing on a beach together.'

He blinked. Cailean *openly* engaging in horseplay? Unheard of since he tasted war. Surely Sorcha had not already changed his brother?

'They've kenned each other a lot longer than Mordag and I have.'

'Aye, but I bet you saw it well before their marriage. Maybe even punched some sense intae the man?'

It was Alasdair's turn to snort. 'What does that have tae do with me?'

'Ye ken well what I'm talking about. Ye've been out here all night because o her. And it's about time. Ruth wouldnae have wanted tae see ye hiding away like ye have been.'

He would hardly call mourning hiding away, but the man was right. She had wanted him to seek happiness; used what little strength she had left to insist on it. But while he could bed Mordag, could he really find happiness with her? Only to lose her like he had Ruth?

Chapter 21

Mordag led her mount over the rough ground and let her mind wander. The further from court, the more Alasdair changed. Sure, he still had those moments where he acted like, well, a boy. But at other times. What was it? Caring? She snorted. He wanted her maidenhood, that was all. But then why did he listen so, and answer questions without growing annoyed? She shook her head. That trick and his warning. He was talking about himself, and she had fallen for it. Thrown herself at him. She would not let that happen again.

In front of her, he had stopped to take a drink. To make matters worse, he was wearing that damned grin of his, like he knew exactly what she had been thinking. She huffed and caught up to the toad; taking the flask, she drank heartily, before changing the focus of her damned mind. 'When ye were talking tae that man yesterday, ye mentioned a Raven. Who is he?'

The grin disappeared and his jaw set hard. 'He's Robert's spymaster; every man under Brus is ordered tae obey his words.'

'Oh. What does that have tae do with Sorcha's land?'

'That is a good question and one ah'm sure only he kens the answer tae. I'm just there tae discover her ties tae Robert.'

'Her ties? Nowt else?'

His smile returned before he brushed a strand of her hair off her face and placed his hand under her chin. 'Aye, tae make our home, my beautiful wife.'

Mordag quickly leaned away when he leaned in. Nice try. He broke away, but not before she saw the flash of something in his eye. It was neither annoyance nor anger, but something else. No. It was not that: neither of them cared about the other. Disappointment. There, that was what it must have been.

They carried on together. The silence, however, was starting to annoy her. 'What of the condition o our home?'

'I truly have no idea, but I ken my strong shield-maiden will soon have it fit for a king.'

She hesitated as the warm glow she had felt the night before filled her chest. He was trusting her, not just to run the household as his wife, but to set it right. There had to be a mistake. He did not know her; she could do anything, ruin him even. She glanced at him. He was watching her. She saw no trickery. Again, that warmth, that desire to be close to him. The one that had her feigning sleep just so she could stay close. Suddenly unsure, she spoke up once more. 'Alasdair?'

'Aye?'

'What's a shield-maiden?'

He had not laughed at her question. Instead, he regaled her with sagas of the fiercely brave women found amongst those who had once raided their lands. It made the final leg of their journey pass quickly and before she knew it, they stopped so the men could don their mail. Their smiles and kindness suddenly gave way to a chilling hardness. Seasoned men, the lot of them. She shuddered, and then Alasdair cursed. The daft toad's ringlets had got caught. She rolled her eyes before batting his hands away and reaching inside to free him. Once he was free, she tugged the mail down.

Their eyes met.

How had he thought her a fiercely brave woman when now, inches from his face, she wavered? Kiss the damned fool! No, he only wants to warm his sheath, do not give in! He smiled and placed a kiss on her forehead, just under her fillet. Damn him, that's not what she wanted! Or was it? He turned to the men and, like them, changed. So that was in him too? She shivered and stepped away. It was too much like her father.

'I doubt we'll get much resistance, but if there is trouble and I go down, Seumas is in command.'

If he went down? What was he talking about? His death?

'Osgar, Daniel, I'm holding ye personally responsible for my wife. If anything happens, ride for Iain Abrach land.'

Damn that. He was not going to die! He was not going to leave her to go back to her father. She slowly approached him after the men had dispersed. She could not meet his eye, but managed to kiss the corner of his lips. What a traitor she was!

'Promise me, ye will no start anything?' she asked, suddenly unsure of herself.

'I dinnae plan tae, but ah must be prepared.'

*

The men encircled her and led her horse as they rode towards the manor. Though high, the sun was still to her back. As the dwellings got closer, the lack of men was glaringly obvious. The people she could see were Alasdair's age or younger. Thank the Virgin, most of their stares were curious and the children ran alongside. Alasdair's men must have seen it too as her reins were handed back and they separated. Alasdair called her forward. She would show a united front, for the sake of peace. Damn it, she'd strip naked and run into the loch if it secured it!

They drew to a stop and she studied her new home. A cruck-built, stone and thatch hall. It had been extended at the back – shaped like a T, her brother would say. To the right of the hall stood a kitchen, and further away, a small kirk. *It was perfect!*

'Thank the great merciful Lord, the king has finally answered me pleas and sent aid!' a harried-looking man proclaimed as he hurried from the manor.

'The king's steward, I assume?' asked Alasdair.

'Aye, lad, and ye be?'

The toad held up a hand to quiet the steward and dismounted. He approached her and aided her to the ground before taking her by the hand, all proper like at court. They walked past the ant-like man and onto the step of the hall. Together they faced the gathering people. He gently squeezed her hand.

'I am Alasdair Macmaghan, second son o Grann Macmaghan, brother tae Cailean Macmaghan, Chief of Clan MacMhathain and Earl of Kintail. This land, through his marriage tae Lady Sorcha Gilchrist, is now under his control. This is tae be my home along with my wife, Mordag Nicnachten.'

She ignored the few who shouted out their disgust. Those who knew of the Macmaghan brothers demanded to know why the king's 'hounds' had been rewarded again. But many more just looked relieved. These were tired, hungry people, despite the richness of the loch and land. Only the steward looked happy.

'Send word tae *every* man, of age or no,' Alasdair ordered, 'they have two days tae appear in front of me and swear an oath tae their new chief. Those who dinnae will lose their home and it will be given tae a man who is proven more faithful.'

So much for being careful. The whole thing stank of hostility. Strangely, there were no angry cries of defiance. Several men eagerly approached, wishing to pledge there and then. Alasdair bade them follow him inside. She turned, only to be lifted from her feet.

'Damn it! Alasdair Macmaghan, ye're a maddening man!' she hissed in shock.

'Aye, and dinnae deny it. Ah ken ye like it!'

Mordag scowled at him as he crossed the threshold. Only then did the *sumph* set her down. She intended to give him a mouthful, but the hall distracted her. While sound, it lacked what made a place a home. Beneath her feet, the old rushes were sticky and compacted. The walls needed fresh limewashing and dusty cobwebs hung in unattended corners. What had they been doing here? A lone banner bearing royal heraldry hung limply at the end of the hall, behind the laird's chair. It looked even more rickety than that knight! Up above it was the original laird's chamber, exposed to the hall below with a single rail to prevent accidents. How many children had fallen from it?

A shiver ran up her spine; there was so much to do, and she was in charge! She glanced at Alasdair. Why was he chuckling?

He nodded. 'I'll be here a while, so go ahead.'

Well, she did not need his permission but did so anyway. First, she would clear the rushes so that dry ones could be fetched before winter. Then she... No, that could wait. She pulled back a motheaten curtain at the end of the hall. A strongroom, and steps leading up to the space above. Just past them were two doors into the expansion. The first, she discovered, was being used as the steward's chamber. The second had nothing but old storage and another door. It was a back entrance. And they were both in a state similar to the hall. Could men not run a household at all?

She paused by the steps and ran her hand over the posts there. In the place where crests would have likely been, the wood had been crudely destroyed. She took a closer look around. There were the poles and hooks for hangings, but nothing there. Odd.

Ah, the old laird's chamber was now an antechamber of sorts. And from it were two more chambers. Both their doors had been sealed with a lock. There must be keys somewhere. And the dust on the floor! Did no one come up here? The rail, thank the Virgin, was sturdy.

Below, a man was giving his pledge to Alasdair acting in proxy. Always on the dagger, or rather its cross. What was wrong with the real thing, or a Bible? The steward was fussing over some manuscripts, while a spry, grey-haired, learned-looking man tried to calm him down. How the king's man had not yet keeled over with apoplexy was beyond her. A glance confirmed her husband had finished.

'My lord husband…'

Alasdair looked up and grinned; she rolled her eyes. It was the correct way to address him in public, was it not?

'…me way's blocked. Do ye have the keys?'

As Alasdair reached for them, he was interrupted by the learned man. 'My lady, please allow me tae assist ye.'

An Edinburgh accent. He appeared quickly by her side.

'I be Jock, the seneschal, my lady.'

'A pleasure.' For once, she meant it. He looked like he would not hurt a fly. 'I gather this area has not been recently used?'

'Nae, my lady, this whole floor is – was – off limits to all but meself. King's orders.'

He unlocked the furthest door and stepped back to let her enter. The bedchamber was also covered in dust, though it was a relief to see dustsheets covering the furniture. Except for the empty bed frame. A patch of newer limewash covered where a crest had no doubt sat.

'I'm afraid this was locked away tae await the Lady Sorcha. The mice had made a nest in the mattresses when I arrived tae take over me duty, so ah removed them.'

'And the other chamber?'

'Similar tae this one.'

It was a mirror of the other but with different furnishings and no bed. She pulled down a dirty horn window panel. It was aligned with the morning sun. To wake to it, yes, this would be their chamber. She took another look around. There was too much for her to do alone.

'Fetch women from about us; ones ye ken tae be sensible. And, if possible, related tae men who have pledged, or wait tae. We will pay them double what we would pay a maid daily, tae come and help make the hall liveable. Also, put word out that I am looking for a couple of maids tae employ. One should preferably have experience tending tae a lady.'

The seneschal smiled and bowed slightly. 'Aye, my lady, and if I do say so, tis about time!'

That was her first order as lady of her own household! It felt like... how could she describe it? Like a chicken let outside? No, that sounded foolish, and she did not squawk. Either way, she was ready to face the task ahead of her.

*

Mordag was washing the panel with ash and hot water when the women arrived. They greeted her and immediately joined in. Her mother, God rest her soul, had been right. A lady led by example. There was also something about sharing work that brought barriers down. In between waulking songs, sung to keep them all motivated, the women gossiped.

'Ah care not who lives here, ah'm just glad tae see this place come alive again.'

'The elders are mourning for a time past.'

'Och, no just the elders.' The woman who said it was

the oldest of the lot. 'Please be careful here, my lady. While we are happy tae move on with our lives, others are less so.'

Mordag paused in her work to smile gratefully at the woman. 'They wish tae return tae a time before the Herschip?'

'Aye and nae – many here are Comyn. And some feel drawn tae the spirit of what it was before, or what they think it should be now.'

Should be now. Her father was one of them.

'Well, let's hope that with time, we can all warm tae each other and live in peace, aye? After all is said and done, we have lost enough loved ones.'

Many voiced agreement but cast worried glances. What was scaring them? The foolish talk of men?

An excited shout came from the corner of the room. Someone had uncovered a nest of mice, making them shoot in all directions. She cursed and joined in with the mad dash to catch the pests. Rags tossed, feet stomped, brooms slammed on the floor and a bucket was overturned. Several of Alasdair's men filled the doorway and looked around in confusion. One let out a high-pitched yelp as something shot over his foot. Mordag burst into laughter – warriors indeed! The confusion on the men's faces made it worse, and soon the whole chamber had joined her.

Alasdair shouted from the hall below. Without thinking, she pushed past the men and strode to the railing. 'I'm afraid yer men are nae match fer four-legged foes!'

Chapter 22

In the shadow of dusk, men made their way to a lone longhouse. Not one of them arrived with more than a single companion. They glanced around, as if fearing the land itself, before entering the dwelling. Inside, only the thinnest of ales welcomed them as they gathered around the peat hearth. Further away a woman, whose face was the gauntest of the lot, was searching a child for lice. When the last had entered and sat down, a man who could have been fifty or seventy spoke up.

'Our men will have arrived at the earl's lands, and thanks tae the Macnachten, we now ken it is his brother who arrived today. As disappointing as it is tae ken that the earl is hiding the lady away behind his strongest walls, we do have an advantage. Macnachten's own daughter shares the brother's bed.'

The men talked amongst themselves; some cursing Cailean, others praising this new fortune. A man, whose right arm hung limp, spoke up. 'She'll comply with whatever we demand?'

'She will if she wishes tae live.'

There was a dark chuckle amongst the men. Another, from the back, asked, 'What of the Gilchrist man?'

'What o him? He's naught but a prattling *sumph*. We're lucky he didnae betray us when he arrived at court. Leave him tae rot!' retorted the maimed man.

The one who had spoken first held his hand up to shut down any further responses. 'Nae. He may still be o use as a thorn. Ah'll think on it.'

'And what about those of us living on the land? He's demanding that all men – fighting age or no – come and pledge their fealty to the MacMhathain chief. He'll take our homes if we dinnae,' another asked.

The leader's look soured. 'I'll no stop ye from taking a false pledge. But we can also find a place for ye until we can reunite ye with yer home.'

Some agreed with leaving the land altogether, forfeiting on their rents. Others would not abandon their families. A few looked pained: their sons, brothers or fathers favoured the changes. And one or two were outraged at the thought of taking a pledge they would not keep.

The group continued to talk long into the night of new plans and the success of their cause. When that finished, they spoke of broader topics like the harvest and weather. The woman had left them to their vigil, joining her children in their only bed. All were eager for the return of a group of fitter men – the fat milking cows, chickens and nanny goats arriving at Druim Earbainn had not gone unnoticed. After everything they had endured while that land prospered, they deserved the beasts.

A lone man burst through the door. He was missing his weapons and his green *léine* was half-red. The whites of his eyes were a stark contrast to the darkness around him. Out of breath and swaying slightly, he stood before them, clutching his useless hand. Their leader broke through the crowd and cursed vehemently.

*

The reivers were in high spirits as they gathered on the edge of Druim Earbainn. The harvest moon was high and there was only a light scattering of cloud, making it ideal. Creeping forwards, they stuck to the shadows cast first by nature, then by the dwellings and workshops surrounding the manor. Fearing guards, dogs, and anyone who may still be awake, they used hand signals. The men had not needed to worry. There was no guard and the dogs greeted them with wagging tails. From somewhere on the hill behind, an owl hooted. Two older, more experienced men stopped. They glanced at each other and shook their heads.

Their young leader came back to them. 'Why are ye no moving?'

'Tis no right. Tis too quiet.'

'And the owl. There'll be death this night if we continue.'

The first nodded in agreement.

'Christ's teeth, tis a perfect night and they're sitting there for the taking! I'll tell David of yer cowardice; see how ye feel when ye've no animals tae feed yer children.'

The men struggled with their doubts. One had lost a nanny that spring, and the other's chickens had stopped laying through age. They gave in and continued on towards the barn, where scouts had confirmed the animals were kept, though they let others be the first to reach the doors.

The doors swung open silently and another reiver voiced doubt. The hinges had been creaking earlier that day. In their excitement, three of the youngest did not heed the warnings and ran into the dark barn. Chickens scattered before them, but before they could capture any, they were met with the cold, hard steel of two warriors. The first of the three fell, his unarmoured gut pierced. He lay there long enough to see his friends draw their swords. It was a hopelessly unbalanced match; he closed his eyes, praying for a swift end.

Outside, the reivers found themselves surrounded as more men stepped out from where they had lain in wait. All drew their weapons, holding them out in front of them, but none moved to attack.

'Och now, this is no very nice, is it?' came Alasdair's voice from the deepest of the shadows. He stepped out into the moonlight and held their gaze with an icy one of his own.

'MacMhathain scum.' The young leader spat on the ground.

'Hardly fair tae call all who bear my clan's name scum, now is it? My name is Alasdair. So shall we try again?'

The lad growled and stepped forwards only to be stopped by the oldest man. 'No need tae bait the lad.'

'Bait? I merely wish the right person tae be insulted. Now, tell me who sent ye.'

Alasdair's voice now matched his eyes. In response,

the young leader raised his blade and shouted with blind fervour, 'For the Red Comyn!'

He charged forwards, aiming for the man in front of him. No others followed. The attack was poorly executed; a quick parry sent him stumbling onto the blade of another. The other reivers quickly threw their weapons away and knelt. Seumas gestured for them to place their hands on their heads before Alasdair's warriors finished the disarming.

He joined Alasdair, who looked enraged. 'I didnae expect them tae be this close.'

'Them? What have ye no told me?'

With his back to the reivers, Alasdair lowered his voice. 'Brus fears rebellion; everything pointed tae the north-east.'

'God's bones!'

'Aye.' He again faced the group and nodded to the man who had tried to stop their leader. 'Bring him here.'

There was no emotion on Alasdair's face as he stared down at the man.

'Ye will return tae wherever ye came from and warn them that Druim Earbainn is protected. No thief, for ye are no reivers, will be tolerated. I have the blessing of both the king and the chief of Clan MacMhathain tae mete out justice according tae our laws.'

'Aye, my lord, merciful ye be!' tried the man.

'Ensure he cannae brandish a weapon again. And see he doesnae linger.'

'What? Nae! My lord, please! I tend the land tae feed my family!'

The man was dragged off by the two who had brought

him to Alasdair. He stayed silent, staring coldly at those who still knelt. The reivers shifted uneasily. Some prayed under their breath, while others held their heads high. If that was to be their fate too then they would accept it as men. A scream of agony rent the air.

'Line them up.'

Doors to the dwellings opened and families approached the scene. A woman let out a wail of horror as she recognised one of them as her youngest son. She was held back by her eldest; he had been one of the first to pledge. When most had gathered and the two warriors had returned, Alasdair addressed his new people.

'Hear me now: these are yer enemies, no me. No only are they the reivers who have been robbing food from yer mouths, they are, by their own admission, claiming retribution for John Comyn o Badenoch. By order of our merciful king, all enemies not deemed worthy of ransom are tae be put tae death.'

A couple of watchers spat on the ground. For many who carried the Comyn name, this was the final insult. A few who had yet to pledge to the MacMhathain chief decided they would in the morning. His man had done more for them in half a day than others had done in years. Alasdair nodded to his men. They withdrew their daggers and, one by one, slit the throats of the kneeling rebels.

Chapter 23

Alasdair inhaled deeply before walking away; he would look weak if he purged. Killing in battle, or as a spy, was vastly different from ordering a person's death. Lord have mercy on him, the speed of everything meant he'd had no other choice. The boats arriving in the late evening, making them early, the steward's talk of reivers, and Mordag's warnings – he'd simply had to face the threat head-on. Never again would he be so naive as to assume where enemies lay! It was *pure luck* that they revealed themselves as being so close, let alone living on this land.

He left Seumas to clean up and found Mordag at the back door. In only her shift and a plaid, she stood pale and sombre. Did she fear her role in the incident? Or the wrath from her father should he find out? She swallowed and stepped aside for him to enter.

'It had tae be done; more would die if they lived.'

Was she trying to console him? He nodded and held out his arm to encourage her to go ahead. Together, in silence, they made their way up to the bedchamber she had cleaned for their use. He stripped and climbed under the covers. Mordag no longer needed him for warmth yet, while she avoided his kisses, she curled into him. And he clung to her. Christ, just by association she was in as much danger as he. She had been right; it had to be done for both their sakes.

He woke with a start to an empty chamber, except left on the table nearby was drink and an apple. He blinked. She had noticed his preference for the fruit? Please let this be a sign of her thawing and not some notion of a dutiful wife. Forgoing his knife, he bit into the apple and headed to the door. In the pile of chests and furniture just outside the chamber, he found clean garments.

He fancied himself still asleep when he arrived below. His men were cleaning away the old rushes and there were tiles underneath! Daniel shot him a pleading look – it was hardly the work of a warrior – while Seumas grinned. He returned the smile as he passed but left them to it. Until he knew the lay of the land, he had no feasible defence strategy and nothing else for them to do. Assuming it was possible to do anything with but a handful of men.

Jock joined him as he headed outside and spoke in low tones. 'That *cumberworld* steward has already turned tail an fled back tae the safety o Robert's court. I'm havin that chamber cleaned out for ye. Thought the Raven would want somewhere his man could privately work.'

Alasdair pulled up short and glanced around. The old Raven was involved? Now he considered it, it did reek of him. Had he overestimated Robert's hand in everything? Was it he who ordered that Sorcha be hid away, or the Raven? Perhaps she was Robert's bastard after all.

'Who dae ye think it was that hired me? No one else kens,' chuckled Jock.

'I'd like tae keep it that way.'

'Aye, my lord.'

'Mordag is illiterate, so I would like it tae be an area where she is welcome to sit with me as I work.'

'I'll add a couple of those lovely folding chairs yer brother sent down and a wee table.'

He nodded before pausing again. 'Jock, I have more oaths tae take. Will ye ride with me afterwards?'

'Aye, my lord.'

Forget defence; a strategic withdrawal is what he needed more. Yes, they would hide in plain sight and observe. Possibly more. And who better to help him than a fellow spy?

He approached the line of bodies. They could not be buried in the kirkyard but, as local men, they had loved ones. It was a small mercy to grant their folk the chance to bury them elsewhere.

'Dae ye recognise their leader?'

His question was directed at a few men who stood nearby. One stepped forward. Lack of food had aged him beyond the fluff on his chin.

'Aye, that be Donald, Caitlin's nephew. She drove him out last summer when he kept gabbing about the Comyn Clan rising again.'

Jesus. It was no longer for Sorcha's benefit alone that he needed to find out who once owned this land. The old steward had been useless, stating there were no records left. And he dared not yet question the locals. But why would a spymaster hide such information? Perhaps the land had been sold to Sorcha's family, making it unimportant. He ran his hand through his hair and stared at the cage hanging near the dock. A rare but odd remnant of whatever had once occurred here.

'If they're no claimed by compline, have them buried away from here.'

*

After checking that the animals were well, Alasdair returned to the hall. Well, he would have, if the women were not scrubbing the floor. They had nigh-on threatened to geld him! Jock's terrier sat on the step, whining. In a barrow nearby sat the bodies of yet more four-legged invaders. He knelt next to the beast and scratched it behind the ear. 'Ye did well, then got put out, eh? Well, now ye have me for company.'

The dog regarded him before running away. Typical. He grinned as he stood up and dusted off his trews.

'Uh, ye wished tae hear me oath?' A man tentatively approached.

He nodded and gestured for the man to go ahead; he looked around in confusion before removing his blade and kneeling.

'I swear by the holy cross o our Lord in Heaven tae give Cailean Macmaghan me fealty and tae pledge me loyalty tae Clan MacMhathain. In land and life I am his man as he is mine. Should I raise me hand against him, let the iron of this blade pierce my heart.'

For the next hour, he was kept busy with what looked to be the last pledges. A leaden weight settled in his stomach. If no more approached him then the evictions would begin on the morrow. A flood of water poured from the door and ran over his feet; Jesus, his boots were soaked! Retreating to dry land, he settled on one of the benches that also awaited the cleaned hall. A group of the keenest men approached him while he was checking his boots.

'Is this a bad time?'

'Nae, ah just got in the women's way. What concerns ye?'

'I – we – would like tae cut ties wi our past an prove ourselves tae the chief. Perhaps ye could petition him on our behalf? We wish tae take the clan's name.'

The boots could wait. He motioned them to sit. 'Truthfully, I would be glad tae, but if ye take the name now and something happens, then ye endanger no only yerselves but yer family. I'll no risk that, so instead, I'll ask ye to hold off for now.'

The men looked at each other gravely before dropping their voices and leaning towards him. Another shook his head. 'Ye dinnae ken. For years we took pity on them and fed them what we could, starving ourselves in the process. Then we learn that they were the ones stealing the rest!'

Lord, give him strength! The last thing he needed was for a blood feud to erupt. He would not be able to tell who was rebel and who was retaliating. But perhaps he could placate them with something else. Something that would give him the eyes and ears he needed.

'I forbid ye from starting a feud. However, I do have a way ye can help.'

*

A couple of days later, Alasdair and Jock entered the steward's old space. It was now warmly furnished with his tapestry. In one corner sat a large table and the other, a comfortable place to sit. It was, in essence, no workspace but a solar. He nodded his approval at the pieces which had been chosen to house his manuscripts and household accounts, before freezing. Why had Cailean sent down *that* chest? He had not thought about her since their arrival.

'It's ideal, only see that that chest is moved tae storage.'

'I'll move it now, my lord, and I cannae take all the glory.'

He lowered his head before defying his age and grabbing the chest. Alasdair inhaled shakily, stunned by sudden guilt. Ruth had deserved a life like this, but she would never have coped. The journey alone would have been too much. Not like his sturdy Mordag; she had thrown herself head first into the work. And whatever his new wife felt for him, she had understood the importance of appearing united.

'Alasdair? Are ye well?'

He forced the guilt back down. 'Aye, my shield-maiden. I'm just tired, as no doubt ye are. Ye have done wonders, Mordag.'

She hovered there, struggling to accept his words. He closed the distance and took her hands.

'Tis true. Let's take some time for ourselves and dine alone tonight.'

She looked even more dubious, but slowly agreed.

It was just what he needed. Her company, hearty food, and peace. And he kept to the safe topic of making the manor their home. Mordag had hired maids, a laundress and someone to tackle the mice properly – the latter's wages nothing more than a daily fish or bowl of whey.

He observed her for a moment. 'Is there anything ye wish for? Either tae make yer work easier or because ye have always wanted it? I cannae promise ye will have it quickly, but ye will have it.'

He was, after all, comfortable enough, having spent little beyond necessities over the years. And he doubted Mordag would be excessive. It had taken a lot of encouragement when they visited the pedlar.

'I... I would like a raised garden fer herbs, like what ah saw at Pillanflatt. Twill keep the dogs from digging it up and make it harder fer pests. Ah ken there's a garden there already but tis a mess. Starting over would be easier.'

'That's easily arranged. And there will be time aplenty tae prepare it ready for the next growing season.'

'Aye.' She smiled shyly.

It was nothing like the beaming smile she had given on that first day, but it was just as lovely. He gently encouraged her to continue. After an obvious internal battle, she added, 'Thread and an embroidery slate.'

'I'm afraid I'm no familiar with the latter.'

'A frame fer stretching cloth. I can only do certain stitches with loose cloth. Me father refused tae replace me old one when it got damaged.'

'Ah! Aye, my mither had one. That tapestry is one of her pieces. While I cannae promise ye gold thread, I will happily give ye what ye need tae decorate our home.'

Mordag was now blushing, and he could not help but grin. Every spare moment his mither had, she was found embroidering something. As a boy, he'd once asked her why, and the question must have been badly timed, for she'd replied that it felt good to stab something repeatedly. Indeed, if – *if* – they had children, he would bet his last coin that Mordag would say the same to one of them.

Someone knocked and he bid them enter. Arthur came in, placing a strongbox and key on the table before handing two missives to him.

'The box and the first missive are for the lady, my lord. The second is from the chief. His boat sails on the morrow and he wishes there be a response on board.'

'Aye, we cannae keep the crabbit bear waiting.'

Dismissing Arthur, he let his brother's missive sit and wait. The one for Mordag bore his seal but not his heavy hand. He motioned her to come closer. 'Would ye like me tae read it to ye?'

'Aye, please.'

She abandoned her seat and approached him; he pulled her down into his lap, her legs hanging over the arm of the chair. She squeaked in shock, but she was not angry with him and simply rolled her eyes.

'Ye *sumph*.'

'Och now, here I am being nice… oomph.'

She dug her elbow into him. 'Just read the thing.'

He grinned as he broke the seal; he rather enjoyed her insults.

'Tae my dearest and newest sister…'

Ah it was Sorcha's hand! She warmly welcomed Mordag to the family and expressed her wishes that they would soon meet. Unfortunately, she was not in any position to give marital advice, but if Alasdair was anything like his brother, then there would be many a small irritation.

'Ye must be,' muttered Mordag.

'Jesus, I thank ye!'

But she's not to grow too irritated by it for they were akin to puppies, not knowing any better. Now *that* made his eyes roll and Mordag laugh.

'I like her. And she kens ye well!'

As there were no living daughters, Sorcha had been gifted most of her mother-in-law's possessions. They included more pieces of jewellery than she could possibly wear – *that* was a well-meant white lie. With Cailean's blessing, Sorcha had selected several pieces she thought suitable, and they were contained within the box before them. Mordag gasped, and Alasdair paused. Sorcha could not have known of his wife's lack of suitable things, yet it was a well-chosen gift.

'"With my warmest regards, Sorcha." Oh, there is a postscript: "Please tell Alasdair that the great cow feud of Clan MacMhathain continues".'

He both laughed and groaned in sympathy for his brother. Mordag stared at him.

'I'll tell ye that story later, I promise. Why dinnae ye see what she has sent ye?'

She opened the box and suddenly sat up straight, perching on his knees. From the box, she carefully removed one of his mother's silver girdles. Each circle that made it held Celtic knotwork. The matching velvet bag lay beneath. A plain circlet of silver, two rings and three brooches formed the rest. Jesus, one of the brooches was his favourite piece – two golden hands clasped together and encircled with red stones. Cailean had to have chosen that.

'They're beautiful, and far too good tae be worn daily.'

'Aye but when ye do wear them, they will look alive on ye.'

Mordag looked into his eyes and started to close the gap between them. Just when he was sure they would kiss, she withdrew. He struggled to keep from sighing. Something scared her, and forcing it would destroy any chance they had. He had made an oath to wait, but it was a heavy penance. She turned back to the pieces again.

'Can we pen a reply?'

A simple 'we', yet it meant so much. He would treasure it, and that she made no effort to move from his lap.

'Aye, let's do it now and send it back with my reply tae Cailean.'

She cleared the dishes while he retrieved his writing materials and readied a quill. A breeze could have blown him over when she willingly returned to his knee! He encouraged her to sit sideways, against his left arm.

'Now what would ye like it to say?'

Mordag thanked Sorcha kindly for the gifts and well-wishes. And proclaimed her surprise at their unexpected nuptials. She complimented the land and expressed her desire to return the manor to its former glory. Then it went downhill for him as she agreed that Alasdair was akin to a puppy, and sought Sorcha's advice on bothersome Macmaghan traits, like 'his damned grin' and him talking in his sleep. Best not admit that his brother was the opposite. Besides…

'Ah dinnae talk in me sleep!'

'Aye ye do. Mostly mumbling, like, but ye do. Tis even worse when yer tired.'

She then concluded the letter and took the quill from him. In a shaky hand, she wrote out her first name.

'Me brother taught me this, so I wouldnae have tae put a cross.'

Ah, smart lad. Crosses were the easiest to forge. He then added his own small postscript, thanking them for that one brooch.

'Ah thank ye, Alasdair.'

Reluctantly, he let her go and she settled with some sewing. He agreed that the jewellery would stay in the strongroom until needed, but she and only she would hold the key to its box.

Alasdair opened the second missive, scanning the words. As he suspected, it started with a lecture, but he was not expecting the softening towards the end of it. Cailean hoped he could find happiness again. After that, it was all business. How was the land, his reception, and so on. In return, Cailean could offer little news aside from…

'Mordag, we have another problem.'

'It cannae be any worse than what's already happened, can it?'

'I'm no sure. It's likely tae affect us, but how ah cannae say. We're at war with a clan, only we dinnae ken which.'

'Jesus, Joseph and Mary!'

'Nae, ah doubt they're involved.'

His jest fell flat as the heavy weight of the news hung between them. He returned to the letter. Allies had been alerted and the chieftains were in agreement. He snorted to himself. With the peace treaty and the neighbours being on somewhat friendly terms, they'd be chomping at the bit! He slumped and sighed, only to sit up again. Douglas, of all people, had known both Thomas and Annabelle, but how to get it out of him?

Sinking back into the seat, he closed his eyes and once again ran his hand through his hair. A fingertip brushed over the scar and he froze. The night he had hurt himself there, he had been eavesdropping on his father's meeting. There was a small, black-haired man with him. What had his name been? *Thomas!*

Chapter 24

Cailean scanned the loch. Sorcha's followers had announced themselves with cowardly attacks. One secluded property per night until last night. That one was too close to his seat. They mocked him. Yet each attack would take a handful of men at most. Their ability to go unnoticed too. It had to be those mercenaries. Cailean cursed.

'*Mo ciann?*'

He dismissed Donald's concerned question. Should he risk more tracking parties? It would leave larger areas unprotected. Or treat it as a diversionary tactic?

The boat landed at Eilean Donnain's back gate. A siege was unlikely, but he got out and no further. There was a grated tidal pit which carried waste from the garderobes. Their greatest weakness. And few were above such tactics.

'When was the grate last checked?'

'I'm no sure. I'll go ask the smith tae dae it.' Donald went ahead.

He followed, more slowly. Wagons checked, food tested…

'Sir Cailean, a moment of yer time, please.' The chaplain interrupted his thoughts.

'Aye?'

'I dinnae care for the harvest home tae be on the same day as Michaelmas.'

'Same rule as last year.'

The man smiled and dipped his head.

'Ah thank ye.'

Masses first, then festivities. It never changed, but he always asked.

A boy shot past him. One of Donald's. A group following slowed, passing shyly then speeding up. The lad found his father and climbed up. He had balls – Cailean would have been beaten, but his cousin was encouraging it! He feigned a fall under the onslaught and was abandoned. Cailean snorted and leaned on the wall behind him. When had he last watched children play? Christ, he could already be a father. What kind did he want to be?

'The smith will take a look next low tide.'

'Dragon?'

'Eh? Oh, aye. Ah was his keep.'

'For a great lump of rock, ye fell too quickly.'

Donald laughed, then gave him an odd look. What? He could jest! He patted him on the shoulder and headed inside.

Sorcha too was planning Michaelmas. A task she enjoyed, judging by that smile. He helped himself to her drink.

'Good morrow, my lord husband. Was the journey advantageous?'

'Twas not as I had hoped.'

'And the family?'

He shook his head; slaughtered like the others. 'It's no yer fault, Sorcha. I provoked them.'

He predicted correctly; she was biting her lip. Compassion could be both admirable and a weakness. He feared hers could be the latter and had revoked her permission to travel accordingly. He changed the subject to Michaelmas. She laid out their plans. Cailean nodded as he watched Douglas. Could he actually do what Alasdair suggested? They were not *that* alike! He apologised and excused himself.

Slouching and pouting, he headed towards the man. Hell would freeze over before he looked angelic. *This was ludicrous.*

'Uncle Douglas, Father will no talk tae me,' he whined.

'He's a busy man, Alasdair. What is it ye wish tae ken?'

He blinked, and overheard Donald choking.

'That man that was here, ah think he was called Thomas?'

'Aye.'

'Who is he?'

'Be a good lad and bring me a drop of the good stuff. Then I'll tell ye.'

Good stuff? His father's *uisge beatha*? The *tyke*! Cailean had taught Alasdair how to filch it. Insisted he did not share it around. That explained their father's suspicion. And was he still doing it?

*

Now, Cailean stood in 'Grann's side-chamber', filling a cup with his *uisge beatha*. He handed it to Douglas.

'What was it that ye wanted tae ask me?'

'That man, Thomas, who is he?'

'Oh him. Horse trader. Twas how Brus met him if ah'm no mistaken. Mighty useful, ye ken. From what Grann says, the man's reputation allows him tae come and go as he pleases in both Scotland and England.'

'So he works for the king?'

'Och no; no fer that toom tabard.'

God's balls, he had gone that far back? How old was he when this began? And they had been allied to Clan Bruce for that long? Thomas too? Cailean obliged with more *uisge beatha*.

'So what was it ye wanted tae ken about Robert's eyes?'

'Ye mean Thomas?'

'Aye, the canny fox.'

Cailean stood up and looked out of the small window. They were going in circles. He sighed and pinched his nose. What more could he do? He lacked Alasdair's finesse. Douglas shifted behind him. 'I ken that look, Grann. What's troubling ye?'

What? Unless... Did he dare?

'I'm no sure about Annabelle.'

'What about her?'

'Tell me everything.'

'God's teeth, no again! Fine! We accompanied Thomas tae Methven as Brus and yerself wished. It was no pretty – Valence had wreaked vengeance on those he believed had helped Robert. Whether they had or no. She was unfortunate; wrong time and place. And a sight fer sore eyes she was. Why, if ah hadnae been married meself...'

He turned to stare, not trusting his ears.

'...Well, Thomas got lucky, did he no? You letting them stay here, then him getting her pregnant like that over the winter. Forcing Brus's hand and all. But why are ye bringing all this up again, Grann? They havenae learned who she is, have they? I'll swear on my blade, *I've told no one.*'

So they wintered here. How convenient that both sons were at foster! He clenched his teeth. What else had been kept hidden? And why had no one else spoken of it?

'Douglas, who is she?'

The old man was staring into his cup. 'Her family name? Ye're really asking me that? God's teeth, I'm no a changeling, Grann! Why, it's... it's...'

Douglas looked confused, then frightened. Tears started to well. Cailean cursed; he had pushed him too far.

'Ah dinnae ken... how could ah no ken?'

*

Cailean slid the ledger away. He was still sickened by what he had witnessed. A man recalling just enough to understand his fate. Weeping and begging for 'Grann' to kill him. Perhaps he would have, but Cailean could not. Was it not enough that his father's death still haunted him? The apoplexy caused by his mither's death. His slow withering away. More attacks, then nothing. Some claimed he'd died of a broken heart. Too much drink more like. Dear Lord, let him die by the sword.

Enough of this! He needed to be surrounded by life.

A hall full of people sat weaving garlands and chaplets, directed by Sorcha. Laughter all around. Children playing, forced inside by rain. He settled on his seat and just watched. Sorcha met his eyes. She spoke to someone, then broke off. He lost sight of her. Where had she gone? There! A chaplet now upon her head. He lost her again. She was closer, a second chaplet in hand.

'That's no going on me.'

'Aye it is.'

She pounced; he caught her and pulled her onto his lap. She surrendered, laughing. He claimed his prize, a kiss. The crown landed on his head. Breaking the kiss, he snorted, 'Bested by my wife.'

She tilted her head closer. 'Then let us find somewhere more discreet tae discuss yer ransom.'

Just the thought made him hard. What better distraction? He nodded his approval, but it was too late. The hall had grown quiet and cold. Sorcha swore under her breath – in French *and* Latin – as she pulled herself free. What now? Bernice stormed towards him. His vigour died. He should have known; she was incorrigible. He grasped his wife's hand. Let Bernice see their united front.

'I'd invite ye tae speak, but I ken ye need no encouragement.'

The tense hall chuckled nervously.

'Have ye turned yer back on God, Cailean Macmaghan? Unruly children, pagan crowns, revelry the day before the feast of St Michael!' Bernice crossed herself. 'We should be solemnly remembering the battle Archangel Michael fought against Satan!'

'Children need tae play. Tomorrow's mass is place enough for solemnities.'

He would give her no more.

'Ye've changed, and no for the good. Grann would be appalled. Letting the place fall intae ruin. I blame it on ye marrying that she-devil bastard!'

Cailean shot up. Damn the vile bitch! Sorcha tapped his back, and slowly, he eased his tense muscles. He would not lower himself. A glance confirmed that Sorcha was pale but enduring the attack.

'Aye, ye forgot that all could hear your wee talk with Douglas, ye fool. I should have recognised the brat. Looks just like her whore mother.'

'Enough! Yer spiteful tongue is nae longer welcome here. Leave for yer convent today or be confined tae wait yer judgement under the law of scold and the law of trespass.'

Why was the hall still so silent? Damn it, they were all agape!

'Ye would no dare!'

'Ewan, see that the abbess leaves or confines herself.'

Ignoring the hag's ranting, he focused on Sorcha. His movement a signal to the others. Noise returned.

'What is she talking about?' asked a shocked Sorcha.

'Yer parents wintered here, tis all.'

Her forehead creased. Bernice's final screech upon retreating distracted him. He turned back to Sorcha. She was gone. What was wrong with her now? He intended to find out. He took a few strides forwards and stopped. The children still huddled together, terrified. Damn it, she would have to wait. How did he do this? Bend down to their height, right?

'Ignore her. Ah like seeing ye play.'

They did not look so convinced. He looked around, at a loss. The children were the future of his clan. They should not fear approaching their chief. One of Ewan's twins was holding a carved warrior; he nodded towards it.

'Ah mean it, ah even had one just like that.'

That worked. A poppet was thrust into his hand. He admired its gown while the lad's chest puffed up.

'I'm gonnae be yer bestest man when I'm older!'

'Am no!'

'Am so!'

Cailean blinked, the corners of his lips lifting. A memory from long ago resurfaced. His father scolding him and Alasdair. 'Tae be great warriors, ye must ken the first rule. Dinnae argue with the person watching yer back.'

*

When would the accursed rain stop? It had followed Cailean for the entirety of his trip, collecting rents. He rode through the gate, not expecting a welcome. Sorcha has still been angry when he left. Lord knew why as she had kept silent. He had removed Bernice and kept her safe. What more did the woman want? He pulled his mount up, a little too sharply. She was there, hooded and mantled. A ray of sunshine. He dismounted and splashed through the muck.

'My lady wife, ye look well.'

'My lord husband. Ye look… well, the fires are blazing, and the butler already prepares some spiced wine.'

Like a drowned rat. He nodded his approval.

'Then let's get within.'

He stopped in the keep's antechamber. Sorcha reached for his sodden plaid. What was she doing? He sat on a bench to remove his riding boots. She knelt to take them off. Then slipped his dry house shoes on.

'Sorcha?'

'Please, let me do this. A good wife...'

She was trying to make amends? He thanked her and still she continued. Leading him toward their stairs. He stopped her the moment the door closed. 'Enough of that; welcome me home properly.'

He pulled her close and claimed her lips. How he had missed her! Her sweet taste, the smell of her skin. She pressed herself against him. And her passion! The door opened, a page hurried past. They broke off and he glared at the boy's back.

'Oh... Ye should probably drink that before it cools.' She spoke softly.

He did not want it. Just her. 'Fine, but ye'll join me.'

She smiled and started for the steps. Glancing back, she added, 'Welcome home, Cailean.'

He growled and chased after her. Her sweet laughter ringing in his ears. He dropped his belt and sword. Pulled his wet *léine* over his head. And stumbled over a yelping something. God's balls, what were the hounds doing in the bedchamber? He forbade it. Both dogs tried their luck. Approaching once more, but lower, they licked at his hand. The *tykes* knew they were in trouble. Sorcha sat up on the bed, meeting his gaze.

'They kept me company. Like ye, they let out many *ryfftys off wynd an snorand.*'

He blinked, taken aback by the sudden change from Gaelic to Scots. Was she teasing him? Her eyes were sparkling. She must be.

'Ye missed me then.'

'How could I no? Ye are my husband.'

In three large strides, he caught her, pushing her down onto the bed. He tugged at her kirtle's lacings – her gown lay discarded somewhere near the door. But Sorcha was having none of it. She pushed him back until she sat upright again. *She* was the lady of Eilean Donnain; *she* had kept it in his absence. And while she could not stay angry at him for keeping knowledge from her, especially after hearing what it had done to Douglas, she could not – no, *would* not be treat thusly again.

She would make him see that.

She teased his lips, biting them. He growled a demand for more, yet she pulled away at every attempt he made to deepen their kiss. Yes, feel her frustration! She tugged his undershirt free and dipped her hand inside his trews. She ran a thumb over his head and he became as stiff as his member. He was so close! Now, she kissed him hard, meeting his need with her own.

He tore her hand from him, pushing her back into the bed and pinning it above her. The lacings gave way, then her chemise, torn asunder. She laughed, a sound so deep and rich. No longer a maidenly sigh. Cailean had stopped! His eyes on her breasts. Dear Lord, have mercy, he was not done yet! But the cold air on her nipples followed by the warmth of his mouth! She lifted up as he feasted upon them, gasping and panting for breath. He pulled back again to stare at her. *She did that to him.*

'Every night. I could think of naught else. I need tae be inside ye now!'

The animalistic lust of his voice! Oh, damn the toying, she had to be on him! He grunted in shock at the ferocity of her push, landing on his side. She gave him no choice, for already she was mounting him. Let him watch her as *she* rode *him* to their release! His teeth gritted as he helped guide her onto his member. A hand on his chest, she rode him hard, staring straight into his eyes. Yes, she was his lady, his wife!

He grabbed at her hips, but she needed no urging. So close now! Her lustful cries rent the air, her pace descending into unruly spasms as her legs ceased to function. Cailean grabbed her and they rolled together. He grunted as he thrust hard into her before he too was overcome by his seed spilling.

*

Sorcha slipped from the bed, her fingers trailing over Cailean's prone body. What had come over her? She had meant to be apologising for her behaviour. In all possible ways. Instead, well, how could she describe it? A release, and something more. A gaining, perhaps. Of what though? She unpinned what little of her styled hair remained, letting it free. A sleepy sound of approval from Cailean.

'Come back here.'

'We have work tae do, and Ailis will be here soon enough.'

He grunted as he got up. She heard him pour the now-cool wine into a goblet and drink heartily. Sorcha picked up her comb and ran it through her hair, wincing as it found the inevitable knots.

'I doubt she'll be up any time soon.'

Padding feet; the smell of his sweat, horse, wine and their lovemaking. His arms around her. She wanted to give in, sink back into bliss with him. But she feared what he would say next. Alas, the comb slipped from her hand and her head tilted to the side. He nuzzled her hair.

'I did what ye suggested. Even used yer arguments about her status. Iain's father has sent word tae Glasgow.'

She gasped. In part because he had listened to her idea of a betrothal between Iain and Ailis! And because his fingers had suddenly dipped south. His other hand curling in her hair, pulling her head back. He bit her collar bone, his damp hair trailing over her breast. She hissed. The pain travelling downwards, inflaming her. No. There really was too much to do. She pulled free, turning to face him. His eyes stormy, his grip possessive.

'I told ye. In here, I'll listen tae ye. In all regards and all moods.'

He kissed her hard. She relented, pressing into him. She felt him twitch against her stomach. He was ready for her. He broke the kiss. She panted softly.

'Now, I've been without my wife for too long.'

He was already pulling her back to the bed. She knew what was coming. He wanted to put right the wrong of her straddling him. Elizabeth's ladies had warned of using it too often. 'Men,' they'd stated, 'dinnae like a woman taking control when they're ploughing.' She opened her mouth, to promise not to do it again. He put a finger to her lips.

'I want tae watch ye...'

She had intended to moisten her lips but caught his finger by accident. He started to tremble. Wait, had she done that to him? That strange feeling of gaining something was back. Was it the control they spoke of?

'...watch ye ride me.'

Chapter 25

Pathetic. Licking rainwater from the walls like that. But what else was there to watch in this godforsaken place? Michael sneered and shouted at the half-dead, moaning sops to shut up. Not that they ever listened. The lice were fat enough; feed the rats instead. He shifted, the threadbare blankets under him hiding the coins the women paid to keep him away. Nowhere near enough to pay his debt, but enough to keep him fed. The men would be there soon. Selling the watery gong they called pottage, and the piss-water that passed as ale. A farthing for a bowl of one or the other, or a half-penny for both and a chunk of the baked grit they claimed was bread. First thing he'd have when he got out would be a proper meal.

Damn that foolish bitch, what was taking her so long? She should have freed him by now. His hands itched to take down the arrogant Highlanders. His cock hardened at the thought of finally ploughing her. He would make them all pay. From those that threw the rotten food to the king himself! He laughed as he saw in his mind's eye what he would do to each and every one of them!

Now, about that delectable young morsel that had just arrived. Such a ripe age and so ready for the plucking…

'Oi, Laird O Nochtthenes…' a guard called.

God damn them to hell and back! The name came from them learning he had forfeited his lands. The *cumberworld* who sired him had not paid the taxes.

'… get yer arse here.'

*

In his five years as a mendicant, God had greatly tested him by sending him to the most wretched of places. And the land of the Scots had fallen to such a state since Edward of Caernarfon had relinquished it. Whereas others had condemned them to their fate, the friar could not. Christ had not given up on the condemned thief, saving him even as he died. He must do the same. And had he not just been rewarded for doing as Christ?

He shuddered, recalling his time in Inverlochy. That poor woman with those bedraggled, hollow-faced orphans clinging to her skirts. She had approached him with her plight, begged him to aid her for no one else would. Her patron had been falsely imprisoned in Glasgow at the false accusation of a greedy innkeep. She could not leave the children to go and pay his debts. Would he carry the coin to pay the debt? And give him the sack containing his belongings? Of course he would!

He weighed the few coins he held. He should not have accepted them, but the ungodly practice of Samhain was almost upon this vile kingdom. They would not show him mercy when he condemned their false worship, and he needed to eat. But first, in honour of his act, he must preach the Gospel of Matthew. Remind people here to love thy neighbour. Something dark and foul-smelling fell over his face.

Ice-cold water shocked him awake.

He gasped and blinked the water from his eyes. Where was he? What had the unholy sons of Lucifer done to him? All he could see was a single tallow candle and – he groaned – a well-built thug in the shadows. Lord save him! He tried to move, but his hands were bound to the solid object holding him upright. The man spoke in the barbaric tongue.

'I do not speak your language.'

'Sassenach?'

'Yes! Yes! Please do not kill me! I work only for our Lord the Almighty!'

The man spat out a string of words, stirring movement in the room. There were others? The friar's lips moved in silent prayer. They had warned him not to come here. Warned him about what the Scots did to any English they encountered. He had been so unwise to think he would be different. If he got out of this alive, he would go somewhere safer, like Wales! He tried again.

'I swear on the cross, I never lifted a blade against any man. I only want to bring joy to Christ's flock! You have all been through such a hard time!'

The sound of a drawn sword, the whisper of air moving and then a painful prick at his throat. He squeezed his eyes shut. The stench of him shaming himself. He cracked an eye open; the blade was gone. He bent over and finished purging what little his body had left to hold. Voices filled the air and, suddenly, his hands were freed!

'Apologies, brother. We had reason to believe you were not who you appeared to be.' Latin? He followed the voice. Dear Lord, he was a priest! 'The man you freed from that debtor jail is a most heinous sinner.'

'But… but…' he stammered.

It made no sense. How could it be? Though, yes, the devil tempted through all means possible. How many souls had he dragged into his fiery pit through so-called good and holy work? His hands, awkward from being bound, sought his cross. He had been a fool, blinded by his arrogance. But she had looked so feeble. He shook his head. A wolf in sheep's clothing deceived just as well.

'May the Lord forgive me for I have sinned most grievously!'

'Consider this your time for confession.'

Chapter 26

Mordag placed the table linens in the chest, saving their first use for the morrow. They were the manor's first new items suitable for a feast, though not extravagant. All other items were already owned, borrowed, or salvaged. After seeing the coffers, she'd asked Alasdair why. He wanted their wealth to 'grow' with the people. Odd.

She locked the chest and nodded to Caitlin.

'Let's hope the weather holds, my lady.'

A peek out the door revealed a red sky. Let the omen hold true.

'Still, it will do no harm tae keep a brazier burning,' Mordag added.

Caitlin agreed, only to tut at her daughter. The child was tugging at Mordag's skirt. She held out a late-blooming flower.

'Fer me? I thank ye.'

She took the bloom, but the girl shook her head and pointed to where the Samhain bonfire was being built.

Alasdair stood in naught but his undershirt and trews, sweaty and likely reeking. Their eyes met and he nodded, that damned glint in his eye.

'Well, ah thank ye for bringing it tae me,' she corrected herself, and got a blush in response.

'Away tae ye pa now, Maggie, yer sop will be waiting.'

The girl rushed off in the direction of the kitchen. Whether she reached the cook or not would be a different matter.

'God willing, ye'll soon be watching yer own, my lady. And, if ye dinnae mind me saying, perhaps ye can share yer secrets wi us?'

'Secrets?'

'He being such a goodly sort. Ye must be doing something right.'

She watched Alasdair. He had returned to piling the wood. Guilt sat heavy, like a bad dish. She could not continue to fool herself by thinking that the cleaning was for him. And yet he still behaved fairly. Yes, that grin was annoying, but he had not forced his marital rights. Shame on her for letting it go on for so long. But could she really give that to him? She had to. It was the only thing she held.

'Come with me, Caitlin.'

*

His footsteps were getting closer. Mordag swallowed and turned so her back was to the door. *Be as strong as a shield-maiden.* But what if he did not like what he saw? She flicked her hair back over her shoulders. It was too late now. The door slammed back against the wall. Alasdair's breathing heavier than normal. Had he run?

'What's wrong, Mordag? Caitlin was adamant that ah come.'

She glanced over her shoulder, keeping her eyes low. 'Please shut the door.'

Her voice trembled. May the Virgin give her the courage she lacked. Slowly, she spun and dropped the plaid covering her nakedness. She hesitated, painfully aware of his eyes roaming her. Then lifted her eyes. He was taut as a bowstring, the blue of his eyes piercingly intense. His nostrils flared like a stallion's. There was nothing boyish about him now. And how had he closed the gap so quickly?

'Are ye sure ye want this?' he asked, his voice almost a growl. 'I'm no sure I can stop if I start.'

Mordag licked her lips and wrapped her arms around his neck, her breasts pressing against his undershirt. *More*, her body sharply demanded. Her hips against his. Against his erect *slat*. Christ, she had done that?

'Aye, Alasdair. Make me yer wife.'

She scarcely noticed the change in her voice. He growled, really growled, then forcefully pressed his lips to hers, like she had, that night. A shiver ran down her spine. Yes, like in the drover's hut. He grasped her backside and lifted her. Her legs knew what to do. They wrapped around his hips. So strong! But what to do now? Scared but eager for something. She rubbed herself against his shirt and gasped.

He lowered her onto the bed, tore the shirt from himself and unlaced his trews, his eyes not leaving her. 'Jesus, Mordag, my shield-maiden, ye daze me more each day.'

Her eyes fell across his body. His nakedness, no longer repulsive. When did that happen? And damn it, she just had to touch him! She reached out, but he stopped her with his hands, pinning hers above her head. No! Oh his lips! They trailed down her neck, breast, navel. Her mother had not spoken of this. And still lower! She could not think clearly. Wait, her hands were free?

'Holy Mother of Christ!' she cried out, grabbing at his hair, digging her fingers into his curls.

He was using his tongue down there! On the spot a woman must not touch, lest they became... She hissed and twisted. Alasdair's voice, vibrating against her. What was he saying? He grabbed her hands, forcing them from his head onto the sheets beneath. She tore at them. Her body wanted more. But what?

He knew. A finger? No, it was not enough. She reared up, groaning. Where was this going? No, where was she running to?

'Alasdair!'

She panicked as something swept her away. No matter how she bucked, she could not fight it off. Her body was not hers. Where had Alasdair gone? He was back, on top of her. Something new pressing against her maidenhood. Something bigger and much thicker than his fingers. Something gave way inside her. Her maidenhood! He had breached it! She cared not, wrapping her legs around his waist.

Mordag opened her eyes; when had she shut them? He was ploughing her with gritted teeth. She lifted her head, shamelessly begging for a kiss. He obliged, his control gone. She bit him by accident. He groaned. She bit again, holding onto his lip. Another, more desperate growl. He tore himself away and stared deep into her eyes. Thrusting harder. Once, twice. Something hot spilled within her. His seed!

He fell forwards onto his elbows. She felt him shaking, slipping from her and falling onto his side. He panted into her ear before nuzzling gently there. So soft after all that hardness. She giggled.

'Me wife finally conquered me by letting me take her maidenhood and she giggles! I am a ruined man!'

That only made her giggle more. How giddy she was! If only she had known the truth. She stretched slowly, cat-like. She felt so alive, and so tired at the same time. The air felt cold. She shivered and rolled onto her side, finding herself welcomed by his arms. She buried her head into his chest, giddy and strangely vulnerable. Finally, she found her voice. 'Ah've been a lousy wife, Alasdair. Ah should not have forbidden ye.'

His body shook with laughter, and she recoiled in horror. He pulled her back. 'Dinnae fret, my love. I was thinking of all the ways we can make up for lost time.'

The laughter slowed; his hand, playing with her hair, started to droop.

'Like what?'

'Mmm. Plenty of time tae show ye…'

His hand stilled, his breathing lengthened. Christ, had he really fallen asleep? Hah! Those women she overheard that time were telling the truth. Men *were* useless afterwards. But what of her? Would she be useless to him now that she had given him what he wanted? She shivered; a different chill penetrated her and tightened its grip.

*

To be fair, he had kept his word. Several times. And now Mordag gripped tightly to him as he helped her down the steps. Her damned legs, he had ruined them! Through the hall's main doors, a bright but cool day greeted her. They would need extra plaid for the Samhain vigil. A chorus of greetings from Alasdair's men distracted her.

'Och, it's nice tae see his lordship gracing us with his presence,' came Daniel's sarcastic greeting.

Had Alasdair meant to meet with them last night? The warrior was hit hard around the head by Seumas, who bent down and said something in his ear. Embarrassed horror replaced his look and he quickly hid it behind an earthenware cup. 'Ah mean, tae many weans.'

Just what had that meant? Had Seumas known? Unashamedly, her husband grinned like the cat who'd got the cream. She rolled her eyes and accepted the cup of ale he handed her. Well, that had not changed.

'Ye're hopeless,' she muttered.

'Aye, but I ken my lady wife wouldnae have it any other way.'

'Och, ye do, do ye?'

He leaned in to kiss the corner of her mouth. She stilled, not sure if she liked this public display. He drew back only a couple of inches. 'Aye, just as sweet as the first time.'

The damned cheek! Just who did he think he was? Jest with the men if he must, but she would not let him flaunt…

'My lord, they're arriving,' Jock apologetically interrupted.

She pulled back sharply and caught the glint in Alasdair's eyes. Oh, for goodness' sake! She huffed as he backed away, dipped his head and began to follow the seneschal. Wait, he would be… Damn, he was gone. Rent collection could last all day. He needed to eat.

Mordag grabbed half a bannock and followed, only to slow to a halt. The men were still watching her.

'If ye've nowt better tae dae than *glowren*, me raised beds need filling wi soil.'

All of them jumped to attention, and Seumas coughed. 'Right ,men, err, training, yes, important training.'

She smirked; she was well aware that they were busy with something else for Alasdair. Still, she rather liked making them sweat.

Thrusting the bread into Alasdair's hand, she gave him a sharp look. He got the message. In a line in front of them stood most of the men living on the land. Less than there had been last year, or so Jock had said. Her husband's evictions. Taking his lead, she smiled a welcome as the first individual approached.

'Ah, Ròidh, what have ye got there?' asked the seneschal, taking the role of scribe for the day.

'Four bags o grain and a chicken, like last year.'

How much had he said? That was nigh-on robbery! No wonder they were gaunt, what with that and the reivers. She was more than ready to give Alasdair a mouthful, only he stood bent over some parchment, discussing something with Jock. They nodded and he straightened.

'You were one o the first men tae approach me tae give their oath. Ye trusted me where others didnae, and now ye get the reward for the risk ye took. We will take two of those bags as rent and naught else.'

There was murmuring along the line. She could only guess the surprise and relief they felt. Ròidh stumbled his thanks and praised them both. What had she done? It was Alasdair's doing. After he stepped away, that was her turn. She pointed him to the ale set out nearby, and reminded him that he, and all attending that day, were welcome to stay for the Samhain feast.

And so it went. After Alasdair had renegotiated their rent, she directed them onwards and accepted their gratitude on his behalf. Occasionally, she was called over and gifted small items from the wives or daughters, as her mother once had. Each one she thanked for their generosity.

Mordag came to a sudden halt, her heart breaking. A boy and two girls had approached the table, hollow-eyed and barely dressed. The boy held a scrawny chicken close to him, while one of the girls held a small bunch of dried heather, held together with a poorly woven ribbon. He silently held out the chicken.

'Bessie's son. They lost their father tae wasting sickness last year. He was a shepherd and she a weaver, but now she's trying tae handle both,' murmured Jock.

Her hand fell on Alasdair's arm, gripping it tightly. Memories threatened to overwhelm her. His hand landed on top of hers, squeezing it. Did he know what she was feeling?

'Tell yer ma that we'll no take rents from her this time and that I'll be up tae see her myself,' Alasdair instructed the lad.

The boy's eyes widened. 'We dinnae want yer charity,

mister chief, sir. We're hardworking and will pay like the rest.'

'Aye ye will, just no like this. But that's tae be discussed with yer ma.'

He did not belittle the lad. Just spoke firmly. Mordag swallowed and had to look away, but not before she caught the boy sizing him up, then giving in. She felt a tug. The girl was there, holding up the heather.

'For you, lady. Ma says white be lucky an good for a newly wedded. An ah made the ribbon meself.'

'That is so kind o ye, and ah see a good weaver in ye too.'

Her compliment brought forth a large, bright smile. She had to do something, as they would not stay for the feast.

'Ye ken, ah think it just might be lucky. Our cook made way too many bannocks today and we just cannae eat them all. This heather must have sent ye tae help us.'

She guided the girl away, towards the hall. The boy hesitated, before his hunger overcame his pride and he followed her. Mordag glanced back to Alasdair, their eyes meeting. What passed between them – well, she could not place it, but it had not been there before.

*

Mordag kept a careful eye on the children, stopping them from bolting the food. She'd better send them home with some steeped mint; one of them was bound to need it. Turning to call to Caitlin, she found a lanky figure blocking her way. He had grown and the fluff had spread from his top lip.

'Angus!'

What was he doing here? And had nobody altered his clothing? She pulled him to her and held him tight, only to break off and look at him again. Her brother grinned.

'Ye look happy!'

'O course ah do, ye're here! But why? Is our father here? I didnae think he'd pay me dowry.'

He pursed his lips, shook his head and opened his mouth to speak. Only, he seemed to think better of it. He glanced over his shoulder, at Alasdair, silhouetted in the door. He was still busy doing the rents. Something had changed in her brother. He was guarded. What had been going on?

'Is there somewhere discreet? I need tae speak tae ye both.'

'This way.'

First she called Caitlin, then quietly led him into the chamber Alasdair called a solar. Then, not liking Angus' pallor, she raided Alasdair's *uisge beatha*, pouring a toothful into a cup. And almost shrieked when her husband stopped her. How had he got there so fast? And more to the point, how had he known they were there?

'He sent ye tae keep her in check, didn't he?' Alasdair's voice was low and oddly detached.

Angus nodded. What were they talking about?

'Blood first. MacMhathain are the false king's *tykes*. The lot,' Angus admitted. 'Only, ah cannae do that. Not after seeing ye both.'

Jesus, Joseph and Mary! She returned to the *uisge beatha*, to find it gone. Alasdair invited Angus to sit. What about her? Oh, damn it! She perched on Alasdair's knee, only for him to pull her closer. Really? He might as well have pissed on her.

'Will you both speak plain Gaelic?' She held up her hand to stop Alasdair. 'Ah ken he disnae like Robert, but the Comyns are in no position tae claim anything.'

Her brother was shaking his head. 'Something's changing, Mordag. Ah dinnae ken what, but you're in danger here.'

'The rebellion is centred on this place, Lord only kens why,' interjected Alasdair.

Angus had dropped his gaze; he always did that when he was fighting himself. And her husband was giving nothing away. Or was he? His eyes were as dark as they had been that time they were caught at court. She loved her brother, but this was another way she could repay Alasdair.

'Angus?' she prodded.

'Not here, her. Lady Turberville.'

'Who?'

'The Countess o Kintail.'

Chapter 27

Alasdair had needed time alone after that revelation. Mordag had all but dragged her brother from the chamber at his request. He had not quite caught what she said. Something about short garments? Alas, that was the least of his concerns. Baron Macnachten was deeply involved, yet intelligence suggested the remaining Comyn heads were not. Either they were much better at hiding it or thoroughly disinterested.

Yet that paled compared to his missing the connection. Seeing it for what it now was: a babe contracted to a boy who was loyal to a fault and likely to stay that way. And one who happened to need rewarding handsomely for saving his king's life.

So who were the Turbervilles? What were they to the Comyn? And what was their status to warrant such actions on both sides? His eyes fell on the bestiary; damn that thing. Every attempt to open it had failed. It must contain the answers he sought. Yet in the back of his mind, he knew it would not be as simple as that. Angered by his inability to do what was expected of him, he grabbed his writing material. At least he had a name this time.

A knock at the door. What was needed now? The rents were done and Jock knew not to disturb him. He hid the missive he was working on behind a fresh piece of parchment. 'Enter.'

Mordag and Angus again, though now the boy wore his old *léine*, dotted with pins. He had torn it just the other day. Fixing it would have made it too tight on him, ,but not Angus. The boy could have it. Alasdair waited for Mordag to get her sewing items. Neither moved; they shared what he recognised to be Mordag's stubborn countenance.

'Angus believes he can find out more. Play the dutiful son who is eager tae dae his bidding. He'll bring word when he visits tae remind me o me place,' stated Mordag.

He blinked. Angus could do what?

'Fer surely the king and this Raven me sister speaks o would want tae ken?' added Angus.

Alasdair's first instinct was to scold her, but he held back. The Raven was no secret in itself. But, Christ's teeth, he could not in good conscience send a pup to do his bidding. If Angus wished to prove his loyalty to Robert, it must be by some other means. He placed his quill down and folded his arms.

'Nae. More than nae, I forbid it! Ye're too young, Angus, and this is no trifling matter. They will kill ye, and Mordag too, when – not if – they discover ye.'

'You're an ambassador, and ye've no been killed.'

If only it was that simple. Clever or not, the boy was showing his swaddle.

'Ambassadorial spying is different. It's expected. What yer father plans is treason, no stately prying. And ye have absolutely no experience or ability tae mask yer intentions. Let alone any other forms of control.'

Proving his point, Angus's face darkened before shifting again.

'And dinnae even think about going behind my back.'

Were it not so serious, he would have laughed at Angus's shock.

'But yer brother had saved Robert's life by my age!' the boy protested.

'Aye and it almost killed him, ye *sumph*. My answer is still nae.'

Lord have mercy, was he as argumentative as Angus at that age? No, he would not permit himself to answer that. He looked to Mordag. She had fallen uncharacteristically silent, and her face was pale. He pushed back his chair, intending to comfort her.

'Alasdair's right, Angus. It's far too dangerous fer ye,' she admitted.

'And ye,' Alasdair practically growled at her, lest she be thinking of anything foolish, before taking her in his arms.

She did not protest but clung to him instead. He closed his eyes and kissed her forehead. His plans, should they need to leave quickly, were coming along nicely. But with God as his witness, he swore a silent oath. He would do everything he could to not let it come to that. Pulling slightly away, he grinned at them both.

'Let's no talk of this anymore. Ye have a *léine* that needs sewing.'

'And trews lengthening,' Mordag added with a mutter.

*

Samhain, Alasdair's favourite festival. For what other night was a child permitted to stay up all night *and* make as much noise as he could? Now, most of them slept on benches, laps, or wherever they had fallen. He grinned. They were not alone. Jock had surprised him by running sprightly around the manor with his torch aloft. Of course, Seumas could not bear to be outdone; the two had provided ample entertainment with increasingly difficult challenges. Though he had drawn the line at caber-tossing. Seumas could barely toss straight when sober.

He took the proffered cup of broth from the cook, turned, and was crippled by something hard hitting his knees. A boy of two was struggling to look up at him from beneath a helmet.

'Och, Jamie, what ye doing in that?'

The boy lifted his toy sword high and struck it down on the metal of the helmet. Alasdair exchanged the cup for the boy, making him laugh.

'Ye ken ye're no supposed tae hit yerself over the head with yer sword, right? Ye're meant tae hit others with it, like that man over there.'

He pointed at the passed-out Seumas before setting Jamie down again. The babe lifted his sword high to charge – but before he could hit Seumas, the helmet made him stumble. It flew off the child's head towards… Christ's teeth! Seumas's pained yells filled the air. He quickly grabbed the broth and hurried towards Mordag, discretion being the better part of valour and all.

She shot him an odd look, but welcomed him back

inside the plaid they shared. He gave her the drink before holding her to him closely, awaiting the first light of dawn. Silence fell upon everyone.

Turberville.

English, likely, but what did that matter? There had been a blurring of familial names long before Edward's coup. Many had owned land on both sides of the border. His eyes fell on the cage. But was it a long shot to dismiss England as a source? He considered Angus. The lad sat alone, staring into the flames. Had he not proven that information could come from the unlikeliest of sources? But who to approach there? That kingdom, though appearing strong, was in utter turmoil.

He blinked as those around him stirred. Ah, first light! Gently, he nudged Mordag, and she lifted her head drowsily. 'Tae bed with ye. Ah'll join as soon as ah'm able.'

*

Someone woke Alasdair with a gentle shake. Had he fallen asleep at his studies again? Cailean? No, it was too light; he blinked sleepily and sat up. He was at Druim Earbainn and the hand that shook him was Mordag's.

'What have ye been doing? Ah was worried sick. Jock found ye. Ye look awful.'

He blinked and gestured to his work, only the table was bare. Where had the Raven's messages gone? And the seal stamp itself? Jock? Wait. Had she also said she was worried sick? He grinned up at her; she did care for him!

She tutted. 'Ye're fevered from lack o sleep.'

'Tis no sleep that fevers me, Mordag.'

She was already pulling him from his chair towards the door. Bone tired as he was, his loins stirred. The vigil had barely affected her. In the full light of day, she looked as radiant as ever. And she was leading him to their chamber! He was not dreaming; she too wanted him.

He struggled to watch her through unfocused eyes as she undressed him. Christ, he had never been this lucky! He pulled her to him, nuzzling her neck. She tutted again and turned, evading his grasp.

'Mordag, please.'

She turned back towards him and smiled, pressing on his chest. But still did not speak. He was as weak as a newborn babe. He fell back onto their bed. She lay next to him and ran her hand through his hair. It felt good but was not what he wanted. He wrapped his arms around her as she did it again, silently begging. She gave him a kiss, as soft as down feather.

She was toying with him! And he naught but a mouse caught between her paws. Fine, he would do as she wished. Let her play with his hair as much as she wanted. If only his eyes were not so damned heavy…

Alasdair nuzzled his head into the pillow, vaguely aware of the noises below. Something soft and round warmed his exposed back. Mordag? No, he was alone. He shifted slightly and it let out a loud purr. What was the cat doing in their chamber? He tried to wave an arm to shoo it off. It got up, spun around and started pawing his back. He winced as sharp claws dug into his flesh. Enough, he was not a pin cushion! He pushed himself off the bed and cursed bitterly as the cat tried desperately to cling to his skin.

'Away with ye!'

The tabby-striped creature took not the slightest bit of notice. He snorted and got up to relieve himself. Mordag walked in while he was at the pot. He glanced back at her. She was carrying their freshly laundered clothing.

'How long did I sleep?'

'The call tae nones has no long passed.'

He groaned; he had wasted most of the day. Finished, he took the proffered undershirt and pulled it over his head. It smelt of the bush it had been laid out on. She had likewise laid out a fresh *léine*, trews and his belt for him. He blinked. The apples, the clothing. And luring him to bed to settle him like a bairn. Was she mothering him? Surely he did not come across as that lost?

He ran his comb through his hair – wretched knots – and watched her. She had changed from her older kirtle into the blue gown. Gone was the headscarf, replaced with a flowing veil and the silver circlet. Magnificent! She glanced at him and blushed. Definitely not mothering. He put the comb down and held out his hand.

'Come, my lady wife, let us brighten the lives of everyone below with yer presence.'

She rolled her eyes but took his hand. Together they descended for the saints' feast.

The hall had returned to its normal state. Well, as normal as it could be with a bench. It would still be some time before the new head chairs arrived. With luck, before spring. Mordag was his queen, no less, and looked just as regal as she sat. He gave those attending a brief speech on remembering the sacrifices of saints, as they were already struggling to stay awake. Let them eat and retire early.

He sat and waved Jock away. While the man did far more than a seneschal's duties, he really did not need to cut and serve the dishes. There was no one to impress and the manor was not the stately hall of Eilean Donnain. What his brother would give to swap places with him!

'What's making ye laugh?' asked Mordag.

'The irony of one's order of birth.'

He placed the meat of a salmon onto their trencher.

'What about it? Do ye no longer wish tae be here?'

'Och no; no that! Rather the opposite. Have ye ever heard of the Sword of Damocles?'

'What has a man's sword got tae dae with birth order?' She suddenly put down her spoon. 'It's no another one o yer damned eu… euphantisms, is it?'

His lips twitched; she was trying her best.

'No – well, yes, but no in the manner you're thinking.'

He took a sip of wine to moisten his throat. A shout announcing a messenger bid his story to wait. The messenger bore no patch, so had not come from Robert. He walked around the table to meet the kneeling man.

'Who sent it?'

'The seneschal of Pillanflatt, my lord. He said it couldnae wait, and ye would, well, ye ken.'

John? Why would he send something so openly?

'Jock, pay the man well. And feed him too,' he called out before addressing the messenger. 'If ye wish tae make more then dinnae wander away.'

He tore the seal and scanned the contents. It was the hand of his interrogator. It spoke of rats having escaped terriers. And of one particularly large specimen that was spotted scurrying north. He cursed violently.

'What is it?'

Mordag's voice sounded as taut as he felt. He set his jaw hard and drew her away from the hall. But stopped near the safe room's door, so that Jock could overhear too.

'Pray, Mordag. Pray that a single strand of horsehair can keep us all safe.'

Chapter 28

The snow descended the hills early and Cailean did not like it. The cows were safe, but some sheep still remained, and travelling was disrupted. If it lingered, they would be nigh cut off until spring. A glance confirmed most were equally unimpressed. Aside from the children. From the ramparts, he had a good view of their game. His inner bailey, it seemed, was now a tourney field. The children gathered at each end with Donald and Ewan adjudicating. They knew better than to stand dead centre. He should not, but why not?

'Release!' he roared.

Snowballs flew. Sure enough, the children aimed for the men. Cailean left them to it. By the time he made it to the hall door, the children had charged. Somewhere beneath them, his men.

'I ken that ye will make a great father someday, my lord husband, but I also fear the mischief ye encourage amongst them.'

He glanced at the pile of plaids that hid Sorcha. And she still looked pale.

'Better they tire themselves out here. Come, ye should be inside.'

She gave no protest.

Cailean set her in her chair, next to the fire. Ordered hot spiced wine and kept a watch. She had been sleeping well, he knew, for the dark mornings made him linger. Often, he lay holding her sleeping form. It felt right. Other times, he kissed her awake. No matter how sleepy, she never denied him.

'Jesus, the weans are brutal,' Ewan drawled.

'Did ye hear what set them off?' replied Donald.

'Nae. But then, I wasnae expecting an attack, was I?'

Cailean blinked and tore his eyes from Sorcha. Donald and Ewan settled nearby, removing sodden and soiled garments. He raised an eyebrow at them. They did not notice – the wine had arrived. Sorcha was reluctant to take any until their eyes met. Better.

'*Mo ciann*, were ye no on the ramparts?' asked Donald.

'Aye.'

'What did ye see?'

'Future clansmen following orders.' Why were they gawping at him? 'Well, ye were stood out in the open.'

Donald struck his knee and guffawed loudly.

'Well, I'll be damned. He tricked us, he did!' proclaimed Ewan.

He openly stared. Ewan's speech had sped up to match that of a normal man's. He was that enthused by a jest?

Their smiles suddenly departed. Now Cailean smiled. There were only two who could do that. Himself and… Bridget screeched, followed closely by Iona. The women hauled away their husbands; giving lectures as they went.

He chuckled and then winced. They had spotted their children.

'Och, perhaps ye were right.'

Sorcha did not reply. He frowned. A glance confirmed what he suspected. He took the goblet from her still hand. The bed was better than a chair.

*

A one-off, Cailean had assumed, brought on by the weather. A sennight later and if she stayed still, she slept. And slept at night, too. He dared not kiss her awake now. She also lacked appetite. He'd sent for the healer to find her gone, visiting her expectant daughter. Where? Somewhere near Diùirinis! He glanced at Sorcha's trencher; she'd barely touched it. At least she was not getting worse.

'With yer blessing, my lord husband, I shall retire early,' she said quietly.

What could he do but nod? He had a guest to entertain. Father Messi. Intended for his aunt's convent, he had landed there instead. The damned weather! Cailean feigned interest; how did anyone sit through his conversation? Then he suggested an after-dinner game of chess. Yes! Anything to shut him up! He sent a page for his board and instructed the staff to leave his table up.

The boy returned empty-handed, his face flushed. Hamish caught the lad first, intending to box his ears. His hand hung in the air. He let the boy go and hurried towards Cailean. The seneschal bent down and spoke into his ear. *She was what?*

'Apologies, father.'

Not giving the priest time to finish his sentence, Cailean bolted towards his chamber.

Shoving open the door, he heard Sorcha's retching. She had her head over a bucket and behind her, Ailis lingered. At the fire, his alewife was heating some brew.

'How long?' he demanded, rounding on her.

'*Mo ciann*, me lady has been sick fer several days.'

'And no one thought tae tell me?'

'We were forbidden. Besides, it will pass soon enough.'

He blinked. What was she blathering about?

'Cailean, dinnae worry yerself,' Sorcha panted and held out her arm.

He rushed to her, pushing Ailis aside. He helped his wife to the bed, then unpinned her hair, its vibrance striking against her white skin. She looked… she looked like… but Ruth had burned with fever. Sorcha's forehead was cool. She pushed his hand away.

'I'll be fine. I trust Tealag.'

The alewife was approaching the bed, the warmed drink in her hand. He kept his guard up.

'Tis naught but some malt and ginger tae settle my lady's stomach,' Tealag explained.

He reluctantly let her past. Sorcha took it and sipped. She pulled a face but did not put it down.

'See? I'm fine. I'll no break while ye accommodate our guest. And I'll be right here when ye come tae bed,' she insisted.

She was right. He could not neglect his duty. 'Fine, but if ye're sick again…'

'…I will send word,' she finished for him, and settled

back into the bed. He sighed, stood up and collected his board. He felt so useless.

*

'Ye appear most distracted, Sir Cailean. Is it yer wee wife? I had assumed it was her normal complexion, but now I fear it is no?'

Cailean sighed. He had played poorly, only avoiding defeat by chance. How could Tealag not be concerned? Come to think of it, neither were Bernice or Iona.

He studied the board. 'The weather changed, she became listless. No interest in food.'

'Ah. Aye. I have heard of that before, my dear man.'

He looked up, no longer interested in the game. The priest gave him a comforting smile.

'Saw it in an English knight at Stirling Castle when I had the displeasure of overseeing their spiritual needs during those final months. She is from the borders, is she no? Were I a betting man, I'd wager she is more used tae rain than snow.'

Cailean stared, not understanding.

'The knight hailed from somewhere near Dover. His humours simply struggled with the change in weather. He barely rose from his bed and had tae be tempted tae eat. Come spring, he was hale again. Ye wouldnae ken him tae be the same man.'

That must be it! Her humours had proven fickle before, so why not now? The women must have recognised it. His lips twitched upwards. He motioned to the board.

'Shall we start afresh?'

'Aye, let's. I wish tae see yer true skill.'

They reset the board. Cailean's curiosity got the better of him. 'Tell me, did he ever adjust?'

'Och aye, he resides here permanently now. Pretty little place, right next tae a nice brook.'

He sighed. 'Bannockburn.'

The priest agreed, his smile most unchristian.

*

Early winter brought the people together. They gathered in Cailean's hall, in clusters. He divided his attention between them, but always returned to Sorcha, and his closest kin. Now, he sat watching his hounds enjoy the attention of some children. He knew they secretly played with the hounds; but tonight, they had finally braved asking his permission.

Donald cursed. He glanced across to where his cousin sat with Sorcha.

'Send me intae battle one-handed, and I'll come off victorious. But this – well, ye defeat me every time!' He laid down his king.

'Dinnae lose faith, Donald. My gameplay, just like yer swordplay, comes from an early, vigorous, training.'

Chess, stalking indoors, well read. His brother was identical. No, not from childhood like her, but later. After his fostering. Cailean had never given it a second thought, but now it irked him. Why? The children were called to their beds; they shyly thanked him. His lips twitched as he nodded. He only half-listened to the gameplay discussion. His mind was back at Henderleithen, how Thomas had appeared feeble.

'...Chess is more than battle... I sacrificed that pawn tae gain...' Snippets of Sorcha's discussion. The 'we' that priest spoke of, and her brother's attack.

'Ah had planned... but when ye...' Donald's reply. Adapting to a new threat, the mercenaries.

'...I could see yer plan...' Sorcha again. Thomas and his father knew each other. Strategised in this very place. Thomas raised Sorcha for the king. His father knew who she was. He stayed silent for the king. Cailean looked at the rook Sorcha placed on the board. Who were they to Robert? *Rook, knight, pawn...*

'How could ah no see it?' asked a frustrated Donald, breaking his thought. His cousin stared at the board.

'We are good at seeing what we wish tae see, or so Pa would say,' replied Sorcha.

Cailean snorted; Alasdair said the same.

'Nothing, just thinking of me brother,' he responded to their curious gazes.

Sorcha smiled warmly.

'Lord willing, in the spring.'

'Unlikely. We have our duties.'

'Forgive me, *mo ciann*,' Bridget interrupted, having recently joined the group, 'but I have held my tongue fer too long...'

He caught Donald's eyebrow rising, and silently agreed. Bridget was never quiet.

'...Duty be damned. There is far more than it. And ye have sacrificed more than most, but after what Donald told me, ah thought ye'd finally seen that.'

'Dinnae bring me intae this, wife!'

'Hold them all close. For ye will never ken when

"duty" will rip them from ye.' Her eyes flicked between him and Sorcha.

Was that not what he was doing? Damn it. The whole clan was Cailean's family! He intended to silence her, but she had stormed off, Donald trailing. He could not hear what they said. Or rather argued. Yet Sorcha would not meet his eye. What in the Lord's name?

The door to the hall crashed open.

'The earl, is he here? I must give this tae him at once!' a stranger, staggering, exhausted beyond measure, cried out.

A runner? Sent in this weather? He rose. 'I'm here; speak.'

'Ah cannae.'

Sinking to his knees, the runner held up a missive.

Cailean took it and glanced at the seal. God's balls! How far had he come? He broke it and read. The handwriting was spidery. Different yet familiar. A hand ripped the missive from him. *Sorcha*. How dare she be so impudent?

'Upstairs.'

His growl died on his lips. She was not reading it; instead, she pieced back together the seal. Her body was shaking. She set upon the messenger, thrusting the missive under his nose.

'What sick game is this that ye play? Who sent ye? A man from Glasgow? Tell me! I demand tae ken!'

He grabbed her. She fought him bitterly, spitting with rage. This – it could not be her humours, could it? From melancholic to caustic?

'Ah... ah cannae!"

'Tell me!' she shrieked.

This was beyond acceptable. He hauled her towards their chambers, calling for the man to be cared for. Up the stairs, she kicked and writhed. She screamed curses he recognised from a flyting. Aimed at him and not the poet's intended. What had possessed her?

He threw her down onto their bed. She rose. He grabbed her and threw her down once more.

'Enough, Sorcha!' he roared into her face.

Had she been a man, he would have used his hand. She stilled; her fight frightened out of her. Her veil half hanging off. Her eyes; she was crying. Because of him? No. It was a part of her rage.

'Please, let me go! Ye dinnae understand. I need tae ken!' she begged pitifully.

'Ken what, Sorcha?' What little patience he had left dwindled.

'Why the letter has Pa's seal!'

He reared back. Was she deluded? Thomas was a horse trader. Yet what minor laird would be granted a secretive wardship? And who was the most secretive man in Robert's employ? The changed handwriting. And Sorcha did not jump to conclusions – she thought it from Michael. God's balls, Thomas was Robert's spymaster! And worse: his replacement was warning that Michael was free.

Chapter 29

Sorcha set her drop spindle down and stretched her weary body. Last winter she had spun for hours with little difficulty. Now, she felt overburdened after just an hour. Despite Cailean's insistence, it felt more than just her humours. But what did she know? The nausea came and went as it pleased. And, most inconveniently, it was triggered by smells that had never previously bothered her.

She stopped just outside the door, having sought fresh air. Oh, for goodness' sake! Had they not shifted the dung to the mainland yet? The weather had broken days ago! She tried to swallow her ire. Whatever ailed her, it was making it hard to control herself. She had nigh-on lost all when she saw the seal. Not that Cailean was telling her much about that; he uttered nothing more than it being a seal held by whoever held office for the king.

A load of gong, by all accounts. He was hiding something from her.

No, that was foolish. He likely thought it unimportant,

like he had Douglas's revelation. Sorcha sighed. She must trust him to do what was right. She smiled politely as a guard passed. Oh, this was useless! The air from the solar window should be sweeter. Let it also rid her of whatever plagued her mind.

She glanced through the latticework before climbing the steps. Another meeting with another chieftain. In the chamber, Ailis greeted her and continued to sing softly. She was still giddy with the news that betrothal negotiations had begun. Sorcha could not help but smile. The lightness paired perfectly with the breeze coming off the loch.

'Spring cannae come soon enough, Ailis.'

'Aye, my lady.' Followed by a giggle, no doubt caused by the knowledge that spring would bring a return to court. One that would coincide with both fathers meeting.

'Ye ken, I'll be expected tae have a new gown for the royal christening.'

Why had Ailis stopped singing? She found the girl blushing. 'Aye, my lady.'

'I dinnae see why my maid shouldnae have one too.'

Indeed, Ailis would need it, for her gown had grown tighter across both bust and hip. Her maid's eyes widened.

'My lady is most kind.'

She nodded before returning to look out the window. Whereas she had first found being surrounded by water unsettling, she now welcomed its music. She closed her eyes and focused, clearing her thoughts. The window shut abruptly. Cailean. When had he joined them? She leaned back into him, welcoming his embrace.

'Leave it open,' she murmured, as he pulled her away.

'Nae, ye'll catch your death.'

She stiffened before forcing herself from his arms. Cailean's eyebrows creased. That was it! That was what was irking her. Not her damned humours.

'Ailis, go and find Iain,' she ordered coldly.

The door had barely shut when his ire let loose. 'God's balls, Sorcha, what is it now? I only came up here tae see ye well.'

'What is it now? Really? Can ye honestly no see? Because tae me, it looks like I'm captive on a damned island. In someone else's tower!'

She stalked back to the window and flung it open. As if to prove her point, he followed and shut it again with a growl.

'I'll no hear this. Tis yer humours. Naught else.'

'Naught else? Do ye take me for a *sumph*, Cailean? First, I can only travel on yer land or tae court. Then I mustnae go any further than the dock. Then the castle walls, despite the raids having ended – aye, Donald told me, because ye will no speak of it with me. And now – now I'm no even allowed tae open a window!'

'Ye. Are. Ailing,' he spat out, between gritted teeth.

Why was he so pig-headed? She stormed into their bedchamber, Cailean hot on her heels. Sorcha spun around sharply, forcing him to stop, and stomped her foot in warning.

'*Win aff your heich naig* fer once! I am no aboot tae *funder under a dadding wyndis*!'

He blinked slowly. Lord give her strength! He had spoken Scots well enough at court! She flung both her arms up.

'I had more freedom at Henderleithen!' she hissed.

Cailean grabbed her forearms, his fingers digging hard into her skin, eyes coldly staring into her as he swung her around. A vein pulsated in his neck. He did not shout.

'Dinnae speak o what ye dinnae ken, woman. I have done nought but protect ye at the expense of me own clan. Me own brother!'

Sorcha shook her head and tried, viciously, to remove his grip. She knew that look. It often came before… He tightened his grip and even shook her. She hissed and squeezed her eyes shut, ready.

'That man ye insist on calling "Pa" was no decent man. He was yer damned guard. And a poor one at that. Ye were nought but a pawn tae him. He kenned that Michael beat ye and he permitted – encouraged it!'

A sharp crack was followed by a stinging pain in the palm of her hand. A red weal appeared on Cailean's face. She gasped. *What had she done?* He pushed her back, growled and stepped forwards. He looked… he looked… She swallowed, ready to accept it. His eyes widened and he shook his head.

'Damn ye, Sorcha!'

He was gone, torn to shreds by her own vicious doing. She staggered and sank to the floor as an icy hand of coldness choked her from within. Michael was right; she was nothing but evil. A roar from below and the sound of approaching thunder. Let it take her, she had naught else now. She'd driven away the one person she had left. The one she loved the most. The sound stopped next to her, and from all sides, hands grasped her.

*

'Please, my lady, ye need tae rest.'

Sorcha did not take her stinging eyes off Cailean, clinging to the window instead. It was past matins and still he was out there. Man or post, it mattered not. He attacked them all without mercy. And when his weapon broke, he simply picked up another. Her vanity, her selfishness, had done this to him. It had destroyed what little they had built together. She shook her head. She was not worthy of rest or peace while he battled below. He staggered, falling against the wood, clinging to it.

Someone placed a plaid over her shoulders. It was one he had recently worn. She turned to tell them to take it away, but they were no longer there. The chamber sat empty; even Ailis had fled her side. It was only right. She was to marry into the clan and she, Sorcha, was an outsider. A fraud, a border Sassenach. She would use what coin she had access to and return to Elizabeth's side, if she would let her. At least there she could never hurt Cailean again. And Alasdair, he could keep her lands. An apology, for she could not do what he had instructed. She could not draw Cailean out.

She must leave. His bedchamber was no longer the place for her. Tonight, she would take a pallet in the solar. And the day after, the barn, if he permitted it. Stopping at her chest, she lifted its lid, for she still had an old kirtle in there, somewhere. She would need it to keep warm.

'Donald… was right…'

Sorcha cracked her head on the lid in her haste. Pain seared through it and streaks of light danced in her vision.

No, she had not misheard, Cailean was really there, standing in the doorway. Sweaty and swaying, his *léine* long gone and his undershirt ruined. He did not move; reluctant almost? Did her wish her to leave by the servants' door? To be bolted shut after she walked through? Their eyes met; she reared back. So often she had seen what lay beyond his stone-faced countenance. But what she saw there now… It was raw pain, need and – no, her eyes were deceiving her. Unless he hoped to move a mistress in.

Her lips moved, her voice, trembling, spoke of its own accord. 'I love ye.'

She caught him as he fell into her arms. Down they went together, clinging like drowning seamen did to flotsam. She was too weak-willed and too greedy, for she could not do it. She could not leave him. There was something wet on her neck; it trickled down between her breasts and was joined by more. She clung to him tighter as his shoulders shook, her own face growing wet.

She should be begging him for forgiveness. Promising to never let her ire get the better of her. Or to raise her hand. Yet her tongue would not let the words out. Instead, Alasdair's words haunted her. Was this what he meant?

Her lips finally parted. 'Tell me.'

Cailean's words came slowly at first, then faster like a surge of water along a river after a heavy deluge. She said nothing. He spoke of his fears, his shyness, living in the shadow cast by his grandfather's greatness and his father's ambitions. Driven to protect his clan and to serve the rightful heir to the crown. *At all cost.* She cradled his head in her lap and gently stroked his hair. How they'd got there, she could not recall.

'From the moment I saw ye, I wanted ye. No matter the cost. When he…' Cailean paused and sighed. 'Ah should have gutted him that night.'

Her hand faltered and she quickly remedied it. He had tasted freedom, only to realise the illusion upon the arrival of their betrothal contract. Exactly how she had been feeling. So why was it an illusion?

She tested the waters. 'He's no here though. And I'm safe with ye and our clan. Whatever ails me will no kill me.'

Cailean looked away before looking back. 'That missive, it brought word. He's free, Sorcha. And we dinnae ken where. Or who with.'

She squeezed her eyes shut in a wince. He had been protecting her. Her hand rested over his scar. Where she had struck him.

'And tae think I lashed out. I am so very sorry, Cailean.'

'No. I shouldnae have grabbed ye. Nor hid things from ye.'

'Ye were only trying tae protect me and I was being pig-headed.'

'It's no excuse. I hid other things from ye too.'

'Like?'

Again he paused, though this time she sensed he was looking for the right words.

'Ah ken Thomas was like a father, but he was more. He was Robert's eyes and ears. That seal was the mark of the Raven.'

Sorcha sat up sharply. She could feel him staring. No. That was just a story. But then – 'The Lion, the Raven and the Phoenix.'

'What?'

'Pa used tae tell me this story...'

She recited it.

'Yer mither never contradicted his words?'

'Never. I was too young to see it, but I do now. Caelian, her death...'

She looked away for she had but a taste of Pa's grief. After a moment's silence, Cailean replied, 'I was wrong. Him and my father. God's balls, I cannae think straight!'

'I think Alasdair will ken.'

She did not know why. Perhaps it was because he was so similar to Pa. Cailean nodded in agreement and suddenly looked drained. She quietened and stroked his hair again.

'*We* will write tae him.'

Sorcha did not reply.

He must have been exhausted. His breathing slowed and his head became heavier. She would not disturb him. Instead, she stared at the window where the darkness of night was becoming a murky grey. *A new day, a new clarity.* She mused, turning the night's events over in her mind and looking at them from different angles. One thing became clear: though he spoke not of love, Cailean needed her as much as she needed him.

She blinked and looked down at his sleeping form. Once, she and Evelyn had quietly observed a marital quarrel. 'When a person tries tae build a relationship alone, they always collapse under their own strain,' Evelyn had said. 'A bridge must be built together, meeting in the middle for it tae be stable. That is how a good marriage thrives'. Could it be that they were now building the same bridge? She dared not hope, but at the same time, she knew that when the day came that Cailean admitted his love, it would mark the placing of the keystone.

Chapter 30

Winter was easy to hate. Mordag loathed leaving a warm bed when nature called. She detested how the shortened days left her with little vigour. And no amount of soaking rid food of the salt it was preserved in. She shot back into the bed and, frozen, pressed herself against Alasdair. Her cold skin made him stir enough to mutter her name and fling an arm over her. Her shivers soon stopped, but sleep eluded her. Alasdair had begun his usual mumblings by the time her lids felt heavy. She snorted softly.

'…Ruth…'

What? Mordag's eyes shot open; he was still fast asleep. No, he had promised her. But since she gave herself to him – the late nights, the scratches on his back. She had thought it other things, but now – foolish, foolish woman! Just as a fox could not befriend a hen, a whorer could not be loyal.

Damn him! He had played her too well! She rolled over, pulling free of his arms. Why was she crying? Damn this Ruth! But no, she could not damn her. Men always took what they wanted. And he wanted a warm wife as well as a mistress. Well, he'd get one or the other. And it would not be her begging him! Damn it, stop crying. He is not worth tears!

Sleep never returned. Instead, she feigned it when he woke. He pressed himself into her back, his hardness against her backside as he kissed her neck. How she did not tense, or worse, she had not a clue. He growled, it felt spitefully right, and then felt her forehead. What in God's name was that about? Whatever it was, he got up after it. Gone to seek his strumpet no doubt.

She only 'woke' properly when Caitlin entered, bringing blessedly warm water. They had the carding and spinning of the unsold wool to do, though her maid first had the chambers to straighten. Mordag briskly rubbed her face dry and caught Caitlin's off-guard look.

'Ah've told ye before tae speak yer mind.'

'Aye, my lady, but there is a time and place for it. This is no that time.'

'Ah'll decide that.'

The older woman sighed. 'Fine. Have you and Alasdair argued? He's no one tae be so foul but he just snapped at Jock.'

Hah, Ruth must have been busy! She brushed it off, saying he'd just woken up that way, but Caitlin looked unconvinced. Mordag dressed quickly and hurried to the hall, ignoring the ache she felt within.

She smiled out of politeness as she joined the others. Picking up a pair of paddles, she lapsed into silence, not joining in when the singing started up. Unable to stop herself, she eyed each woman in turn. None of them were called Ruth, unless they had given a false name. Most were nothing special either. A cad he was, but if the court rumours were true, he was picky.

Mordag sighed and stopped. She just could not find any appeal in working. What was wrong with her? It was a perfect distraction. Setting the paddles down, she headed for a side table. It contained drinks, and a few morsels to stop them from flagging. Nothing tempted her.

Sensing his eyes, she looked around and met his stare. Annoyed, she spun back around and filled a cup with ale.

'Good morn, my lady wife.'

His hands snaked around her hips and drew her towards him. She pulled herself free, spun and thrust the cup into his hands.

'My lord husband,' she must keep her tone neutral, 'I trust ye slept well.'

'Mordag...'

Damn it, what was it with her forehead? She forced his hand down off it and refused to look him in the eye. Get away from her! She sidestepped around him, coming face to face with Seumas. He was shaking his head in a warning to her. What did he know? He was not married to the toad; no, he most certainly encouraged his friend to whore. She glared at him and marched past.

*

Yule, a time of laughter and loving, or so Mordag had been taught. She alone watched them put the log on the fire. The hall was full of good cheer, the people oblivious. She hardly saw the toad now. When he invited her into the solar in the evenings, she begged tiredness. And was still 'asleep' when he woke in the morning. If he was there at all. He no longer bothered her, going to *her* instead.

Yet she could not shake the icy pain inside her, made worse by her body demanding his touch. Why would it not accept that she was never his? Damn it, she should not linger. The eggs needed collecting and the cleared path had become ice. Something else to focus on.

She grabbed her mantle from its peg, put it on and wrinkled her nose. The store chamber was doubling as a guard hall, but the path to the barn used its door. Granted, the men kept the area tidy but, well, they always transformed into boys when unsupervised. Naked, stinking, foulmouthed boys. Thank the Virgin it was empty. She hurried through and reached for the latch.

A hand pushed it back down. 'Ye're no going out in that, Mordag, let someone else do it.'

The toad. A tired toad. She swung around to confront him. 'Ah'm perfectly able tae do it meself.'

'I've no doubt of that, but ye've been exhausted.' He ran a hand through his hair. 'We both have. Let's just go and hold each other, aye?'

Was that what he called it now? She pulled away and lifted her chin high. Damn her body, she was repulsed and wanton. She could no longer keep it to herself.

'Dinnae ye dare touch me, ye good fer nowt *tyke*! I ken exactly what ye've been up tae and I'll no settle fer it, ye hear me?'

His eyes widened and he took a step towards her, hand out. She easily dodged his grasp; at least her father had 'taught' her that.

'Mordag, I dinnae ken what ye've heard but...'

'Nae, dinnae ye "Mordag" me. Fer once, ye will listen tae me, Macmaghan. Ye broke yer promise tae me. Ye promised tae be faithful, but Father was right, ye MacMhathains are slimy creatures no even fit fer the bottom o me shoe!'

He pulled up short, his head twisting slightly. It poured from her like foul pus. With it, the releasing of the pain. Good. He should see exactly what he had destroyed.

'Unlike ye, I keep me promises so ah'll share me bed, but there'll no be any "holding". No now, no ever! Fer that ye can go tae that... that bitch Ruth!'

Silence.

Alasdair stood as still as a rock. His jaw tightened. Triumph upon seeing the pain in his eyes fell lacklustre at her feet. Why was she not happy? All mirth in his eyes gone. She tensed up. A sound of someone stirring to her left broke the silence, but she could not take her eyes off him.

'Seumas, escort the lady tae her chamber and hold her there. I will speak tae her later.'

That icy cold voice. Alasdair turned away and madness gripped her.

'I'll no be spoken about as if ah'm no here and—'

He spun on a penny and she recoiled.

'Nae, wife. Ye'll do as yer damned told for once, for ye ken nothing. Do ye hear me? Nothing!'

His shouted words washed over her with pure rage. It ripped the breath from her. Seumas caught her and she tore herself from his grasp and spun around again. An empty space where Alasdair had been standing. The pain she thought gone returned twofold. A damned convent was better than this!

'Lady Mordag,' Seumas warned.

She rounded on him, screaming at him to not touch her. It did nothing but make him fold his arms. Mordag stormed out of the chamber and up the steps, her skirts in her hand to make it faster. And slammed the door in his face.

How dare Seumas open it and come in? She grabbed the nearest thing – a bowl of dried flowers and herbs – and flung it at him. He avoided it, considered the door and then, incredibly, stalked after her.

'Ah dinnae ken what sort of man yer father was, but if ye were my daughter…' he growled menacingly.

Her anger grew, only to fall the closer he got. She stepped back nervously. What was he going to do with her?

'Good job I'm no, then – yer poor daughters!'

She had to get to the door. He caught her and threw her onto the bed. No! This was not what Alasdair said! He was to guard her, not to… She rolled over and climbed backwards until her back was pressed into the headboard. He stood looming at the end of the bed. She had nowhere to go. Please, Alasdair, where are you? Please come quickly. He could have her and all the women he wanted, if he would just stop this brute!

The anger on Seumas's face melted into horror. He shook his head. 'Christ's bones! Ah wasnae going tae dae that!'

She did not believe him. He moved away, back towards the door. She watched his every step but stayed silent. Her voice was better kept for screaming. He placed his head on the door, muttered something, and twisted around to face her.

'Mordag, if ah may?'

She did not permit or deny him. Just stared.

'Ah dinnae ken what ye've been through, but ah ken what Alasdair has overcome. Ah only swore tae our chief that ah'd keep him from any physical harm. But damn it, he's my best friend and ah'll no stand by and watch his heart break again. No after seeing what Ruth's death did tae him.'

Her mouth dried up. What was he talking about? Ruth was not his lover?

'She was his sister? Nae, his wife?'

Seumas cursed again. 'He didnae tell ye? Christ's bones. How did ye learn her name? No, dinnae tell me. He said it in his sleep, didnae he?'

Mordag nodded and slowly sank back down onto the bed. She kept her eyes on him, not really believing her ears. But the tone of his voice rang too true. She gestured to a stool but still stayed silent. She could not trust her mouth. He sat and rubbed the back of his neck.

'Ruth was his wife. Only ah didnae ken it at the time, but their parents did. Their love, it was naught but the intense love pups feel. And one a sickly wee runt at that. But after Grann's death, Alasdair must have worn Cailean down. He can be like that.'

He smiled and her lips flicked up briefly in acknowledgement, but he was staring at nothing.

'They had a beautiful wee ceremony in July. She was dead by January.'

Mordag closed her eyes. What had she done? Found him guilty without a chance to defend himself. *Just like her father.* She inhaled shakily. The pain inside her had shifted. Not for her but for Alasdair. Hot tears trickled down her face. Poor, innocent Alasdair.

'How did she die?' she somehow asked.

'Ah dinnae ken, I wasnae there at the time. He only told me once that she fell ill at the start of Yule. He never partook in the festivities after that.'

He had not been angry, but worried. Thought her ill and, worse, at Yule. She sat on the edge, her feet hanging over, clutching a pillow. She really was her spiteful, bitter father. Clinging to a belief forced into them both by other people. And what now? She had dealt him a bitter blow, tearing open old scars. If they were that old.

'How long ago was it?'

Her voice was flat to her ears. He had little more he could share, but he was kind enough to share his thoughts. He explained that while others had moved on, Alasdair had not. Despite appearances, her husband had never introduced Seumas to any woman. Until she came along, forcing him.

'Even that was me own hot-headedness,' she murmured.

'Aye, but ye make him happy. Anyone can see that.'

'I'm sorry, Seumas. Ah see now that ye tried to warn me. But it's up tae me now, ah must be the one tae apologise.'

And how to do it? Would he even accept it? All that poison. She glanced up. Alasdair's man and friend had not moved.

'I'll help ye, lass, for his sake, but if ye ever do anything like this again…'

'Ah'll flay meself. And, Seumas?'

'Aye?'

'Yer daughters are lucky tae have ye.'

*

The deft fall of Alasdair's axe split the wood asunder. He tossed one half aside and repeated the process with the other. For once, his hands itched to work alongside his mind. Mordag's attack had blindsided him. All because he had dared to display a modicum of concern. Yes, he had been distracted by intelligence, especially with news from France, but he was not oblivious. She had drawn within herself and slept more, terrifying him. Yet she still curled up to him when he found the strength to get there.

He softly snorted; to think his first fear was that she knew he was Robert's spymaster! Not some nonsensical rant about broken promises. He hesitated. Damn everything, she had ripped his heart clean from his chest. Who had told her about Ruth? He brought the axe down hard. And what possessed her to call Ruth a bitch?

He screwed his eyes shut. Those final days still haunted him. The fever had left her weak and clinging to life. Then the wasting. No matter what she ate, she had vanished before his eyes. Yet, she still professed that he made her the happiest woman alive. What a fool he had been that last day. He should never have ridden out. He could still feel the weight of her lifeless body in his arms. He should never have hounded Cailean.

Mordag had destroyed all but a modicum of his control. Christ, was this his reckoning? Had he not vowed at Ruth's grave to stay unwed? And worse, he had not thought of her until Jock asked about the damned Yule log. He reached for another piece of wood.

'If only Cailean did that when upset. The clan would no need fer firewood.'

'And there'd no be a tree left in Lochalsh. Ah thought I told ye tae stay with Mordag.'

He didn't raise his head, just kept chopping the wood. He heard Seumas settle on a stump and felt his eyes bore into him.

'Ye did, but she's no goin anywhere. I knocked – no literally, mind – some sense in tae her head. Ah'm here to do the same tae ye, though yers will be literal if necessary. Aye, I ken ye're my superior, but yer brother gave me some leeway.'

Alasdair spat and brought the axe down again. 'Why am I no surprised? He kenned I was no fit for this job.'

Everything was bitter. His marriage, his work for the king, this place!

'Och no, in that he was right. But ye're a damned *sumph* for no telling her. She's damaged as it is. No wonder she's put two and two together tae get five.'

'Ye're blathering,' he growled.

'She heard ye say Ruth's name in yer sleep. And because she kenned not of her, well, what did ye expect would happen?'

The axe hovered. Christ, no wonder she had lashed out, claiming broken promises. And then ordered him to join his lover, not his late wife! He laughed bitterly, lifting his face to the sky. *Sumph* indeed. Silence descended. He chucked down his axe and sat on the block. His head falling to his hands. He was exhausted. Seumas nudged him with a flask. He took it and almost drank it dry.

'In her own way, she was right. I still feel for Ruth, Seumas. I cannae shake her and give Mordag the full dedication she deserves.'

His friend coughed and shifted, 'It's no me ye should be talking this out with, but I've said it before, Alasdair, ye cannae live in the past.'

He nodded, returned the flask and stood up. He needed to speak with his wife.

*

Alasdair cautiously opened the door; no projectiles and no screams. Just silence. Movement on the bed caught his attention. Mordag nudged the cat away from her. She looked nothing like his proud shield-maiden. Perhaps the cat had mistaken her for a mouse. He slowly crossed the floor, unsure how to proceed.

Mordag got up and rushed towards him; he opened his arms. He blinked, clearing his vision. Where had she gone? He felt a tug on the bottom of his *léine*. She was on her knees! Her words a disarrayed bewilderment of Gaelic and Scots. Some, like forgive and wrong, he managed to make out. He took her hands and guided her to her feet.

He rubbed a tear from her cheek with his thumb. 'We've both been *sumphs*, aye? Shall we start again? Greetings, my lady, I am Alasdair, Son of Grann. What would ye like tae ken?'

It had not meant to be humorous, but it made her laugh. 'Oh, Alasdair!'

This time, she filled his arms and they kissed. Whatever he wanted to say fled him. She broke off and stepped back, blushing. Christ, he wanted her more now than ever. Dare he even try? She did not stop him as he pulled her gown off, then her kirtle and finally her chemise. She shivered as the air teased her skin.

He trailed a finger down to her nipple, already erect, and circled it. Her soft gasps of pleasure his reward. He cupped her breast in his hand. It fitted, as though made just for him. He greedily pressed his lips to hers. She relented, bending backwards, her womanhood pressed against him. He knew that beyond, inside the folds of her rose, she was ready for him. But she pulled back and reached for his *léine*. He grabbed it himself.

'Let me,' she insisted.

Alasdair dropped his hands. She undressed him like he had her. Taking her time, her fingers catching in his chest hair or running along the few scars he had. He closed his eyes and breathed in her earthy scent. She spun him around and guided him back towards their bed. Under her spell, he would let her do anything she wanted. Feeling the mattresses on the back of his legs, he sat on the bed and opened his eyes to look up at her.

Mordag's lips parted, only slightly; her eyes clouded with her lust and more. She pressed up between his open legs. He fondled her round buttocks and nibbled his way down the valley between her breasts, but she did not mount him as he wanted.

He bit back a growl. She was on her knees again. Her

hand curling around his erect shaft. He unintentionally bucked into it, commanded by the softest of squeezes. Wait, no, he dared not... Her soft lips, the heat of her mouth. Christ's teeth! *Where had she learned that*? He inhaled sharply and leaned back. He had never received a whore's kiss, let alone from the mouth of his wife! It felt – Christ, he had no words!

His breath quickened with the bobbing of her head. Every fibre of his being strained. Damn it, he was going to unman himself and spill his seed down her throat if she continued. He could not debase her like that!

'Mordag, please!' he croaked.

She complied, rising. In one swift movement, she straddled his lap and they joined together, his shaft buried deep within. Gone was their tenderness. He held her hips, wanting her to ride him hard and fast. To take his seed from him. She needed no such encouragement, nor even a touch between her lips. She bucked in his arms, her beautiful body alive as she cried out her release. He juddered and joined her with a cry of his own.

*

They lay on the bed, Alasdair holding her tight to his side. He watched her fingers weave in and out of his own. She still wore the pearl ring! He kissed the finger it sat on. Whatever he had with Mordag, it was different from what he had felt for Ruth. Seumas was right. It was time to see her as his future. He sighed softly.

'Ah'm sorry, ah should've told ye sooner. I've just never been able tae find the words.'

'Are there any words that rightly fit the pain of death?' she asked softly.

'For bards perhaps, but no us.'

'I'm sorry too, Alasdair. I jumped tae conclusions, despite how well ye've treated me.'

He kissed the top of her head. Lying back, he closed his eyes. He felt the cat land on the bed, pad over it and climb onto his stomach. He hissed and winced as it clawed at his skin.

Mordag gasped, ''Twas the cat!'

'Hmm? Oh, aye, it'll no leave me be.'

She knocked the cat off him and examined the scratches. Ignoring them and propping himself up on an elbow, he added, 'In truth, I've no treat ye well either.'

If he was to keep what he and Mordag had, he needed to be truthful. They were bound now, one under the eye of God. Nothing further could or should come between them.

'I've hid that I kenned about this uprising before we met. I was working on it – spying on yer father – when he thought me whoremongering. And when we met in the alcove.'

Her eyes widened, but she did not pull away. His head lowered.

'Ah dinnae ken Robert's plans, but ah dinnae want more war or, heaven forbid, a second Herschip. And while I'm no his pet, my hands are no clean.'

She took her time, as if digesting the words. 'Me father's his own man and I, me own woman. Me place is with ye now, no matter what. You are my husband and...'

He lifted his head.

'...I cannae lose ye. Ye mean that much tae me.'

Chapter 31

Michael crushed the early blooming flower under his foot. It was time for him to leave. They had been right about the farm; it was too isolated to be visited during the snow. But that had melted, the bodies thawed and stinking. People would grow curious and come looking. He needed somewhere else to hide until he could flush the bitch out.

He strung the carcass of the last animal up. A goat. When had he last eaten a decent meal of meat? Or worn the clothing he was entitled to? He would never again wear this stinking, barbaric dress, even if it was warm. No. For him it would be scarlet, damask, gris and cheveril. She could wear sackcloth for all he cared. If he let her live.

'Yes, she'll live like I did. In a damp cell with naught but sackcloth and oat water,' he told the carcass. 'Then when I want her, I may permit her tae wash. If only so I can better see my skill.'

The beautiful sight of a body bruised and broken, it healing, him doing it again. Over and over. He licked his lips. His prick growing hard. He cursed, spat and grabbed himself. He needed a *queynte*. Who cared whose? He could imagine hers until he got his way. He shuddered and flicked the result off his hand before turning back to the job.

*

Goat was not a good meat. It was tougher than hide and tasted awful. Still, Michael packed the roasted and dried flesh. Better than eating grass or oatcakes. He would never eat the damned things again. His people would grow only wheat and would grind it into the softest and whitest of flour for his table only. Served alongside dishes of venison, porpoise, chicken. His mouth watered and his stomach grumbled. Damn it all, he was wasting away!

He carefully picked his way down the hillside. Was she still in that island fortress? That's where they had said to find her, but the earl had multiple homes. So why would they stay at one? Michael would regularly travel, make a great show of it. People would cower at the sight of him. Men would beg him to take their daughters. Yes, daughters or life. He laughed.

In the glen, he dropped his pack and grabbed his flask before kneeling beside a stream. He caught his reflection and sneered. A ragged beard and hollow cheeks. She had done this to him. He tilted his head slightly. Hooves and wheels were coming towards him. Michael placed his hand on the sword; a simple carter would not know how to defend himself. And waited.

No, it was not a cart but one of those fancy boxes nobles used. What was that doing in this godforsaken place? Never mind, he'd take it. It would come in useful later. The wagon stopped. Could it be his lucky day? Did it contain the bitch? He bit back a snort as a man set down a stool. Putting on airs, wasn't she?

'You there. I havenae seen ye here before. What's yer business on my nephew's land?'

Damn it. That had to be the ugliest, tallest old hag he had ever seen. Rutting the goat carcass was more appealing. But a dusty *queynte* was still a *queynte*. Michael spat and turned slowly, showing his sword.

'None o yer business, ye old hag.'

The woman pursed her lips, then narrowed her eyes at him. 'I will ignore that insult, son of Thomas Gilchrist, for I think ye and I may have a common interest.'

He snarled and pulled his sword from his sheath. The man was quicker than he thought. His weapon drawn, he was between Michael and the witch, advancing slowly.

'Ye'll no speak that *cumberworld's* name around me, woman. Ye ken no what I want.'

'Oh, but I do, and I ken how to get her away from the keep.'

His lips curled with another insult when he stopped. He let his face distort into a twisted smile and tilted his head.

'Perhaps ye're of some use after all.'

The woman nodded sharply.

'Put away that stick before ye hurt yerself and get in. I havenae got all day.'

'As ye would like.'

He bowed as that *sumph* Alasdair once had, sheathed his blade and grabbed his things. He would hear her out and if he did not like her offer, well, it would be easier to plough and kill her in that box.

*

A Yule Alasdair had enjoyed – something he had not dared to think possible. But with Mordag closely by his side, he had. He made time to laze with her upon learning of her hatred for darkness, though often the lazing became lovemaking. She, in turn, had given him the strength to open Ruth's chest and lay her to rest. It now sat awaiting the day they would have a daughter of their own, her legacy a future dowry.

He glanced at Mordag; she sat studying the illustrations decorating the book he had first read to her from. A gift paid for from Cailean's first spoils of war. His brother had been sick of the piles of manuscripts littering their chamber. His eyes fell from her to the piles around him. Some things never changed.

Alas, not one of them was of use. Not even the ones the Raven had requested from the king's records. Nor were the responses he'd received. Sorcha's sire was a dead end: a knight named Turberville had been based in Scotland and died shortly after Methven. A bastard recognised by his father but not his half-brother, the one who now held the former's titles. But little else of note was found.

Cailean's latest pile of missives had arrived afterwards, in one go thanks to the weather, and now it was clear he could have saved himself the work, had either of them thought to ask Sorcha. He ran his hands through his hair and snorted, earning a glance from his wife. He reassured her with a smile. But it did confirm why a lowly laird was caring for Sorcha.

He had finally met his mentor and had not realised it. The one who had encouraged him to use sleight of hand to begin with; to practise on his family, to write with both hands, and to exploit weaknesses like Douglas's fondness for *uisge beatha*. The one who had been near every battle, and knew their father, a Bruce supporter since the death of the maiden. A perfect rook indeed, for no matter how much animosity lay between two kingdoms, merchants and craftsmen still crossed borders freely.

The story, quaint as it was, held little of use besides explaining how Thomas and Annabelle had met. Not who she was, for he was now certain it was her line he must follow. Just that she was some phoenix. A creature that rose from ashes. And judging how she had been found, it was fitting. But what of that other nonsense? Lions, bears, eagles, dragons…

No. It could not be *that* simple. Could it?

Alasdair grabbed the bestiary. Eagle, dragon, raven and bear. How often had Thomas written to him that the best secrets were kept in plain sight? He snatched up the missive written in Sorcha's hand. *Noble eagles*, *mighty bears*, *cunning ravens* and *cruel dragons*.

He pressed the beads in turn. A soft click. He tugged at the lock; nothing gave way. Christ's teeth, what now? He lifted the tome to get a better look and the spine fell away, revealing another underneath. Something glinted in the discarded piece. Attached to the fake spine was a long, slender rod, its tip as fine as a pin, though rounded. Some sort of key? To where?

Acting on a hunch, he stood up and approached the nearby window, opening it to let in the winter light. The lock had no keyhole, though the light revealed it had been shoddily cast. No, it had not. No one would spend so much on binding it in such a way, then ignore this section. Certainly not a man with as fine an eye as Thomas had. There had to be more. He ran his finger over one of the patchy areas. Was that a small hole? He chuckled wryly.

Back at the table, he pushed the pin in. It met no resistance until it had passed the normal length of a pin for cloth. He pushed against it and gently tugged the strap. It came free.

'Jesus, Thomas, ye wily old cur!' he exclaimed.

'What?'

He started, having completely forgotten about Mordag. 'I will finally have some answers.'

She smiled, closed the book and stood up. 'In that case, I'll tell Jock tae send in some food for ye.'

His eyebrows knitted, only for his nose to note the smell of food coming from the hall. Mordag sniggered and left.

Alasdair returned to the book. The sheaves of sewn parchment were not glued in, but held by leather strapping. He flicked through the pages of writing, much of it scratched or crossed out, some passages circled. Were these Thomas's notetakings?

Choosing a page at random, he read. It was a list of notable names from a southern family. After each was an animal – the animals from the story, plus a new one, wolf. Some were marked with a cross, signifying death. Many had notations too – but he could have howled. It was all in code. He leafed through more pages. Code, all of it, and not just one code either. Was nothing to be easy for him?

Angered, he searched and found his family's name. Grann, bear and cross. Niall, wolf and cross with a question mark. He crossed out the question mark; his uncle was long dead. Cailean, bear cub scratched out and replaced with blinded bear. Odd. Then some coded words. Alasdair, fledgling, and a lot of code. But there, at the end in the simplest form of French, Thomas had scrawled a few lines.

'I know that when you read this you will be struggling and full of questions that I will not be able to answer. I can only apologise. It was my selfish actions and Robert's covetous need to secure his succession that started this. Try as we might to predict what would occur, Grann struggled under the pressure and it ultimately destroyed him. I hope you can someday find it in your hearts to forgive me.'

He stared at the words long into the night.

Chapter 32

Glaistig strode around the bailey, followed closely by Taranis. Then came the young bay Thomas had gifted Cailean before his death. It had been dubbed Raibeart by his men. He groaned, recalling their reasoning: 'A lowlander come north to learn how tae fight'. They appeared to have wintered well. The mare perhaps a little too well. He nodded to the men; they led them towards the gates. Sorcha was looking thoughtful. He crossed his arms.

'They said Taranis didnae mount her,' she thought aloud.

And how would they have known that? They had found the horses well after the attack. 'Is it no too soon tae be showing?'

'Aye, but I just ken she is.'

He chuckled softly.

'What makes my lord husband laugh?'

'Tis the good Highland air and spring's arrival that's done it. I see it in you, too. Ye have put on weight and have a glow tae yer cheeks.'

And her intense appetite; making up for lost time. She blushed and took his proffered hand.

'Myself perhaps, but no her, for I ken my mare. She's pregnant.'

He relented; time would tell. A cry came from the ramparts. Someone was approaching.

'I didnae ken ye were expecting guests,' Sorcha murmured.

'Neither did I.'

He helped her over the worst of the mud, stopping in front of the keep stairs, then cursed as the wagon entered. Bernice preached restraint but rode ostentatiously. Sorcha's grip on him tightened. Then she mirrored his curse, albeit in quiet French. He still had not told her that most there understood the tongue. He enjoyed the subtle show of spirit.

'Aunt Bernice, what a surprise.'

'Cailean, I had tae come. We must allow bygones tae be bygones. So I forgive ye. Besides, Easter will soon be upon us and ye must be properly prepared. I assume my chamber is still available?'

His eye twitched; again, she ignored Sorcha, but he stilled his tongue. Over Yule they had devised a ridiculously childish plan. Would it work? Still leading Sorcha, he followed his aunt into the keep, and heard her shriek of horror. He glanced at his wife but said nothing.

Inside, he admired the two new tapestries of Aphrodite and Eros. Sorcha broke the silence. 'Beautiful, aren't they? A wedding gift from the Good Sir James.'

'Aye, most discerning,' Cailean agreed, then directed

his words to Bernice, 'though I thought ye were retiring tae the guest chamber.'

The abbess turned and looked aghast at them. Speechless! He called for Hamish to escort her. She stammered and stormed off alone. In the right direction! Perhaps childish plans had their use. A second, fainter screech came from above.

'Oh, how lovely! Yer aunt appreciates the work we had done tae the chamber.'

'Let it hasten her departure.'

*

Cailean tossed aside the latest missive from Alasdair. It bore little news. Sorcha's past was as attainable as a *spunkie's* light. Though his brother had expanded on her story. Apparently, Thomas and their father were not motivated by duty. Ever the romantic, Alasdair had implied love. In the case of Sorcha's stepfather perhaps, but not Grann. He stopped by the chessboard and considered his next move. The game was drawn out, interrupted by their work.

He had to inspect his vessels with the boatwright and had agreed to Sorcha accompanying him. She was rushing to get ready and soon shooed Ailis's hand away. Her mantle covered most of his favourite dress. Pity.

'Donald is tae stay with ye at all times. If ye feel ill at all, ye are tae return here.'

'I havenae in several days. And I'll go no further than the last house. In truth, I'm eager tae meet the healer. My stocks are low.'

'She is – well, ye'll discover for yerself.'

He escorted her to the bailey; Donald fell in at the hall door. Outside waited their mounts. A rouncey for himself, and Glaistig? He glanced at Sorcha.

'She's pregnant, no injured. It'll no harm her and I dare not think what she would dae if put out tae pasture for a couple o years.'

He winced in agreement and helped Sorcha mount. They needed to leave quickly; the tide would soon turn. Cailean held his horse in check, ready for when it felt grass on the other side. Old nag or young colt, spring made them all foolish.

'Give them their head,' he called as soon as he could.

Sorcha streaked past, laughing. His mount squealed and shot after them. He smiled. How could he not? The feeling was infectious. He glanced back at a guffawing Donald. Something wanted him to shout out a challenge. A race to catch Sorcha. He bit his tongue. They were too close to the local dwellings now. Maybe later, if she was still about.

He pulled up and looked around. Only older folk watching babes. Cailean frowned. He glanced towards the water. The boats lay abandoned. As did other chores. These signs, paired with a lack of word sent to him meant one thing. A child was missing. And during boar farrowing season. Damn it. He quickly dismounted and secured his horse. The folk always organised at the same place.

Indeed, his *tacksman* was near the tinder store. He perched over a rough map drawn in the mud.

'Who's lost?' Cailean asked.

'*Mo ciann*,' greeted the man. 'James's eldest lass,

Martha, didnae come home last night. He's been searching fer her all night but ye ken what it's like at this time o year.'

Cailean nodded. The grounds would be a mess of tracks. He had James, his woodsman, mark out areas for thinning during the winter. What the families cleared, they were permitted to keep. They were also permitted to hunt small game.

'Ye should've sent word. Where are they searchin now?'

The *tacksman* pointed at the ground with a stick. 'Tae the east o Claw Rock.'

He nodded and took off at a jog, taking the worn path to the landmark, his hand on the pommel of his sword. To get that far and still not find her – he could not shake his gut feeling.

*

The sun was already at high point and no trace had been found. Cailean had long given up calling the girl, Martha's, name. The lack of progress was hindered by sows' nests, making them double back and swing around. Judging by the silence, others too feared the worst. He prayed now that they would find a body, for the sake of her parents.

From a dip to his left came a shout of alarm.

In it, someone had made a camp. And next to the fire lay the body of a girl of no more than ten summers. Cursing, he ordered the others to stay back and approached. Her *léine* and shift torn, but not by animals, though scavengers had been there. Marks around her neck, likely between her legs too. He had seen such corpses before, though never outside of war. His mouth went dry even as he growled. Whichever coward had done this would dance on a rope.

James pushed past him, let out a strangled cry, and fell to his knees. He grabbed his daughter's body and clung tightly to it. No one spoke. What could they say? Cailean hardened his jaw and looked around. A lad was vomiting; his first body. And the rest were ashen-faced. This was not the work of one of them. Were Sorcha's followers back? He placed a hand on the woodsman's shoulder.

'I will pay for her burial and masses.' His voice quiet.

'Why her?' He choked on his grief. 'She wasnae yet a woman!'

'We will have earthly justice. The Lord will dae the rest,' Cailean promised, helping James up. Their kin surrounded him, leading him away. One or two gave worried glances; they had daughters of a similar age. He lingered, first checking the ashes – burned out, not extinguished with water – then scanning the ground. Only one flattened area in the shape of a man's body. One person was responsible. And not someone accustomed to camping. Not Sorcha's followers. Her brother?

He clenched his fists.

There had been no word. No sightings. Could he have survived the winter? He had enough fat on him. But not out here. Sheltered by someone? On what promise? He needed to send out more scouting parties. If it was him, he was bound to be somewhere nearby. Though not that close to Eilean Donnain. To have survived this long, he needed at least a grain of common sense. And what of Sorcha?

He hurried after the others.

*

Martha's mother's keening greeted Cailean. He lowered his head, feeling the sound pierce his heart. Twice he had not taken Michael seriously. He would not fail his people again. He inhaled slowly. Sorcha was safe with Donald; they needed him more.

The *tacksman* stepped up to his side. 'Twas no a beast, was it?'

'How dae ye define a beast? Call the pledged men. Have them bring their weapons,' he instructed. 'Also send a lad tae the keep. Same order. And the priest. He's no left yet. Find my wife too and send her home.'

The man motioned to another standing nearby. 'A beast hunt it is, then. As fer the lady, ah havenae seen her, *mo ciann.*'

Good, she must have already returned to the keep.

Back at the tinder store, he extended the map in the mud and waited. The men came readily with their arms, though most had forgotten protection in their haste. Word had spread; they wanted vengeance. He must tread carefully, or innocent blood may still be spilt.

'I believe this is the work o one man. An outsider. But I cannae be sure. Yer weapons are for yer own protection. The individual may have assistance. Therefore, I forbid, on pain of banishment, death by yer hand. Am I clear?'

A few glances, but mostly nods and spoken confirmation.

'Ye will bring any persons found acting unusually, or strangers, tae Eilean Donnain. Understood?'

Again, a mix of confirmations. The crowd parted and

James walked through them, axe in hand. 'Ah'm ready, *mo ciann.*'

Cailean closed the gap between them. He put his hand over the axe head and pushed it down. 'Go home, James; yer wife and yer other weans need ye. And ye ken ye're in no state tae be out there. Ah'll no see blood on yer hands.'

James twisted his head in rage, but the argument did not come. Eyes filling with tears, he pulled away. The *tacksman* stepped in and murmured softly, agreeing with Cailean. He watched them both leave together. A man broken by grief.

Cailean called the others closer, and gestured to the map. 'Start from here and fan out. I'll have most from the keep start here. We'll pincer them. Force them either up the hill or, more likely, down here. Ah'll have men waiting here and here, tae be sure. Let's flush him out!'

They shouted their agreement; he sent them off towards the west end of the woodland. Where were the others? A vanguard at the least. He headed for his horse. It was alone: Donald and Sorcha must have returned to the keep. So why could he not shake the feeling in his gut?

The rumble of a galloping horse made him look up. A riderless Glaistig with reins dangling perilously, stirrups flying, a foaming mouth and white eyes. He held out his hands and stepped into her path. She slid to a halt and half-reared. Any other warhorse would have killed him. He calmed her with a trembling voice and forced down nausea. She couldn't have thrown Sorcha, she was too skilled a rider. Dear Lord, let her have spooked and broken her restraint.

'Easy now, ye ken me, Glaistig.'

She snorted and danced on the spot but did not flee. He reached for the reins, grabbing them. The mare jerked back, then stood trembling. They were intact. Ripped from her hands? He swallowed, his chest unbearably tight. He murmured again, this time nonsense. The foam around her mouth was tinged red. Had she bitten herself? A hand on her neck. She was soaked with sweat. He reached over to cross her stirrups. Even her saddle was wet. The sickly-sweet smell of iron assaulted his nose. No. It could not be. He turned his hand over.

Blood.

Chapter 33

'Is it no too early tae be harvesting sorrel?'

Sorcha's curiosity got the better of her. The woman she addressed had to be the healer, for her dwelling had the largest and most developed herb garden. She gently pulled Glaistig's head away from a bush of mint. Best to keep a hold of the mare; Lord only knew what mischief she could cause.

'For healing, aye, but nae fer removing rust from my linens. Besides, these leaves came too early and have been nipped at by the frost,' the woman replied, before straightening up.

Though her face was toughened by the sun, there was an astute kindness about her. It reminded Sorcha of Evelyn.

She smiled a toothy grin. 'Greetings, my lady, ah wondered when ah'd be seeing ye.'

Unlike Evelyn, the woman brazenly stared. Sorcha struggled to stay composed under that gaze. Stroking the mare's cheek, she gathered her courage from around her feet.

'Yer garden is impressive. The local healer, I presume?'

'That and other titles, aye. The name's Peggy.'

'A pleasure tae meet ye, Peggy.'

'So is what ah hear about ye true? That ye ken herbs enough tae do a better job than I at easing Cailean's face?'

Heat flooded her cheeks, though Peggy's direct nature was a welcome change. Her ladies would never use two words when twenty were better. Sorcha glanced over her shoulder. Cailean was gone but Donald sat within sight on someone's stool, whittling.

'I doubt it. I merely have plenty of practice in easing scars, bruises and the like. Little else. Though I must confess, it is why I sought ye out. I need tae replenish my stock.'

The healer folded her arms and lifted an eyebrow.

'And no else?'

Sorcha bit her lower lip, for the question felt accusatory. She gave a shake of her head.

'I cannae think of anything else.'

'So nowt tae ease yer morning sickness or aid yer sleep for when the babe starts tae move? I'd bet my last herring that be any day now.'

'I see that talk of my winter sickness has reached here. It isnae pregnancy, for it was no confined tae mornings.'

The healer's eyes narrowed, and her hands went to her hips. Oh Lord have mercy, she had insulted the woman!

'May God strike me down if ah'm wrong, but ah've helped many older than ye in tae this world, lass. Ah ken well the signs, and it often starts in winter on account of men having too idle a hand! As for the sickness, did yer mither no teach ye that it is rarely confined tae mornings?'

'My ma died when I was a bairn.'

She had responded instinctively, even as her free hand and eyes landed on her stomach. Could it be true? She would like a son for Cailean growing safe inside her. Did she dare to believe it? But her menses continued, albeit lightly. She lifted her gaze, meeting Peggy's eyes, which were softer now. If it was true, then both she and Glaistig would be pasturing now. On the unlikely chance Cailean would let her ride, it would be a quiet palfrey.

'Och, lass, ah'm sorry. No doubt none mentioned it at the keep either. The foolish lot!'

Again, she shook her head, unable to find her tongue. Peggy glanced past her. 'What is it, Donald? Ye're flitting like a midge.'

Sorcha searched Donald's face. If he'd heard their conversation, he did not show it, though Peggy's words had him turning quite red.

'I need tae piss,' he admitted.

'Honestly, Donald, ye're no a wean and ye dinnae need tae be telling the lady. Or has Bridget got ye asking fer permission now?' snapped Peggy, before Sorcha could reply.

She dipped her head; it was not Donald's fault he had his orders.

'Nae, it's no that…'

'Hold yer wheesht and go relieve yerself, ye big oaf. And no in my garden!'

He responded like a scolded pup. Though as he left, he cast Sorcha a look. She met his eyes and barely nodded. She would not move from that spot. Certainly not now she had more than herself to think of. Peggy wheezed in merriment.

'Once ye've helped birth one o their babes, they darenae give ye grief. Now will ye come in for a drink while we sort out what ye be needing?'

She declined and gave Peggy a list of the herbs she needed. Her hand settled lightly on Glaistig's nose. What would her son be like? His father's height, with eyes as deep as a sea? Perhaps hair as red as hers? He would be a warrior, no doubt, but would he love learning too? And would he develop a compassion for the clan he would one day lead? Yes, with their guidance, he would. She was sure of it.

She was forcibly pulled from her daydream by a firm grip on her arm. Instinctively, she tightened her hand on Glaistig's reins.

'Annabelle, they're coming! We must find Thomas.'

'What? What is it, Douglas?'

And what was he doing here? She dug her heels in, but the man was strong for his age.

'I told ye, they're coming. Now stop messing and follow me!'

It was no use: the more she struggled to stop him, the harder he got with her. And the deeper his panic seemed to grip him. He pulled her away from the scattering of dwellings and into the woodland. She caught sight of an oblivious Donald relieving himself. Douglas's crazed eyes stilled her cry in her throat. She would have to go with him and let whatever had seized him pass by.

'Who is coming? Where are ye taking me?' she pleaded, to no avail.

Douglas was silent, concentrating on hiding their tracks and distorting their path with his free hand, while his grip on her remained firm. He was as if possessed, dragging her through the undergrowth. It tore at her mantle and ripped her veil from her head. She cried in pain but was ignored. Glaistig dawdled, unwilling to scratch herself. The buckle at the end of the reins dug into Sorcha's hand; she felt it slip. *No!*

'Please, Donald, wait!'

'There's no time!'

Glaistig vanished.

*

They could have been walking in circles for all Sorcha knew. It was all foreign to her. Then they stumbled into a small clearing. Douglas lost his grip and she kept going, putting some distance between them. Only when she felt far enough away did she look around. Nearby was a spring. The light shining through the trees gave it an etheric glow. She struggled to catch her breath and forced down nausea. He bent double and smashed his forehead with the palm of his hand.

'Ah dinnae understand. Tis… tis the fae stank, but that's at home,' he admitted.

She blinked and reached out for him, intending to close the gap. Whatever was affecting him was wearing off.

'I thank ye, Douglas, I'll take care o her now.'

Her blood ran cold. Slowly, Highland clothing, scraggy beard, small eyes and a sword. Her chest contracted painfully. Why was he here? Foolish question. She knew he would follow her. But how had he survived? She could not tear her eyes from the rage she saw in him.

'Thomas?'

Douglas.

'I said get lost, old *sumph*!'

Michael had tricked him, but how? She heard Douglas unsheathe his blade. Cailean had let him keep a real one? She had thought it fake. Yet he had explained that Douglas was once a great warrior. Dare she hope? She stepped back as they started to circle each other. Douglas held the blade over his shoulder, level with his forehead, its tip pointed at Michael.

'Ye're no Thomas,' he spat.

She backed even further away, a foot landing in the spring's water. She felt it soak through her boot but she did not remove it. Michael leapt towards him. She flinched as the blades struck each other. It was hopeless: with what little eye she had, she could see they were evenly matched. Michael was heavy-handed, slowing him down, but Douglas had lost his reflexes. Again and again, they parried.

She needed to keep her head. But what could she do? She spotted the hole their arrival had made in the undergrowth. Slowly, she inched around the outside of the clearing until she was at the point at which she had entered.

'Run, Sorcha!' Douglas ordered, his voice as sharp as any hale man.

Shocked into action, she fled to the sound of a gurgled cry of pain. It was not Michael's – of that, she was sure. She wove in and out of trees – something caught her, and she struggled. The pin holding her mantle broke, freeing her.

'Ye'll no get away this time, ye little bitch,' Michael called, taunting her as she struggled through some brambles with her gown.

Was this the way she came? It mattered not; she just needed distance to hide.

'Ye owe me and it's long time I collect me due.'

There! A gap blocked by a small log. They had crossed that, right? She leapt over it and landed wrong. Pain seared through her ankle. She slowed, limping. *No!* Hot tears stung her eyes; she gritted her teeth and tried to get away.

Michael charged into her back. She fell forward, her scream knocked from her. Unable to curl, she landed face-first on the ground. Blind hot pain tore through her gut. She clawed at the ground in front of her, pinned by his weight. He shifted.

No!

Michael ripped her caul from her hair, cursed and reached again. He spun her around; a hot wetness expelled itself from between her legs, soaking her riding trews. Her son! He could do as he pleased with her, but he would not take her son from her! She bucked fiercely as Michael straddled her, hissing and clawing at him, aiming for those foul eyes. She gouged his cheek. He swore bitterly, raised his hand and struck her.

Something in her cheek cracked and light blinded her. Shocked, Sorcha gulped in air, only she could not breathe – his hands were clamped around her neck. It was hopeless; her vision blurred around the edges. She fell limp, her head turning away from him.

'I should kill ye now, ye pathetic whore. But ye're too useful tae me alive,' he snarled. 'Ah'll kill yer earl then marry ye myself, bitch. But first, I've no ploughed ye. I will see what I've been missing and show ye what a real rutting is.'

Sorcha could not respond. Her eye was swelling, forcing tears from her. Her lifeblood and son were slowly leaving her. May Cailean forgive her. If her son could not survive then Michael's threats meant nothing. She had no strength, no fight. She was no wild cat. Michael grunted and shifted to free his manhood.

'Fight, damn it, fight me, ye whore!' he screamed, forcing her to turn her head, smashing his lips against hers. She did not bite, focusing on the branches above his head. She heard him cut through her gowns. Cailean's favourite, destroyed. Another curse – one of surprise at what greeted him. Oddly, she remembered he'd never seen her with unbound breasts. He pawed at them. She mouthed the lullaby Cailean had sung for her and waited for the familiar feeling of floating away, but it did not come.

Through the brush, something chestnut flashed. The ground below her thundered. Sorcha snapped back at the sound of an enraged squeal. Glaistig! She felt his weight lift enough for her to drag her legs out. Her breath rushed back into her, along with her will to live. Her ears rang with Michael's pained screaming.

Curling into a ball, she saw from the corner of her eye that the mare had him by the shoulder. Gripping him with her mouth, shaking him like she was trained to. Only she had never been taught to do it riderless. Her mare had become a warhorse! Refusing to let Michael go, Glaistig lurched forwards. He had nowhere to place his legs but under her forelegs.

Sorcha's stomach lurched and a cramp seized her gut as the bones in Michael's lower legs snapped. His renewed screams scared Glaistig. Without her mistress, the mare faultered and dropped his now limp body. Backing away, her eyes rolled and she snorted. Twice she reared from fear alone.

They could not stay there. If Glaistig did not accidentally trample Sorcha, then she would surely bleed to death. Unfurling herself, she reached for the nearest tree. Inch by painful inch, she pulled herself up. Gritting her teeth, she howled with effort, making Glaistig shy away. *Come back!* They may still save her son!

Her vision swam, her throat restricted again. She wept bitterly as she leaned against the tree. Her mare was just too far away.

'Glaistig!'

She called the snorting, dancing mare. Glaistig did not move. The blood. The scent must have been overwhelming. But what could she do?

'God damn it, Glaistig, dinnae do this to me now. Please!'

She spat angrily, only for it to end in a ridiculous plea. Sorcha softened her voice, though not her cursing, and held out her arms. The mare did not know what she said. She tossed her head but stepped closer. It was working. She reached for the reins and fell onto her neck. She could not risk screaming as she pulled herself into the saddle. It came out as a desperate growl.

'Home!'

Glaistig whipped around so fast, she could only cling to her neck and keep the reins from tangling round

Glaistig's legs. It seemed like an age before the light around her grew brighter. She heard a man's shout and then, as they burst into the open, a woman's. Her horse put her head down and bolted.

Sorcha could not stop her. Only cling on to her saddle, now slippery with her blood. She choked on her fear and on her helplessness. Glaistig was heading straight for her stall inside the walls, beyond the flooded causeway. Please, please slow down. She could not have made it this far only for them to both die of broken necks! Shouts ahead of her. People had seen what was happening! They formed a line in front of the water, waving their arms about.

Her mare lifted her head, changed her leading leg and must have thought better of it. She slowed. She was stopping! Good. Good girl! Glaistig turned sharply again. Sorcha's legs could not hold her. She slipped sideways, falling to the ground. She rolled away and came to a stop, facing the direction she had come. Her body screamed with pain, blackness crept in. Someone was coming towards her at a gallop. Cailean?

Chapter 34

'Where is she?' Cailean crashed into the ominously quiet keep.

Pale faces and missing women met him. The pounding of feet from above answered. Their chamber. He tore towards the head of the hall. Donald stepped in front of the door; his *léine* stained with blood. *Her blood.* He felt lightheaded, then seized the fear gripping him.

'Get out o me way,' he spat through clenched teeth.

'Nae. She lives, but if ye go up there, ye'll only hinder Peggy's work.'

His fists balled. Who was he to be telling him what he could do? And how had he allowed this to happen? He clenched his jaw and stepped forward. He would… he would… Sorcha's scream of pain hit him like a punch to his gut. Followed by an invisible axe to his chest. He reeled backwards and screwed his eyes shut.

He had failed her. She could be dying up there and he was not at her side. The pain. Battle wounds paled in comparison. Was this love? Lord help him. He loved her.

He shook his head. How could he have not known? And now he may lose her because he could not protect her. What twisted fate was this?

Donald, the voice of reason, placed his hands on his shoulders. 'She is strong, Cailean. Saved herself.'

'What happened?' He forced the question to his lips.

Donald looked at the others over his shoulders and dropped his voice.

'Give me yer weapons.'

What was Donald implying? An insider? He growled, twisting his lip. His cousin remained steadfast. Cailean's hands were leaden as he struggled to remove his sword belt. Ewan took it and his unsheathed dagger.

'She didnae say much. Couldn't. But on the crossing over, she spoke of Douglas.'

Not a chance in hell.

'He's missing, *mo ciann*,' Ewan added, confirming what his cousin said.

'But he...'

Donald nodded; his expression guarded. Who? Who had betrayed him? Cailean swung around. No one would meet his gaze. They had abandoned their work to wait. Helpless like him. Except for *her*.

Bernice sat at a table, calmly writing a missive. Damn her insolence! She should be up there, helping. He stormed over to the table and kicked its trestles hard. Parchment and quills flew. Ink splattered Bernice's gown. A small, useless win. She jumped up to screech at him.

'*Mo ciann*,' someone called, and Bernice fell silent.

He spun around. Ailis was at the door, clutching bloodied linens. Her eyes and nose red, swaying in shock.

Cailean fought the urge to grab and shake her. Another of the clan beat him to her side.

'What is it, child?' they asked softly.

Ailis inhaled a sob. 'She's losing the babe.'

He struggled to breathe. Sorcha had been carrying his child? Why had she not told him? They'd vowed to not keep secrets. He wanted to turn. To run. Anywhere but there. Voices around him.

'Ye didnae ken?'

Donald.

'The healer said my lady didnae ken till today.'

Ailis.

Murmured choruses of disbelief; of *we thought it obvious*.

Was it? He sank to his knees and started praying. Tears flowed. Let them see what they had done. Let the traitor know how much they had ruined him. Sorcha's keening from above. Too similar to that of James's wife. How many more innocents would die? And what for? Some sick game? Please, Lord, let her live. He could not lose her.

'Christ, Cailean. Look at what she has done to ye. That she-devil has ripped yer manhood from ye. Yer grandfather would be disgusted tae ken that such a weakling now rules his lands. Ye dinnae deserve tae share his blood, let alone be the chief. My Niall wouldnae have made those mistakes.'

A spoken smack to his face.

'Be silent, woman. Ye'll no utter that name here,' growled Donald.

'That name? *That name?* He is yer father, Donald, and ye will show his memory the respect it deserves!'

'Deserves? He would've seen the clan torn asunder! Kermac was right tae choose Grann over him. He is nae father of mine. Just as ye are nae mother! Leave now, ye *crabbit auld schow*.'

A strange madness seized Cailean; bitter laughter escaped his lips. Now it made sense. She was just as ambitious as Niall. Only no longer for her husband.

'Nae. Confine her tae a chamber. None are tae leave,' he quietly ordered.

*

Silence followed, both below and above. Cailean prayed, paced, sat and stood. Nothing eased him. Nothing would, until he could be with Sorcha. He could not eat the meal the cook served. Nor could many others. He ran his hands over his eyes. Runners arrived from time to time, bringing no news, he assumed. They went to Donald first. He himself was in no fit state to lead.

He jumped up as the door opened. Iona and Bridget stepped wearily into the hall. Their sleeves rolled back. Hands newly washed, gowns ruined. They ran into their husbands' arms. Why had they said nothing? Was she? He swallowed; he could not say the word. Bridget pulled back but did not leave Donald's arms.

'Forgive us, *mo ciann*. Ye can go up now.'

His feet moved by themselves. Slowly, then sprinting. Sorcha was alive!

He slowed only at the door to their chamber. A maid passed with a bucket, another, a pile of cloth. Sorcha's garments. Ruined. What had happened to her? Peggy appeared in the door, carrying a bundle. His breath caught. She stopped, but held it away from him. How had she known?

'She wasnae even halfway, *mo ciann*. It didnae – couldnae take a breath. And it's best ye dinnae look.'

Cailean hesitated, not wanting to listen to her wisdom. He shook his head.

'It was expelled cleanly. That is, nothing left behind, an with no aid from meself. Barring fever, my lady should live and bear more. Though,' Peggy's voice became hard, 'if I hear ye've been punishing her in any way…'

He met her eyes. How dare she think, let alone voice, that? Yes, that was his child, but Sorcha lived. God willing, there would be more! The woman nodded. Damn her.

'Anything else?'

'Aye. Her other injuries are extensive, though none as brutal as her face. With time they'll heal, but her mind – well, I cannae speak for that. Some lasses recover from such abuse and heartache. Others never do.'

'I'll no leave her side, Peggy. She's been through enough hell. Now, if ye dinnae—'

'Her scars. Michael?'

He knitted his eyebrows and folded his arms. 'She spoke of what happened?'

'Nae. Just insisted ah told ye it was him. When I saw the scarring – well, abusive men rarely let their victims go.'

He cursed. Sorcha was his priority, yet he could not ignore what she said.

'We will speak more o that on another day,' he promised, as he entered the chamber.

The shutters were up at the windows. A pungent mix of herbs choked him. Crosses, an image of the Holy Mother and, above where Sorcha lay, a paternoster hung. The things his mother had used, though the girdle was missing. She was on her side, under fresh linens and in a chemise. And somehow looked even smaller. Her hair hung limp.

He stepped closer. Angry bruising, mostly down the left of her face. A split lip. More bruising on her neck. Her eyes, though dulled by herbs, held an anger he knew too well. Michael would dance thrice over. As would those who aided him. Damn it. He needed to hold her; for his sake as much as hers.

Cailean edged his way onto the bed and carefully pressed himself against her back. She flinched. What other damage had he done? Then raised her arm. He avoided her lower torso, lightly resting his hand on her ribs. She pulled him tighter around her, despite the pain it must have caused. Her hands bandaged, nails torn. He would *never* forget this.

'Ah'm here, Sorcha,' he murmured, with a softness that belied the anger within. 'I'll no be going anywhere else.'

'I want him tae suffer, Cailean.' Her words were slurred and venomous. 'I want him tae ken what I feel.'

He pressed his lips to her hair.

'He will, my love.'

*

The night dragged for Cailean. Sorcha fretted if she could not feel him; cried out if he left the bed. He had missed the pot when she first did it. Ailis had not begrudged the mess; nor he, her fussing around them. She did what he could not. Men were occasionally let in to give reports, their concerned glances comforting, reminding him that his people cared.

They reported that Glaistig had calmed and was uninjured. He ordered her closely watched. Should she colic, it would finish Michael's work. Furthermore, they reported Douglas had died, sword in hand. A better death than that which nature had intended. But nothing of Michael.

He did not believe that he was still out there. His men had returned home without a word and bad news spread fast. Had he escaped the pincer, he would not have reached any border. Cailean watched Sorcha's chest rise and fall. She had not stirred for a good while and it would soon be dawn. Damn it, he needed to know. He edged away. Nothing. He got up. Still nothing. He went no further than the door, finding two of his *leuchd-crios* on guard.

'Is Donald about?' he asked.

'Here, *mo ciann*,' a tired voice responded from the dark solar.

Movement and cursing. How many were sleeping there? Donald approached, pale-skinned, with dark rings under his eyes. Aye, he was holding back.

'Light a fresh candle,' Cailean instructed, while checking again on Sorcha.

She had shifted but was not distressed. He lingered, feeling her head for fever. There was none. Did she finally feel safe? He returned to Donald's side.

'What have ye no told me?'

'Ah'm sorry, we thought it better tae keep it till morn.'

He nodded; he would have done the same. 'Ye caught Michael?'

'Aye. Alive, though he's no a pretty sight – ah've no seen injuries like that off a battlefield. And, well, his doing it now is no coincidence.'

'How bad?'

Donald listed them; Cailean blinked.

'And bringing him here was no easy task. Lots of jostling, ye understand?'

His jaw hardened. He never condoned torture; men tended to bear false witness in the hope of ending it.

Donald shook his head, his eyes empty as he stared at nothing. 'They didnae have tae ask him anything. He was soon freely cursing "the old hag in the cart".'

Well, that confirmed it. 'Donald, I'm…'

'Nae, Cailean. Dinnae say it. I should have seen it. My branch is rotten tae the core. If I had realised what I ken now, I'd have never—'

He stopped him. 'I ken I havenae said it before. I'll say it now. Yer as much my brother as Alasdair. And good things can grow from the mess rot leaves behind.'

He said no more. He did not have to. Instead, he poured a drink from a forgotten pitcher and sat down. He motioned for Donald to do likewise.

'So the longer we delay, the less likely justice will be delivered.'

'Aye.'

'Send word tae those who can reach us quickest. It's best I dinnae judge them alone.'

'Aye, *mo ciann*.'

"And Donald… those injuries?'

'Not our men, nor Douglas.'

Cailean inhaled and shifted in his seat.

'Glaistig,' Sorcha croaked.

God's balls, she was trying to get up. He frowned, but helped her. She clung to him as she got her breath back.

'Were it no for her attack…'

'Dinnae linger on what ifs, ye'll tear yerself up,' he said softly.

She nodded and gestured to the screen.

'Ailis, come and help yer mistress.'

While Cailean wished she would return to bed, Sorcha insisted on sitting with him when she'd finished. Slowly, she recounted what happened. The hatred was still there. Was anything of the woman he loved still a part of her? He glanced at the chess board between them. At some point, it had been disrupted.

Donald changed the subject. 'The funerals will be held later this day. I ken ye sent for the priest, but it'll no be led by him. He says it is better led by the shepherd they ken best. Instead, he is holding masses for their souls.'

He winced; Sorcha flinched. No amount of prayer would save their child. Born without breath, dead before baptism. Condemned to purgatory evermore. He caught the silent tears rolling down his wife's cheeks. She was still in there.

'Douglas will protect the babe as he did ye.' His eyes met Sorcha's, giving what small comfort he could.

Lone 'molehills' occasionally appeared in the graveyard, but never when there was a legitimate burial prepared by Peggy. Not that Sorcha could attend the funerals. He would take her there after her churching.

'My lady!'

Cailean swung around. Ailis hurried to take down screens and throw open the windows. All of them. A haunting melody drifted through the window. He tilted his head to listen. There was more than just the *sennachie's* voice. Sorcha grasped at his hand. He set his other hand on top.

'What is that?' she asked.

His cheeks felt as wet as her own. 'A coronach. They're lamenting *all* the lost lives.'

'Oh, Cailean!'

Chapter 35

Prodding the plain liver, Sorcha sighed. It looked as appetising as the black pudding, both of which she was to eat for a sennight. Had she not suffered enough? She looked up and caught Cailean's eyes. Watching her like a hawk. She reluctantly ate a mouthful. He was, at least, trying – unlike the women. She'd woken to Peggy prodding her, had Ailis insisting on doing the trivialist of things for her, and endured no end of 'words of comfort' from her ladies after the funeral.

Cailean had ordered her left alone this morning. Not to mourn; there was no time for that, no matter how much her heart bled. No, she had to be strong for the trial. Just as she'd had to be strong after Thomas's death. *Just like Elizabeth.*

She swallowed the last piece and hastily pushed the stinking plate away. Ailis took it.

'Ask the cook if he kens how tae make it more palatable,' she instructed the maid.

'He kens; blame Peggy,' Cailean interjected.

The healer was right; even he obeyed her instruction without question.

'There is no difference whether it's spiced or no,' Sorcha protested.

Cailean paused in his dressing to kiss her head. She suppressed a wince, having not explained that her scalp was sore. It was hard enough to get him to kiss her properly, or to hold her firmly. She knew he feared hurting her, but she could not find the words. The ones to describe how she needed to chase away the memory of Michael's hands on her.

He continued to dress. She watched him pin the plaid to his shoulder, then tuck it into the back of his belt. The emptiness in her clamoured for him to undress and take her to their bed. She looked away. No, it was more than the erasing of Michael's touch. She discreetly wiped her eyes and stood up, smiling crookedly. It hurt too much to lift both sides of her mouth.

'I'll be in this meeting for a couple o hours, then the trial will begin. Try tae get some rest.'

'I'll do my best, Cailean, but Peggy's coming tae try and get more splinters from my hands.'

Her large, fiercely proud warrior of a husband blanched. He mouthed some excuse about not being late, before gently brushing her lips with his own and fleeing the chamber. After everything that had happened, she thought nothing could surprise her.

His bulk was replaced by Peggy's light frame. The healer pursed her lips; Sorcha bit her tongue and sat down again. She unwound the bandages and placed her hands into the bowl of warm water Peggy placed in front of her, though she shied away from the woman's prodding hands.

'Ah recommend ye try tae welcome touch. Ah ken tis difficult.'

'It's no that,' she snapped, before sighing. 'Yer prodding an poking will no change anything about my bruising. And I ken the other warning signs that ye're looking for, I'm just no used tae the hands of healers. What I want… what I need are Cailean's hands. I need him, to prove tae myself that I'm still alive. That Michael hasnae won. That he hasnae taken everything from me.'

Lord have mercy, she was crying, but it was not like before. This time she felt the pain course through her. Spill out of whatever basin she had been collecting it in.

'And… and I'm empty here. My body kens he's no there anymore. It grasps at nothing.'

She gestured to her stomach.

'Ah cannae imagine what ye must feel, child. But the grasping – it is no more than yer womb purging so that it can welcome another child someday. If ye rush it, it may no heal properly and ye may bear nae more children. As for the rest of ye – well, yer cheek bone is broken and ye have at least one, if no more, broken ribs. Ye of all people ken what they need.'

Time. Damn him. *Damn him to hell.*

*

Sorcha faced Cailean's chest but did not rest her head upon it. Her veil shrouded her from view, and her rebandaged hands held it over her upper chest and neck. She wore her loosest gown and her hair in a simple braid. She'd heard the hall fall silent as they entered, and felt their eyes on her. Cailean, his back turned to them, lowered her into her chair. Both he and Ailis took their time arranging plaids and furs around her. She grasped his hand; he could do this. He nodded in return, and she lowered her head.

'I thank all who join us. A vile, cowardly act has occurred. One that cost us the lives of an innocent girl and a great kinsman. It also tore my heir from yer lady's body, almost killing her.'

That was her cue. She lifted her head, listening to the gasps of horror. No amount of healing herbs had lessened the extensive bruising.

'This was done tae a grown woman; imagine what happened tae the child.'

She fancied he sounded just like those exotic lions, though sobbing distracted her. She looked away and locked eyes with a woman being held up by her husband. Martha's mother. Cailean's opening words receded into the background, as did the sounds of the crowd. It was just the two of them adrift together in a sea of pain. Sorcha inhaled and nodded slowly. *Be strong, do not let him see your suffering.* The mother understood and stood upright. Sorcha blinked and stared ahead. The sounds returned. Cailean was calling for Michael to be led in.

Her hands dug into a fur. There was no leading – instead, they dragged him in, holding him up under his armpits. Michael's legs were immobilised by thick wooden splints. And he stank, not just of his own waste but of chickens. Where had they been holding him? No, she must not let her compassion take hold. *He killed her child.*

Taunts tainted the air. Something bounced off one of his guards, who coarsely questioned the thrower's parentage.

Her mouth dried when Michael lifted his head to stare at her. His eyes still burned with hatred. She seized it, nursed it and flung it back at him. Lifting her chin, meeting him head-on, and she caught a flicker in his eyes. Yes, see how he had not broken her! He was nothing to her!

'Law dictates that a man must stand tae face his charge,' stated Cailean.

Out of the corner of her eye, she saw him flick his wrist. Michael's face contorted with pain as they swung his legs around, forcing them to bear his weight. He blinked, breaking their gaze first. A trestle was brought for Michael to lean on.

Donald stepped forwards and held up a piece of parchment.

'Michael Gilchrist, ye stand charged with the patricide o Thomas Gilchrist, and the murder of Douglas MacMhathain, Martha Macmaghan, and the unborn heir o the Earl of Kintail. Ye also stand charged with the attempted seizing and molestation o Lady Sorcha Macmaghan. What say ye?'

A chuckle started on Michael's lips; it grew into a dangerously maniacal laugh. He lifted and rolled his head. Again, he looked at no one but her. Sorcha's newfound strength faltered.

'I've nought to say in this rat's arse of a court.'

Lord have mercy, he was possessed! Father Messi's hand clamped onto her shoulder, his paternoster falling down so the cross landed between her collarbones. She sensed, rather than saw, others crossing themselves. She broke Michael's gaze, meeting Cailean's reassuring one instead. He nodded.

'Bring forth the abbess.'

Her husband's voice was as unyielding and unemotional as a sword. She grasped it and used it to bolster herself.

Ewan broke off and left the hall. It fell silent. She, like the others, was listening intently. Sure enough, there was a screech followed by a scuffle. She scanned the hall; the sight was almost farcical. Numerous pairs of eyes looked heavenwards, following Ewan and Bernice's progress along the ceiling and then in the direction of the steps. He frogmarched her into the hall, but not down the middle – up behind the crowd until they arrived at the dais.

'What is the meaning o this, Cailean Macmaghan? How dare ye lock me away an then pull me in front o court like a common crook!' Bernice shrieked, her face bright red. She caught Cailean's nod to Ewan, who spun her around to face Michael. Sorcha would never do justice in describing the way Bernice's face paled. Likely the woman thought him dead. A murmur rippled through the crowd. Loathe as she was to admit it, Michael had been right in one regard. The trial was as much for show than anything else; no one could doubt their guilt.

'Who is this vile creature?'

So this was what Pa meant by a guilty person being a little too quick to deny association.

'Shut up, ye old hag. Because of you, I'll hang. If ye'd done what ye said ye would then neither of us would be in this damned mess!'

'How dare ye? I did everything right! It's no my fault that the only thing ye can kill is a useless child!'

Sorcha jumped to her feet as the hall descended into chaos. Martha's mother was being held back by her husband. Hidden blades had been drawn from Lord only knew where. Shouted orders from the *leuchd-crios* and castle guards. Retorts from the others. Someone pushed her towards Cailean. Her legs tangled in the plaid and furs. She fell forwards, into him. Pain sliced through her chest and seized her stomach as he tried to catch her. Michael's insane laughter; Bernice's shrieks.

'Silence!'

The shouts of the men stopped immediately. The curses of a fighting, heartbroken mother fell into loud, gut-wrenching sobs. Sorcha's heart threatened to burst through her chest. Even Michael and Bernice had been silenced. Cailean's *leuchd-crios* surrounded their chief and his wife swords unsheathed and facing outwards. Likewise, guards had circled the accused. So fast. The only man with a sheathed weapon was her husband. Did his level of control know no bounds?

Another wave of pain. She doubled over, clutching her stomach and fighting for breath. She dismissed Peggy, who had not been allowed to approach anyway. Cailean was looking at Sorcha; the blue of his eyes almost black. His anger not directed at her, but because she was roughly handled in the commotion. Of that, she was sure.

'Tis nearly over,' he murmured.

She nodded, stood up and took a step back. Her correct place, just behind him.

'I'm going nowhere. I am yer *fiadh-chat*, am I no?' she responded, equally quietly.

The tips of his lips flashed upwards for a brief moment, then he returned his attention to the clan.

'Sheathe yer blades. Ye shame me by bearing them in this hall. Be damned grateful this isnae the fort!'

The slightly slower, though still resonant sound of all manner of weapons returning to sheaths filled the hall. A good many men appeared shamefaced, though whether that would stop them in the future was another matter. Slowly, the guards relaxed. And last of all, upon a single word from Cailean, his *leuchd-crios* sheathed their swords. From behind her came a quiet apology from Mata – it must have been him who pushed her.

'I ask ye once more, Michael Gilchrist. What dae ye say in yer defence?'

'Go tae hell!'

'Twice the accused has forfeited his right tae a defence. Ye leave me with no choice. Michael Gilchrist, ye are found guilty on all charges. Ye are to be taken from this hall and hung by the neck from the ramparts. Yer body will stay there as a warning tae all until it or the rope rots. From there, the carrion and beasts o the land will do with ye as they see fit.'

Cailean held his hand up to still the already moving guards.

'Ah personally request that ye lower him slowly.'

Sorcha forced herself to watch them take him away. To remember this moment, yet she felt no satisfaction. Just a strange distance from a man who was no longer her brother. The brother she knew would have soiled himself. He would have begged forgiveness. Wheedled, manipulated, or run away. The person being led to his death – well, she doubted he would accept the last rites.

And what of Bernice? Would she hang too? She had done little more than incite. Ewan pushed the abbess forwards.

'Ye have no jurisdiction over me. Ye cannae charge me.'

'I dinnae intend tae, for ye are correct. Law dictates that as a member of the clergy, ye are tae be tried in their court. But there is still a measure of justice I can mete out.'

Sorcha's eye twitched. His tone did little to soften the sting of his words. She watched the abbess's face. Relief, then confusion and then fear.

'No – no, Cailean! Ye cannae dae that. I have nowhere tae go!' Bernice's voice grew more hysterical as she pleaded. 'Please, my nephew, I'll pledge my life tae ye. I'll do whatever penance ye wish o me, but no that. Please, I beg ye, no that!'

'Bernice Nic Choinnich, I hereby strip ye of yer name, yer kin, and of yer ties tae Clan MacMhathain. Ye will find nae food nor shelter with any clan member, under threat of banishment. Ye will be deprived o all the clan has provided ye and ye will be cast out tae be driven from these lands...'

Ewan unsheathed his dagger and started to hack at Bernice's gown, tearing it from her body. Once it was on the floor, he ripped off her wimple and veil, revealing that the so-called pious abbess had allowed her hair to grow long. Another came forward and bent down in front of her. He grabbed at her feet and cut the shoes and hose from them, leaving her with nothing but her shift.

'...Should ye set foot on clan land again, any man may strike ye down without fearing punishment. I turn my back on ye, woman o nae clan.'

There was a shuffling of feet as those in the hall moved as one, turning to face away from Bernice. Sorcha barely got a glimpse of the distraught woman's face before Cailean had spun her around so that they too had turned their back on her. She could hear the abbess choking on her tears.

'Cailean, Sorcha, please dinnae dae this tae me!'

Sorcha shuddered. The only time she had heard her name on the woman's lips, and she wished it was not. Someone struck the abbess, hard enough to make her stumble by the sound of it. Surely not Ewan? He was so gentle!

'Ah suggest ye leave now, before the causeway is fully flooded,' came Ewan's drawled-out warning, followed by the sound of her running feet, and, from beyond the great door, children mocking her. *They knew what it meant?* A handbell sounded, breaking the hall from its spell.

Cailean was pale, almost grey. She couldn't leave him like that.

'Come.'

Ignoring the questioning looks, she guided him back through the door and up the steps into their chamber. She closed its door in Ailis's face and drew the bolt. Just the two of them. He had been strong for her, so she needed to be strong for him.

He sat on the bed, rubbing the bridge of his nose. A distant look in his eyes. It must have been his first banishing, so tight was the clan. Well, at least those of it she had met. She pushed herself between his legs, ignoring her own pain. Cailean blinked and came out of his thoughts. He looked up at her. Not that he had far to look.

'Sorcha... I... ye dinnae need tae dae this.'

'But I do, my love, so share yer burden with me.'

Chapter 36

'So when are ye going tae tell him?'

Mordag tried to hide her filched, honey-smothered bread from Caitlin.

'Ah dinnae ken what ye're talking about,' she replied innocently, while smiling knowingly. Along with craving the sticky sweetness, Alasdair's pawing of her breasts had become painful. And Caitlin knew she had not bled. Her maid snorted.

'If he has half the learnin he appears tae have, he'll ken soon enough,' Mordag added as she walked back outside.

They were supposed to be tending to her raised beds but the honey from Lochalsh was the best she had ever tasted. She must get Jock to plead a need for more. Discreetly licking her fingers clean, she sat on the edge of the first raised bed. What herbs she had managed to rescue from the old garden now lived here. The yarrow was thriving and, with luck, would flower well. And the horseradish had survived its splitting. She teased free the few plants she knew to be weeds, if only to take her mind off the honey.

Around her feet, Jock's dog snuffled. Then suddenly froze, his head cocked to one side. She stopped. Were they back? He shot forwards, yapping in excitement. For a second time, she abandoned her work, greeting the two men on horseback – or rather, the annoying one.

'My lord husband.'

'My lady wife.'

Alasdair grinned, dismounted, then lunged towards her, catching and kissing her like a common man. She huffed at the indignity before surrendering to his lips, secretly delighted by his lack of airs. It had only been a few nights, but it had been too long. She drew her head back, her eyes scanning him.

'Was everythin all right?'

'Aye. Tis as I thought.'

She frowned. He had told her of his plans with Jock.

Mordag glanced past him at the old seneschal. He was greeting his new wife, Bessie. The widowed, and far younger, weaver had taken a liking to him. She remembered Alasdair's face when they had been found in an 'embrace' and dragged before him. He had been forced to accept their claim of marriage through the old way – a vow before God and no one else. And why was he speaking so loudly?

'Just dinnae kill me when it affects us too,' he suddenly murmured.

She tilted her head. What had he done now?

'Och dinnae look at me that way, tis no my fault that someone has upset the Sluagh Math,' he said, loudly again.

She crossed herself. He leaned in to kiss her cheek – no, to whisper in her ear.

'Our men are going tae have some fun; encourage them tae think the land is cursed.'

A feint? As if reading her mind, he nodded. She gestured with her eyes to the hall, before speaking just as loudly.

'Likely ye, with yer big feet. And, Christ give me strength, did the horse drop ye in fox dung? Ye fair reek! Caitlin, heat some water up and have one of the men prepare a tub. I'll no share a bed with that wretched stink!'

Alasdair stepped back, laughed heartily and gave a courtly kneel. He took her hand in his, kissing it.

'As my wife commands it, it shall be done!'

He garnered a few half-hearted laughs from onlookers, already fearing the unseen. She rolled her eyes and pointed. Now that really had been too damned much!

*

Mordag checked the scent of an oil before pouring it into the tub. The heavenly smell twirled around her as Caitlin added a final bucket of hot water.

'Thank ye, Caitlin, I'll help him bathe.'

'Ah!' Caitlin nodded in understanding.

Mordag tutted in response. She would tell him later. After the bath, when she lay in his arms. Alasdair also thanked the maid as she left. A boy carrying the food and drink entered, looking extremely uncomfortable. She lifted the cloth. Bread, meat, cheese and a *large* pot of honey.

'Forgive me, my lady, but cook said tae tell ye that that was all the honey he could now spare. If ye take any more, he'd no have anythin tae cook with. Same fer bread. There would be none left fer the meal.'

She hurriedly dropped the cloth and took the tray.

'No matter, twill be fine.'

The boy quickly fled. She placed the tray on the table and turned, bumping into Alasdair. He was already stripped to his waist.

'What was that about?'

He reached past her, taking and examining the pot. She quickly snatched it from his hand.

''Tis nothing, really.'

He watched her closely before reaching for the cheese and unsheathing his knife.

'But there is enough there tae last until... Wait... are ye eating for two?'

No, this was not how she wanted it to go. She had only been jesting when she spoke of him figuring it out for himself! She stammered.

'Well... maybe... oh, damn it. Aye!'

Alasdair went stone still. She could see every one of his emotions playing out on his face. Shock, disbelief, realisation. He started to laugh, haltingly at first.

'I could no bring... Didnae dare hope tae... Ouch!'

He dropped the knife and the cheese, lifting his hand. She caught sight of blood – how had he cut so deeply?

'Och, Alasdair! Ye clumsy...' she grumbled, as she reached for the cloth that had covered the food. Turning back, she found an ashen face. He swayed and took a step back.

'Mordag, I...'

'What's wrong? Alasdair? Yer scaring me!'

Mordag gasped as he tumbled to the floor. She fell next to him, reaching for his head, and shouted for help. He was a dead weight. She ran her hand over his face, felt his breath on her skin. Thank the Lord he was breathing! An illness?

Seumas burst through the door. He looked from her to Alasdair and sighed.

'Dinnae just stand there! Do something! Where's the nearest healer?'

'Och, he's fine. He'll come round shortly. Now, where's the blood?'

Had she not been cradling Alasdair's head, she would have launched herself at the incompetent warrior.

'Ah thought I told ye...'

'Ah ken what ails him, Lady Mordag. He's had it since he was yea high.'

He motioned loosely at his thigh. She wouldn't have believed him, but for the calmness of his voice. She sniffed. 'His hand. He cut himself when he – when I confirmed that ah'm carrying his child.'

Seumas' hand stilled over the cloth. 'Well, that would do it. The damned *sumph*. And may ah be the first tae congratulate ye.'

She smiled weakly. Alasdair groaned softly.

'Shh. Ye had a wee tumble.' Mordag soothed him as he lifted limp hands up.

'Dinnae ye dare look at yer hands,' growled Seumas.

Immediately, her husband dropped them, and an idiotic grin spread across his face. She blinked in disbelief.

'Tis true? I'm going tae be a father?'

Her mouth fell open. The fairies must have taken him! Seumas grunted from where he was binding the wound.

'As usual, there's nowt wrong with his thick skull.'

Frustrated at being left out, she finally snapped. 'Will someone tell me what is going on?'

Alasdair sighed heavily. 'I cannae abide the sight o me own blood.'

Now he said it, it seemed obvious. Still annoyed, she snorted. 'And? Ye should have told me! Tis nowt tae be ashamed of.'

Why was he staring at her like she had grown another head?

*

As much as she tried, Mordag could not convince Alasdair of that. As for the babe growing within her, it had sent him back to his writings. Spurred on to break some code. Could men not be satisfied with one written word? He was so distracted by it, a louse made better company. So she spent her time in the hall, listening to talk while embroidering swaddling for the child.

'Old Fionghan had gone out tae piss last night and swears he saw a beast in the loch,' Jock declared.

'That man cannae see straight, the amount he guzzles. Twas probably a lost seal. Ye ken we've had them before,' retorted Caitlin. 'If ye want a truthful encounter then how about that *bogle* Una saw?'

'But Una jumps at the sight of her own shadow.'

'Well, aye, but—'

'Ye cannae deny something got the linens,' interrupted Bessie.

Mordag winced. A whole day's washing wasted, and

she knew the real culprits. When things returned to normal, she would have them help Una for at least a day. Jock caught her eye. He was grinning. Damn it, he was as bad as Alasdair! She shook her head, put down her sewing and grabbed a cup. She drank heartily, only to spit it out as Bessie's lad burst through the door, shouting.

'Jock, Jock! The sheeps are different colours!'

'Ye only just noticed?' he retorted.

'No, no. Their whites have changed!'

Wearily, she eyed the seneschal and got up. If they had destroyed the wool, well, fae or no fae, there would be trouble. She and the others followed the excited boy outside. He pointed at the hillside behind the village. Mordag shaded her eyes. Sure enough, the animals were streaked with differing shades of blues, greens and reds. Bessie cursed and fled to the hall, likely checking on their supply of dyes.

'Oh, fer goodness' sake! This is too far,' she muttered so only the seneschal heard her, then spoke louder. 'Catch them and check if it's set, or can be washed off.'

She left them to it, making straight for the solar. Alasdair was surrounded by scraps of parchment, his hands blotchy with ink, oblivious. She reached over and slammed the book he had open. He jumped and let out a loud curse.

'What did ah dae tae deserve that?'

'No ye, yer men.'

He blinked and she snorted.

'They've gone and dyed the sheep. Damn it, Alasdair, it's no funny. Why are ye laughing?'

'Because it's my fault, or rather my child self's fault. It'll no harm them.'

She hmphed and folded her arms; his explanation had better be good.

'I convinced my brother that it was a better idea tae dye the wool while it was still on the sheep. To prove it, I stole some dye from the stores and had him catch one. But no matter what we did, the dye wouldnae go into the wool. Then Cailean remembered something important that we had not done. And I'm sure my men havenae done it.'

She groaned.

'Ye pissed on it, didn't ye?'

'Aye, we both did. That wasnae the worst part though. That was our father riding intae view with the Domhnaill and them both finding us at it. Cailean was due tae leave with him the next day.'

Slumping onto the stool opposite, she shook her head. She should have guessed from his other stories that it was something he would have done.

'I swear, Alasdair, if it doesnae come out…'

'…ye can recreate the beating ah got, aye.'

He came and knelt in front of her, placing his hand on her stomach.

'Try no tae stress, for his sake. Shall we go and see if they make a rainbow?'

He really was a rogue, but she could not stay angry. To be honest with herself, she would have loved to have seen the look on the young Alasdair's face when he got caught. She shook her head but smiled.

'What of your work?'

That wiped the mirth from his face.

'Oh, I cracked it, I was just reading. It has been interesting, but of little use yet.'

*

Again, Bessie's lad disrupted Mordag's work with shouted news. Though good news this time: the boat from Lochalsh was here. She set down the wool she had been untangling and led her group outside, calling for fresh ale to be brought. A part of her swore her stomach was already swollen and she had to stop herself from smoothing her skirts.

Odd – nothing was happening at the dock. They all stood around, looking uneasy. One quietly spoke with Seumas. Normally happy to receive word from his wife, he looked worried. Forgetting the bump, she lifted her skirts, intending to hurry towards them. Alasdair cut her off.

'What's wrong?' she asked, trying to look past him. He pulled her away, into a firm embrace. And held her, not moving. Unable to shift herself, she looked over his shoulder. Daniel was now ranting. Only the odd word reached her ears. Something about an old hag.

'Alasdair, what is it?' she asked again, softening her voice. He broke away, looked at her and embraced her again. In that brief moment, she saw tears. It was bad news.

'No here, inside,' he murmured.

They passed quietly through the hall, avoiding the gazes of the curious. Up the steps and into the chamber. Mordag met Caitlin's eyes and the maid left without a word. She turned to face Alasdair, only he was not looking at her. He took a few steps forwards, then knelt, pressing his head to her stomach. She noticed a missive for the first time. It did not bear Cailean's seal. Taking it from his hand, she looked over the scribbles. Like the seal, they looked nothing like the others she had seen.

'Tis from my cousin. Sorcha was attacked by a man she considered her brother, Mordag.' His voice cracked. 'She survived but she was pregnant.'

A giant hand squeezed her chest.

'*Was* pregnant?' she asked, though she knew the answer. Mordag screwed her eyes shut and let her head fall back. She softly recited a prayer. It was hard to feel for someone she had never met, but Sorcha's words had been kind. And – she shivered – just the thought of losing *her son* was enough to overwhelm her. The pain Sorcha must be feeling. She wrapped her arms around Alasdair and their son.

'I failed them at the worst possible moment,' he muttered.

'What? No! Ye couldnae have done anything. They are there, we are here.'

'Ye dinnae ken. I could have stopped it.'

What was he talking about? He had mentioned nothing about stopping a brother. She searched her mind again, just in case he had. Oh, that!

'That day at Robert's court?'

He lifted his head, to stare at her in confusion.

'Angus was watching it and told me all about it. Ah assume that man was her "brother". Was there really any other option?'

'Nae, but if he was nae able to pay his way out…'

'From what you've told me, if no him, then someone else might have attacked her instead?'

Alasdair fell silent for some time, sighed and slowly stood up. When did he start looking so old?

'Aye, if they conspired with our aunt as he did. Either way, this changes things and no for the good, Mordag. I need tae get back to work. Prepare...'

'Now?'

She did not want to be alone. And he still did not look good. Alasdair hesitated, then gestured with his head to the bed.

'Nae, no right now.'

Good. She still felt chilled and just wanted to be held. With the rebels on their doorstep, it could have easily been her.

*

Alasdair slipped quietly from the hall, intent on spending time in the solar. It had been a rough evening. Now where was that scroll? He searched through the piles of rolled-up pieces until he found it, then settled in his chair. Bernice's actions had caused a damned mess. Thanks to past infighting, the nearest line to theirs was several generations back, or Donald.

He ran his hand through his hair and then unravelled the scroll. With both his parents being traitors, his cousin's honour would prevent him claiming his right to be chief, should the need arise. Without Donald, he would be deemed the most suitable. And with battles looming, Cailean would likely be confirming that by proclaiming Alasdair *tanist*. He made a note on the parchment and silently cursed clan politics.

The door opened; looking up, he was surprised to see Mordag. She approached without speaking, and he welcomed her into his arms. He could hardly blame her for not wanting to be alone. She stared at the scroll, then traced her fingers down the lines. She must have seen a tree before.

'This you?' she asked, pointing a finger at Cailean's name. He moved it across.

'I was just about tae add ye.'

'But ye are alone?'

'Aye, I said—'

'No, should Ruth no be on here?'

He wrote in her name and put his quill down. The scroll was not a full tree, marking only lines of continuance and meant to quickly guide a reader. The full tree was at the fort and in the *sennachie's* mind. He calmly explained this to Mordag, and that it was his wish to go against it by pre-emptively adding hers and Sorcha's names.

'It seems cruel tae leave off names. Is this a common practice?'

'Aye, they leave off likely branch ends and dinnae add marriages until issue is confirmed tae save space. Most copies outside personal familial records are like this. Ruth was no expected tae live tae adulthood, sickly as she was, let alone have a child.'

'It's just no right though: if no one kens outside the family, then people can get missed or forgotten about. Did ye no say that Edward stole records? And castles being razed and the Herschip. How many people have been forgotten because their history either died with the people, or was destroyed?'

He did not react; he was too busy staring at the tree. A sickly girl unlikely to live; a land full of people with the Comyn name. No records past John's death, but the manor had been prepared for someone after it. A part of a rushed dowry; a way to ensure it stayed tied to Scottish folk and not a lowly English knight? And, being English, he was unlikely to have close ancestry. Had it really been staring him in the face all this time? Or was he grasping at smoke? Something sharp jabbed him in the ribs.

'Ye really need tae stop doing that when ah'm talking tae ye.'

'Yes, no… Christ's teeth; Mordag, yer magnificent!'

'What?'

She stared, dumbfounded, then suddenly lifted her chin. 'Och, aye, of course ah am, ah have tae be, tae put up with ye!'

'No, ye dinnae understand. It makes sense! That's why I cannae find anything!'

Despite everything, he could not stop the grin. He could finally be useful again! He pulled her to him and kissed her, letting his love flow freely. She reeled from his lap.

'He's addled! He's finally succumbed to it!'

Alasdair laughed – he would have done more but he needed to act fast. He needed to confirm it and then send word to Cailean. But where would he be? The court was at Dunfermline Abbey, and his brother would be bound for it. For the christening. And how to get confirmation? Of course, Thomas's bestiary! He jumped up.

'Dinnae wait up for me. It's going tae be a late night.'

'Aye, it looks like it. Just, dinnae spend all night here.'

Her words made him pause. It was hard to overlook how much she had changed since they had arrived there. He treasured the words she had uttered after their argument. And now, that tone she used. He took her hands and kissed the wrist of one, then the other.

'Wild animals couldnae keep me from yer side.'

He grinned as she huffed, ever her wont to have the last word.

'Wild animals, no. Yer collection of writings, maybe.'

She rolled her eyes and left.

Eager to keep his word, and desperate to confirm his hunch, he grabbed the bestiary. And struggled to get the fine needle into the hole. He forced himself to slow down. Opening it, he leafed through the pages until he found those discussing Clan Comyn. In particular, the Badenoch line. There, next to a name he did not recognise, Thomas's scrawled 'Raven' and, miraculously, no cross.

Thank you, you canny old tyke!

Chapter 37

'He did it!'

'This better be good.'

'Left behind an eager wife fer this.'

'Christ's knees, yer wife eager? She been skimmin the ale?'

The hastily formed group chattered in nervous excitement. Wild rumours had spread like fire since the arrival of a boat at Druim Earbainn's dock. Now they would learn the truth. Their leader arrived. His anger radiated far enough to silence the group without a word.

'He damned well failed! And no only failed, but got himself caught and hanged!' he snarled.

'And? We didnae expect him tae succeed, did we now?' his limp-armed companion asked, exuding derision.

The leader swung around, getting in his face.

'What part o caught did ye no hear? The fool likely sang like a thrush.'

Quickly, the man backed down.

'Aye, didnae think o that, did ye?'

'Tis worse, David,' came a cracked voice from the back. The men parted to let an old, frail man through. He looked the leader in the eye.

'News arrived that the false king now has heirs – aye, heirs. His English whore bore him twin boys.'

David shielded his face. When he looked up, it was grim. Everyone knew what that meant. Double the security if they made it out of the dangerous years of infancy.

'Then we have nae choice. We'll get our woman back the Highland way. And once we have her, those that doubt will rally tae our cause. We will place the true heir on our kingdom's throne!'

Around the abandoned outbuilding, most raised their fists in defiance and cried out their agreement. Those with experience of battle looked on sullenly. They knew better.

'We have a hundred in Buchan and a further hundred coming from the other branches.'

'But no official support,' interjected the only survivor of the reiving attempt.

'Aye. Tis similar with Macnachten. He'll be sending his heir down with fifty men, but no himself. No doubt so he can pledge innocence if it disnae go in his favour.'

'The louse-ridden, worm-gutted gowk,' said another, to much agreement.

'Finally, the Dubgalls are bringing 200 o their own.'

One of those with experience cursed. 'Four hundred and fifty men. Hardly enough. They say the MacMhathain can call over 1,000, and that's without reaching out tae the likes of the Domhnaill.'

David's eyes flashed dangerously.

'It will be more than enough. We ken these lands

better than all o them, do we no? And we'll have the hill! So wheesht or get out!'

The man pursed his lips. 'What's yer plan?'

'The slopes are too steep there for them tae amass anywhere but the woodland or the north-east slope. They'll no slog through the woods, they're too overgrown, even *his lordship* hasnae touched them.'

He looked unconvinced, but the others agreed with David. Shaking his head, he broke away from the rest and headed outside to get some fresh air. He was shoved out the way by a livid scout barging in, his clothes covered in muddy splotches. He pushed his way through the crowd and set an accusatory glare on them all.

'Who decided tae harry the manor by driving their sheep over the damned hill?' the scout demanded. 'Was it you, Fergus, or perhaps you, John? Ah ken ye've always hated me.'

'What are ye blathering about, ye fool? Ah've no moved me sheep yet,' retorted John, with Fergus in agreement.

'Yer herds are gone. And I was nigh-on trampled by the devils, runnin towards the manor with no man guidin them.'

'God's arse, the damned fae!' exclaimed Fergus.

Both men shot from the building to find their lost beasts. Just cursing the fairies was enough to unsettle many of the men there. They crossed themselves and murmured about how active the creatures were being. Some speculated that it was an ill omen.

'Fer Christ's sake, tis naught. Now will ye listen tae me...' roared David.

Chapter 38

The normally patient Alasdair found awaiting the reply agonising. Time appeared to stagnate and, no matter what he did, his thoughts often returned to Sorcha's bloodline. An illegitimate daughter was no issue; bastards had been crowned before. And were often self-made. Or a sibling? One barely of age or, as in Ruth's case, too sickly to think useful. Either way, not needed until Comyn supporters had no other choice. He put the axe he held down and slowly stretched his back.

Alas, he also could not shake the feeling that a hushed expectancy gripped Druim Earbainn. Something was coming; it was just a matter of what would arrive first. He glanced around at those he could see. To 'encourage relations', he had distributed plaid, but they were not all the same. Only those he could trust received plaid woven in Lochalsh. To distinguish it from export, the weavers all followed the same weave; one Cailean's warriors knew well. Those he distrusted received plaid woven by Bessie.

His and his men's armour lay ready. No longer were

they seen in more than twos or threes, and many slept away from the manor. Things were now beyond his control, so he had devised several plans for Mordag's safekeeping, as much as he had loathed the thought.

Alasdair looked to the pile of wood; that was enough for now. Though he itched to do more, the smells from the kitchen were far more enticing. Besides, he was not avoiding anyone. Although Mordag's moods did change like the wind, especially now the honey had run out. Fine, maybe he was, a little.

He threw his *léine* back on and, now walking towards the hall, fastened his belt. A boy passed by with a pewter platter; he unashamedly grabbed a still steaming pastry from the top of it.

'Hot, hot...'

He tossed it between his hands, drawing giggles from several nearby children. He grinned, winked – then, forgetting, bit into it and succumbed to several choice curses. They howled with laughter at his expense. Despite his pain, he smiled. Children always found the good in a situation. And Lord knew, he needed that at a time like this.

'Clear the way, clear the way!'

Cries and galloping hooves, then Arthur, followed closely by Angus. Both soaked with sweat, as were their mounts. They reined in and Angus caught his eye. The lad shook his head.

'Go home and stay there,' Alasdair ordered the children, dropping all playfulness.

They ran off. The kitchen boy was returning, empty-handed.

'You! Find Seumas and Jock. Now!'

He snatched the missive from Arthur, with a warning that he would be needed again, and motioned to Angus to follow. He tore open the seal as he strode into the hall.

'Out!'

Around him, people abandoned the space. He scanned the badly written reply, which confirmed what he suspected. Sorcha shared the Red Comyn's bloodline. Indeed, she had as strong a claim to the throne. Correction. Whoever married her had a claim. And if she bore them a son – *Christ's teeth!* That was why Robert had chosen Cailean – he would *never* pursue it.

The hall door shut behind him.

'Where are they massing?'

'Here; they want tae battle on land they ken well.'

'I thought as much. How long?'

'Ah've no idea, but ah'm meant tae be with them.'

Great, just great. As soon as they realised that Angus was gone, they would move. He needed to get Mordag out of there. Riding was too dangerous, and they would be coming from the north-east. Plus, if she left in too obvious a way, the scouts on the hills would know that he had been alerted.

'The path's clear and marked, my lord,' said Jock, already a step ahead of him.

'Good, but the men—'

'I'll take her,' interrupted Angus. 'If ah meet anyone, they'll no ken what ah'm doing. And it's no as if I can go back.'

Alasdair hesitated, looking him over. He had filled out some over the winter. And judging by the way he now held himself, it was not fat. But Angus was still a boy and, he'd wager, had not wet the blade he carried.

'They'd both be safe,' added Jock.

But he had no other choice.

'Fine. Jock, explain how he can get through the woods. Ye're tae continue on down tae Clan Iain Abrach. Tell them I sent ye, they ken I might send folk their way. And tell Fraoch to get his arse tae Cailean instead o charging up here.'

For the first time, Angus looked doubtful.

'He'll no tan yer hide. Wouldnae dare… I need tae get Mordag.'

*

Mordag gasped and sat up. She must have fallen asleep, only to be startled awake. She caught Caitlin's reassuring smile. Whatever it was, it had not been meant for her. Now where had she dropped her lucet? A cough from her maid again; she followed her gaze. It was on the table. She did not recall putting it there.

'Ah dare say a dog was caught helping himself,' Caitlin muttered.

'Och, aye. More than likely.'

'But it is almost time for the meal.'

She blinked away the remaining sleepiness and tucked a stray strand of hair behind her ear. With a nod, she got off the bed.

'Me surcoat and a veil, please. And how is the weather looking?'

''Tis holding. Why, what are ye planning?'

She smiled as the gown was placed over her head. 'Fresh air more than anything else.'

'So nowt tae dae with that wager ye have with Seumas?'

Caitlin had finished sitting it right and now stared at her. Her smile transformed into a smirk. What concern was it of hers that they were betting on how quickly it took Alasdair to fill the shed with firewood? It was not even coin at stake. If she lost, she was to do his sewing, and if he lost, he was to whittle some toys. The older woman chuckled and motioned for her to sit.

Alasdair entered just as Mordag felt the last pin slide into place. Her greeting died on her lips, and she struggled to stop a shudder. He stood differently and there was no soft sparkle in his eye as he ordered Caitlin about. Wait, what was it he said?

She swallowed. 'Tis time then?'

'Aye.'

She secured the mantle she felt placed on her shoulders, then pulled the hood Caitlin gave her over her head, all the time watching Alasdair. He was rooting around in his chest. She refused to take the bundle her maid offered her. As soon as he finished, she flung her arms around his neck.

'Ah ken I promised tae go, but I dinnae want tae leave ye.'

'If there was any other way...' His voice; its normal softness gone.

He tightened his hold, then released her. She could feel he was just as reluctant. He was scared and trying not to show it. What was he hiding? She clasped his face in her hands.

'I will see ye soon,' Mordag vowed, as much to herself as him.

She kissed him slowly, wanting to sear the moment in her mind. She guessed he felt the same as, again, they struggled to separate. But it had to be done. He pressed something hard and cold into her hand.

'We will do what we must and hope for the best, Mordag. Take this. Tae our allies, it's as good as my ring. Only Cailean has one that's identical.'

It was a brooch. In its centre, two rampant bears guarded each other's backs. She nodded and pouched it. Taking her bundle from Caitlin, she shared a look, wishing the woman well. Then Alasdair led her from their chamber for what she prayed would not be the last time.

*

'Angus!'

Had he risked himself coming there? Mordag would tan his hide! She hurried up to her brother, patting him to make certain he was there.

He chuckled weakly. 'Aye it's me.'

'Yer tae go with him, Mordag. He kens where tae take ye,' instructed Alasdair.

'But what of—'

He cut her off. 'No enough time. Go.'

His voice sharp. She stepped back. She had promised, but damn it, she needed to know something, anything!

'Please, Mordag, trust me. Get our child tae safety.'

She swallowed. He was right. It was not just her anymore. She shook her head, clearing her thoughts, and nodded. Right, they needed to go. She strode towards the door, Jock and Angus scrambling after her. She pulled it open and stopped, looking at him one more time. The man that stood there was no sop of a courtier but a Highland warrior preparing for battle.

Angus grasped her hand and led her away from her home. A jolt passed through her. The only place she had felt truly at home with the only man, besides Angus, she had ever felt comfortable with. They had to return there, both of them. She could never go back without Alasdair. And he could not die, he was going to be a father!

She stumbled, and forced herself to look where they were going. Wait, what? Why the woodland? She cursed as she nearly tripped over another root.

'Slow down, Angus, ah cannae keep up.'

'Then run.'

'I cannae... I cannae risk falling.'

He glanced back at her, confusion on his face. Damn it, Alasdair had not told him.

'Hush, we're here. And dinnae blame the lady, she's in a delicate way,' interrupted Jock, standing in front of a wall of brambles.

What was he on about? They had barely stepped into the woods, and she could not walk through *that*.

'Remember what I said about the markings, or ye'll get lost.'

'Aye, and just what do ye—'

Jock hushed him again and crouched down. He felt amongst the leaf litter for Lord only knew what. Finding it, he lifted it. A sheep hurdle! It pushed back the overgrowth, but not enough. It was just too deep. Angus pulled her along its length, then bent down. Oh, there was another one! And this time, it revealed a path, not much wider than herself. She hurried onto it.

Behind her, both of them carefully laid the hurdles back down. Then Angus brushed past her, grabbing her hand and dragging her once again. She had to stop him; her mantle was getting caught. Muttering to herself, she freed it and used the same hand to hold it close to herself. Worse, the path was not straight; it wound around, having joined some animal's trail.

Then it spilled into a proper clearing, with paths leading off in all directions. Angus crouched and started examining the bases of trees for something. She was tempted to snap at him to stop being so daft, but Jock's words echoed in her ear. He was looking for something.

'What did that man mean by ye being delicate? Ye've no been "delicate" a day o yer life.'

She snorted. 'Ah thought ye were clever from all that learnin but obviously not.'

'Well, there's nowt wrong with yer tongue. Ah, this way.'

He set off down a path, not giving her time.

'Fer goodness' sake, Angus, ah'm pregnant!'

Now *that* got him to slow down.

*

She took Alasdair's heart with her. Or at least that's what he had to think if he was to keep focused. He swung around and stormed back upstairs. There was still too much to do and Lord only knew how much time left to do it in. He tossed his armour and a bundle onto his bed. This was not going to be comfortable, but it was necessary.

He discarded his trews, swapping them for braies and hose. And tucked a particularly wicked, thin blade into the sewn-in sheath at the top of the latter. It killed well, left little trace, and discreetly handled most locks. His cotehardie also had numerous hidden pouches. And this one was trimmed with ribbon and buttons, making it harder to detect anything placed in them, should he be caught and searched. Then his mail.

Grabbing his weapons, belt, helm and bundle, he moved to leave, only to stop and stare. In the haste, Caitlin had not tidied up Mordag's things. Alasdair grabbed an embroidered fillet, shoving it into his pouch, and left the chamber. He swept his eyes over it before closing and locking the door. This was their home, and he would do everything in his power to see them back there in time for Mordag's confinement.

Jock was waiting for him at the bottom of the steps.

'They're away?'

'Aye, my lord. And the horses are being saddled as we speak.'

'Good, come.'

He entered the solar and took the bestiary from its place, handing it to Jock. It was too big for him to take with him. Jock handed him the keys to the strongroom. The rebels may take the manor, but he'd be damned if he was going to finance their uprising.

'Ye ken what tae do.'

'Aye, my lord, and...' Jock hesitated. 'Take care o yerself. There's plenty here who wish tae see ye return.'

He smiled, though he knew it did not reach his eyes.

'You too, Jock, ye're just as invaluable. Send Arthur in and have these attached tae my saddle.'

Chapter 39

Emerging from the trees, Mordag caught sight of the wide but shallow river she knew to be the one they had passed on their way there. Only she was at its mouth. It really was not that far, so either the child took a greater toll on her than she thought, or she had grown soft. Who was she fooling? Her workload was nothing like before. She hurried to the water's edge and set down her bundle. In it was an empty flask she intended to fill.

Angus crouched down and took it from her, filling it. He had become a nanny goat!

'I dinnae want tae rush ye, sister, but we're no safe yet.'

'I ken, ah just need a moment.'

She sat there, sipping from the flask before she held out her hand. He took it and helped her up.

'We'll cross over there. Then back along it and along the loch edge until we get close tae the inlet of Loch Leven. It'll be easier on ye than going over the hills.'

She nodded, turned, and came to a dead stop. Two

men she had seen before stood above them. Only they looked far from friendly.

'Look what we have here, Fergus. A lost ewe and a bollockless ram leading her.'

'Strange, ah wouldnae have thought he'd let her from his sights.'

'Must have been desperate, what with the others coming. Dinnae recognise the whelp though.'

'It matters no, John. Now be a good laddie and step aside.'

Mordag grabbed Angus's arm and he looked back at her. She slowly shook her head.

'Run. They want me, no ye,' she hissed.

Her brother ignored her and freed himself before drawing his sword. 'She's no yers tae take.'

The damned heroic fool, he was going to get himself killed! Alasdair should never have agreed to this. She could only watch in horror as the men took up their own weapons and split up. Within a couple of swings, it was obvious they were fighting as dirty thugs, one getting to him when his back was turned to attack the other. And they were toying with him. It quickly wore Angus down.

'Stop!' Mordag shrieked. 'Have mercy! He is just a lad and ye're easily besting him.'

She shot between them, her hands held out, trying to stop the fight. John and Fergus shared a glance with each other. She flung herself at Angus, clinging to him. If they really wanted her, they'd not attack. She could feel his anger radiating from him, but he was too tired to speak. The men approached slowly. Ripping his sword from his hand, she threw it away.

'Have ye no honour that ye must strike down a defenceless lad?'

'Ye dinnae ken what honour is, Nicnachten,' growled Fergus. 'But we're willing tae give ye what ye wish. He'll die soon enough o blood loss or exposure.'

Mordag grabbed and hugged Angus once more. Into his ear, she whispered, 'Stay hidden until the MacMhathain gets here.'

A strong, rough hand grabbed her and pulled her away. She glanced back over her shoulder and saw Angus knocked down with the butt of his own sword.

'Nae!'

'Wheesht or we'll give ye something tae cry about.'

She bit her tongue, for the sake of her son.

'There's a wee boat down there. It'll be quicker than taking her back round the hill,' mused John as he approached and bound her hands together.

'Will they be there yet?'

'Doubt it, but we can wait it out there. Tis downwind. We'll likely hear their cheer when they gut the bastard.'

She swung around and retched. They were going to kill Alasdair! And they were laughing at her reaction. The louse-ridden, devil-spawned bastards! If she had only held onto the sword, she would have gutted them herself! Again, rough hands grabbed her, pulling her away with them. She glanced back, hoping to see Angus move. Instead, she saw a small boy emerge from the heather and move towards him before looking towards her. Bessie's son!

*

The hall was once again full of people. Alasdair took careful note of those who stood around, smirking. He had finished his missives and secured his sword to his side. Tucked under his arm was his helm and padded coif. Hidden about his person was the seal and other writing paraphernalia. Arthur knew where to find him, for he had no intention of joining Mordag at Glencoe. He caught a nod from Seumas. His horse was ready.

'Stop!' he roared, silencing the hall. 'Spread the word. This is no yer fight and I'll no see unnecessary bloodshed. Send yer women and children tae safety if ye can, but dinnae dae anything rash. Remember, life is worth more than possessions – yers or mine. Go now!'

Those that had their own homes melted away while those that slept in the manor left the hall. He joined them at the front and mounted. Just in time, for he could hear the rebels' approach, their confidence obvious by the sound of their singing. He pulled the coif, then his open-faced helm over his head. With luck, he would not need its protection. He urged Legs forwards, only to stop just shy of the dwellings.

The 'army' was coming towards him. They wore an assortment of badly kept armour, the traditional yellow padded *léines*, or bits of leather cobbled together. Their weapons weren't much better. He doubted they could afford much else. And he was not surprised to see them marching without a banner.

Alasdair remained still, waiting for them to stop. They did, to jeers that were quickly silenced by a man of similar age to Robert. He stepped forwards.

'I see ye MacMhathains have some sense left in yer. Get from here and cower like the *tykes* ye are.'

He refused to rise to the reproach.

'I'll go, but no before ah have yer word that ye will leave those who live here alone. Yer fight is with us, no them.'

The man smiled coldly.

'How nice of ye tae think of *our people* like that. How many women there carry yer bastards? Those babes will be killed. No more. On *that* ye have my word.'

Alasdair had seen and heard enough. He nudged Legs around the army. His men followed without uttering a word. He could only go the way they had come. Mind, that let him observe more. Groups were climbing the hill, setting up around the ridge. They could not be more exposed if they tried! He glanced back at Seumas, who shook his head in disbelief.

They rounded the east of the hill, then crossed the river that skirted its southern side. It was too easy; no one had stopped them. Osgar called out from the back. His hand fell to his sword hilt; he pulled the blade free and reined around. An arrow bounced off the back of his helm even as he spurred Legs into action. Too damned close!

'Split up and ride hard!'

He aimed at the nearest man emerging from behind a gorse bush. He urged Legs to charge on a slight diagonal and straightened up at the last moment. As he expected, fear of being crushed unbalanced the man. Alasdair brought his sword down and sliced at an exposed elbow, leaving it useless. As the makeshift poled weapon fell, it hit and bounced off his mail and, by chance, fell crooked against the only exposed part of his leg.

Alasdair cursed, more from the sting than the depth of the cut, and pushed Legs away, leaving the injured man to fight his own wayward weapon. He spun around – Seumas was surrounded. Spurring Legs into another charge, he aimed for the man whose back was to him, at the gap between his gambeson and kettle helm. This time, luck was in his favour; the sword came down at the top of his neck. It tore at the cloth, not skin, but it was enough of a blow to stun.

Righting himself, he looked back. It caused ample disruption, allowing Seumas to break free. The warrior shot after him, yelling something. Alasdair could not make it out. He looked ahead, spotting the low-hanging branch when it was too late. The helm took most the blow, but twiggy branches got under it. One dug into his skin, cutting a gash between his eyebrows before his momentum freed him.

He cursed bitterly as blood poured down, obstructing his view. Wiping it away was pointless. He did not dare rein his horse in, but he couldn't guide it either. And he was feeling lightheaded. Mordag sprang to his mind, her lectures on how it was not a weakness. Her look on her face when she admitted to being pregnant, her fear for him.

Alasdair gritted his teeth and felt the reins snatched from his hands.

'Hold on!'

Never had Osgar's voice sounded so sweet! He grabbed his pommel; under him, Legs slowed down, changed direction, and sped up once more.

*

Her gut was empty, but Mordag still retched when she heard the cheer. It could not be true; he would not roll over and die. Her captors laughed at her distress but, oddly, had not defiled her. She bet her father was hoping to marry her off again. Only this time he could claim she was fertile. She placed her hand on her stomach and squeezed her eyes shut. She could not cry in front of them. Their son would be named after his father. And if what Alasdair said was true, then Cailean would take care of them both. If she got out of this alive.

The manor was swarming with men when they arrived. They were not how she thought armies looked. But they had that gleam in their eyes; the same one the foraging parties had when she was a child. She shrank back, even as they dragged her by her bound hands up the dock. A man with only one usable arm was in charge.

'Ah, the Nicnachten whore! No wonder we couldnae find her. David will be pleased.'

'Good, maybe now he'll let us…'

Her skin crawled under Fergus' leering gaze. The maimed man grinned and approached. He grabbed her chin and looked her in the eye. His breath stank of gong.

'Dinnae ye worry yer pretty head, *lady*, we'll put ye somewhere where no man will touch ye.'

She pulled her chin free and spat at his feet. He sneered.

'You, go an get the key for the cage, so all can see what we do with the bitches who carry MacMhathain whelps.'

Mordag swallowed the panic rising inside her. That

damned thing. She should have begged Alasdair to knock it down! She could not show fear, so seized her contempt for their cause, brandishing it like a shield. The bottom of the cage was covered in old, half-rotten straw. Someone tossed out the useless old bucket and replaced it with a new one.

Lifting her chin, she walked proudly towards her prison. She would sooner starve than reward them by begging. It was smaller than it looked. She could stand or sort of sit in it, but certainly not lie down. And it was exposed to *everything* and *everyone*. She imagined John being cut down by a MacMhathain warrior and stared at him as he cut her binds. He met her eye and hesitated. *Good.* Someone else shoved him back, swung the door shut and locked it.

Grabbing the bars, she stared at them in defiance as the cage was lifted up. When she refused to break down, the men gathered around it wandered off. Hah! These were the type of men she had grown up around. But now they were gone, and they took her defence with her.

She shivered, drawing her mantle around her and her hood up. There was no sign of Alasdair's body, or spilt blood on the ground. Didn't armies like to show off such kills? She should be grateful she was not staring him in the face! Just that thought left her swaying and choking down a sob.

Perhaps they had not killed him? And the cheer was just for winning the ground? Could she afford to cling to such hope? She had to. Had to imagine him getting away, then returning to free her and their home! Tears pricked her eyes. She had to know! Turning just her head, she strained to listen to the nearest men.

'So what now?'

'The seneschal didnae have the keys, so they're breaking down the door.'

'They still at it? He said it would be easy.'

'Aye, well they reinforced it and added extra locks, didn't they?'

The strongroom! She slid her hand inside her gown and found her keys hanging on her kirtle's girdle. Two rings. One for chests and the strongroom's door, the other, smaller ones her personal keys. She unhooked the first set and, under the hood and gown, lifted them up to her neckline. Jesus, Joseph and Mary, they were cold! Still, the tightness of the top of her kirtle saw them sitting snugly between her breasts. Just in time, too.

A group of men approached and, judging by their behaviour, the man at the front was the biggest cock. She lifted her head and glared daggers at them. If this was to work, she had to keep it simple. And believable.

'Lady Mordag, ah do apologise for how me men treated ye. But ye must understand our concern. Ye being so close tae our enemy and all.'

Yes, the leader – and better spoken, like her brother. Learned?

She snorted coldly. 'Aye, ah shared his bed, when he bothered tae return to it, and aye, ah did what God dictates, but dinnae align me with that whorer. Did me father no tell ye how we met? Ah was trying tae hide and he was hiding so he could spy.'

A murmur confirmed that they had heard the story. The group shifted and out poked a weasel face she recognised. The man whispered in the leader's ear.

'Aye, I heard about the arguments, and the rutting. Ye're pregnant, are ye no?'

She tossed her head, feigning anger at his words.

'He had learned well how tae use his *slat*, unlike most men. Why shouldn't ah enjoy meself? As fer anything else, well, he watched me closely. Didnae allow me tae wander – ah even had tae sit in the same chamber when he wrote.'

The leader checked her words with the weasel. He had no choice but to agree, not knowing what they really did behind closed doors. The man's face darkened.

'So he didnae give ye the keys?'

'Only the ones he deemed worthy.'

'Prove it.'

She sighed and rolled her eyes. 'This better get me out o here.'

Letting her mantle fall away, she pulled the skirt of her gown up, revealing her kirtle and girdle so all could see only one set of keys hung from it. She dropped the skirt and reached for the keys. Unhooking them, she held them up.

'Nought but keys fer my chests and boxes o linens, see? Or were ye hoping fer more o a spectacle?' Mordag sneered.

'Nae, that's enough. Alas, I cannae free ye. The *tyke* got away, and with ye carrying his heir, he's bound tae come charging back.'

Alasdair was alive! She struggled to control her face. Again, the leader apologised. Her ruse must have worked so well that he thought her angered! She followed up with a few choice curses. It worked well enough that a few men crossed themselves.

'Just ye wait till me father hears…'

'Yer father is a nobody! Twas I who ordered ye be spared from the hands o me men.'

*

The lochan sat only a couple of miles away, yet it was hidden from view behind a large hill. Better yet, there were trees to hide the horses in and an old, abandoned shieling. Alasdair had earmarked it before winter as a place to hide in. He and the three others accompanying him rode up to the shelter and dismounted.

He needed to collect his thoughts, so led Legs to the water's edge. The missive would take a while to reach Cailean, especially if he had left court. Then his brother would take time collecting men and resources. A couple of months? He glanced to the sky. The weather was likely to be unfavourable. They would have to rebuild the shieling. Maybe get word to Ròidh to bring a few cattle. Make it look innocent enough.

His men already knew what lay ahead. They were to take turns scouting, watching and, if possible, discreetly disrupting the camp the rebels were setting up. It would be too risky for him to go. He led Legs up amongst the trees.

'We'll turn intae herdsmen, trying their luck with a new place tae graze their coos,' Alasdair said, as he unburdened Legs's back. Furs, plaids, Highland clothing, basic food and his weapons, along with the saddle. Or at least he tried to. He was exhausted, the rush of preparing and battle having long left him, and they slid sluggishly to the floor.

'Aye, but tonight we rest.' Seumas sounded just as sluggish.

'And tend wounds. It's no just yer face,' Osgar added, as he approached to take Legs's reins.

'What?'

Alasdair looked over himself. He spotted the wound on his leg before he recalled it. Though dried, he knew it was his blood. That was enough. Legs's back tilted violently in front of him before blackness descended.

Chapter 40

Somewhere to the north of Douglas-held lands, Sorcha walked arm-in-arm with Evelyn. She tried to listen to the older woman's plans for the gardens, but her mind drifted. The christening had been difficult. Every wail created a fresh wound in her heart. Then there were the festivities, which she had no choice but to attend. And her duty to Elizabeth. Never had she been so grateful for wet nurses, though she was relieved to see her queen recovering well.

As for Evelyn, the widow had insisted they accompany her to her son-in-law's hall house and visit for a few weeks. Predictably, she had known what Sorcha needed and Cailean had agreed to her going. The lands were akin to her childhood home and quieter. Furthermore, as a guest and in a place where she was not expected to be found, she was free to do as she pleased. Sorcha was drawn to Evelyn's grandchildren, enjoying their simple company and delight in nature. Together, they went on many a walk.

Evelyn stopped under a newly replaced arbour. 'Twas

a shame tae cut it all back, but the old framework was nigh rotted. It will grow back, and likely stronger for it.'

Ah, her old chaperone had seen her mind wander. She dipped her head apologetically. 'God willing it will bloom again this year.'

The older woman snorted.

'It definitely will if last night was anything tae go by.'

She looked out across the garden. There was nothing to apologise for; she and Cailean had been reunited the day prior and her body still demanded both a child and his touch.

'My healer thinks it will be winter before my stomach swells again. She insists men's idleness secures it.'

Evelyn roared with laughter.

'When I come visit, ye must introduce me tae this woman!'

Sorcha smiled.

'Ye're welcome any time, Evelyn. Ye've been like a mother to me.'

The older woman blushed, her eyes watering. 'Ah, we have company!'

Sorcha expected to see the children. Instead, her husband and Sir James were approaching. She dipped slightly in greeting. The older earl insisted on giving her the kiss of peace, just to tease Cailean. She could not refuse, but ruined his game by breaking with propriety to embrace a now-chuckling Cailean.

'Alasdair was right, ye two are cut from the same cloth.'

'We hold no secrets between us, my lord. Cailean has told me of yer antics.'

Cailean coughed. 'Well, no all of them, but enough.'

Sir James laughed heartily. 'Then it is little wonder that ye did no stray far from his side last night! Now, Evelyn, ye had something ye wished tae show me?'

Evelyn, who had been shaking her head with mirth, suddenly looked confused. 'Aye? Oh, aye! The new tabard. Come, James, tis this way.'

Both departed far too swiftly for it to have been genuine. She felt Cailean's hand on hers, already guiding her in the opposite direction.

'I should have kenned.' She smiled as he sat on a bench and pulled her onto his lap.

'Can ye blame me?'

'No at all. Oh, what is that?'

He had pulled something small from his pouch and was holding it up. A gold ring, and far too small for his hands. She took it from him when he wordlessly offered it to her. A *signet* ring decorated with their initials and a lovers' knot.

'Tis beautiful, wherever did ye get the time?'

'I ken a man in Edinburgh. Ah sent word tae him when we arrived in Dunfermline.'

She let him take it from her and slip it onto her little finger. Until then, she had nothing beside her writing to identify herself.

'I now ken whose missives I should open first.'

'Och, Ewan will be upset tae hear that.'

Their laughter was cut short by their kiss; one she was in no hurry to break. They would not be disturbed. Nor was she eager to progress any further. She just wanted to enjoy his company. Likewise, Cailean made no move. They broke the kiss and she rested her forehead on his.

'Were it my wish, we would be returning home together.'

'Our wish, *fiadh-chat*.'

'What holds his attention so that it keeps ye at his side?'

'He anticipates war if Edward doesnae pay homage tae Charles.'

She pulled her head away, sickened. More war with England. On their borders or in France? Would Cailean be expected to go? The greed of kings knew no bounds.

'I doubt it will come tae anything – England's too busy fighting itself.'

'But Robert must have men ready.'

'Aye.'

She sighed and laid her head on his shoulder. They may have some time together when she returned to Elizabeth, but that would not stop her from savouring this. He asked her of her plans. She would go to the fort, perhaps visit the chieftains if it was safe to do so. He did not deny her, but she could tell he was unhappy. Just the closest ones, she added.

'Besides, since Alasdair spoke of the Kyle, I've wanted tae see it.'

The corners of his lips rose a fraction. 'Aye, ye should see it. Have the boat land there instead.'

It must be quite safe at the Kyle. She shivered and Cailean set her on her feet.

'No, no yet.'

'It's no that. Something's happening.'

She inhaled sharply; Cailean was not wearing his sword. He drew his dagger and crept forwards. She heard it now, footsteps running towards them. She tucked herself in behind him, so as to not be a target.

'Cailean!'

Donald's voice.

She caught her husband glancing back at her and she nodded. He wanted her to stay there. He stepped out of his hiding place. She heard the feet, for there were more than one pair, slow and then stop, followed by Cailean's customary curse and a flutter of parchment.

'Sorcha, come out,' he called.

She stepped out of hiding, in front of Cailean and the tired-looking Arthur. Cailean did not notice her, he was too busy reading the spidery handwriting. He looked at it, then at the seal, and again at it. He cursed and continued reading. No one spoke.

Cailean ground his teeth: this was Robert's plan all along. It had to be. Keep any uprising hidden; make it seem like 'yet another clan feud'. It just so happened to be Cailean's clan and Comyn supporters. Bound to happen with the giving away of that land. It must be why he was told nothing about Sorcha. The doting knight riding off to do his king's bidding. And at what cost? Alasdair could be dead. Did James know? Randolph? Or, worse, Aonghus Óg?

Why had his father left no clues? If it was not for his brother – or his brother's new alias – he would know nothing.

Cailean looked around, frustrated. If they did know; if Alasdair was dead... Damn it, he needed to think straight! He pushed the parchment into Sorcha's hands. Then held up a hand to silence Donald. *Think fast.*

'Arthur, ye ken where he's staying?'

'Aye, my lord.'

'Rest here tonight, then ye're tae take him my reply, understood?'

The messenger nodded. Again, he held up his hand to keep Donald quiet. Sorcha gasped, swayed and lost her colour. He grabbed her arms, but she shook her head. Still, he held on, though not holding her up.

'Tis true?'

'Ye read it yerself, confirmed by a distant relative.'

'If I had known…'

'I'd still have wedded ye, Sorcha. Comyn's niece or no. This is no yer doing.'

'*What?*' interrupted Donald, staring in disbelief.

He took the missive back. His cousin was a slow reader, and it was not his to share.

'John Comyn was my uncle,' Sorcha quietly admitted.

Donald's eyebrows shot up. Cailean guessed his next question, answering it. 'They're gathering in the Comyn name. They'll have taken Druim Earbainn by now.'

'Alasdair?'

'I dinnae ken.'

His attention was back on Sorcha. She could not remain here. Or at court. It was too exposed. She was healed, but could she take it? She would have to. He gave his orders.

'Donald, get the men. Have the horses saddled and get supplies. Nothing that needs cooking. I'm sure ye'll be denied naught.'

'And what dae ah tell the men?'

He closed his eyes and inhaled. Should he do it? It

would be his first time. If they were a handful, he would look a fool. But if he underestimated them, he would lose far more.

'Cailean?' Sorcha gently prompted.

He growled, better a fool.

'We're lighting the Crann Tára.'

*

Sorcha reined in her mount at the top of a hill and looked around her. *This* was Lochaber. A patchwork of moor, woodland and water, interspersed with dwellings. Sprinkled patches of blacks, browns and whites gave away the location of sheep and cattle. Unlike the land around Eilean Donnain, these expansive, rolling hills had a touch of softness to their ruggedness. Though she doubted she would have spotted it last year, or appreciated it as she did now.

This was her home; these were her people. They were going to war for her and Alasdair. How many would die? She forced down her emotions, brought on by fatigue. It had been a hard ride and voyage – the hired boat crew had not hidden their stares or curbed their tongues. And the way they had watched Ailis. She shuddered. Yes, her clansmen would die, but they fought for their honour. No one could be permitted to sully the MacMhathain name.

And no one could ignore the Crann Tára.

She had left Cailean and most of the *leuchd-crios* at the shore on his insistence. They had been making crosses and wrapping bits of linen drenched in chicken blood around them. She glanced behind her, spotting dots of flames moving away, in different directions. They had been lit.

Ewan coughed. 'That there is Loch Achaid na h-Inich. Tae its right, just behind that hill, is the field.'

'And above that, Fort MacMhathain,' she added, though she struggled to make it out, so well did it blend into the landscape.

'Aye, my lady.'

'Then let's ride on.'

With only a few miles to go, Sorcha kept the pace brisk. Soon they were rounding the last hill. Below them sat the field where the clan would gather, its edges sloping downwards towards the stream that ran through it. She could make out the fort too, though it hardly looked imposing.

Riding down and across the field, she travelled more slowly. For the first time, she heard Ewan shout. He was ordering every person he came across to remove the grazing animals from it; telling them that the cross was lit. Everything from confusion to fear to determination crossed the faces of those he told.

While Eilean Donnain was overt in its defence, the fort was unassuming. Several feet of raised earth, topped with a palisade and squat towers, made deceptively high walls. No wonder Cailean preferred it. She made straight for the stone hall house.

Inside, colourful murals and display of weapons greeted her. There would be time later to better study them.

'Ailis, the chief's chamber is through that door on the dais. Find whoever's in charge of keeping it and see it is made fit for use.'

'Aye, my lady.'

'Ewan, ye have yer orders, I suspect?'

'Aye, my lady.'

'Just hold on a wee moment!'

She faced the unknown voice. A grey-haired, squat man met her gaze head-on.

'Lachlainn...' started Ewan.

'Just who are you, tae burst in tae here and order folk about, lowlander?' Lachlainn demanded.

'*Lachlainn...*'

She almost stepped back but forced herself to take a step forwards. What was it with confrontations in this clan?

'The only lowlander with the authority tae dae so,' she brazenly challenged back.

'Och aye? Whose?'

'Lachlainn, *this* is Lady Sorcha, Cailean's wife.'

The change in Lachlainn was immediate and he fell to his knee. She waited patiently.

'Forgive me, my lady. I was told of ye, but we were no expecting ye.'

'I forgive ye, for I assume ye are the seneschal?'

After receiving confirmation, she explained why she was there. With her permission, he rose and saw to his job, but not before he had sent her a runner.

'I want ye tae send out word tae all the local healers, midwives and women who can help. If they have the supplies to spare, we need herbs for healing wounds, bruises and broken bones, fats for ointments, and old linen. I'll no see any man healed by hot metal if I can help it. Also, if any can spare their time, they will be cared for.'

The runner hesitated. Dear Lord, must she repeat

herself? No one questioned Cailean's orders. His eyes widened and he hurried away. That was – well, unexpected.

*

Men were already arriving. Cailean leaned on the wall of the tower, watching. They camped in groups based on their locale. Their fires bright sparks against the overcast sky. He would divide them: half to remain, guarding the lands and Sorcha, the rest with him. He listened to his marshal list his calculations. Robert had better compensate him well. And pigs would fly! He ground his teeth.

He had left Sorcha to manage the commonplace affairs. She shouldered them and the battle preparations well. Alas, she saw more of Ewan than him. When he was in their chamber, he was either sleeping or holding meetings. Now, though, he had to wait. For men and supplies to arrive. For news. He could afford her some time, if she would let him.

He found her sitting on his chair in their chamber, taking household counsel. She didn't notice his arrival.

'I'm sure, given the circumstances, the Good Lord will understand our restraint.'

Easter was that close?

'I agree.' Cailean waved them down. Stepping behind her, he added, 'This is no going tae be inexpensive. We also need tae prepare for battle here. When I leave, Sorcha will go tae Eilean Donnain.'

He shot backwards, to avoid being hit by the chair.

'I wish tae speak with my lord husband alone,' she declared.

'Ye may go,' he added, before stalking into the screened-off half of the chamber. What madness had seized her now? She had to know she could not stay there. He fought not to pace. He could not get worked up before hearing her argument. Instead, he leaned against the bed post. He heard the door close and the swish of approaching skirts.

Sorcha pulled up short. He caught her muttered curse. His stance was too much like Alasdair's. Madness seized him and he tried his brother's grin. Or half a grin. Damned face.

'No, please no,' she pleaded, 'I like yer smile more.'

'I'll only stop if ye tell me what this is about.'

She sighed. 'Dinnae be angry with me. But I have tae come with ye.'

He straightened and stared; he would sooner bow to Edward. 'No. And dinnae even try.'

'Ye yerself said Eilean Donnain cannae be easily raised. And a siege is pointless.'

'Aye, tis why you're safe there.' Why was he allowing this to continue? He had heard her, as promised, and given his ruling.

'I am, but what o the clan? Those closest have accepted me, but the others? Most of them dinnae ken me.'

He tensed; they were her clan too. And yet she sullied their honour?

'Dinnae look at me like that, Cailean. They would fight tooth and claw, I ken that. But if driven back…' She sighed and stepped away. He pulled her back and into his arms.

'Ye fear they will harm the clan tae get tae ye?'

He had considered it; the tactics had worked for his ancestors. Though it had taken a lot of innocent blood spilled. How much would it take for an outsider, even if she was their chief's wife? He held her tighter as his rage increased. Had Robert considered this? Brushed off his clan as easily as her life?

Cailean needed to hit something. Hard, repeatedly. Before he said or did something traitorous. He pulled away, muttering an excuse. Sorcha's grip tightened. He stopped; he would not drag her. But damn, if she did not let him go…

'What are ye playing at?' he growled, then noticed her face. It had hardened.

'Dae ye think ye're the only one frustrated, Cailean? I was tae be the son who stopped Robert. Then I was tae be the political pawn o their enemy. But I cannae go out and hit a pell, can I?'

'Then what is it ye want, Sorcha?'

'*You.*'

When had he started kissing her? Or her him? They parried hard and broke off. Panting. Madness indeed. He ripped his belt and *léine* off. His fae, his *fiadh-chat*, wore only her shift. He could not wait for her to unpin her hair. He lunged; she avoided him.

He snorted. 'I thought ye wanted me.'

'I do, but I didnae say I'd make it easy.'

Challenge accepted. He lunged again. She shot back past the screens. She was light on her feet. They reached an impasse at the table, circling around it. He stopped and pulled off his boots. Then dropped his trews. And tried again. Freed. He caught Sorcha easily. They both fell onto the floor. He claimed his kiss. As hungry and hard as the first. Felt her press against his growing erection.

His fingers found her lower lips, parted them. She was heated. Instead, he toyed with her. Flicking, then rubbing when she came near. She fought both him and herself, cursing and clawing him through the linen. Sweat gathered on his forehead. He was fighting his own wants too. And, damn it, she knew! She rubbed herself wantonly against him. A wild cat in heat.

He would not buckle first!

He did not; neither did she. They grabbed each other, rising up as one. Then sinking back to the floor. Their chests pressed together. He urged her with his fingers. His release came swift, drawn out by her cries and grip.

Cailean held her there, long after he had slipped out of her. Her hot breath on his neck. Better than the pell.

'Thank ye.' Sorcha's voice lacked any strength.

He should thank her. But all he could think of was the truth. She had to go to war with him. And, God's balls, he had to win. Only that would free them from this damned chess board.

Chapter 41

The kirk was empty save for Cailean. He knelt in front of the altar, his lips moving silently. Praying for victory, for Alasdair, and for a son. The Lord knew what was at stake, but he was hardly worthy of asking. He had killed dishonourably and would again. That was the nature of war. Alas, this was as much of his own making as Robert's. Something had to change.

He looked up at the cross and made a vow. He would try and distance himself from the king. Focus solely on his growing people – both blood and *sencliathe*. He muttered 'amen' and rose. They were waiting for him. Thirteen hundred men of fighting age and strength.

Leaving the kirk, he descended to the gathering. He needed to speak with the chiefs, chieftains or *tacksmen* of each area. They had already sent reports – numbers, age and experience of their men. And now they needed their orders. He met each of their eyes.

'Who are we missing?'

'Artair and Muireach – they have withdrawn their men from the field and are up in the woods, *mo ciann*.

Each had a man come down with a similar sickness.'

He nodded; a wise precaution. Stepping back, he signalled to Donald to join him. And ordered him to remove two from his list. Cailean could not wait for them. Then he addressed the others.

'The men we fight rally under a dead man's cause; dinnae trust them tae behave with honour. Donald is remaining here. If he touches ye, ye and yer men are tae stay with him. The rest will travel with me.'

'And how will we travel?' someone questioned.

'I havenae fully decided yet.'

'Well then, tis a good job I'm here then, isn't it?' another called out.

'Fraoch! Ye canny devil!'

The men parted, letting Fraoch through. He clasped hands with his old foster.

'A runner from Alasdair told me of yer issue. And, well, ah cannae let ye have all the fun when it's so close tae me home now, can ah? As fer how ye travel, I bring galleys with the Domhnaill's blessing.'

He did not trust his ears. He grabbed the man – 'He lives?'

'Aye, as lucky as a cat that one,' Fraoch said laughing.

He knew that sound; the tic appeared when he was not telling the full truth. Damn, more restraint for now.

'Enough space for several hundred?'

'Aye, if we're friendly like, and add yer boats too. He guessed yer plan correctly.'

'He would.'

He ground his teeth while making calculations. The storeman needed another day at the least.

'We will leave for Loch Alsh two days from now.'

Cailean moved from the gathered men, making way for Donald. He would also leave, but only to spread out at the land borders. If the rebels came, they would be on foot. A sea battle would be too risky for them. Shame. As Cailean waited for his cousin to finish, Fraoch joined him.

'Ye'll tell me the rest back at the hall.'

'Christ, ye're worse than me father!'

*

Cailean watched Sorcha fill Fraoch's goblet. He knew that look too, and glared at the younger man. Now he was threatening to tell stories about his fostering. Fraoch had been a contrary brat with a point to prove. It was often the case with bastards. Despite it, he had been handled no differently. That settled him, though his headstrong inclination remained.

'Enough, Fraoch. Tell me what ye kept back,' Cailean interrupted.

All humour left the man's face, and he looked back at Sorcha.

'Ye can speak freely in front o her.'

'Alasdair is fine. Took a couple of wounds upon leaving, but naught serious. He's playing wi coos nearby while organising the scouts. No seen him for meself, like. The runner worries though. His wife was on her way tae me when she was snatched.'

Cailean cursed; he sought out Sorcha. She sat nearby with a manuscript, oblivious. Alasdair had shared his good news but left it at Cailean's discretion. He had been struggling to find the right time.

'What have they done tae her?'

'She's in a cage, near the dock. Yer brother was nigh maddened by the news. They had tae bind him tae stop him rushing back, apparently. He still escaped and had tae be bound again until they got his word.'

His brother did what? Did he? Of course he did. He shook the thought from his mind. It was not the time.

'She cannae stay there. No in her condition,' he muttered.

What to do? Locks could be forced, but that was loud. He could meet up with Alasdair. His brother would have a key. Yes, go ahead in a *birlinn*, land at Glencoe. Donald coughed. What now? He refocused his gaze on his cousin. Donald nodded at Fraoch, who held up a key, grinning. He snatched it with a growl.

'It's no the time for games.'

'Ah ken; ah meant no trickery. I do have an idea though.'

'Say it.'

'I owe Alasdair, Cailean. He helped me no too long ago. I could take somethin tae Druim Earbainn, something distracting, then get her out while they're busy. Ah thought silver, but it might be used tae hire mercenaries. Or coos perhaps. Me men will relish getting them back. Ah would have done it by now if it were no for the runner making me swear that I'd come here first.'

He snorted. ''Tis good Alasdair forbade ye. As ye nae doubt ken, there's now coos aplenty there, and silver is foolish. They're led by a cause, not coin.' He paused, thinking, before adding, 'Wine. He's no been bringing more than the odd barrel in.'

The others stared at him in confusion. 'He's no been flaunting coin.'

'Ah, clever one that one,' interrupted a thoughtful Ewan.

He had forgotten he was there.

'I dinnae have the stock,' bemoaned Fraoch.

'I do, only yer no taking it.'

All three protested loudly. That got Sorcha's attention. He could feel her questioning gaze. She did not interrupt; he would speak with her later, alone.

'There is a good chance they ken ye, Fraoch.'

'Let me go,' volunteered Ewan.

'No. You and Fraoch will bring the men and protect my wife.'

'They ken our seamen, if no ye, *mo ciann*,' Donald added.

Cailean stared at his old foster. The younger man drained his goblet and stood up.

'Fine, ye can use some o me father's.'

*

They might not know her, but most knew the circlet. Sorcha wore it as she walked through the clansmen. She found the number of women and children also in attendance surprising. Ailis followed closely, along with a strapping man she had ordered to carry and distribute the bannocks. It was not much, but they were freshly baked. Her maid also carried small sprigs of tansy, meadowsweet and other lice deterrents. She had very little so only gave them to those who asked.

The task was a good distraction. She did not begrudge Cailean for holding back the news, for she doubted she could have handled that *and* the christening. She agreed that he had to help Mordag. Another innocent babe would not die because of them. He had left shortly after speaking with her, intending to stop first at Eilean Donnain. She hugged his plaid tighter around her. There were no hounds this time to keep her company.

She pressed a sprig into a warrior's hand while his companion took a bannock. Pleasant as they were to her face, she had noticed the growing mutterings around her. The men had seen Cailean ride out and noticed he had not yet returned. By the time she had run out of her supplies, she could no longer ignore the growing unrest amongst them.

'Ewan, I need tae speak with the men.'

'Is that wise?'

'Whatever Donald told them has no worked.'

'Ah'm sure they're just eager for battle.'

Enough tiptoeing! She was not blind. Ewan backed away before she could say anything and ran off to do her bidding. Finding the other man sniggering, she glared. He quickly fell silent. Only Ailis seemed of sound mind.

'Come, let's go.'

She strode towards the head of the field. Most stepped out of her way, though once or twice she had to raise her voice to be heard by those with their backs to her. A few called out, demanding to know where such pretty lasses were going in such a hurry. They weren't worth her breath.

They had already gathered by the time she arrived. Donald amongst them.

'Which devil called this meeting? There's nought left tae discuss.'

'I did,' she said coolly.

He spun around and quickly lowered himself.

'Forgive me, my lady, but I dinnae understand.'

The others dipped their heads in greeting.

'There is unrest amongst the men. I assume it is because o Cailean's absence?'

The men glanced at each other.

'Tell me!'

One of the chiefs, Iain's father – the resemblance was uncanny – wrung his hands. 'Tis like this, my lady. They ken he's gone ahead but they want tae ken why. Donald will no say...'

'Word cannae reach the curs!' he protested.

She held up her hand and Donald fell silent, letting the chief finish.

'...Well, they dinnae like it. Cailean has always marched with his men.'

Sorcha sighed; Donald's heart was in the right place. Many a night Cailean had voiced fears of other insiders. None had been found; besides, a spy could not outpace their boats. Not now.

'Enough time has passed. Tell them he has gone tae dae what his brother couldnae. He has gone tae rescue Alasdair's pregnant wife.'

Some of the men looked horrified while most voiced confused mutterings.

'He's endangerin himself fer one—'

'Ah thought his wife died years ago.'

Oh, of course!

'His *second* wife.'

Those who were confused looked relieved. She listened to their hushed exchanges. Some thought it foolish, while others understood. Had they had a child ripped from them too? What was she thinking? Nowhere was truly safe for a child.

Another spoke. 'Ye were right tae tell us, Lady Sorcha. While we may have our doubts, our men will be heartened tae learn of his actions.'

She lifted her chin a bit and smiled. They turned fully towards her and seemed to be waiting. But what now, that was all she had to say. What would Cailean say?

'Go now and tell them, for tomorrow we leave tae join him. He will be there tae lead our men tae victory.'

They dipped their heads again and dispersed. She watched them go. They had not grown angry with her for not knowing her place. She glanced back at Donald, who had been joined by Ewan. Both had ridiculous grins on their face.

'Did I dae something wrong?'

'No at all,' Ewan replied, scratching his cheek, 'though Cailean will be sore he missed it.'

'What?'

'Ye'll be leading them tomorrow. They'll expect it now,' answered Donald.

*

They were right. Sorcha stood at the front of the prow of the lead galley. Though she dressed simply, she wore her hair in a single plait encased in fretwork. It kept it modest and tidy, as well as marking her out from the other female followers. At least it was not raining, though there were clouds on the horizon. She came away, heading back to her place. Unlike her husband, she could not stand there for hours.

Ailis was distracted. She had been doing a poor job since Sorcha woke that morn. Absent at first, then clumsy and inattentive.

'What ails ye, lass?'

She snapped out of her thoughts, blushed, and avoided her gaze.

'War, my lady. I ken my Iain isnae fighting, but it disnae mean he's safe.'

Ailis really could never hold a lie.

'I ken that's been on yer mind, but this sudden change is no because o that. If ye're sickening, it's best I send ye back. I'll manage.'

How could Ailis blush any redder? She claimed good health, then stammered over her words. Sorcha hid her impatience as best she could as each stroke of the oar took them further away.

'I... I kept Iain's company last night!' Ailis exclaimed.

She hissed, 'Ye kenned him carnally? Yer maidenhood is gone?'

Pride and fear crossed her maid's face; she nodded her confirmation. Stepping back, Sorcha rubbed her temple. She had trusted Ailis, and this was how she was repaid? She held her hand up to silence the justifications spilling from her mouth. Betrothal and love mattered little – it was her moral duty to keep maids in her care chaste. They could not linger, but this needed to be addressed *now*.

'Ewan, have the Choinnich boat pull alongside. And ye, lass, will come with me.'

He was quick to see her order carried out. She joined him at the side of the boat with Ailis. She held her hands in front of her, her head high.

Iain's father was there already. 'Lady Sorcha, is all well?'

'I was left with no choice, Choinnich. Iain, join yer father.'

The chief folded his arms and stared in disbelief at his son. 'What have ye done?'

Oh, he knew why he was called up but wisely chose to stay silent. She sighed.

'Did either o ye think of the consequences? Even now, yer seeds may have taken root. Ye cannae afford tae keep a wife yet or, heaven forbid, ye could die in the coming days and leave her shamed!'

Iain kept his head up, only for it to be forced down when the Choinnich smacked the back of it.

'Damn it, I'd expect this behaviour from Brian, no ye! Lady—'

She silenced him. She was not yet finished.

'No tae mention the shame. Iain, ye disobeyed Cailean and cast shadow over yer father's good word. And, Ailis, what have I done tae deserve this? No, dinnae speak. If I let it pass, I will be seen as a careless mistress. No lady will send their daughter tae me. Ye leave me with no choice.'

Ailis paled as Ewan stepped behind her. Sorcha nodded to the mast, grateful for his understanding. Back on the *birlinn*, the Choinnich had a firm grip on his son's shoulder. It was hard to tell if Iain was angry with her or himself. She could not be swayed.

'What is yer wish fer my son?'

She shook her head and sighed again, 'He is tae see why men should no dally with ladies' maids, even if that maid is his betrothed. The rest, I leave tae yer discretion.'

The chief nodded. 'Ah agree. He'll no only be punished by me for his wrongdoings tae me, but also by Cailean, lest any man think he can get away with wronging another.'

She gave a sharp nod and faced Ailis. Sorcha held no love for the task. Holding out her hand to Ewan, she was determined to prove she was no beast.

'Yer belt please, it's wider and will hurt less than my girdle.'

Chapter 42

Watching cows gave a man too much time to think, and that was the last thing Alasdair wanted. He scratched his newly grown beard, catching a louse under his finger. How much longer was he to idle, sprouting lice, while Mordag sat in that cage? He could not be seen near there, nor did he trust himself. Instead, he waited for reports, sent out missives and watched cattle. Not a warrior, not a leader, and certainly not master of anything. Far too much time to think.

He got up, rearranged his plaid, and called to the beasts. They would soon be due back at the shieling. He patted the shaggy, wet rump of the one the others followed. Obligingly, she set off. A vast improvement from their first sennight there. He had never herded cows alone, and some time had passed since he last reived. Perhaps he would change that. Though reiving would not be enough if they hurt Mordag or their unborn son.

No, that patch of grass was no different. *Keep moving, you damned beast.* He turned back, intending to gently knee the beast in the neck, and stopped. Three men, still quite a way off, were approaching. He could not hurry them now. Choosing to lean against its back, he did not need to feign his interest. Herdsmen are an inquisitive bunch.

'Ye there,' one called. 'Where can ah find Lochan Lunn Da-Bhra?'

Ah, Sir James had got his missive.

'Now wha would a lowlander like yerself be wantin wi tha puddle?'

He broadened his accent and scratched his chin as he spoke. And caught the flash of annoyance crossing the man's youngest companion's face. Who had thought it wise he join them?

'Business. There's a man out here with coos like yerself; his brother fell ill while escortin a bull tae a buyer.'

'Ah see. Well, ah'm headin tha way meself. So ye may as well come along wi me.'

The young companion stepped forwards, likely intent on chastising him, but was stopped by the speaker.

'Aye, we may as well, like.'

He got the cows moving again after cursing the lead beast. As they led the way, he spoke of there being much movement of late and how he did not like it. He would leave soon to find 'safer pasture'. The Douglas men listened then, when prodded, spoke of general information they had come by. It made the journey back seem much faster.

Daniel must have heard the cows, for he exited the shieling and reached in its heather roof for the sword concealed there.

'Hold off, they're Douglas men.'

Their leader grinned while the young one's mouth dropped open. He smiled in confirmation, but it lacked any mirth. That was hard to find.

'Ah'll handle the coos then.'

'So ye're the fabled Alasdair?' asked the – until then – silent one.

He nodded and motioned to the building. They could speak more freely in there. They went ahead as he scratched around his neckline. If they were here, then surely Cailean could not be far behind.

Settling beside the fire, he apologised for their lack of hospitality. The men brushed it off and shared their ale flasks with him.

'We're tae tell ye that he's done as the Raven asked. It's all ready,' the leader stated.

He nodded, passing a flask back.

'I assume it's with other men?'

'Aye, we're around fifty men in total. Thirty or so are tae get a taste. Oh, and that priest.'

'What?'

'The Douglas is callin in a favour. He wants the men tae see battle. Their fathers are ageing, and they be mighty wet behind the ears, what with the new peace treaty and all.'

Alasdair brushed off the excuse Sir James had used.

'Why would The Douglas send a priest?'

'He didnae. We caught up with the priest. When pressed he said he was headin tae yer side on the Raven's orders.'

What? He had specifically warned the network to stay away. Who would be so bold? And more to the point, why? No, he did not have the strength to contemplate that right now.

'Ah well, ye're tae head for Glencoe. It's where Cailean will land. Angus?'

From the darker end of the shieling, his brother-in-law emerged. The lad had been fevered when he arrived, accompanied by the old woman that lived just past the edge of his lands. She had stayed until the fever broke, then left them with strict instruction. Alasdair had until that point been sleeping with the hidden horses, unable to hear his ramblings about Mordag. Now, though, Angus was recovering his strength.

'Aye?'

'Ye're tae go with them and meet up with Cailean. Tell him what ye told me.'

For once, the lad did not protest but nodded and headed back, presumably to gather his things. Feeling their questioning gazes, Alasdair added for his guests' benefit, 'He's my brother by marriage and a defector.'

'We can trust him?' asked the quieter second.

'With my life.'

That satisfied them.

'We'll stay tonight if tha's alright and set out come dawn.'

He nodded his confirmation to the leader. It would look better, should anyone be watching.

*

The shouts did not stir Mordag – they did it every damned time a boat passed by. She kept her forehead pressed against the bars. The baby did not like it but her back needed a rest. And her feet were a hot, swollen mess. She snorted as she recalled the bitter cold of her first night. She had prayed that they would show mercy and free her. How wrong she was. How long had it been now? She had lost track of time.

At least they allowed Caitlin to tend to her. First with plaids, food, clean straw, and bucket emptying. Then they lowered the cage and let her out every so often so that her sores could be cleaned and dressed. But only when they knew she was going nowhere fast. Caitlin forced her to walk back and forth, and to accept dry plaid. Without her, Mordag and her son would be dead.

She stared at Alasdair's brooch. It was as filthy as herself, but it was the only thing she had. He was still alive somewhere and was coming to get them. Caitlin had promised that. The shouts grew louder. Irritated, she looked up. The boat was not passing but coming towards the dock. She could not, would not, shout a warning to the fools.

Her sore fingers tightened their grip on the brooch. It was not one of Cailean's boats. Were they now being supplied that way?

'Ho there!' cried a man aboard, as the rebels gathered nearby. Was he blind? They hardly looked welcoming.

'Who are ye?' responded the man with the single useful arm.

'Och dinnae be so fearful, Fraoch sent us tae deliver the wine he promised Alasdair.'

She sat up straighter, only to be growled at by her guard. Damn him, she was not foolish. Had he not been told? The boat was waved in. One of the swine even caught the mooring rope! The sailors landed and jumped out, most taking the chance to stretch their legs while their captain spoke. One especially tall, rough brute approached her; his clothes were stained badly and his hair wild. She recoiled from the dirty, unshaven face. He was hideously scarred and sneering at her.

His paw gabbed her foot – she cried out and tried to pull her dangling legs back inside the cage, but he was too strong.

'Oi, get yer hands off her!' shouted the guard.

The captain of the vessel laughed aloud.

'Och, dinnae worry about the half-wit. He'll no hurt her. He just wants a feel, the lassies'll no approach him, ye see.'

Damn him, those eyes were not dull! But the men laughed and turned away, leaving him there with her. His paw crept further up her leg. She cursed him viciously. Why did he look so familiar? She felt something metallic slide into the top of her hose. A key? Why was he staring at her brooch? She pulled her hands away. Those eyes, that face, even the scar… Jesus, Joseph and Mary! It was Cailean!

He gave a short nod and in a slurred, quiet voice added, 'I'll be back after dark, but ye need tae unlock the door tae signal us.'

What signal? The minute she opened the door, they would grab her. He tugged her shift under her skirts. No time, instead she screeched and kicked him. Damn, too hard! He reeled back amidst laughter.

'Stay away ye louse-ridden, *slat beag fleoidhte*!'

She forced herself to her feet. The men around her roared as the hurt giant fled back to his boat.

'That one has a tongue on her!' cried the captain again.

'Why dae ye think she's in there?' came a reply.

Mordag rolled her eyes and feigned boredom as they unloaded several barrels of wine. If anything, they were too eager to finish and leave. Thankfully, no one seemed to notice; they were already eyeing up the barrels. Surely the men weren't *that* foolish? Mind, she needed them to be. She watched the boat leave while keeping an ear open.

'Ah've nivver had wine before.'

'And ye willnae, it needs tae go tae David.'

'Now why should it? Ah see it as ours. Spoils o war, like.'

The man used his good hand to scratch his chin.

'I suppose a couple of barrels willnae harm. Mind, only a couple!'

She bit her tongue to keep from snorting and watched them crack open the first. Anything that could hold wine was dunked into the casks. The wind carried the strong scent to her; whatever it was, it was not cheap. She stared in disbelief as they took deep gulps. Did none of them know to water it down? Grimaces and gasps of disgust followed.

'They really drink this swill?'

'Och aye, tis no wonder they feast hard!'

'Need it tae take the taste away!'

'Dinnae hog it, let others try.'

They were like children given a pot of honey to share. Men abandoned posts to raid the manor of its jugs. They filled them up and scurried away. Another barrel was quickly cracked open, and then another. Mordag could not grasp what was happening, despite it being as plain as day. If men were so easy to fool, then why did war go on for so long?

*

Sure enough, by nightfall Mordag had lost her guard. A noise loosely described as singing came from the hall and she had witnessed several scuffles break out. Now she waited for them to sleep, just as the rest of the women did. They had realised quickly enough what was happening, and had barricaded themselves in their homes, including Caitlin. At least this way she would not be labelled a conspirator. Mordag glanced at the hill. Oddly, no one had come down. Perhaps they too were drinking the barrels that had been hauled up there.

She shook her head as a man stumbled towards a house. He pulled up his *léine*, started to piss, stumbled and fell. He groaned but did not get up. Would he ever get up again? A splash behind her had her swinging her head around. How many had jumped or fallen in now? If their own follies killed them, she supposed, it was better than dying painfully in battle.

The singing slowly tailed off and only a few stragglers remained. At least the one that had fallen near her was alive; his snoring hid the sound of the key turning in the lock. She winced as she slowly swung the door open. No one came running at its sound. She peered out into the darkness, expecting to see a boat approach. Nothing. Not even the sounds of oars in water. Where were they? Damn them, they had promised. She could not leave the door open for much longer.

Something was coming towards her. Ah, it was just Jock's terrier. The dog sniffed around the drunk man before cocking its leg. She bit her lip. He groaned, muttered something, and fell back asleep. That was too close. She could not wait any longer. Sitting down, she dangled her legs over the edge. The drop was only a few feet. She could do it. But her baby? She rubbed her stomach. What choice did she have?

Mordag slid out of the cage. She landed on her feet, but the pain was too much. Falling to her knees, she clawed at the ground to stop herself yelping. She could not walk, and she could not stay there. They would find her. Gasping, she crawled as best she could to the wooden dock. Still no sign of a damned boat! Tears stung her eyes. Had Cailean been lying?

Maybe if she got to the woods? But she could not take the direct route. She must. Her son had not survived that fall for her to give in. Biting her lip, she rolled from the dock onto the loch's shore. Her hands and knees screamed at her. She ignored them, and the taste of her blood.

Falling to her elbows, she continued to inch forwards. She *must* continue. She glanced to her side, at the prone body. One of the swimmers. Damn it, she had barely passed it! Choking on her tears, she pressed on, only to fall over after a few feet. It was just too much. She blinked as something moved in the distance. Was Jock's dog coming to piss on her too? No. It was too big – a man. She had been spotted. She laid her head down. Waiting for the rough hands.

They did not come.

Someone carefully lifted her up. Her head fell against wool. And something muscular behind it. She looked up; blue eyes.

'Alasdair?'

'Hush, lass, ye're no safe yet.'

No, those were slurred words, and that was a scar. Cailean. Only he looked nothing like earlier; he had shaved and washed. He looked so much like her husband. *She was going to see Alasdair again!* She let out a strange, strangled laugh as she heard him wade through the water. Then multiple hands grasped her, pulling her up and into their boat.

Chapter 43

Closing the bed curtain, Sorcha left Mordag to sleep. She had insisted on coming with them to the camp. Unfortunately for Cailean she had sided with the stubborn woman, for every time she woke, she asked for Alasdair. And with no sign of fever, it was better she stayed under their watchful gaze. Leaving Ailis to clear up, Sorcha stepped outside.

Her tent was in the middle of the encampment, surrounded by only a few rough shelters. Hardy men indeed. Only a couple of other tents stood towards the back. She stretched and adjusted her bycocket. Around her was a quiet anticipation. The men, for the most part, were seasoned warriors. They knew it could be days or weeks before a battle. She inhaled and tried to feel as they did, but it was useless. She would not relax until it was over.

From her pouch, Sorcha withdrew a missive. It was Evelyn's seal and delivered by the Douglas men. Breaking it, she opened the parchment and found only a few words written by her friend. They wished her well, and success in her endeavour. She did not recognise the other hand, but the writer identified themself. What was Sir James doing writing to her?

She sat on a nearby stool. He had known Pa, and it was his love for the man that made him act, now that her past was exposed. She pursed her lips; how kind of him to wait! Sorcha scanned the rest of his words and stopped. He was telling her how she could ensure this would never happen again. Why, it was so simple! And if they had only told her…

She lowered the missive and stared at the nearby campfire. It would not have worked before. They would have called it coerced. She shook her head and read through the rest of the missive. It confirmed her thoughts and added to it. Win or lose, she was to make a spectacle of it and his men were there to ensure it happened. If they lost, it would be the last thing she did.

Lord have mercy, she needed to do something. A walk, perhaps. Where was her guard?

'Now tha be a sight for sore eyes.'

Father Fraser! She laughed with disbelief. 'What? How? I thought ye still in the lowlands.'

She tripped over her words, then gestured for the priest to join her. The impeccably clean man smiled sadly before sitting down.

'After yer father's death I found I couldnae linger there, so I left. And when I heard yer husband was tae war, well, I had tae see for meself that ye were well.'

She had raised her hand to summon drinks. It stilled a moment before she continued her order. His words felt off. She smiled politely.

'Well, as ye can see, I am indeed most well. Do ye intend tae stay with us long?'

'For as long as ye need my counsel, Sorcha.'

'*Lady* Sorcha, father. For sure ye ken my husband is an earl.'

'Of course, child, forgive me. I forgot myself – it feels like only yesterday that ye were running around the fields.'

She recalled those childhood memories of his visits, having always treasured them, but now she could see the truth. His smile. It was hard; cold, even.

He sipped the drink, then chuckled. 'Ah, mead. I've no had it since ye left. So tell me, is it true that Michael is now working for someone?'

'Not now, no, he's…' She stopped. How had he known that? She had never written to him. '…Hanging by his neck.'

The priest shook his head. 'Such a lost sheep. How did it happen, if ye dinnae mind my asking?'

She answered him truthfully. It was common knowledge both at home and court. Yet she could not shake the feeling that he knew already. He at least looked genuinely saddened when he heard of her loss.

'I will pray for ye, Sorcha.'

Pray for what? Her health, her soul, or something else? Sorcha rubbed her forehead; it was starting to hurt. Her heart still outraged by the thoughts she was having.

'I can see this whole affair troubles ye, Lady Sorcha. Is it yer husband's war?'

'Aye, he… he fights the people Michael assisted.'

'And who are they?'

Sorcha inhaled sharply, her head winning its battle. If

he knew of the war then he should know who they were fighting. She shook her head and stood up.

'I'm afraid I need tae lie down. The journey here was most taxing.'

'I'm sure it was.'

She was lying now? Standing, she waited for him to rise. He did, albeit slowly, and openly staring at her. Had he realised? She glanced around and spotted Cailean walking past.

'My lord husband! Ye remember Pa's friend, aye?'

Father Fraser faced Cailean. 'Ah, greetings again.'

'Father, what a surprise.'

Cailean looked from him to her, then back again. He dismissed his men and folded his arms.

'Indeed, indeed. I'm sure we will talk later, Sir Cailean.'

'Ah'm sure we will.'

'Lady Sorcha.'

She partly lowered herself. 'Father Fraser.'

The priest walked sedately away while Sorcha stayed still. There was no need to feign now.

'I dinnae trust that man,' Cailean muttered.

'Once, I would have called that foolish. Now I'm no so sure myself.'

*

Alasdair's wife and son were free! To have seen the rebels' faces when they discovered the ploy. It had been reckless, for sure, but it had worked. He had intended to leave the shieling then and there, until Seumas stopped him. Yes, they had rescued her, but there was no army yet. So he'd lingered, keeping the cows company for a few days more. Lucky beasts.

Now, he was riding fast along the edge of the river. To the south of its opening was the MacMhathain camp. It was tempting to push his horse harder, but he resisted. Not that he expected trouble. His scouts had confirmed that the rebels were still in disarray, leading to patchy scouting and guarding. If only they had been ready. Mind, this might afford him the chance to visit Mordag. He could make it to Glencoe and back in a few hours.

Osgar suddenly stood in his stirrups and dropped his reins; he waved to a man standing on a rise. The man waved back, spun around and waved to someone unseen.

'Why'd the chief bring him? Tha useless arse couldnae fell a sapling.'

'He lit the cross. Besides, yer brother can run an see.'

Alasdair's response was met with a snort and a grin. His men were as eager as himself – some had taken a liking to the women of Druim Earbainn. He had given them his blessing over approaching Cailean to discuss staying there and marrying when this was over. It would be good to have them there; perhaps there would be friends for his son.

Rounding the rise, he was not surprised to see Cailean already waiting. Dour-faced and cross-armed. Great, the opportunity to leave camp just fled. He reined in Legs and Iain ran forward to take his reins. The lad was unarmed, save for his dagger. Odd, and why was he tending the horses? He brushed away the thought and dismounted.

Facing Cailean, he dipped his head, ready to apologise.

'*Mo ciann...*'

'Alasdair!'

He lifted his head and was caught in an embrace. Laughing, he returned it.

'It's good tae see ye too!'

There was a hint of a smile on Cailean's face before he barked, 'Leave us.'

Even for his brother, that was abrupt. Was Mordag unwell? Did he want to chastise him for losing Sorcha's land? He searched for clues, but his brother's face was of stone and his eyes hard. When only a few of the *leuchd-crios* remained close by did Alasdair try to speak, but Cailean stopped him.

'When did Thomas make ye his successor?'

Damn. How had he figured that out? As if answering him, Cailean produced a missive from his pouch. The one he had hastily sent. Taking it, he glanced at the seal before opening it. He had written it with his left hand. Thank the Lord that was the only one he sent with his personal seal!

'Who is asking me this? My brother or my chief?'

'Yer brother.'

'Shortly after our mither's death, our father gave me a missive from the Raven and told me tae follow his word. I only thought I was tae be a spy.'

Cailean's eyes softened.

Alasdair sighed. 'I believe they kenned this might happen and were doing their best.'

Now, his jaw hardened, and he pinched his nose. No longer the brother but the chief. 'I'm grateful, truly, for Sorcha. But if anyone tries tae manipulate me like this again…'

Alasdair withdrew his dagger and held it pommel up.

'May my own blade pierce my heart if I allow that tae happen again. Ah may work for Robert, but I'm pledged tae ye, *mo ciann*.'

His brother came close, staring deep into his eyes. He held his gaze, and grinned when Cailean nodded.

'Ye can lie freely tae the faces o others, but ye've never been able tae hide it from me.'

'No from our mither either.'

Alasdair sheathed his blade. He'd been patient enough.

'What about Mordag? Is she hale? And the child?'

Something flashed across Cailean's face. Surely not a smile? Or was it a grimace? He jerked his head and, like a puppy, he followed. Yet his brother said nothing. Instead, he talked of his lighting the cross, of Fraoch, and his anger at having to bring his wife along. Alasdair tried to sympathise, but Mordag... And besides, he had planned for Sorcha to be there.

More infuriatingly, his questions were being ignored and the men they passed insisted on cheerfully greeting him. He was close to the end of his tether when they stopped in front of a large tent.

'As for Mordag, see for yerself.' Cailean gestured towards the tent.

He looked out the side of his eye, not trusting his brother's words. But they were genuine. He could have hit him. Instead, he shot into the tent. Mordag, his wife, she was both a sight of beauty and rage-inducing at the same time. Her long hair fell in two plaits over her shoulders and swung freely as she clung to both Sorcha and Ailis, struggling to stay upright.

The next thing he knew, she was in his arms and he

was kissing her cracked lips. He tried to be gentle but could not stop himself. Neither could she. He broke off to stare at her; she likewise.

'It… it… Ye look like a sheep's arse!'

He grinned; she was still his Mordag! Behind him, Cailean laughed.

'Cailean!' chided Sorcha.

Still unable to take his eyes off Mordag, he called over his shoulder, 'Me wife's right.'

Snapping from his trance, he bombarded her with questions. How was she, what happened, did she need to sit down? She clamped a bandaged hand over his mouth.

'Hauld yer wheesht. Ah'm just a bit sore from being in the cage, nothin more. Now help me tae that bed and ye can greet yer son properly. Ye woke him up.'

'Oh… aye!'

His son! In his haste, he had forgotten. She slapped his hands away, stopping him from lifting her.

'I need tae walk.'

Chastised again, Alasdair walked her slowly over to the bed. The only bed in the tent. They had given it up for Mordag? He looked back at Cailean, catching his eye. His brother nodded, acknowledging his silent thanks. After taking some time to settle, she took his hand and placed it on her bump. It was faint, but he felt it. He gave a small laugh; his child, his son had fought and won his first battle!

'He's as strong as his mither,' he murmured.

'He has his father tae thank. We did as ye taught us.'

'Hmm?'

Distracted by her proximity, and the wish to hold her

forever more, he had not fully grasped what she meant. She smiled shyly, looked away and then met his eyes.

'Ye, Alasdair. Thanks tae ye, ah made them see what they wanted tae see. And then, kenning ye were out there. I… I love—'

He did not let her finish the words he had never expected to hear her say. Overcome, his lips covered hers. Slowly and tenderly. Savouring their reunion.

'I love ye too, Mordag. And as God is my witness, I will punish them for what they did tae ye.'

*

Two pairs of judgmental eyes inspected Alasdair. He fidgeted uncomfortably under their gaze, in clothing that hung off him. Ailis had been ruthless when combing out and oiling his hair. It now sat, somewhat tamed, in a tight plait. His beard too, had been cleaned, oiled and trimmed. He had kept it at Mordag's insistence. Apparently, it made him look more his age, but now all he could smell was rose.

'Yer maid does good work,' remarked Mordag.

'She is, for the most part, a good lass. I'm just sorry that Cailean's garments are all we have. With luck, his own will be clean by the morrow.'

'Aye well, we cannae be picky at a time like this now, can we? He'll do.'

He sighed. 'Ye both had yer fun?'

Sorcha and Mordag smiled, then looked at each other. Nodding, they dismissed him.

He had quietly thanked Sorcha the evening prior, having assumed it must be difficult for her. She had looked him squarely in the eye and set him straight. How much she had changed since they last spoke, and he had feared it was not all for the good. Her playfulness with Mordag, at his expense, had helped alleviate that fear. Not to mention, it had been good to see his wife's lighter side. Though he was already dreading future reunions.

Now it was his turn to change.

Alasdair sought out Cailean, who was busy talking with Fraoch and Angus. In front of them was a rough map, drawn in the dirt. His brother just nodded in greeting, while the other two grinned.

'No more woolly sheep's arse? Now tha be a shame. One of me men needed tae practise his shearing.'

'Ah, Fraoch, how is yer wife these days?'

He grinned as the younger man cursed and spat. His wife near fell over herself every time she met Alasdair. Cailean coughed and motioned for Angus to continue.

'Their leader, he'll no be swayed. Insists that this point is the most advantageous. Believes ye will only come from this side.'

Angus used a stick to gesture first at the top of the hill, then the gentler, bare-sloped north-east side of the hill. To attack there, they would have to first march most the way to Inverlochy.

'Archers?' asked Cailean.

'Aye.'

'I thank ye, Angus; Mordag is expecting ye.'

'Ah want tae fight with ye. Surely, ye trust me. I'll pledge tae ye!'

'Nae!' Alasdair's voice mixed with Cailean's. Permitted

to continue, he placed his hand on Angus's shoulder, leading him a few paces away.

'For a start, Mordag will wring my neck if ah agree tae ye fighting. Which ye ken is reason enough, but dinnae forget yer tae be yer father's *tanist*.'

'I doubt my father or clan wants me back now.'

'Even so, Cailean will no take yer pledge till he kens for sure. So go tae Mordag for me, she is bound tae be bored or worse.'

His voice of reason convinced Angus, who started leaving, only to stop. 'Wait, what do ye mean, "worse"?'

He grinned. 'Ye'll see!'

That handled, he returned to find them waiting for him.

'I assume we're no doing that?'

'Aye.' Cailean stared again. 'We'll split intae three. Meself, Fraoch and—'

'And I.'

Alasdair met his brother's eye, expecting to meet resistance. Instead, the corners of his lips raised and there was a glint he had not seen before. He trusted and wanted him there?

'And my brother,' confirmed Cailean.

Chapter 44

Cailean had prepared as best he could; now it was in God's hands. He gently kissed Sorcha's forehead, rousing her from her sleep. She woke and smiled sleepily at him until she too remembered. He started rising from the furs that marked their 'bed'. She stopped him. He let her pull him down into a deep, slow kiss.

'I will pray for ye.'

Her eyes glistening, her voice wavering. He struggled. What did a man say to his wife at times like this?

'The Lord kens I fight for a just cause.'

She did not look convinced. He kissed her again before rising. Like Alasdair, Ailis had ensured his hair would not get in his way. He dressed quickly, forgoing his *léine*, and left the tent. Iain had already risen, and laid out Cailean's armour and weapons. He nodded, and Iain reached for the gambeson.

He was not alone with his thoughts. Most silently dressed around him, the yellow of their layered linen *léines* mockingly cheerful. They would fight with honour today and they would fight well. But he would still lose men. Good, honest men.

Dressed in mail, tabard and padded coif, Cailean knelt. Iain handed him his unsheathed knightly sword. He focused on the cross of the hilt and prayed. If it be his or his men's time, let it be quick. Let the battle be swift and may his plans succeed. Finally, he prayed for Sorcha. If he failed, let her be safe. Crossing himself, he rose and handed back the sword.

A calm coldness descended over him. He was ready. Iain finished buckling the sword on him. Alasdair joined him at his side. Identically dressed, save for the markings on his tabard.

'The things we do for our wives.'

Cailean glanced at his brother; his jest was unusually flat.

'Watch yer back out there,' he warned, 'and find me on the field.'

'I'll be at yer side in no time, ah'm sure.'

He nodded and accepted his helm from Iain, followed by his two-handed greatsword.

'Ye have yer orders.'

'Aye, *mo ciann*.' Iain nodded and departed.

Looking back at the tent, he was not surprised to see Sorcha and Mordag. They stood wrapped in plaid. He nodded to them both and left. His aim, the men who were slowly forming near the loch's edge. In the distance, masts were approaching. He left Alasdair to walk in the opposite direction.

*

The men Mordag watched leave were no longer husbands. Alasdair, who had tenderly kissed not just her lips but her stomach, did not even grin. Though she found it annoying, she prayed she would see it again. He would be a cruel ruler if He allowed them to reunite only to be torn apart by death. She could feel Sorcha's shudder. Was this her first time? Alasdair had said that the countess had been sheltered.

'They have tae dae it. Though ah agree, it's no nice tae see.'

She awkwardly patted Sorcha's hand, trying to hide her own fear. Men, she knew, would be trying to kill the man she loved. Where was the fairness in that? Damn it, she knew better: nothing about war was fair. She watched the men filter by. The older ones serious, the younger ones not hiding their smiles. *Their first time.* She could not return their bright greetings. Neither did her sister-in-law.

'Court, war. Tis all the same, is it no?' Sorcha asked bitterly. 'And worse, I have a part tae play in it too.'

Mordag started to agree, but trailed off.

'What dae ye mean?'

They were interrupted by men approaching, taking up positions on either side of the tent, or settling in front of the fire Ailis had yet to light. If the men were disappointed to not be fighting, they did not show it.

'Come, let us dress. There'll be plenty o time tae tell ye.'

She looked at the few stragglers remaining and

nodded. Who knew when the battle would begin. Or how long it would last. Thanks to love, she would do nothing but worry. At least her brother was not fighting; she had seen him leave with Iain. Likely to climb the larger hill next to them for a good view.

Oddly, Sorcha insisted on helping her wash and dress. Ailis was still nowhere to be seen. Mordag had rested enough but her sores were not healed, and she still struggled to walk further than a few steps. Muttering incessantly at being so useless, she tried her best to do as much as possible. Sorcha tutted but did not stop her.

'Win or lose, it will end today. I ken the men want us tae flee tae Glencoe, but I cannot. I'll no begrudge ye going without me.'

She looked down at Sorcha, who was buckling her boots. Though Sorcha's voice was determined, she caught a hint of fear.

'It'll no come tae that. We'll be using that cart tae join them.'

They damned well would win; Sorcha met her eye and nodded. 'Aye, though I'll no be sat in any cart.'

She looked ready to tell her as she got up, but then Ailis entered. The maid was carrying one of the richest gowns Mordag had seen. Heavy green silk, patterned with vines and brocaded with gold thread. The flashes of white lining she recognised from court. Ermine. Her jaw dropped.

'Yer wearing that?'

'Aye, amongst other things. Ailis will do yer hair first. I'm afraid mine will take considerably longer.'

'Now ye've really got my attention.'

*

Creeping through the woodland, Alasdair signalled to two men in his division. When he had told Cailean of his work within it, this was not what he had been expecting. But it made good sense.

The men, in turn, called forward their men and together, they split from the main group. He led them right up to the edge of the trees. Through the overgrowth, he could see the rebels preparing. All he did was show the men with him where the sheep hurdle lay.

Several more times, he repeated the process until he too was crouched waiting next to one. As he suspected, they weren't watching the woodland. Seumas nudged him before handing him a piece of bitter vetch. He slowly chewed it while trying to not watch the rebel pissing several feet away from him.

His mind wandered to the manor below. Had the message reached Jock and the others? Were the women and children safe? The rebels' scout had retreated when he saw Fraoch's assorted group of men leave. So if they had not, hopefully, the rebel camp's movements would alert them.

He slowly pulled the targe off his back. Something was happening. Had they been discovered? He strained to hear it over the noise of the camp. No, the cries were urgent but not of alarm. As they grew closer, he relaxed again. It was a call to break down the camp and for followers to disperse. From where he hid, he could feel their expectant excitement. How long had they been waiting for this day? Likely since they learned about Sorcha, but was that when she was a babe, child or adult?

If they caught the leaders alive, he would have to ask them. Along with a multitude of other questions. Robert would want a thorough report. Though, outside of that, this was to be taken as 'just another clan dispute'. For one so astute, the king could be thoughtless in his choice of words.

'Where are they going?'

'Tae the other end of the hill. They'll be back,' he answered.

Seumas' whispered question had broken his thought. Probably for the best. If they were lining up, then they had seen Fraoch. He motioned for Osgar to come forwards.

'Send word round, the battle will soon begin. And remind them not tae move until they hear the pipe.'

The man nodded and crept away. Alasdair turned back just as more shouts drifted towards him, followed by the low beat of a drum. The battle was starting.

Chapter 45

The men standing on the top of the hill were dressed in whatever they could find or make. Their weapons just as rough. Some were lucky to have their family's weapons, hidden from Bruce's Herschip, others had found them over the years, and still more carried whatever could wound. Yet each man walked with conviction; God would see them victorious. When word reached them that the MacMhathain camp was moving out, they were ready.

They lined up on the north-east side, those with targes at the front. Their leader there with them, in the centre. Confused shouts spread throughout the men. Their enemy was lining up halfway up the south-east side! The commanders were thrown into disarray. This was not what David had said would happen. Leaving their men to rearrange, they rushed to join him. He stood under an old, tattered standard of John Comyn's.

'What is the meaning of this?' one demanded to know.

David looked at the gathering men. The maroon and

azure of Macmaghan, the azure and argent of Douglas and, at the fore, the yellow of Domhnaill.

'There's too few for them tae be all. A vanguard? Either way, hold yer ground. Let them exhaust themselves on the hill.'

'And he sends out others tae do it? Pitiful.'

'Maybe. Keep a watch. And have the archers come forwards.'

David stared thoughtfully. After a minute, he was striding forwards, clear of the new line. Fraoch, in a yellow tabard, likewise stepped out. He held up a hand and gave a cheeky wave before shouting, 'Nice day, is it no?'

'Leave while ye still can, we will show yer men no mercy.'

'No mercy eh? Hear that, lads?'

The men behind him laughed; one called out, 'Eh, Fraoch, they think that scares ye!'

A whisper started to spread throughout the rebels. The Snarling of Glencoe was fighting with Robert's hound.

'So be it!' cried David.

He retreated back into his men, while calling the archers to ready. Fraoch called for drummers and shields ready. Arrows filled the sky before raining down on the men. Most found nothing but shield. Others slipped through gaps, piercing whatever flesh they found. The line did not break. At another command, they started walking, climbing up the steep hill.

The drumbeat continued, almost drowned out by the sound of rebels hitting barrel-lid targes in their attempt to intimidate the slowly approaching wall. Volley after volley of arrows rained down. Shields started to look like hedgehogs. Behind them lay the dead, dying and incapacitated. Rebels stared in disbelief; they were fighting madmen! And worse, the arrows were struggling to find their mark the closer they came. Some archers stepped forwards, trying to use knolls to get a better downward trajectory.

'Archers!' called Fraoch, his command echoed by others.

They stepped forward and readied their bows.

'Release!'

'Shields!' came the counter order.

The arrows flew higher than the rebels' volleys, arched over and descended at a steeper angle, into an unprepared mass. They cursed; it was not right! They had the upper ground, thus the upper hand! Yet the men fell.

'Boats! Boats! David, they're landing boats behind us!'

A runner shot through, shouting to their leader. Yet more curses flew.

'Archers tae the back!' he shouted. 'Infantry, hold yer ground!'

The runner went on to spread his orders.

Down below, Cailean's division had already killed their first man. He'd died caught with his trews down, defecating. Archers kept the others back as he and his men jumped into the shallows of the loch or climbed over debris. The arrows stopped just as Cailean led the first charge against those guarding the buildings. Vastly outnumbered, those still standing tried in vain to meet the attack, only to drop their weapons when, from the nearby dwellings, men sprang out to attack them. A few stopped to take them prisoner, the rest passed on with Cailean to form a line just past the buildings. Behind them, a man with only one working arm fell to his knees in defeat.

'Shields and pikes ready!' roared Cailean.

At the top of the hill, the archers were slowly descending, trying to get in range.

'Hold steady,' he added, to already well-disciplined men.

His *leuchd-crios* lifted their shields over his head as arrows started to haphazardly rain. Marta, still holding the standard aloft, took one to his upper arm. The flag wavered but did not fall.

'Missed the bone,' he hissed. 'Someone snap the damned shaft.'

A man to his right complied.

Above them, the Comyn standard appeared. David tried to form a line, expecting the men below to march up as Fraoch's men were doing. The line grew restless, just like their counterparts on the other side. Fraoch was drawing closer and still they had not been allowed to break. The Snarling sent word to his drummer, who rolled the drumbeat.

In answer to the roll, Cailean ordered his piper to play.

From the woodlands, Alasdair and those with him charged. Roaring a war cry, his axe fell on a startled rebel. Hot blood sprayed across him as the man fell. The man behind him was more prepared, parrying the blow and bringing his own axe down. The blow hit Alasdair's targe, sending a strong ricochet up his arm. He pushed through it, trying to unbalance the man.

The charge cry confused the rebels, who thought it their own. Commanders cried for the men to descend on Fraoch's division. Without the room to charge, their attack was weak. It struggled to break through the front line. As one man fell, another quickly took his place. Fraoch was there, alongside them, a broad grin on his face as he pushed his sword through a gap and met resistance.

David swung around when he heard the first cries. 'Hold, damn it. I said hold!' he screamed.

The men fought their own desire to charge. The MacMhathain was down there; he needed to die. When the second roar came, it was too much. They broke, charging down the hill towards the waiting men. A grave mistake. The hill made them run faster, its steepness stripping them of control. Those who fell tumbled hard. Some came to a skull-smashing stop against hard rocks or in bushes, a broken mess.

'Raise pikes!' Cailean roared as they neared. He thrust his sword over the shoulder of the man in front, holding it there. Those who could no longer stop themselves saw their death before they ran onto the pikes, their armour useless against their own momentum. Some, with their last breath, tried to swing a blade. A few got lucky. Further up the hill, those who had managed to stop looked on in horror. Even the archers had stilled their strings.

'Forward!' Cailean cried.

The men walked over the bodies, finishing off any that still breathed. Above them, men retreated, only to find their rear in disarray and the enemy on the side of the woods. David swung his head around and caught the blade of a young warrior. He spotted an opening and grabbed his dagger, plunging it into the man's armpit. His army a tumultuous mass of confusion. If they continued, they would be overrun.

'Fall back! Regroup at the bottom!'

His desperate order was picked up. Those who could, spun and fled down the south-east slope of the hill. Their enemy did not follow. They now held the high ground.

*

Alasdair walked amongst the fallen, his axe in his belt, his dagger in hand. He had forgotten this part of battle, likely purposefully. Kneeling in front of a rebel with his gut hanging out, he smelt the contents of his bowel. Deftly, he slit his throat. A small mercy in the grander scheme. Gurgling to his right caught his attention. A Domhnaill man lay with an arrow in his neck. He was reaching for Alasdair, his eyes silently begging. Christ, had no one seen him? He dropped his dagger. Taking the man's hands in one of his own, he nodded. His other hand grasped the arrow.

'*Mo Charaid, sgiath gu h-ard os cion na h-eileinan fhraochadh.*' He leaned in and spoke softly as he pulled it free.

The man's eyes widened and watered as he returned to the heathery isles, first in mind and then in soul. So much death fighting an ideal that had withered away so long ago now. And how many more would succumb before the day's end?

Yes, he could now lead men into battle, but did he care for it? No. His father's spirit would have to make peace with that. He would no longer feel shame. He sighed and let go of the lifeless man before reaching over and shutting his eyes.

Embittered, he headed towards his brother's banner. He needed to shut his emotions away like Cailean, or he would be useless. Slipping between his guard, he found him, flask in hand. He was staring at the reforming lines of the rebels. Alasdair snatched the flask from him.

'This better be *uisge beatha*,' he dryly jested.

Cailean spat and shook his head. He would never drink it mid-battle. It was good to see his brother hale. Alasdair's men were to handle the stragglers, not lead the damned charge. Alas, they had not broken as early as he expected. He looked again to the reforming lines. That damned pennant still flew, but their next clash would crush it. He sighed. The rebels had to know they were outmatched. Damn their honour. If the flag fell first, the conclusion may not be a routing.

'Ah've seen whores' sheets wi less holes.'

Fraoch's thoughts as pertinent as ever; their line did look ragged. His ally was leaning against one of his men. He could not see a wound. Nor could he tell the blood apart.

'Damned fox hole. I didnae see it behind me.'

Cailean raised his eyes to the sky. 'Ah thought I'd taught ye better. At least it wasnae a damned tree.'

His brother protested; he ignored him.

'Ye're sitting the rest o this out. Up tae ye whether yer men do or no.

Fraoch defiantly pushed his help away, but as he stepped forwards, his leg buckled. 'Damn it, fine. But take them, their blood's up.'

Leaving him, Cailean walked with his brother towards the head of the gathered army.

'We'll join together now. Form up and charge as one. Watch for their poles.'

'God willing, it'll be over quickly.'

'Aye.'

*

Sorcha looked into the small looking glass. Ailis had done wonders. The intricate plaits wove around one another but did not hinder the coronet sat upon her uncovered head. The maid draped a heavy mantle across her shoulders and secured it in place. A suitable weight for what she was to do. She put the glass down and caught Mordag's eyes. At first, the woman had thought her crazed. But some careful explaining had brought her around. Now she openly stared.

'What troubles ye, Mordag?'

'Naught, only – ye look like a queen.'

She lifted her chin just a touch higher. 'Tis a good thing, is it no?'

'Aye. And ah'm no missing it. Ah'm coming with ye!'

Lowering her head, she let Ailis attach the belt around her waist. It was done. Now all she needed was news.

'Of course ye are. We'll no part, no now.'

They would see she favoured Mordag and feel her righteous wrath for what they did. Oh, she even sounded like a queen! Her cheeks reddened. This was too much to assume. Had she not once thought being a countess far above herself? Thank the Lord it was for a single day. She would make sure of that.

Sorcha sat down grasped her own hands, her knuckles whitening. They had received no word. Was Cailean safe? Did he lie injured? She looked away. She must not dwell. Yet she could not speak. And Mordag no longer offered any words of her own.

How long had passed before Ewan appeared? Hours, surely.

He likewise stared, but said nothing about her dress.

'My lady, there is word.'

'Well? Dinnae keep us. Do our husbands live?'

Too sharp, but he surely understood. She struggled to keep her hands still, irritated by Ewan taking his sweet time.

'They're well. The armies clashed and we drove the rebels back. They have reformed. It will be over by the eve.'

Her heart leapt at the news, though she forced it still. Good news, yes, but the battle was not over. Much could change.

'I thought they wouldnae surrender,' Mordag added bitterly. 'Me father will be pissing himself if any o his men are caught.'

If only she could speak so crudely. 'Cailean told me it was why he sent Angus. Youth led astray.'

'Jesus, Joseph and Mary. Forget the king, if ah get me hands on him…'

'I'll join ye if either o our husbands are hurt.'

They exchanged weak smiles before she rose and approached Ewan.

'Have Taranis and the cart brought around. We intend tae ride to our husbands' sides.'

'My lady, ah cannae—'

'An order, Ewan. And tell the others to expect Douglas men. Ye're tae do what they ask.'

She waited again, this time less patiently, for Ewan to acknowledge her. He was struggling to grasp what was happening. She did not blame him,

'It's of the utmost importance, Ewan. I do this tae protect Cailean and the clan.'

Her sincerity must have shown, for he nodded and left.

*

The commanders of the rebels tore through their remaining men. Any found with targe were forced to the front. Followed by archers and pikemen. Any protesters found their honour and courage shamed. Though no one said the words, they all felt it. Stay and die or run away to an unknown fate. Robert had been brutal before; would his men be the same? Or worse, their chiefs, when they learned of their involvement?

David tore a shield from the hands of a young lad, placing it into the hands of another.

'He'd no stop a charging piglet,' he ranted angrily. 'Use sense, men!'

There were mutterings, while the rest agreed, ridding others of their protection. The boys had likely taken discarded shields anyway. Their leader pushed himself out front.

'Remember, we fight fer the true rulers o the Scots! As long as there is a Comyn heir, we fight!'

Roars erupted; the impassioned drowning out the

weaker ones. Opposite them, Cailean did not need to rouse his men. They sensed victory. The lines murmured with anticipation. Archers had put their bows away. They knew what was coming. To Cailean's right stood Alasdair. He nodded to his chief.

'Forward!' Cailean shouted; his command echoed down the lines.

They started walking forwards, banging shields and weapons together. Anything to make a din. Opposite them, the rebels tried to make a combined wall of shields and pikes.

'*Acha 'n dà thearnaidh!*'

Cailean's cry was drowned out by the spreading roar of the others. The lines burst into a run, straight towards their foe. The front lines were forced to brace while many at the back dropped their arms, turned and fled; the cry and sight of the charge overwhelming them.

The momentum of hundreds of men crushed the thin defensive line, penetrating it deeply. Their blood up, they turned and attacked the front line from behind. Hacking at them and showing as much mercy as a tidal wave. More turned to flee. Those towards the back were luckier than those in the middle. The front men were as good as dead.

Cailean pushed the makeshift poleaxe away with his blade. He slid down its shaft and rammed the pommel into the man's face. Its weight crushed his nose, forcing bone and cartilage back up into the skull. Blinded, the man dropped the pole and sought his dagger. It was too late, for Cailean kept the blade close, lifting it above his shoulder. It swung downwards, the blade's impetus enough to slice through bone. The body crumpled.

He searched the masses for the Comyn standard. It was close.

'To me!' he shouted.

Alasdair and his *leuchd-crios* fell in close. As a single body, they swept forwards, towards their target. Any Cailean met were bounced back along the group. The closer he got, the more skilled the men they faced. One parried his blade, trying to get in close with his shorter sword. He caught the blade against his crossguard. It was one of the mercenaries. He smiled coldly.

Grabbing his own blade, he used his weight to push the man's weapon against his chest. It would not cut through his armour. Instead, he suddenly slid the metal up. And thrust the point of the crossguard into the man's eye. He fell onto Alasdair's axe, his screams silenced.

It left the standard-bearer exposed. And next to him, their leader. The flag fell as the bearer chose to save himself. Wide-eyed, the rebels' leader looked around. He screamed for reinforcements. Cailean did not look to see if they came. The standard had fallen. Even the loyalist of rebels would know the cause lost.

'Surrender,' he growled.

Again, the exhausted man looked around. He wavered, then lifted his sword above his head and charged. Cailean met the blow and sent him spinning off. His men fell upon him, disarming but not killing him. A pitiful end to years of trouble.

Now he looked around the field. Small pockets of resistance were being dispatched; the majority had thrown down their weapons. Most of his men stood around, guarding, or tending to the wounded. He glanced at the sun. It was still high. Absurd indeed. No one bothered to cheer.

'Round up those still standing. Disarm them and march them back tae Druim Earbainn,' he ordered.

'And the wounded?' asked the approaching Choinnich chief.

'Tend tae those who might survive. Let their followers deal with their dead.'

He would see his own returned home. Cailean turned and silently walked away, Alasdair still by his side.

Away from the bodies, he stopped. 'What does Robert want now?'

His brother did not answer. He was bent double, breathing hard. Then his legs went and he fell, cursing. Cailean sprang forwards, looking for a wound, but was waved off. Ah, the lethargy. Not just weariness of tired muscles. Brought on by blood settling, it soured moods and left a man unwilling to move. He sat on the churned ground and waited.

After several minutes, Alasdair spoke.

'He wants the leaders questioned, then hung for treason. If he had his way, the others too. But I'll sway him. Survivors can dissuade others.'

'Ye think there will be more?'

'From this lot? Nae. But others still evade him.'

He shook his head, dismissing Alasdair's words. 'Ye ken the people. Will ye return tae the manor?'

'Aye, *mo ciann*. In a... in a...'

He patted his brother's shoulder.

Chapter 46

How was he to get to the manor? It took Alasdair several attempts just to stand. Such poor form. Yet his brother did not seem upset. He was still debating the trek ahead when Iain rode up. The lad led Legs and another horse behind his mount. He stared in disbelief.

'Ye kenned?'

'It's no unknown, but nae,' replied Cailean.

Alasdair cursed his clouding mind. Cailean would have had horses waiting anyway. It took just as long for him to mount Legs, perhaps longer. He had to get back to the manor. Prepare for prisoners, see to the wounded. And Lord only knew what state the manor itself was in! Then there was Sorcha and Mordag. When he was finally in the saddle, he found himself alone. His brother, still on foot, had left.

He rode for home.

On the quick journey back, he braced himself for what he would find – but the raised voices of angry women had not crossed his mind. Shouting at someone, they were demanding that another was handed over to them. Rounding the dwellings, he found Fraoch standing on one leg, with the rear guard. They were protecting a man with a limp arm.

'Infant murderer! Rapist!'

'Caged our pregnant lady!'

'Stone him!'

Christ, they wanted to lynch him! He pushed Legs up between Fraoch and the women. They threw insults until he pulled off his helm and cap. Quickly, the women fell back, though their anger remained.

'Look at ye. Ye stand here demanding mob rule while yer men and the men that overthrew them lie exhausted, injured, or worse out there!'

His angered shout, spurred by a sudden vigour, had the desired effect. The women quietened. Some, having been swept up in the fervour, looked ashamed.

'He will be punished, but no like this. Lawlessness ends now. Now go!' he ordered them. Only a few grumbled, and a hard stare from him encouraged them on their way. He swung Legs around, to face the man. The one Mordag said had ordered her in the cage. He expected rage to seize him, but it did not come. His hatred transformed into a cold hardness.

'Let him experience what he did tae my wife. Put him in the cage.'

'Gladly.'

Damn it. Just like Mordag's treatment, it was as much for the man's protection as it was for punishment. Yet he felt no satisfaction upon watching him dragged there. Nor any desire to see him remain there indefinitely.

'One o these days it'll be me saving yer arse,' spat Fraoch.

'Ye already did, in bringing those boats.'

He slid from Legs and was lucky to not fall on said arse. He grinned at his muttering friend – the first one that day. And left him to it with Legs for company.

Approaching the hall, he was joined by Jock, his front covered in blood not his own.

'A sight for sore eyes! Ye look as hale as ever!' Alasdair could not hide his relief.

'Aye, my lord, always was a lucky devil. Under close watch and nowt more.'

He clasped his hand, not caring about the filth for he was likewise covered. Jock led him through the hall, where the worst of those already collected lay.

'Turn out the barns, make them ready for more. The stables too. The horses can go on lines,' Alasdair instructed. 'And the space above, though no the bedchambers. How are they?'

'Still locked, as is the strongroom. The former were being kept for the Lady Sorcha, the latter, well, it was going nowhere so they gave up trying.'

More likely waiting to pick the keys off his body, the overconfident fools. Though he was grateful that Mordag and Sorcha had ready chambers. They – for he doubted Mordag would stay behind – must have set off by now. A slow journey with a cart in tow. Plus, she would be keeping away until it was obvious that as many rebels had been secured as possible. He started searching for the rear guard's commander.

*

Wincing, Cailean nodded his thanks to Mordag's maid. The woman had helped him strip and bathe. His muscles now stiff; his body various shades of purple. And a cracked rib or two. Thankfully there were no cuts deeper than a scratch. Now he was back in his stinking armour and awaiting the arrival of the camp.

By none prayer, all that remained of the battle was the inanimate. To be picked over or picked up. Cailean's losses were minimal, though the full toll would not be known for weeks. He cast his eyes over the assembled chiefs and chieftains. With their united cause completed, their bickering had returned in earnest.

'I intend tae keep a core. No more than a few men from each o ye.'

'Fer how long?' asked one.

'Ah doubt more than a month.'

'And those on the borders?' asked another.

'I'll do the same. The chance of retaliation is low, but ye never ken.'

He stood up, finished with them and their damned rivalries. No one would be honoured over another.

'Alasdair?'

His brother was pinned to the bed by a red cat. He was the only one without a quarrel with someone. Long may that last. Nor was Cailean fooled by his uninterested act.

'Aye, *mo ciann*?'

'Walk with me.'

He sorely wanted the rebel leaders hung by nightfall. His brother rose; the cat, unimpressed, glared at him.

'Ye can have him back later.'

Since when did he make promises to cats? Damn it, now Alasdair was grinning. He snorted and strode from the chamber.

'Where are the heads tae go?' Cailean asked once outside.

'Tae Inverlochy and Edinburgh. Only, hold off, will ye?'

'The Raven's workings, aye?'

His brother's face did not change but his eyes did.

'What is it?'

He did not get his answer. Excited shouts spread from the north-east of the settlement. The camp was approaching. Yet those who were moving to meet them slowed down. Cailean's men shielded their eyes and stared. He tensed. Was it someone else? Not hostile, though.

'I may have omitted a few things...'

He swung around to stare at Alasdair. What had his brother planned?

'...Just, go along with it, aye?'

He growled; what was he up to? No. He looked too guilty... the Raven must have planned this. Reluctantly, he nodded. His brother motioned towards the prisoners.

There, Cailean was bade to stand in front of them and wait. Over the top of dwellings, he saw an argent standard, bearing a vert phoenix. He knew no such heraldry. The murmuring around him was likewise confusing. The bearers rounded a corner. Douglas men? Then a dark horse. *His horse!*

Sorcha sat astride, resplendent in a gown he had never before seen. She sat tall, majestic even. The fae he once mistook her as. A fae queen! On her head, the coronet of an earl. No, *his coronet*! He struggled to keep face. Damn it, what was this? Behind her came Ewan, then the wagon, and *his* men. His attention returned to Sorcha. She looked nobly angered.

He tore his eyes away at the sound of prisoners moving. Many were kneeling. Was this another spectacle akin to Robert's court? A glance at Alasdair confirmed it was.

Sorcha collected Taranis and they broke into a slow canter, abandoning the standard. She rode forwards, made him half-pirouette and returned. A second half-pirouette followed before she came to a dead halt. At her command, Taranis kicked out and then reared. Not once did her eyes leave the men, and she sat as securely as any knight. Finally, she stilled the warhorse.

Keeping her chin high, Sorcha waited. She sensed Angus placing the stool next to her and Ewan joining him. She could not look down. Elizabeth never watched the pages prepare her way. They helped her dismount before falling back. She focused on Cailean, his face impassive. And started walking slowly towards him, even as another ran ahead to place a sheepskin at his feet.

It was now or never. She stopped short, turning to look out over the prisoners again.

'Ye kneel before me, calling me yer future queen, yet ye bared arms against me this day.'

Those she assumed to be leaders cried out their innocence. She silenced them with a glance.

'Dae I look weak tae ye? Dae I look like a woman who would cower behind walls while others die in *my* name? Is my blood filled with water rather than the strength of my ancestor kings? Or dae I stand before ye, surrounded by warriors of *my* choosing?'

She seized the righteous rage that filled her. Yes, they were Cailean's warriors, but he was the only one that had, eventually, listened. The prisoners mumbled. She let the contempt she felt for those who would harm innocents show on her face. Both sides murmured; Cailean's men uncomfortable as she roused up their prisoners. Yet their commanders remained silent, following their chief's lead. If only she could thank him for not interrupting.

'Well? Do ye really wish tae be my men?'

They shouted agreements.

'Prove it!'

She drew the dagger that had arrived with her gown. The one John Comyn had been wearing that fateful day. Thrusting it up, she showed it to them. Their delight upon seeing it sickened her. To those with fervour, she may well have been him.

'Swear upon my uncle's dagger!' she cried, thrusting it up once more. Those caught up, spat out their pledges. A man shouted in alarm, only to be silenced by his guards. Was he their leader? Did he recognise what she was about to do? It was too late. So assured were the staunchest believers in their cause, they were blinded. It was no different to Michael. Others were more aware, but likely wishing for the freedom it brought, also knelt and pledged.

Turning to face her husband, she caught the flicker of a smile. She returned it with her own.

'I accept yer pledge,' she cried out and lowered the dagger. 'I am no weak woman. I stand here free-willed.

I choose, therefore, tae honour our Lord by following His law. In all matters earthly, it is tae my husband that I submit myself.'

She sheathed the dagger before lifting the coronet off her head. It was not hers to wear. Cailean had to duck low so that she could place it upon his head. Stepping back, she caught his slight nod, but she was not finished. She held out her arms and someone removed the mantle. Angus bent and unlaced her boots, removing them. The fleece was a welcome addition as she stepped out, barefooted, then knelt at her husband's feet. Upon spotting his raised eyebrows, Sorcha's composure almost fled her. It was farcical but memorable.

The men who had pledged in fervour spat curses. Out of the corner of her eye, she spotted the broad grins of those standing closer. Some of their shoulders shook. Her hands held aloft, as in prayer, were enclosed by Cailean's.

'I, Sorcha Comyn, daughter of Annabelle Comyn, daughter of Elinor Balliol, daughter of Dervorguilla Galloway, daughter of Margaret Huntington, daughter of David Earl of Huntingdon, son of Henry Earl of Huntingdon, son of David King of Scots, promise upon the holy cross of our Lord in Heaven tae be faithful tae my lord husband, Cailean Macmaghan, and tae *never* deceive or cause him harm.'

Just as the day she pledged her troth, she tied her fate to his. And with it, the fate of every man that had pledged to her. Only this time, she met his intense gaze, and matched it with her own.

'I accept yer pledge, my lady wife, Sorcha Comyn. Rise and stand by my side.'

Cailean's word sealed their fate. They were now, in essence, his men. She accepted his proffered hand and rose. He stepped next to the fleece so she could be at his side. The silence was almost overwhelming. Her hand on his, she looked out over the defeated men. Though still angered, she felt sorry for them, so thorough was their defeat. And Cailean had yet to punish them.

'Those who pledged tae my wife. I order ye tae return tae the land ye come from,' he started. 'Go to its chief. There, tell him of yer treason. He is tae punish ye as he sees fit. Should ye survive, ye are tae give yer oath once more tae him, if he'll accept it. Only then will ye be free of yer oath tae the Lady Sorcha.'

Curious, Sorcha studied the men. It risked them getting off lightly, but at the same time, the chiefs would want to distance themselves from the stain of treason. She gently squeezed his hand to gain his attention.

'Forgive me, Cailean, there is one last thing I must do,' she murmured, before raising her voice again. 'As ye go, ken this: I renounce my right tae the crown and turn my back on Clan Comyn. A missive proclaiming as much will soon reach the royal records and Comyn chiefs. I am of MacMhathain!'

Now she met Cailean's eyes. His smile was broad. He nodded, unable to speak, as a deafening roar enveloped the land. What need had she for a crown that came with nothing but distrust? She had proven herself to those that mattered the most and they had accepted her. As the roar died down, Cailean dismissed the assembled groups. She watched the rebel leaders led away as men swarmed around them both.

She stayed close to Cailean's side, though the men crowding them stank of blood, sweat and other unsavoury things. It was worse than the boat! Still, she kept the smile on her face. It was truly over now, and she was with Cailean. That mattered the most.

*

Mordag smoothed the sleeveless surcoat over her bump. The gold shone brilliantly. Alasdair had been right. The gown was intended to catch men's eyes, but not lustfully. She realised that after seeing Sorcha the day before. From the way she dressed to the way she spoke; it had all helped her command men in a way Mordag had never thought possible. Now was the perfect time to do the same. Caitlin stood back after finishing her hair. The crispinette was held up by a fillet, hidden beneath the circlet she had retrieved from the untouched strongroom.

'If ah may be bold, ah'm glad tae see ye in this, my lady. It becomes ye.'

'I thank ye, Caitlin. No only for the compliment, but for everything ye did.'

The older woman's smile was warm but tired. 'When men fight, women always suffer.'

A bitter truth, and now she was to watch its conclusion. Mordag nodded grimly and left the chamber. She tried to walk as gracefully as Sorcha, but she was still too clumsy. She would work on it, and her posture too. In the hall, Alasdair stood waiting for her. She had hardly seen him. Something about asking questions for Robert. She greeted him as etiquette demanded and he took her hand.

'Ye sure this will no upset the babe?' he asked quietly.

'Aye. They need tae see ah'm the lady o this hall and will no cower meekly.'

A smile flickered across his face, then he glanced past her to Sorcha.

'Stop acting as though the victory was all yer doing.'

Her chiding only made his eyes sparkle more. She tutted softly as the doors opened. They fell behind Cailean and Sorcha, and she tried to hide her emotion. They were heading for the hastily built gallows. Mordag sensed people following her. She took a deep breath. Hangings had been a common occurrence growing up, but she had never really known those people.

Of the men lining up on the platform behind the scaffold beam, she knew all but two. They were the leader, the man with a useless arm, two men who lived nearby, and her father's man. All stared straight ahead. Only one, the youngest, showed any sign of regret. Tearful, he begged mercy. She had wanted to scream her revenge until she saw him. *That could have been Angus.* She ran her hand over her stomach and gritted her teeth. It had to be done.

A man she recognised but whose name she did not know stood up on the platform and addressed the criminals. 'Ye stand charged with the unlawful bearing of arms against our king, Robert Brus, and of unlawfully seizing the land, arms and peoples of the Earl of Kintail tae aid yer cause. For the good of yer soul, confess now yer part.'

Mordag's heart thudded as the repentant youth sobbed his confession. He was granted mercy from their priest.

'My soul is safe with the Lord,' the leader shouted. 'He

kens a wicked usurper mocks his holy throne. The Brus will fall at Comyn feet!'

How could he have seen through Sorcha's ploy and still be so blind? She stared as the heckling started. Nearby, Sorcha crossed herself. Mordag glanced at Alasdair. He looked as angry as he had the day they argued. She suddenly felt sick, but made herself turn back to the spectacle. The man was silencing the crowd.

Having got no more confessions, he continued, 'Ye are tae be hanged by the neck until yer soul departs this earthly realm. May the Lord grant ye mercy.'

He looked towards Cailean; the earl must have nodded. The man motioned with his hand and the rebels were pushed, or leapt, from the platform. The latter broke their own necks. Two women threw themselves on the legs of their men, struggling with the twisting bodies to hasten their death.

Time dragged on as Mordag watched the life slowly drain from those who were not so lucky. Their eyes bulged; their tongues swelled. All soiled themselves. Her son stirred inside her. It they had not been caught, they would have killed him. Now she and Alasdair had earned the right to raise him here.

She straightened her back and announced, 'Ah will return tae the hall. There is much tae do in there and ah wish tae see it done right. I shall assume they will be cut down before the day's end.'

No one stopped or contradicted her. Druim Earbainn was *her* home.

Epilogue

Pillanflatt, a month later.

Two blunted swords met, dipped and pulled away. One slipped past the guard, stopping short of the groin, its counterpart narrowly avoiding the first's elbow. Cailean watched with folded arms.

'Get that foot in line,' he growled at Angus. 'Iain, ye're no a chicken.'

They were exhausted and covered in sweat. He did not relent. Error through exhaustion killed many. And few battles were as quick as Druim Earbainn had been. He caught sight of Donald, who tormented the lads by drinking loudly from his flask. Distractions were also harder to ignore. There was a thud, followed by coughing.

'Who are ye tae be... Seumas! What are ye doing here?'

'With Alasdair, aren't I? How are ye, ye old dog?'

Their reacquaintance caught Cailean's attention. Alasdair was here. He called an end to the training. The boys fell to the floor in exaggerated relief. He shook his head. Angus encouraged light, youthful rebellion. Better that than Iain's earlier misdeed, rectified through a quick marriage. He left them to their fun.

He found Alasdair nearby, once again in garish garments. Some things, it appeared, would never change.

'Kept the beard, I see.'

'Aye, well, she likes it. Will ye walk with me?'

He nodded and waited for the light conversation.

'Sorcha still at Henderleithen?'

'Aye. The man knew her father so does no begrudge her wishes.'

''Tis only replacing a stone, is it no? His body was already laid next tae her mother?'

'A bit more, since he originally paid for the kirk. And Mordag?'

'She gets larger each day and with it more frustrated. She's healed fine, only tae find our son stops her from doing as she wishes. God willing, I'll be home tae amuse her soon enough.'

His lips twitched; poor Mordag. At least towards the end, she would have Sorcha's company. But not before he got to enjoy the summer with her. Alasdair came to a stop, under a vaguely familiar tree. Before his eyes, his brother tensed.

'I thought it over?' Cailean asked.

'Hmm? Oh aye, that's done. Only mercenaries would dare fight for a Comyn rising now.'

God's balls, his brother's jests were getting worse. He stared past Alasdair, at the water. He would not encourage any more.

''Tis others that I fear. Brus is getting old, his sons are

infants and one already rumoured tae be sickly. His foes once feared him, but I think that is diminishing.'

Cailean continued to stare at the water, even as his jaw tightened. He was only there to give the king his required time while waiting for Sorcha. He lifted his eyes to the sky. There was no 'thinking'. More storms were coming. And what of Alasdair? He was Robert's right-hand man now. No, he did not like it.

'Who is planning what?'

'I'm no sure yet. I need more time but—'

'*Mo ciann!*'

He cursed Donald for interrupting his brother and swung around. All traces of discretion gone.

'What?' he roared.

'Lady Sorcha sends word; she awaits ye in Glasgow.'

He would ride as soon as he could. But first, he turned back to Alasdair.

'Go, enjoy yer summer. I'll see ye when it's time tae wet my son's head, aye?'

He met his brother's eyes; light-hearted words, piercing gaze.

'Aye, until then.'

Glossary of Gaelic, Scots, and Medieval Terms

Acha 'n dà thearnaidh [*Gaelic*] MacMhathain war cry 'The Field of the Two Declivities'.

Birlinn [*Gaelic*] A type of small galley, similar to a Viking longship.

Bogle [*Scots*] A ghost or folkloric being.

Chevalerie [*Old French*] Horsemanship.

Crabbit auld schow [*Scots*] Grumpy old sow.

Crann Tára [*Gaelic*] The fiery cross.

Crotals [*Medieval English*] Harness bells.

Cumberworld [*Medieval English*] Idiot.

Destrier A highly trained war horse.

Dwale [*Medieval English*] An alcohol-based sedative that contained opium, hemlock and vinegar.

Fiadh-chat [*Gaelic*] Wild cat.

Funder ... dadding wyndis [*Scots*] Be blown over.

Glowren [*Scots*] Staring.

Gowkit-cled [*Scots*] Foolishly clothed.

Gravour [*Medieval English*] A long, thin instrument used to separate hair.

Gris [*Medieval English*] The grey-white part of squirrel fur. At its best when taken in winter.

Léine [*Gaelic*] A type of long linen or woollen tunic worn in the Highlands and Ireland. Typically shorter on men and longer on women.

Leuchd-crios [*Gaelic*] Bodyguards, equivalent to English knights.

Lucet A small, double-pronged tool used for making cord.

Lude Smitten [*Scots*] Lovestruck.

Màthair [*Gaelic*] Mother.

Mo Charaid, sgiath gu h-ard os cion na h-eileinan fhraochadh [*Gaelic*] My friend, fly high over the heathery isles.

Mo ciann [*Gaelic*] My chief – honorific for a clan chief/chieftain.

Mummer/Mummery [*Medieval English*] An actor/a play.

Nochtthenes [*Scots*] Worthless/wickedness.

Palfrey A general riding horse with smooth paces.

Pell A training dummy.

Plaid A woven wool blanket or cloth.

Queynte [*Medieval English*] Female genitalia.

Quoits A ring-toss game.

Ranten Drukkin [*Scots*] Ranting/raving drunk.

Ryfftys off wynd an snorand [*Scots*] Burping, farting and snoring.

Rouncey A horse used for both battle and general riding.

Sair heid [*Scots*] Sore head.

Skaithit [*Scots*] Physically hurt.

Scold A woman charged with being a public nuisance.

'S e' Galla Bhruis a th'annad! [*Gaelic*] Literal: 'It's the bitch of the Bruce in you', meaning 'You're Bruce's bitch'.

Sencliathe [*Gaelic*] Men who join the clan via bonds of manrent, marriage, or having 'broken' from other clans.

Sennachie [*Gaelic*] A clan's historian and storyteller.

Slàinte mhath [*Gaelic*] A toast meaning 'good health'.

Slat [*Gaelic*] Penis. *Slat beag fleoidhte,* a small, flaccid penis.

Sluagh Math [*Gaelic*] The 'good folk', fairies or demons.

Spunkie [*Scots*] A coastal will-o'-the-wisp.

Sumph [*Scots*] Fool/idiot.

Sumpter Pack horse/mule.

Tacksman [*Scots*] A renter of land, who sublets to others.

Tanist [*Gaelic*] Heir to the role of clan chief.

Tippets Detachable streamers of cloth and fur. The longer they fell, the higher the status.

Toom Tabard Derogatory name for the exiled John Balliol, King of Scots (1292–1296).

Tyke [*Scots*] A mongrel dog; or derisively implies lineage.

Uisge beatha [*Gaelic*] Whisky.

Win aff . . . heich naig [*Scots*] 'Get off your high horse.'

Author's Note

Where possible I have used Scots Gaelic names for people and locations. When I have used English, it is due to character birth location or to distinguish between characters. I have tried my hardest to be as historically accurate as possible, but Highland society was mostly oral at this time. In those instances where information is lacking, I have used my best guess. I beg forgiveness for any failings.

As for Robert the Bruce, the pedestalling of him as a freedom fighter has overshadowed other, more questionable, actions. The Bruce-Comyn feud predated the English invasion by decades. After his victory against the English at Loudoun Hill, he sent men to Comyn lands and the lands of their allies; the destruction they wrought not only humiliated the Comyns, but deprived them of much needed support and left the land's population struggling to survive for generations after.

Throughout his campaign, Robert used the same scorched earth tactics as Edward, depriving many Scottish folk of their crops and homes. And just as Edward had done, land rights with centuries-old ties were often redistributed to Robert's favourites and supporters instead of being returned to original owners. This created legal cases and blood feuds that would continue long after his death.

Despite the signing of the Declaration of Arbroath, tensions were still high in 1324. There were constant whispers of rebellion which Robert would have been eager to quash, quite possibly through the work of men like Alasdair. Furthermore, the Highlanders and Islanders that Robert had heavily leaned upon during his campaign were starting to distance themselves from him. Cailean's thoughts and actions towards Robert could have been akin to one of those supporters.

While their real chief was no earl, Clan MacMhathain (Macmaghan) was at the peak of its power during this period. Known today as Clan Matheson, their lands were historically tied to Lochalsh and, throughout the Middle Ages, members of the clan served as constables of Eileen Donnain. They were vassals of the Earl of Ross, allied with Clan Macdonald, and could gather as many as 2,000 fighting men. Their chief's ancestor is Kermac Macmaghan and he did help drive the Norse from the Isles.

Acknowlegements

I must begin by thanking my mum; thank you for reading everything and putting up with my absentminded self! I would also like to thank the rest of my family who knew nothing of what I was doing, just the long absences.

A massive thank you to Sir Alexander Matheson, Chief of Clan Matheson, for agreeing to let me use his clan's name and history. I hope I have done it justice and you will permit me to write more books with clan characters.

To my friends Nils, Ben, Sky, and those too shy to be named. Thank you for not abandoning me when I was too busy or tired to game, and for being my personal cheerleaders on those bad days. I owe you all a festival's worth of drinks!

This book would have turned out very differently if it had not been for Sam Boyce of Sam Boyce Writers' Consultancy. As my mentor you saw my potential and as my editor you cut out the nonsense. For that I thank you. And finally, I thank the wonderful staff at Troubador Publishing for your hard work at making my dream a reality. Thank you!

This book is printed on paper from sustainable sources managed under the Forest Stewardship Council (FSC) scheme.

It has been printed in the UK to reduce transportation miles and their impact upon the environment.

For every new title that Troubador publishes, we plant a tree to offset CO_2, partnering with the More Trees scheme.

MORE TREES
LET'S PLANT A BILLION TREES

For more about how Troubador offsets its environmental impact, see www.troubador.co.uk/sustainability-and-community